NIGHT SONG

NIGHT SONG

BEVERLY JENKINS

AVON BOOKS ⟲ NEW YORK

AVON BOOKS
A division of
The Hearst Corporation
1350 Avenue of the Americas
New York, New York 10019

I would like to thank some of the many people who helped me bring *Night Song* to life.

First thanks must go to Vivian Stephens, my agent. Without her my stories would still be in boxes in my basement. Her guidance and support have helped make my dreams come true. Thanks, Coach.

Ellen Edwards, my editor at Avon, saw the beauty in history, the love in the story, and said, "Yes!"

Christine Zika, Assistant Editor at Avon.

Earl Harvey and Kendall McCarthy of Creative Source Management, Philadelphia, are two of the most gracious men on the planet. I owe you two forever.

To Michigan State Police Trooper Lorenzo Veal, a modern-day member of the Tenth, thanks for taking time out of a busy day to talk with me. Thanks even more for the pictures of the Tenth's uniforms.

Corey Thomas of Burrell Communications Group, Chicago, is a woman sent from the angels. I owe you lunch.

To the ladies at Parke-Davis, Ann Arbor, your love and encouragement brought the story to life. Special thanks to Mel and Kevin for their diligent work on the first draft.

And last, a salute to my children, who didn't seem to mind having a madwoman for a mother during deadline time. And to Alex, my own "grand passion," I love you.

Prologue

Georgia, 1864

The overhead door was heavy. Nine-year-old Cara Lee Henson planted her bare feet firmly on the carved step in the earth and pushed with all her might. Her grandfather, Benjamin, had hidden her down here in the underground root cellar more than an hour ago. He had expressly forbidden her to show herself until he returned. Cara knew better than to disobey, especially since he'd spoken to her so seriously, but she wanted to see what was going on.

She pushed harder. The door finally inched up enough for her to see out, and she blinked from the sting of the bright sunlight. There they were, over by the house. Cara's tall, dark-skinned grandfather was easy to spot. He stood like a tree amidst the Bluecoats surrounding him. She could also see the men's mouths moving, but she was too far away to hear what they were saying.

The man talking the most seemed highly agitated because his face was all red and his arms were waving around wildly. Cara supposed he must be the leader because his blue uniform looked cleaner and in better condition than the others. He was also the only one on a horse. Cara struggled to raise the door higher, hoping to hear why the Yankees had stopped here.

Cara's heart began to beat faster when one of the men viciously slapped her grandfather across the face. His head reeled from the sudden blow, but he stood his ground, seemingly unafraid. Another slap followed, and Cara tensed, wondering why they were doing this! Then, because the leader's voice was raised in anger, she heard.

"Where's the master?"

Her grandfather answered but was struck again.

"Where's the master?"

One of the men hit him with a rifle stock, and the blow sent him to his knees. A frightened Cara began trembling with alarm. There was no master. Her grandfather had been freed at the age of twenty. He'd been deeded this small plot of land upon the old master's death. "He's free!" she wanted to scream at them. Her dead parents had been free, Cara herself was free, as were scores of other blacks in the South.

Crying now, she guessed the Yankees didn't believe him. She now understood why she'd been made to hide; some of the Yankees were not the saviors people thought they would be. Her grandfather had put her down here for her safety. She wanted to run to him but froze as she heard the question shouted again.

"Where's the master, old man?" The soldiers grabbed him roughly by the arms and forced him to stand. His head was bloodied, his eyes swollen closed. But Grandfather Benjamin had always been a proud, strong, free man, and in reply gave the only answer he could—the truth.

The soldiers dragged him away from the house. The stand of trees and the blue backs of the men momentarily blocked Cara's view. When they broke, what she saw froze her heart, because even at nine, she knew.

They'd seated him atop the leader's horse. A rope had been tied to a thick branch above his head and the noose fashioned at the end of it lay around his neck. One of the men gave a sudden slap to the animal's rump and sent it racing across the field, leaving her grandfather to dangle, jerk, and finally slump into death.

The Yankees next set fire to the modest, whitewashed house, totally unaware of Cara's silent watching. With what was left of her innocence she said a prayer for her grandfather and hoped he'd be happy in heaven with her parents and grandmother.

As the fire spread to the barn and adjoining fields, she took one last look at him on the end of the rope, then she very slowly let down the door and descended into the solace of the darkness.

Chapter 1

Henry Adams Township Graham County
Kansas, 1882

Over seven hundred Black people—farmers, ranchers, merchants, and craftsmen—lived in the Great Solomon Valley, and it seemed to Cara that every single one of them had turned out this day for the parade honoring the Tenth Cavalry. Making her way through the jostling throng was almost as difficult as it had been to keep her students under control that morning. The children were so excited about the festivities that they'd been impossible to teach, and Cara was pleased just to have been able to keep them inside the schoolhouse until dismissal time.

She grimaced, then laughed at herself. She wasn't quite old enough yet that she could play the disapproving spinster schoolteacher. But she did wish that the town elders could have spent just a little of the money they'd put into refurbishing Main Street toward purchasing urgently needed books, pencils, paper, and maps for her students. Still, secretly, she did share the wish to have Henry Adams Township steal some of the thunder of the rival town of Nicodemus by doing a bang-up job hosting this event.

Nicodemus was famous as the largest Black settlement in the country; it put its smaller sister towns in the shade, and Black people in Graham, Marion, Barton, and Rice counties, as well as those in the colony down in Cherokee County, established by Benjamin "Pap" Singleton and his Tennessee followers, justifiably wanted their day in the sun. And a fine day in the sun this was, too.

The succulent scents of whole pigs and sides of beef cooking on spits over the newly dug pit behind Handy Reed's blacksmith shop were making Cara's mouth water. Red, white, and blue bunting proudly draped the buildings; American flags flew on poles erected at six-foot intervals along the new, half-mile length of wooden walk. All the colors and movement infected Cara with a sense of gaiety. And the fresh-baked pies, cookies, cakes, and lemonade being sold at a booth by the ladies of the A.M.E. Church made her look forward to a fattening treat at the end of the day.

Pushing her way through the throng, Cara at last was able to see her boardinghouse, such a short distance from school and so clearly visible at the end of the street on any normal day. Finally, she made it to the crowded front yard. The owner and operator of the house, Sophie Reynolds, had foregone the parade activities in order to personally supervise preparations for the dinner that night in honor of the Tenth. Cara sighed. In the two years she'd lived in this house, every good thing she'd heard about Sophie from the wagon drivers who'd brought her to the Valley had been confirmed. Known for her good sense, her good heart, and the quality of her establishment, Sophie had won over Cara at once and become a friend; before half a year had passed, Cara had begun to think of Sophie as a second mother.

Suddenly shouts and cheers erupted from the crowd at the far end of the street, and the people around Cara echoed their cries. This was the moment everyone had been waiting for—the arrival of the twenty-four Black members of the Tenth Cavalry. Eager to see them, the men and women in front of the boardinghouse surged forward, capturing Cara in their midst like a fly in amber and sweeping her along with them.

The cheers greeting the mounted troopers slowly making their way along the street deafened Cara. People on the route fell in behind them, tears of pride shining in their eyes. They knew from their own struggles what these men and their brethren in the Ninth Cavalry must have faced as they tried to prove themselves worthy of wearing the uniform of United States Cavalry.

As Cara had told her class that morning, the men of the Tenth were also known as Buffalo Soldiers, a term of honor bestowed upon them by the Plains Indians. These men were legendary. Despite being given used and worn-out equipment, harsh punishments, and an area to patrol and enforce that stretched from the Canadian border to the Rio Grande, the men had succeeded. They were highly decorated and were known as fierce fighters. They had the fewest court-martials and the lowest desertion rate in the frontier army. Yes, the people of the Valley were proud; the Black soldiers were their own, and outstanding examples of what members of the race could achieve in the face of limited opportunity and hardship.

Cara smiled, watching some of the women, dressed in their Sunday best, shower the uniformed men with streamers, flowers, and hair ribbons. A few of the women, caught up in the excitement, ran up to the horses to hand the men wildflowers. Mae Dexter, daughter of the mayor, offered a bunch to the handsome mustached man leading the column. He graciously took the blooms, raised them to his lips, and handed them back with a dazzling smile. Cara seriously thought the girl would swoon right there in the road.

"Isn't he gorgeous?" a woman exclaimed. Cara had to agree. He sat the big horse with ease, and the way he'd brought Mae's blooms to his mustached lips—a shock of recognition tore through Cara. It couldn't be! Chase Jefferson! The man she'd been waxing over was none other than the soldier with whom she'd had the run-in two years back?

A stunned Cara watched Jefferson bring his men to a halt beneath the banner tied across Main Street that read: WELCOME TENTH CAVALRY. Cara's students had contributed the banner, and the letters were a bit lopsided. The troopers dismounted before the newly built dais upon which sat assembled dignitaries and members of the press. Chase Jefferson accepted the town's generosity on behalf of his regiment and the United States government. The mention of the government drew a few hearty boos from the crowd, but the sergeant went on with his short remarks as if he hadn't heard. When he finished, the town elders presented the company with a ceremonial key to the town hall, and the mayor read a proclamation declaring it Tenth Cavalry Day. With the official welcome concluded, the crowd capped off the brief ceremony with more thunderous applause and flag waving.

Chase marveled at the size of the crowd. He and the other troopers spent the next twenty minutes shaking hands, exchanging pleasantries, and graciously accepting an appreciation not shown the Black cavalry in many places. Never in his wildest dreams had he imagined they would be met with such an outpouring of enthusiasm. A fortunate few of his men had relatives either in town or in the surrounding area and would be spending this ten-day furlough in the bosom of family. Those not so fortunate would be quartered at Sophie Reynolds's boardinghouse and at other generously offered homes.

Thinking of Sophie made Chase smile. He hadn't seen her in the decade of chaos following the war, but time and absence hadn't diminished his affection and regard for the woman who had positively influenced his life in so many ways.

Making his way through the crowd, Chase spied one of his men, Euclid Tate, talking with a sweet young thing who was twirling a pink parasol. Chase made a mental note to remind the men that the women were off limits. He did not want the town's generosity repaid with even a hint of scandal.

Chase continued to wade through the sea of well-wishers, stopping to receive a congratulatory word from a teary-eyed matron or a firm handshake from a cattleman. He had to find Sophie's; he needed a long hot soak in a large tub, and a drink. He knew she ran a legitimate business now, and he was proud of her for it, but still he had the fleeting wish that she was still in the old trade. He and his men had been on the trail for weeks. Proprieties and uniform aside, he could certainly use the companionship of a willing woman.

The A.M.E. ladies provided Chase with the directions he sought and a chilled glass of their lemonade. A quick talk with his second-in-command, Trooper Lorenzo Veal, on accommodations for the men and stabling of the horses concluded the last of Chase's official duties. He returned Veal's salute, rehoisted his saddle, and set out for Sophie's.

The crowd had thinned as people drifted off to attend the other afternoon activities, and to rest up for the night's big doings. Quite a few folks still clustered in groups, large and small, talking, laughing, and visiting with their neighbors. Some hailed Chase as he passed, and he responded in kind.

Sophie's place turned out to be only a short walk up the busy street. As he looked over the big, freshly painted structure, he wondered, smiling, if she still kept that brandy she'd been so fond of.

Chase lowered his gaze to take in the wide, welcoming porch with its large sparkin' swing in front of big gleaming windows. Two women stood by the door. One he'd never seen before, but the other—a dark, honey-skinned beauty with an abundance of shining hair pulled back in a style too severe for such a face—he'd thought far too much about during the past twenty-four months. Cara Henson. He smiled. Well, well, well. Did she remember him? Her sass alone made her unforgettable. Sassy, educated, and opinionated, she'd called herself. He'd been sorry they hadn't been able to get to know each other back in Topeka. He'd been even sorrier when Laura Pope had interrupted them that last day.

Cara looked up from her conversation with Reverend Whitfield's wife, Sybil, and found herself the subject of Chase Jefferson's attention.

For a moment the world narrowed to hold only his eyes; she didn't hear one more word Sybil said. He bowed gallantly, flourishing his blue Stetson, his gaze never leaving hers. When he righted himself, Cara's heart was pounding.

"My, my," said Sybil. "I believe you've gained someone's attention." Sybil frowned thoughtfully. "Cara Lee Henson, do you know that handsome man?"

Two years ago, Cara had been closely following reports in the Black press on the fate of the more than forty thousand former slaves who'd pulled up stakes and migrated to Kansas. Called Exodusters, 'dusters for short, the migrants were successfully making new lives in little settlements all over Kansas.

Historically, members of the race had been settling in the West since before the nation's independence. But this present-day journeying, which some newspapers were calling Kansas Fever and others the Great Exodus, began in earnest in 1879 as thousands of Blacks began fleeing the Southern states to escape the violence that followed the Civil War.

Cara, having grown up in the South, knew that after the Civil War the government withdrew the last Federal troops and returned to power the very people who'd split apart the country in the first place. The new elected Democrats gutted Reconstruction, then ushered in the dark, terror-filled era of Redemption. She remembered the fearful nights she and the other children in the orphanage where she lived were hidden high up in the trees behind the house to escape the midnight visitations of the Kluxers. Schools newly opened to Black children were burned, both Black and white teachers were killed. People who spoke out or advocated meeting the violence with violence were also murdered, victims of what the adults then called "bulldozin'." And despite the one hundred and eighty thousand Blacks who'd served on the Union side of the Civil War, and the twenty-nine thousand who'd manned Union vessels, the government did not intervene.

By the mid-1870s the country's newly freed citizens had had enough. They began to heed the calls of young men like Union veteran and former slave Henry Adams to leave the South and head West. By the end of 1879, over forty thousand Black men, women, and children had uprooted for Kansas, in the largest mass migration of the race the nation had ever seen. The excitement of starting fresh and creating a new town had teased Cara to throw her fate in with the bold adventurers, but it wasn't until she was fired for a second time from a teaching job that she developed a full-blown case of Exodusters' Fever. Unmarried at the age of twenty-four, with no kin and only thirty-three dollars to her name, Cara bought passage on the Kansas Pacific for Topeka, the point of departure for caravans heading out to the new Black settlements. She hadn't dreamed when she was preparing to leave Blessed, Ohio, that she would be part of such a very large number of migrants.

Debarking at Topeka, Cara followed in the footsteps of numerous 'dusters before her and went to Floral Hall. There she got shelter and food until she could hook up with a group heading for the town of her choice—Henry Adams, which lay two hundred forty miles north, and whose school board was advertising for a teacher. Optimistic and eager, she waited at Floral Hall, working at a volunteer activity as all residents were required to do. Hers was the food detail. At every meal Cara dished up creamed beef for what seemed a near-endless line of people. On the second night of serving supper, she spotted the army private from Fort Leavenworth she'd met the evening she had arrived at Floral Hall. He had been one of the party that had brought beef donated by millionaire Phillip D. Armour to supply the Exodusters. Private Worth had asked her to marry him—as had two dozen other strangers in the previous twenty-four hours. The aid ladies who ran Floral Hall had reassured Cara on the matter, pointing out that men who were aiming to build towns needed wives, and many women, alone or widowed with children, jumped at the chance to marry one of them.

Worth finally moved up in line to Cara's spot. "Look," he said quickly because so many waited behind him, "can we talk, after you're done here?"

"Yes, Private, but it will be a while before I'm finished, and"—she smiled to soften her next words—"I will not be changing my mind about marrying you. Understood?"

He grinned. "I do understand Miss Cara. I'll see you after your shift."

Cara shook her head at the young man's joy, then turned her attention to the next 'duster in line.

While attending Oberlin, Cara had served in the dining hall to help pay her tuition, but she never remembered those days to be so tiring. Her shift had ended thirty minutes before, and she was seated outside on a crate under the light of the waning moon. A breeze blew against her hot temples and sweat-dampened shirtwaist.

"Are you Cara Henson?"

Startled, she looked up at the mounted man in uniform looming above her in the dark. She'd been so tired, she hadn't even heard him ride up. For a moment she almost succumbed to panic; for in the dark and because of her fatigue, the blue uniform brought back the terror when she was nine, terror that had plagued her in nightmares ever since. "Yes, I am," she said warily. She hoped this wasn't another marriage prospect. Another six men had offered for her this night.

"Do you know a soldier named Benson Worth?"

For the first time Cara realized this soldier, whoever he was, was extremely angry. She sat up straighter, curious. "I met Private Worth a few nights ago, but I don't know if his first name is Benson."

"You don't even know his first name?"

The man's voice crackled with incredulity that made Cara even more confused and a bit irritated. "No, I don't."

"A man is about to be court-martialed because of you, and you don't even know his name?"

Her eyes widened. "Because of—wait." She stood and held up her hand. "Who are you?"

"Sergeant Chase Jefferson, United States Cavalry."

Cara wondered if he considered his position justification for his attitude. "And?"

"And Benson Worth is facing court-martial because of you."

"That's impossible."

"Is it? Why?"

"Because—" Cara didn't know why. She shrugged. "Well, I don't know why, but I do know I can't be responsible."

"Spoken like a true lady."

"Excuse me?"

"Benson Worth deserted his post tonight."

"And that's my fault?"

"Yes!"

"How?"

"Are you denying he had an assignation with you tonight?"

"Yes, Private Worth asked to see me this evening, but it was no assignation—at least not in the way you're thinking. I met him two nights ago over a plate of creamed beef, for heaven's sake." Cara did not like this man at all.

"He says you were considering marrying him."

"What?"

"Are you hard of hearing, ma'am?"

"No. I'm not. Private Worth asked me to marry him, yes. But I declined."

"So you admit you were supposed to meet him tonight?"

"Well, yes, but—" How would she explain the extenuating circumstances to someone who obviously considered himself both judge and jury? She decided she owed him no explanation at all. "Sergeant, I am sorry if one of your men took it into his head that I'd marry him. Private Worth seemed to be a nice young man. I'm sure his superiors will see his actions as those of an impressionable young man and be lenient. Good night."

"Wait just a minute."

Cara grabbed what remained of her patience and turned back. "Yes."

"You have nothing more to say than good night?"

He guided the horse closer but she held her ground. Horses didn't scare her, but she wasn't so sure about the rider. He'd maneuvered himself into the faint light cast by the lantern hanging above the kitchen door, giving her her first full view of his face. His mahogany jaw looked as if it had been chiseled from stone. The lips were stern beneath a full mustache, and his eyes blazed beneath a Stetson. "That impressionable young man may be in danger of losing his career."

"Sergeant, what would you have me do?" she asked, at wit's end.

"I want you on the next train out of here."

Cara had never liked ultimatums. "Oh, really? And if I'm not?"

She thought he would explode. "You always this sassy?"

"Always, Sergeant. My guardians called it my gift."

"Be on that train or I'll put you on it myself. I don't want your kind around my men."

"What kind is that?"

"The kind that takes advantage of impressionable men by offering them—"

"What? Creamed beef? You know nothing about what kind of woman I am. *Good night!*"

The next morning Cara awakened before dawn. She'd always been an early riser, but that morning she got up even earlier than usual. She attributed it to the excitement of her pending departure. She rose, shook out her skirts, and rolled up the borrowed pallet. Walking very quietly so as not to disturb those 'dusters still asleep, Cara crossed the hall to deposit the pallet in its spot in the corner. She waved greetings to some of the workers setting up the stations for the morning meal.

Outside, Cara saw that it had rained during the night. She pulled her shawl closer to ward off the damp. The rain had turned the well-traveled area around the hall into a sea of ankle-deep mud. The privies and the well pump were on the other side of the mud, but someone had thoughtfully laid down planks to cover the distance. Cara blessed the person as she walked on the wood.

When she finished in the privy, she crossed over to the pump, worked the handle, and splashed cool cleansing water over her sleepy face and rinsed her teeth. She dried her damp hands on her skirt and was preparing to return to the hall when she saw a buckboard making its way down the mud-clogged road. The horses were having trouble, balking as the mud oozed high around their forelocks, exhibiting a reaction that struck Cara as amazingly human. The driver of the board was impatient and brought out his whip. Three sounds—the man's vile curses, the whinnies of the terrified horses, and the crack of the whip—tore at Cara's soft heart. She hastily glanced around the yard for someone with the authority to make the man stop his cruelty. She noticed a few people watching the scene, but none seemed inclined to intervene.

When a particularly brutal blow struck one of the horses and sent it sprawling to one knee, she could stomach no more. She jumped from the wooden plank into the mud.

The buckboard had mired itself in the middle of the road. The man's whip continued to fall. His horses continued to scream. Cara, now at the back of the buckboard, climbed in.

She had the element of surprise. She came up behind the man and angrily snatched the whip from his hand. For a moment he was so astonished he didn't move, thus giving her time to fling the offensive whip into the mud. When he finally recovered and turned on her, she saw the drunkenness and rage in his red eyes.

Cara moved back. For the first time she realized what serious consequences she faced. The big-bellied man looked her up and down. Ominous. "Who the hell are you?"

Cara swallowed fear as she held his furious gaze. "Cara . . . Henson, sir."

"Where's my damn whip?"

Cara glanced down into the mud beside the buckboard, and he did the same, just in time to see the whip swallowed by the wet earth.

"Why you little—"

He grabbed her by the arm, snatched her to him, and drew back his fist. A rifle shot pierced the silence. The man held, looked up, and found himself gazing into the barrel of a Winchester. Holding the weapon was a mounted, grim-faced Sergeant Chase Jefferson. Flanking Jefferson were two troopers, also armed.

Cara's knees buckled with relief.

"Let her go, Thomas."

The man refused. In fact his grip became even tighter as he sneered, "You got no authority over me, soldier boy."

"Let her go, Thomas, or I will shoot you where you stand." The soldier had not raised his voice, but every word vibrated with deadly intent. He had not looked at Cara once.

Cara waited tensely, hoping Thomas would not call Jefferson's bluff. She didn't want any bloodshed. Thomas must have agreed, because a moment later he cursed and flung her aside. "Get off my buckboard," he shouted.

Cara did not argue. But before she could jump down, Jefferson moved his big stallion closer to the board, reached inside, and plucked her out as if she weighed no more than a feather pillow. She found herself seated before him on the horse. She twisted to look up into his angry face. "My men will take care of Thomas and the horses. You are coming with me."

He whipped the reins around, and the big horse began a slow walk through the mud. Only now did Cara notice the crowd of people her good intentions had drawn, and to her embarrassment, they cheered and applauded as the soldier carried her away.

But the sergeant was not cheering. In fact, as he halted the horse a short distance from Floral Hall, he said, "You seem to have a real gift for this."

Cara looked up at the eyes glittering below the Stetson and answered innocently, "What, having people cheer me?"

"No!" he snapped. "Causing a ruckus. That man could have killed you."

"Well, thanks to you he didn't. I couldn't let him continue to beat those animals. Now let me down."

He wasn't through. "Being cavalry, I understand why you did that."

"So your point is?"

His jaw tightened. "My point is, he outweighed you by nearly two hundred pounds, and he was drunk. Had he hit you, you'd be picking your teeth out of the mud right now. Next time let a man handle—"

"What kind of man, Sergeant? There were men around, but I didn't see any of them helping those poor horses."

"Oh, are you one of those free-thinking women who don't believe in men?"

Cara's eyes narrowed. She'd had enough of his opinions. "Did I say that? You are determined to stuff me in some little pigeon hole, aren't you?"

"I'm determined to make you see sense, sassy woman."

Cara's chin rose. "Sassy, educated, and opinionated. Men hate it." She stared up into eyes that stared right back. She wondered why her heart was suddenly beating so fast. And why did she feel so warm?

"I came looking for you this morning."

She felt mesmerized by everything about him, his size, his power, his face. A face she found much more handsome than she could have imagined last night. She suddenly remembered what she was about. "Why were you looking for me?"

"You are a muddy mess, do you know that?" His mustache twitched in amusement.

"Thank you for calling it to my attention," she told him stiffly. "If you would be so kind as to let me down, I'll go get cleaned up."

"I think I like you with mud on your face."

This statement caught her off-guard, too. "Why were you looking for me?" she asked.

"To apologize. I went back and questioned Worth again after I left you last night. He changed a few things."

"No!" she whispered in mock surprise.

"Yes. He admitted that meeting you last night had been his idea, and you'd done nothing to encourage him. He also confirmed that you turned down his offer of marriage. Says he didn't tell the truth originally because he wanted the men in the barracks to stop teasing him."

"About what?"

"Being a virgin."

Cara blinked.

The mustache twitched again. "He figured if he told them he had a beautiful woman wanting to marry him, they'd leave him alone."

"If Worth thinks I'm beautiful, he's younger than I thought," she quipped.

"Oh, I don't know," he murmured. "I think he's old enough."

Why, Chase Jefferson was flirting with her, Cara realized. For the first time in her life she wished she knew how to banter with a man. Well, she'd just have to give it her best try. "And so . . ." she prompted.

"And so, what?"

"You were going to apologize?"

He chuckled. "You're not going to make this easy, are you?"

"No, I'm afraid not. In fact," Cara added looking up into his handsome face, "if it weren't so muddy, I'd insist you do it on your knees, but since I'm being gracious, and you did rescue me, up here will suffice."

"This more of that gift of yours?"

She smiled.

However, he shocked the smile right off her face when he took her hand and slowly raised it to his lips. He kissed the fingertips. "My deepest apologies, Miss Henson."

Cara managed to croak, "Apology accepted, Sergeant." Every woman within sight was staring at him. Just as she was. She forced herself to remember where she was and what she was about. She pulled her hand free. "I . . . must go." She wanted no one carrying tales about her behavior to the school board of Henry Adams. She desperately needed them to hire her.

He guided the horse to the planks leading back to the hall with a skill that reminded Cara of her grandfather's way with animals. Jefferson eased her down to the walk, and Cara tried to ignore all the interested faces turned their way. "Thank you again, Sergeant Jefferson."

"My pleasure. Thank you for being gracious enough to accept my apology."

Cara had no idea where the boldness came from, but she heard herself ask, "Is that the kind of woman you like, Sergeant . . . gracious?"

"Sometimes . . ." he replied in a voice so soft only she could hear, "but sassy's nice, too, I'm finding out . . ."

Cara felt heat spread from her head to her toes as she stared up into his dark eyes. "How long will you be staying in Topeka?"

"I'm heading to Texas day after tomorrow. And you?"

"I leave later today, for the Solomon Valley."

There was a shared silence before he spoke. "I see. Then this is goodbye."

Their gazes locked. He was about to speak again when an attractive young woman interrupted. "Chase, where were you last night? I waited up half the night. Oh, hello," she said to Cara.

Cara noted that Jefferson had the decency to appear embarrassed. "Laura Pope, Cara Henson."

Cara in her mud-covered clothes felt like a beggar child standing next to the smartly dressed, dark-skinned woman, but nodded politely.

The newcomer looked Cara up and down, wrinkled her little nose, then said, "You don't mind if I steal my fiancé for a while, do you? My parents are having a dinner party tonight—"

After the word "fiancé," Cara heard little else. "By all means. The sergeant and I are finished."

Hoping the humiliation she felt did not show in her eyes as she looked at Jefferson, she added, "Have a safe trip to Texas, Sergeant."

She heard him call her name as she walked away, but she didn't turn.

* * *

"Ah, so you *do* know that handsome devil," Sybil said. "Just look at that mustache, those thighs. That man could make a woman break every code she's ever lived by."

Scandalized, Cara laughed. "You should be ashamed of yourself, trying to corrupt the schoolteacher."

"I'm not corrupting you. I see a superior model of the Lord's handiwork eyeing a friend who is college-trained, beautiful, and—he's coming this way. Are you ready?"

Cara watched as Chase stepped off the opposite walk and into the street. The closer he came, the faster her heart raced. She had to turn away from those dark eyes. "You, Sybil, my friend, have been in this sun too long. I'm not going to jeopardize my position for a Yankee soldier. I'm going inside. I have papers to correct."

"Coward. Oh, well, you're saved. He's been sidetracked."

Cara glanced over her shoulder. Chase had been waylaid by a reporter from the *Nicodemus Cyclone.* Chase caught her eye for one last, searing look that shook her to her toes.

"My, my, my," Sybil muttered. "So things are that way, are they?"

A very flustered Cara excused herself from the reverend's wife and fled into the safety of Sophie's boardinghouse.

Chapter 2

What a party they were having at Sophie's downstairs. There were fiddlers for dancing, good drink, good food—really good food. Cara knew, for she'd helped set out the buffet. Everyone was having a wonderful time—everyone except her. She sat at the desk in her room on the second floor, the strains of the celebration drifting up through the wooden planks beneath her. The music distracted her, making her tap her toe instead of grading the children's essays. She finally gave up, stood, and stretched.

She'd stayed away from the celebration for a number of reasons, most important her grandfather. Union soldiers were responsible for his death. Although the men downstairs had played no part in the tragic event, she couldn't bring herself to go down there. Seeing the blue uniforms brought back memories of the land she'd never walk again, the grandfather who'd been lost to her, and the nightmares that still haunted her from that terrible day.

The second reason she wouldn't go downstairs was Virginia Sutton, head of the school board, and her morality clause. Virginia owned everything of note in Henry Adams—the bank, the mercantile, the grain exchange. She'd made it plain the day Cara came to town and interviewed for the teaching position that she was reluctant to hire such a naive and inexperienced young woman. Virginia had said flat out that she was concerned about Cara's unmarried state and her possible influence on the children; she insisted Cara be held to the highest standards of morality and conduct enforced through a clause written into her contract. Sophie termed the clause nothing less than Virginia's way of making sure Cara had no fun at all, but Cara had signed without a murmur of protest. Not only had she needed the job, she wanted it. There was nothing she liked more than teaching.

Because of the clause, though, Cara had to be very cautious about her every social contact, especially if unmarried men were to be present. Chase and his soldiers presented lots of problems for her—especially Chase, whom she'd learned was staying in Sophie's boarding-house. But even the most innocent encounter could be misconstrued—by Virginia Sutton, if no one else.

The sounds of laughter and conversation brought a smile to her face; the music seeped into her pores and caused her body to sway to its tempo. She felt lighthearted, younger than she had in ages. It was a strain to hold back, not to join the party and enjoy herself . . . enjoy the company of the most handsome and intriguing man she'd ever met.

She'd tried to rid herself of memories of Chase Jefferson, and after her first few weeks in Henry Adams she'd pretty much succeeded. He was a soldier, a drifter, an adventurous man with no roots whom she'd known for less than a day. She'd decided she was a fool to let such a rogue capture her imagination. And that had pretty much been the end of that. Until today.

Well, there was nothing for it. He was here now. And the question she had to answer was how she was going to handle him.

Chase continued to be amazed and touched by the numbers of people who'd turned out to honor the Tenth. The food had been delicious, his men had been feted and toasted. In the adjoining room, the fiddlers were sawing away, and Chase noted how relaxed his men appeared to be. It would be hard to adjust to the trail again after all this.

Chase was only half listening to the gushing young woman seated by him. She appeared next to him the moment he'd entered the room, and introduced herself as Mae Dexter, daughter of the mayor, and one of the women who'd handed him flowers during the parade. Chase hadn't had the heart to tell her he didn't remember her, but he'd promptly accepted her invitation to share dinner with her and her father. While politely enduring their company, Chase spent most of the evening scanning the crowd for Cara Henson. He'd yet to see her and was beginning to wonder if he'd imagined her that afternoon.

"Are you listening to me, Sergeant Jefferson?"

Mae's question cut into his thoughts. Although her tone had been one of playful hurt, Chase heard the impatient undertone and gave the young woman his full attention.

"Are you married, Sergeant Jefferson?"

"Maebelle!" exclaimed her father, turning from a conversation he'd been having with one of the elders sitting to his left. "I apologize, Sergeant," the mayor said, shooting dark looks at his only child. "Maebelle sometimes forgets she's still a child."

"I am not a child, Papa," she protested petulantly. "I'm almost sixteen."

"No harm done, sir," Chase replied, trying to smooth the waters. "I can answer the young lady's question. No, I'm not."

When she sighed unashamedly in relief, Chase couldn't suppress a chuckle. "I'd like the honor of dancing with your daughter, Mayor Dexter, if I may?"

Father looked first to Chase and then to his daughter. He grudgingly gave his permission, but not before cautioning Mae to mind her manners.

Out on the floor Chase realized he'd made a serious error in his choice of partner. Mae's only topics of conversation were Mae, Mae's new dresses from St. Louis, and Mae. Chase doubted she'd spoken three intelligent words all evening. If he had to stand up with her all night, it would be a long one.

As if she'd read his mind, Sophie claimed him at the end of the dance on the pretense of Chase needing to meet someone. Sophie spirited him away from the pouting young woman and led him into the crowd.

"Thank you," Chase said earnestly as he and Sophie sought solitude behind the closed door of her well-furnished office. "I thought I was going to be stuck with her all evening."

"Well, Mae may be brainless but she's damn persistent. Here—" and she handed him a brandy.

Chase swallowed the fine liquor slowly, then sat back and relaxed. "So, how've you been?"

They spent the better part of an hour catching up on lost time. When they'd last seen each other, the Civil War was still being fought, Chase had been a growing but already handsome eighteen-year-old, and Sophie, one of the most sought-after quadroon women in New Orleans. She'd run a very elegant and exclusive house of pleasure back then, and her beautiful, multiracial girls had been in great demand by generals and businessmen on both sides of the country's conflict. Sophie, Chase, and Asa Landis, now the town carpenter and for more than twenty years the love of Sophie's life, had all been members of the Union Army. They served in the shadowy intelligence network headed by Harriet Tubman, the general.

"So why haven't you and Asa jumped the broom?" Chase asked her as the reminiscing continued.

She smiled. "I'm too old to get married, and so is he. Besides, I like things just as they are."

Chase remembered she'd always been independent. Her being so free-minded often had caused problems, not for Sophie, but for those who expected her to conform. Asa had called her not independent but outrageous the morning she rode through the streets of the city at dawn on horseback, as naked as the fabled Lady Godiva. One of her patrons had bet she didn't have the nerve to do such a thing, and that was all it had taken. She'd done it and, if Chase remembered correctly, had received a new carriage and a matching pair as payment.

"What are you thinking about?" Sophie asked.

He smiled, then spoke, "That morning you rode naked through New Orleans to win the bet."

She laughed. "Asa was so mad. We argued for three days afterward. Told me ladies didn't do that kind of thing. I told him the day I turned into a lady, he could bury me."

"What happened to the girls?"

"Oh, some went North; a few came West. Lost touch with most after I closed the house in '68."

"Did Asa come West with you, or did you find each other again out here?"

"We came together. When he got back from the war, things were fine until the last troops pulled out and the Redemptionists took over . . . It was awful." She paused, shaking her head, her eyes sad. "The killings started during the elections of '78. I wanted to leave, but you know how proud Asa is. He said we should stay and fight, especially after Washington refused to intervene. 'We didn't fight the war just to hand back the vote, Sophie,' he'd say."

"But you finally convinced him."

"No. I finally drugged him and smuggled him out of New Orleans."

"You . . . drugged him?"

"Had to. They'd've killed him. He was too well-known, too vocal. Those sack-wearing, cowardly bastards were dragging men from their homes and murdering them right in front of their terrified families. Asa would've been just one more dead Republican. I was not going to give them that satisfaction."

Chase had seen that same terror throughout the South. The escalating attacks had been one of the reasons he'd joined the army. It provided him with a legal right to carry a sidearm and protect himself. "You *drugged* him?"

"When he woke up twelve hours after I convinced him to have one of my toddies, we were well on our way here."

"You know, Sophie, after all these years you really ought to let him make an honest woman out of you."

"I'm fifty-two years old. I don't need the blessings of a government that can't even uphold the Constitution."

Chase nodded. Hard for him to believe she was over fifty, but in reality he knew it had to be true because he'd turned thirty-five in April. And, no, she didn't have the voluptuous figure that had prompted men to challenge her to ride naked on horseback any longer. Still, her cafe-au-lait skin, her beautiful face held the radiance that had inspired more than a few sonnets.

"Enough about me," Sophie said. "What did you do after Appomatox?"

"Worked with General Tubman on the Carolina Sea Islands for a while, then joined the army in '67."

"How's it been, the army?"

"Rough in a lot of ways. Some of the officers, like that dead bastard, Custer, refuse to command Black troops. In some places, though, the army gives you a chance to be as much a man as times will allow. Many a time we're respected for the job we do. Most settlers don't care what color we are as long as we escort them safely through the territory, build roads, and find new sources of water. Most, I said, not all. Some would rather be attacked by Apaches than have a Black soldier assist them in any situation."

"What about the regular troops, any trouble with them?"

"Depends on the individual. The Rebs that came back to Texas after the war hated everybody in Yankee blue, whether their skin was black or white, so troopers wound up protecting one another's backs. The white troops call us 'brunettes.' Some of our men are offended by the term, others aren't."

"Well, Chase, everybody here appreciates you, believe me. You fellows make Black folks all over the country proud."

A polite knock on the door interrupted them. Sophie called entry, and Cara stuck her head around the door. "Sorry to bother you, but someone said—" Cara stopped abruptly when she spotted Chase.

"Come on in. You told me this afternoon that you and Chase have already met. Sit with us and talk a spell, Cara."

Chase stood, and his heated gaze traveled slowly over the demurely dressed woman who'd been in his thoughts every minute since he'd seen her on the street. *Finally,* he said to himself. Up close she was as beautiful as his memories had painted her. Honey-brown skin, soft, lush mouth. Her eyes, fringed with long, thick lashes, were still a dazzling tawny brown, almost feline-looking, and they held him with the same intensity they had back in Topeka. "I see you made it to the Valley," he told her, realizing his words were inane, but he longed to hear her sweet, husky voice again and didn't mind making himself seem silly, if he could get her to talk.

"Yes, I did. How was your trip to Texas?"

"Long."

"I'm sure the memories of the dinner with your fiancée were a comfort."

"She wasn't my fiancée," he said truthfully. He'd wanted to wring Laura Pope's spoiled little neck for that lie, especially when Cara took off angry.

Cara looked into his face. Not his fiancée? She felt a great relief. They stared at each other. The power of his gaze caught her by surprise. She turned her attention from his mischievous eyes to Sophie. "I—I have some letters to write and the music is distracting, so I'm going to go over to the school." It was a lie of course. She'd intended to enjoy Sophie's company, but Chase was having such a strange effect on her, she felt she had to get away for a little while.

"Are you coming back later?"

"No, it'll probably take me most of the night to finish. I'll just sleep on the cot in the back of the school."

Sophie looked worried. "Cara, there're a lot of strangers in town. Maybe you wouldn't be safe sleeping there tonight."

Cara appreciated the concern. "I'll be fine, Sophie, and I'll bolt the door. Besides, there's no school tomorrow, and I can use the free time to do some cleaning. The floors need to be mopped. I can also wash those windows I've been trying to get at all spring." Cara felt as though she was rambling and blamed it on Chase's presence.

"Well, promise me you'll get someone to walk you over there."

"Sophie, I'll be fine and—"

Chase interrupted, seizing the opportunity. "You have a penchant for trouble. Better let me escort you."

Cara turned on him, intending to decline the offer, but Sophie forestalled her. "Good. Thanks, Chase. I have to get back to the goings-on. 'Night, Cara."

And before the word "wait" could be formed by Cara's lips, the big woman, amazingly fleet for her size, was out of the room.

Cara, temporarily at a loss as to how to disengage herself from Chase, opted for politeness. "Sergeant, thank you for your offer, but now that Sophie's gone, I can tell you frankly that you don't have to accompany me. I can take care of myself."

"I've seen the way you take care of yourself, remember?"

Cara would rather not.

"And," he added, "Sophie's right. You never know who you might run into on your way. Wouldn't do the Tenth's reputation any good to have a woman's virtue tampered with while we were in town."

Cara's efforts to keep the exasperation from showing on her face failed completely. "Very well," she said, her tone grouchy. "I have to go up and get my bag. I'll return in a moment."

The May sky was as clear and bright with stars as any Chase could remember. He looked down at the silent woman who kept pace at his side. "How was the trip out here from Topeka? Any problems?"

"No. Tedious though."

"Do you like it here?"

"Yes, I do. I have some fine students and—"

He stopped. "Students? You're the schoolteacher?"

Cara, who'd also stopped, answered with a chuckle, "Yes, why do you sound so surprised? I graduated from Oberlin, and I've taught before."

"I just never thought of you as a teacher. Seamstress maybe, but not schoolteacher."

"Why not?"

"Every teacher I had was either a grumpy man or an old hag. And you, Miss Henson, aren't even close to either. . . ."

Standing on the dark walk, Cara looked up into his eyes and saw all the things that had turned her inside out the last time they'd met: his handsomeness, his maleness. This man could make a woman break every code she'd ever lived by. For someone as earnest and inexperienced as Cara, it could spell disaster. "The schoolhouse is just a bit farther along," she said and started to move again.

They walked the rest of the way in silence.

When they came to the small stone building, the former church that served as the school, Cara thanked him for the escort and turned away. But he refused to be dismissed so easily.

"You'd better let me go in first. Wouldn't want you grabbed by something in the dark."

Cara looked up at the rakish face and refrained from pointing out it was he she was most worried about. Instead, she took the key to the padlock from the pocket of her skirt and handed it to him without argument. While he went inside, she waited patiently for him to find the lantern, light it, and say she could enter safely.

Once in, Cara stated, "Thank you, Sergeant. I can manage from here."

Chase took his time. He looked over the classroom with its neat line of pews and desks. Student work was nailed on the walls. In the corner sat an old black pot-bellied stove that would be fired up when the weather turned cold. He fingered a globe and opened a dog-eared text. "You really like teaching?"

"Very much," she said, placing the carpetbag that held her belongings on her desk.

Chase leafed through a few more pages of the book before replacing it on the neat stack at the end of a pew. "What kind of things do you teach?" he asked, looking directly at her.

Cara wondered if he'd meant the question to sound so provocative. "I teach history, arithmetic, penmanship. The basics. Sergeant, you have to go. I—I have a morality clause in my contract, and if Virginia Sutton finds out I'm here with you—"

"Who's she?"

"President of the school board."

"Ah." He nodded. "Then she wouldn't approve if I came over there and kissed you, would she?"

Cara felt as though she'd been hit by a stagecoach. She finally managed to croak a reply. "No. She wouldn't."

"And what about you? Would you approve?"

"I'm not going to answer that," she whispered.

"Why?"

"Because you're making sport of me, and—"

"No, I'm not, schoolmarm. I've wanted to kiss you since that night I lit into you about Benson Worth, remember? It was your gift, I think you called it, that got to me."

Cara wondered how to slow this speeding train. "And was Private Worth court-martialed?"

"No. He received thirty days in the stockade. He's up in Minnesota with the Ninth."

Chase let his gaze linger a few moments longer on her tawny beauty. He didn't want to compromise her reputation, but he didn't want to leave her, either. He chose the honorable option. "I'll be back in the morning to check on you."

"That's not necessary."

"It is to me." He walked to the door. "Put this bolt on after I leave, Cara."

"I will." But before she could tell him again how unnecessary it was for him to come back in the morning, he stepped back out into the night.

Cara spent an uncomfortable night on the small cot in the school's back room. When she awakened stiff, sore, and, most certainly bruised, she vowed never to do it again. She felt as if she'd slept on rocks.

She padded barefoot in her flannel gown over to the window where she saw the beautiful sky of a beautiful day. She decided to go ahead with her plans for cleaning the school and went off to attend to her morning's needs.

Cara had just finished winding her thick hair into a chignon when a knock sounded on the door. She opened it to find Franklin Cooper, the mailman and father of two of her students, standing on the other side.

"Morning, Miss Cara."

"Good morning, Mr. Cooper. What brings you out so early?"

"Brought your mail. Sophie said you be here cleaning most of the day so she thought you'd like to have it now instead of waiting until you get back home."

"Why, thank you." She took the packet he offered then smiled, recognizing the fine penmanship of her old friend, William Boyd. Receiving correspondence from him after so many months made the day seem even brighter.

"Sorry I didn't get it to you sooner," Cooper said, "but with the Tenth in town and all—"

"I know, Mr. Cooper, it's all right. How's your wife?"

They exchanged pleasantries for a few moments longer, and then Cooper continued on his way.

Cara closed the door and took the letter to her desk. The last time she'd seen William had been almost six years ago at Oberlin. He'd been a good friend during her two years of study there, even though his family had been related to prominent abolitionists and she'd been a backwoods Georgia girl related to no one. William had not let class differences stop him from forming friendships.

As always, the letter began: "My dearest Cara . . ."

He followed with an apology for the length of time between missives and hoped the following five pages would serve as ample penance. He wrote that he no longer clerked in his father's Boston dry goods store. For the past three months he'd been working for T. Thomas Fortune's *New York Globe.* Cara was impressed. A lot of folks, herself included, considered the *Globe* one of the finest Black newspapers in the country. Mr. Fortune's editorials regularly and strongly denounced the continuing violence and terror in the South.

William then brought her up-to-date on his four sisters. The women in his family had always been socially minded. Cara remembered the stories he had told of his grandmother's work with the Black abolitionists of her era and of his mother's commitment to securing the passage of the Fifteenth Amendment in 1870. His sisters had allied themselves with many other women across the country fighting to secure voting rights for women of all colors. On a less serious note, William described his impressions of New York, specifically the wonder of the still uncompleted Brooklyn Bridge, reportedly the longest and most innovative structure of its kind anywhere in the world. Construction had begun in 1869, and now after more than ten years of deaths, political wrangling, and scandal, it finally appeared as if the bridge would indeed be finished.

Another knock on the door broke her concentration and, still reading, she walked over and opened it. "Morning, Miss Henson."

Cara blinked at the sight of Chase Jefferson filling the doorway. The pages of William's letter slid unnoticed to the floor.

"Sophie thought you might like breakfast."

He stood facing her, as beautiful to her as the fine May morning. His uniform looked freshly washed and starched. His shoulders seemed to block the sunlight. She stammered. "Oh, yes—yes. Do come in."

She stepped aside to let him enter, then waited as he paused to retrieve the letter. She saw him glance at the salutation. His jaw seemed to tighten.

"It's from a close friend," she felt the need to explain, taking the letter from his hand. "We met at Oberlin."

"Where is this close friend now?"

"New York. You can just leave the tray there," she said, pointing to her desk. "Tell Sophie thanks when you get back."

To Cara's surprise, he sat at her desk and began to unload the tray. Only then did she see that there were two plates and two sets of silverware.

"I'll mention it when I get back. Right now, I'm going to eat."

Cara, still standing at the threshold, took a quick glance outside to see if anyone had seen him enter. She had no way of telling, however, so she left the door open wide. "You can't eat here, Sergeant."

"Why not? Wouldn't your close friend approve?"

"William has nothing to do with this. Remember Virginia Sutton?"

"Ah, yes, the president of the school board, the one who wouldn't approve of me kissing you."

"Yes." Cara barely got out the one word. Her throat was constricted, her pulse racing.

"Would this close friend of yours approve?"

"Would Laura what's-her-name approve?" she shot back.

"Most definitely not, even though I've told you she was not my fiancée. How about William?"

"For the last time, William is a friend—a very close friend, yes, but only a friend. He won't care one way or the other, unless the man is a cad."

"Your male friends always start their letters with 'My dearest Cara'?"

"William does, but, Sergeant, why on earth do you care how I'm addressed?"

"Just curious. You planning on eating or not? Food's going to be cold."

"No." Although she hadn't had anything to eat since yesterday afternoon, and she'd felt hungry moments ago, she didn't think she could swallow a bite now. Eating in here with him alone? It wasn't just that Virginia Sutton would have a fit, then gleefully take away her job; it was the intimacy of sharing a solitary meal with Chase that had her at sixes and sevens.

He looked up at her with his great dark eyes and said, "Very well, don't eat then. You just stand and listen to me ask impertinent questions such as: Why isn't a beautiful woman like you married?"

Cara sat.

"Thought you'd change your mind. Coffee?" He held up the small pot.

She usually spurned the brew, never having acquired an appreciation for a beverage whose taste depended solely on the person making it. "Sergeant, you are going to ruin me. Have you been listening to anything I've said?"

Chase liked the soft drawl in her voice. "Can't help but. You've been ranting since I came in. That another one of your gifts?"

Cara shot him a look, then held out her cup. The coffee he poured was reminiscent of the man—dark and strong.

Chase slid his gaze over her decidedly unhappy features while savoring the fat yellow eggs on his plate. At first glance one might think her a contemporary of the mayor's daughter. Like Mae, Cara still wore the fresh bloom of youth, but there the resemblance stopped. The small brown hands curled around the coffee cup were not the pampered hands of a prim miss; those hands had worked hard and long. And her eyes held a wisdom that seemed to contradict the unlined features.

To satisfy his curiosity, Chase reached over and picked up her free hand. It stiffened and her eyes narrowed. He turned it over and looked at the palm. "Where's a schoolteacher get calluses?"

"Chopping wood mostly."

Cara tried to keep her voice neutral but could feel how erratic her breathing had become as he gently rubbed his thumb over the toughened skin at the base of her fingers. "I chop wood for the stove in the winter. I—I've been chopping wood since I was young—well really all my life. I . . . Why are you doing this to me?" Her trailing voice came out in a whisper.

"You think Laura Pope ever chopped wood?" He turned her hand over, and Cara instinctively tried to fist it to hide her nails. He held on. "Probably not," he answered himself.

"Probably not . . ." she echoed, pulling her hand away.

"Where are you from, Cara?"

"Georgia. See how well I answer the questions you put to me?"

He flashed her a smile. "What part of Georgia?"

"A place west of Atlanta called Cherokee."

"Family still there?"

"No, they're dead," she whispered.

Chase heard the pain in her reply. He wondered if her family had been lost in the war or some time during Redemption. "How long you been on your own?"

Cara could feel old wounds opening. "Since I was—can we talk about something else, please?"

"Sure, darlin'. My apologies for prying."

Darlin'? He'd purred the word. Cara gulped.

"Are you married, Sergeant?" she blurted.

"My name is Chase, Cara. And, no, I'm not. Why? Do you know a schoolmarm looking for a husband?"

"You are incorrigible. No, I don't know a schoolmarm looking for a husband, but if I did, would you be interested?"

"Only if she can kiss."

The low timbre of his voice rippled across her skin. The deep mahogany skin, rakish mustache, and assessing dark eyes were disturbing enough, but the aura beneath this easygoing manner pulsed with a male power she found wholly overwhelming.

"Any man ever kissed you, schoolmarm, really kissed you?"

Cara couldn't speak. She could only remember what Sybil Whitfield had said yesterday about Chase being the kind of man capable of making a woman willingly break every vow she'd ever made. "Kissed how?" she heard herself question in return.

He stood then came around to where she sat trembling on the corner of the desk. He reached down and tilted up her chin. "Like this."

Cara hadn't counted on his being this . . . good. The few kisses she'd received in the past had been chaste, sometimes almost apologetic pressings of the lips, administered by men no more experienced than she; but this slow, this languid brushing of his warm mouth over hers felt neither chaste nor inexperienced. Her lips softened like spring rain.

Feeling her lips yield, Chase found the intensity of her response surprising. He'd been wanting to sample her sassy lips since Topeka. He figured once he'd gotten his wish, the need would wane, but her sweet, ripe mouth, tasting so virginal, drew him powerfully. Her warm female body made his manhood harden. Arousal sang deep in his blood, and all he could think about was bringing her to the point of surrender.

And Cara did surrender. Her untutored senses rode the swell brought on by the warmth of his mouth and the heat of his nearness. When he intimately flicked his tongue against the tender corners of her parted lips, then sought out the sensitive skin beside her ear, she responded with moans of yearning.

Gradually, he ended the kiss and stepped away.

Cara was left weak, breathless, shaken. He stood a pace away, his glittering eyes holding hers.

"Your close friend William ever kiss you like that?"

Cara's eye narrowed. "What if I said he had?"

"I would probably say that you're fibbing, schoolmarm."

"And I would say that you are probably the most arrogant Yankee I've ever met. You kiss me until my shoes melt and—if you go on laughing, I will hit you!"

"Sorry, darlin', you were saying that I kissed you until your shoes melted . . . and then what?"

"Out!" Cara told him, pointing to the door. She jumped down from the desk. "You and that Yankee mustache, out!" She felt as if he were toying with her, and she had no experience to draw on to combat him and his kisses.

He had the nerve to chuckle, then replied, "Schoolmarm, you have no idea how close you are to being kissed again. It's that sassiness, I think."

"Sergeant, are you going to leave or am I going to have to get Sheriff Polk?"

Chase found himself amazed by the strength of his attraction to her. It was not something he had great experience with, this need he seemed to have acquired for her, and he was not sure how to proceed, but he found matching wits with her damn exhilarating. "You'll return Sophie's tray and dishes?" he asked.

"Yes."

He picked up his hat and strode to the door, then looked back. "Going to be an interesting ten days, schoolmarm."

Cara pointed to the exit once more, and he threw back that magnificent head, laughing as he walked out into the sunshine.

Chapter 3

Cara was pumping water into the second of two large buckets when Sheriff Polk appeared at the corner of the schoolhouse. The aging but still tough Wayman Polk had treated Cara like a member of his family since the day she'd arrived in Henry Adams, and she was very fond of him. She smiled.

"Morning, Sheriff." The pumping finished, she straightened and wiped her brow.

"Morning, Cara." Polk walked over to her. "Cleaning the school today, I see. Here, let me help you with those buckets. We can talk inside." He hefted the buckets and preceded her through the rear door of the schoolhouse.

"Thanks. It will take that old stove at least half the day to heat this water, and I don't want to still be here mopping after the sun goes down. What brings you here?" Cara asked as he placed the buckets on the stove. She moved around him to stoke the feeble flames of the fire. Wood was a luxury on the plains, and the corn and sunflower stalks they used instead for fuel made poor fires.

"Heard you had a visitor this morning."

She jerked her head up and looked directly into the sheriff's eyes. "Yes, I did."

"And he kissed you?"

Cara's worst fears were being realized and she took a deep steadying breath. "Yes, he kissed me."

Polk's face was unreadable as he stared at Cara. At last he asked, "Do you want to file a complaint?"

"No, of course not." She clenched her hands. "Can I ask who told you?"

"Frank Cooper. He said he came back to the school to give you a piece of mail he'd forgotten to drop off earlier. The door was open, and . . ."

"There we were."

He nodded.

She had to ask the obvious question. "Will Mr. Cooper tell the school board?"

"Probably not. Frank doesn't like Black Widow Sutton very much. He was worried about you is all."

Cara sighed, grateful for Mr. Cooper's taste in people, and that it had been he, not one of Virginia's cronies, who'd seen the incident.

"Now, Miss Cara, if Jefferson is bothering you, I can speak to him. We're proud to have the Tenth in town, but fooling around with our womenfolk is not part of the celebration."

"Thank you, Sheriff, but that won't be necessary."

"Are you sure? I can be discreet."

"This won't happen again. The kissing, I mean." Cara knew that the embarrassment she felt showed plainly on her face.

"Didn't come over here to embarrass you, Miss Cara. It's just people care about you. And with you not having any family and all, well, me and some of the others feel responsible. I don't want to see you taken advantage of."

Cara wanted to kiss him on his gray head for his kindness. "I appreciate your concern. You can be sure that I won't let him take advantage of me."

"Man like that can run circles around a woman like yourself."

"I know, but I'm certain that I can handle him."

"Well, if you change your mind, let me know," said the sheriff, taking his leave.

The sheriff's vow of discretion notwithstanding, Henry Adams was a very small town, and Cara knew that before the week was out everyone within fifty miles would hear about her being caught kissing Chase Jefferson. Damn that man. If Chase weren't so outrageously forward, she wouldn't be the subject of gossip. She got out her mop, pulled the buckets with their still-cold water from the stove, and set to work with a fury.

By late afternoon, Cara had cleaned the schoolhouse from top to bottom—and had almost forgotten about the incident with Chase. She looked around proudly. The old converted church served well enough as a schoolhouse, and she kept it up to perfection. After Asa found the time to patch the roof, it would see them snugly through another winter. But how Cara yearned to have a real school with enough space to accommodate all who wished to attend. Thirty-five students, their desks and chairs, bookcases, the stove and kindling box, cabinets for materials filled every inch of the one-room building.

When Cara reported on cramped conditions and asked for a new building, the school board cried poverty. Everyone in town agreed that educating the younger generation was one of the highest priorities, but they also agreed that there wasn't enough money for a new school. For months Cara had been writing to aid societies back East imploring them for donations to improve their existing school, if not build a new one. She wished with all her heart that the letters she received in return had been filled with a lot less praise and words of support and a lot more bank drafts. To date, she had not been able to procure a penny for her project.

Cara put away her cleaning tools and got ready to leave. Her hands were red and sore from all the scrubbing with harsh soap, and she'd split yet another nail. She wondered what Chase would say now if he saw her hands. She'd wager that Laura Pope never scrubbed floors on her knees. Chastising herself for even thinking about Chase, much less Laura, she closed the door behind her.

Cara carried the tray Chase had left back to the kitchen where Dulcie presided. Dulcie had come to Kansas with Sophie and Asa, and modestly proclaimed herself the best cook west of New Orleans.

"So, Miss Cara, what is this about you kissing a Yankee soldier?"

"How'd *you* hear about it?"

"Frank Cooper. I've known Chase since he was a little boy. You could do worse, you know."

"You're as bad as Sybil Whitfield. She said pretty much the same thing yesterday."

"Then you should listen to your elders. You're a very special woman, *chèrie,* and you deserve a special man."

Cara groaned. "I'm leaving. Is Sophie around?"

"She's in her office. Chase, too."

Cara groaned again as she pushed on the door to let herself out. She definitely wouldn't see Sophie now.

Every available bit of space in Cara's room was crammed with books —packed in crates, stacked in piles, and neatly arranged on shelves. Only Sophie and the women folks lovingly called "the Three Spinsters" had more books. Sophie had one whole room whose walls were lined with bookshelves holding beautifully bound leather volumes. The Three

Spinsters had so many books, they'd turned a portion of their home into the town's first lending library.

Cara was in the process of searching through her library for a book on plants she'd promised to loan to one of her students. She used an old sawhorse as a stepladder to access high places. It was not the most sturdy thing, and Sophie had warned her many times about the dangers of using it, but if Cara balanced herself well, she could reach the crated books on the top shelves Asa had put up for her. A knock at her door interrupted the search. Balancing on the sawhorse, she called out, "Come on in."

"Afternoon, ma'am."

Cara teetered on her precarious perch at the mellow sound of Chase's voice. After the briefest of glances at him she returned her attention to the crate of books. "Go away. The kissing booth is closed."

She heard him walk farther into the room.

"Sorry to hear that." He chuckled. "Real sorry to hear that." Chase liked the view, slightly above eye level, of Cara's hips in the flowing green skirt. "What are you doing?"

"Looking for a book for one of my students."

"Well, come down before you fall."

Cara ignored the advice. "Why are you here, Sergeant?"

"Had a talk with your sheriff about you. He says unless my intentions are honorable, I should keep my distance."

Cara looked down from her perch. "And are they?"

"Suppose I said they were?"

How many women had fallen victim to his fatal smile? From the rakish face to his knee-high boots, he was every woman's temptation. "Sergeant, though I hardly know you, I doubt I'd be wrong in saying that you probably don't have an honorable bone in your body where women are concerned."

To her surprise he laughed. "I thought schoolteachers were supposed to be timid little things."

"Not this one. Timid doesn't jibe real well with opinionated."

"You are something," he said with soft admiration.

His heated gaze made every nerve in her body come alive. She felt her limbs go weak and decided she'd better climb down. When she'd dusted her hands on her skirt, she looked up at him. "I hope you will take the sheriff's words to heart."

"And miss the most fascinating campaign of my career? I've never been one to go against the law but—" He reached out and brushed away a cobweb clinging to her cheek. "How's this for a solution? I won't touch you again unless you ask me to."

Cara shuddered as his knuckle grazed her skin. The gesture almost became her undoing. His words were as innocent as the look on his handsome face, but she realized he was challenging her. For someone who claimed to have been warned off by the sheriff, Chase did not appear to be the least bit wary. He seemed to know she wanted nothing less than to feel his kiss again. Despite the treacherous softening of her will, she said, "You can rest assured, sir, that I won't be asking for your touch."

Chase smiled. "You never know, Miss Cara Henson. Time has a way of changing things."

"Why are you doing this?"

"Doing what?"

"Paying me so much attention?"

Chase wondered if being frank was also one of her gifts. "Would you rather I didn't?"

He had her there, and she knew it. She also knew she was certain how she felt. "It's flattering, but I think this is just a parlor game to you. A way to pass the time while you're here."

"I find you attractive Cara, very attractive, and, yes, I would like nothing better than to spend my time here in your company. But it's not a parlor game. If it were, I'd win very easily."

"Oh, really? You're very sure of yourself, Sergeant."

"Some of us are gifted in other ways, too, schoolmarm."

"Modest, too, I see."

He grinned. "You doubting my abilities?"

"No. I just think no other woman has ever told you no before."

"And you plan on being the first?"

"It might do you good to be denied once in a while."

"Do I hear a challenge?"

Cara had no idea how she'd gotten to this point; she should know better than to toss words with him. "Yes. You hear me saying that this is one woman who can resist your legendary talents."

"You think so?"

"I'm certain."

He smiled again, the mustache twitching. "All right, schoolmarm, you're on. Since I'm not the marrying kind, we'll stick to kissing, how's that?"

The audacity of the man. And the charm of him . . . He was wildly attractive, his challenge exciting, stimulating—and totally out of line with the morality clause in her contract. "You're going to leave town a frustrated man, Sergeant Jefferson."

"No, I won't."

"Especially since you've already promised not to touch me."

"Granted, that might have been a mistake, but it'll make the prize that much sweeter."

"What prize?"

"The kisses I'm going to get."

"My lips are not going to touch yours."

"It's not your lips you should be worried about. A woman can be kissed in a thousand places . . ."

Cara blinked against the dizzying effects of his husky voice saying those shocking words.

"I'll see you later, schoolmarm."

He tipped his Stetson and started toward the open door. At the threshold he turned back. "Oh, by the way, I'm in the room next door."

The news caught her by surprise. "That's good to know, Sergeant."

He left then, and Cara spent quite some time just staring at the space where he'd been, wondering what she'd gotten herself into.

The next morning, Cara sailed out of her classroom and over to the Liberian Lady with a glare in her eye and mayhem on her mind. Previously she had stopped by the sheriff's office, but was told he was in Nicodemus on business. The Liberian Lady, the town's combination saloon and whorehouse, was owned by the nineteen-year-old son of Virginia Sutton.

When Cara barged through the swinging doors, the hands of the man playing the piano froze above the keys. The sudden quiet drew the attention of the nine or ten patrons seated at tables and those standing at the bar.

"Why, hello. If it isn't our little schoolteacher."

Cara turned and looked into the wintry gray eyes of Miles Sutton. He'd come to town six months before and opened the Lady, much to the anger of every church member in the Valley. In those six months, Cara had yet to find anything about him that she liked.

"What can I do for you, love?"

Cara found it difficult to conceal her dislike, especially when he dared to use such an intimate term in addressing her. She started to tell him she was not, nor would she ever be, his "love," stopped herself, and asked brusquely, "Was Issac Brock in here earlier today?"

Miles, drying a glass with a none-too-clean rag, made a show of mulling over her question. "Let's see, Issac Brock. Fess Brock's boy?"

"Yes." She gritted her teeth, then with a false smile added, "Fess Brock's boy."

"Maybe. Why?"

"Because he was late for school this morning."

"What's that have to do with my establishment?"

"He was drunk."

Miles smiled at her and continued to dry the glass. "If he's got money, Cara, I have to serve him."

"The boy's twelve, no more than a child."

"That's not what my girls say. Hey, Arla," he called to a woman seated at one of the tables. "Schoolteacher says Fess Brock's boy is no more than a child. You agree with that?"

Arla looked up from her glass and let out a knowing laugh. "That *child* sure taught me a thing or two."

Embarrassment scalded Cara's cheeks. Arla was one of the three women Miles employed as "hostesses." None of them would ever be mistaken for beautiful, but the men who patronized the Lady didn't seem to care. The knowledge that Miles allowed Issac not only to drink, but also to cavort with the whores, made Cara all the more angry. "Sutton, if I hear about any more of my children being in here, I will have Sheriff Polk close you down. If he can't I will write the Federal marshal in Wichita, and then the governor."

"Whoa, whoa, love, take it easy. The last thing I want to do is get you riled at me. I'll keep the Brock boy out of here." He smiled. "In exchange, how 'bout letting me escort you to the party my mother's giving for the soldiers?"

"There is no exchange for being a decent human being."

"Now, Cara, sooner or later, you're going to realize you and I are fated."

"Miles, you are fated for territorial prison if you serve any more children in here."

"I won't be put off forever, love."

"Good day, Miles."

Issac had come to school retching from the effects of too much of the Lady's cheap alcohol. Cara had put him on the cot in the back with a wet cloth on his head and an old pot nearby to catch his misery. She'd also sent one of the children out to the Brock homestead to fetch his parents. Now, as she returned to the school, the children looked up from their studies. "How's Issac doing?" she asked.

"His ma came and got him. She said to tell you that she'd whip him as soon as he quit throwing up."

Cara nodded, while wishing fervently that someone would take a whip to Miles Sutton.

That evening, Cara sat at her small dressing table brushing her hair. She stopped in mid-stroke as her thoughts floated back to Chase. He made her feel so reckless, so . . . so alive. No man had ever kissed her passionately before. She'd been nearly incoherent when he released her. The mere memory sent a rippling response through her body. She admonished herself for dwelling on his "talents" and vowed to push thoughts of him aside. No matter how he made her feel, she knew he would be around only ten days and then ride away. She meant nothing to him beyond dalliance, and she just had to keep reminding herself of that fact—or endure the consequences.

Cara gave a final pat to her hair and got dressed. Tonight her students were putting on a skit for the Tenth. Later she, Sophie, and other invited guests would ride out to the Sutton spread for Virginia's dinner.

Cara was not looking forward to that part of the evening.

While waiting for her students to arrive, Cara moved about the empty classroom, setting out the costumes and props for the performance, then paused a moment as her mind played back over other classrooms in her past. She'd been teaching for several years, and although none of the positions up until now had worked out, her drive to bring education to the children of her race had not diminished. One woman was most responsible for placing her on the path to teaching— Mrs. Rosetta Sterling. Rosetta and her dear friend Harriet Bat, the orphanage's other staff member, insisted on educating every child who entered their doors, even if the child—due to limited intellect—could grasp only the basics. To supplement the orphanage's books, kept in crates in nearly every room in the old plantation manor, the women wrote North for materials from relief organizations and churches. Writing paper had not always been available after the war, so lessons in penmanship and ciphering oft times had been conducted in the hard-packed earth. The daily lectures held in the mornings after chores had been serious undertakings. Mrs. Sterling allowed no slackers. Both she and Harriet had spent many years lecturing on the abolitionist circuit and loved to debate. Cara remembered spending many nights studying newspapers and pamphlets for the facts needed to do well in the formally conducted weekly Sunday contests.

But during her first few weeks at the orphanage after the death of her grandfather, she'd participated in nothing. Everyone, from the soldiers who'd taken her from her grandfather's cellar a few days after the lynchers had gone, to the laundress who'd fed and cared for her at the contraband camps, to Rosetta and Harriet, thought Cara was mute. Because of her grandfather's death, she'd withdrawn into a world of silence that not even the whirlwind atmosphere of the orphanage with its twelve rambunctious children could entice her to leave.

The nightmares began the second week after Cara's arrival. The terrifying dreams were filled with images of bloodied, blue-coated demons killing her grandfather over and over again. The scenes always ended with the Bluecoats, now horrible-looking skeletons, coming for the little girl in the cellar, and Cara would bolt awake, screaming. The soothing arms of Rosetta were always there, no matter how long it took the sweat-drenched and shivering Cara to drift back into a fitful sleep. One night after a routine visit by some Union soldiers come to fix the orphanage roof, a visit that left Cara terrified and recoiling in a corner, the nightmares were especially vivid. Her nocturnal screams brought Rosetta running more than once. As dawn broke, Cara wakened in Rosetta's lap, the big green rocker in the front parlor cradling them both. She remembered looking up into the compassionate brown eyes and speaking her first words in weeks in a tone as broken as her spirit. "I miss him so . . ." And Cara had missed her grandfather, missed him with all her heart. Mrs. Sterling's reply had been soft. "I know, darling, but we have to go on . . ." And as she held Cara, they both cried.

In the years that followed, Cara realized the words spoken that dawn could have been as much for Rosetta herself as for the benefit of the nine-year-old child. Rosetta had lost her husband, John, to slave-catchers in 1850. The men sent from his Virginia owner came for John in the middle of the night. They quoted a sum the owner demanded in exchange for John's freedom, but the Sterling's entire savings didn't equal a tenth of the price. John's one and only letter to her arrived about a year after his reenslavement. He'd written her of his love and of his impending sale in the Deep South as punishment for attempting another escape. Rosetta never heard from him again.

Harriet Bat filled Cara in on the rest of the story one night as they were writing letters to Washington in support of the proposed Fifteenth Amendment to give Black men the vote. Both Harriet and Rosetta thought the amendment too narrow, but they supported it because equal rights for women were also being lobbied for inclusion. Rosetta had gone to Boston to attend a meeting of the American Equal Rights

Association, founded by Susan B. Anthony, Elizabeth Cady Stanton, and Frederick Douglass. Cara remembered asking Harriet how long she and Rosetta had been friends. Harriet replied, "All our lives, and in fact we're twins."

The revelation baffled Cara. Harriet laughingly explained. She and Rosetta had been born on the same day, six or so hours apart, to parents who'd been the best of friends. Both mothers were helping their husbands bring a group of runaway slaves from Indiana to Michigan when it came time to give birth. The two sets of parents, one free Black and the other immigrant Irish, had been not only friends, but neighbors and staunch abolitionists for many years. The birth of their "twin" daughters further cemented their bond.

Both girls were raised to confront life straight on, so during the second year of the Civil War, when Rosetta showed Harriet the newspaper accounts of the large numbers of runaways being drawn to the advancing Union Army and declared she was going South to look for John, Harriet refused to be left behind. They headed for Washington.

There, Harriet posing as mistress and Rosetta as servant, they toured the camps holding the nearly ten thousand runaways and confiscated slaves, first termed "contraband" by General Benjamin Butler. The camps across the river in Alexandria were not as large as those in the capital but also held thousands of refugees. They did not find Rosetta's John, but they did find appalling conditions in the camps: typhoid, diphtheria, entire families infected with measles. People near death huddled next to the living in dangerously overcrowded buildings. The relief societies and the representatives of the government were overwhelmed by the newcomers arriving day and night. Space was at a premium, food more than scarce.

The two Michigan women stayed to lend what help they could and were assigned to work in the old schoolhouse in Alexandria, headquarters for Black women and children on the Virginia side of the river. Hundreds of women and children were inside the building with nothing to do except to wait for the return of their husbands and fathers working behind the lines of Union troops. The children, like children everywhere accustomed to being outside, had become listless and lethargic from the forced confinement.

The work at Alexandria schoolhouse eventually led to establishing the orphanage. Rosetta brought the first child back to the small room she and Harriet shared because the mother, dying of disease, begged Rosetta to give her daughter a future. Rosetta did. She contacted a childless free couple she knew in Ohio and sent the girl to them via agents of the Underground Railroad. Rosetta Sterling and Harriet Bat found homes for fifty-five other parentless children. They continued to search for John and picked up children throughout their tours of the contraband camps of the South. In 1864, Cara became one of them.

Under the care and love of Rosetta and Harriet, Cara grew from a nightmare-plagued, silent child to an educated young woman of poise and conviction. By the age of seventeen, she'd been arrested twice in rallies on behalf of causes, had more than a few letters printed in local newspapers, and been banned from the local Freedman Society offices for her fiery tirades over the disgusting conditions of the local schools under their jurisdiction.

But neither woman was there now to see how far her life had come. Both were dead, killed in '78 when nightriders torched the free school they'd established not far from the original site of the old orphanage. Cara, working with a relief society in Ohio, had been heartbroken at the news. And she still missed them. Always would.

An hour later, Cara seriously wondered if she'd chosen the right profession after all. The noise and commotion in the schoolroom could only be described as bedlam. The "Indians" dressed in their colorful paint and buckskins were in one corner practicing their war whoops, while the "buffalo soldiers" ran back and forth brandishing their home-made wooden sabers at any girl standing still long enough to be a target. As a result the girls were running and screaming. For what seemed to be the fifteenth time, Cara cautioned little Rilla Walker to stand still so she could repair the hem on her dress. If not for the three mothers who were volunteer helpers, the children would have been in even more of an uproar.

After placing the last stitch in Rilla's hem, Cara removed the pins from her mouth and yelled at two of her more rambunctious eight-year-olds. "Becca Franklin, if you jump from one more desktop, I'm telling your parents. Buffalo soldiers do not abuse property. Or point sabers at their sister's eyes, Frankie Cooper."

Cara wished she'd chosen a nice, quiet Bible play for the children to perform tonight. "Okay, boys and girls, line up. We're going over to the town hall now," she called out wearily. The evening had just gotten under way, and she and the mothers were already exhausted.

While the volunteers scooted the squirming, excited children into a passable line, Cara turned to her desk to gather up her things. She glanced up and went stock still at the sight of Chase Jefferson standing in the open doorway.

"Evenin', Miss Henson."

Every eye in the room focused on the two of them. A moment ago there had been enough noise to mask cannon fire, but now it was silent enough to hear a pin drop on cotton.

Into the breach sounded Rilla Walker's awe-filled whisper. "A real buffalo soldier!"

This would be the children's first close look at one of their heroes.

"Come in, Sergeant Jefferson," Cara invited.

It seemed impossible to deny the effect he had upon her senses. She shook herself, desperately trying to keep in the forefront of her mind that the man would be leaving soon. She turned back to her staring students. "Children, I would like you to meet Sergeant Jefferson of the Tenth Cavalry."

A buzz of excitement went through the children, and she had to clap her hands to restore order. When they quieted, she added, "Now, we have no time for questions this evening, but if you're very well-behaved at tonight's performance, and I know you will be, perhaps we can convince Sergeant Jefferson to come over to school and pay us a special visit before he and his men leave next week."

Cara turned to him. His eyes were riveted on her with such intensity that she seriously doubted he'd heard a word.

She was right.

"I'm sorry, ma'am. What did you say?"

His eyes were working her over unmercifully. Cara heard one mother discreetly clear her throat. "I asked if you'd come by and visit with the children before you leave town." She dearly wished he'd lower the heat of his gaze. It made her want to undo the top buttons of her blouse and fan herself.

"My pleasure," he replied.

Cara turned back to the children, pretending not to see the smiles and raised eyebrows on the faces of the mothers. "Class, I would like you to show Sergeant Jefferson how quietly you can go to the door and line up outside."

To her delight they did it quickly and, more amazingly, quietly.

Chase nodded a polite goodbye to the mothers as they hurried out to join the children, then turned his attention to Cara. She'd donned a white blouse and yet another dark skirt. He knew teachers, especially women teachers, weren't paid well, but to him it was a crime that she wasn't paid enough to afford clothing that befitted a woman of such grace and beauty. She should be draped in the finest fabrics in the latest styles, he thought. He was certain the blouse she wore was one of her best, though. It appeared to be of finer quality than those she'd worn previously and had more lace at the throat and cuffs. The contrast of the white material against the honey-brown skin of her graceful neck made him want urgently to pull her into his arms. He tamped down his desire, cleared his throat, and said, "You look very nice, schoolmarm."

"Are you going to behave tonight, Sergeant?"

"I will behave any way you want me to." His words communicated one thing, his expression quite another.

She rolled her eyes and handed him a small but heavy crate. "Carry this, please."

Chase looked at the brightly colored jumble of items inside. "What is all this?"

"Scenery, Sergeant. And if we don't hurry, the children may start without us."

The short skit opened with a group of buffalo soldiers who happened upon a party of Indians. The groups, wary of each other at first, talked instead of fighting and parted friends at the end. The performance inspired thunderous applause. Chase and his men cheered and whistled. Cara came to the front of the hall for her bows, smiling a tad shyly at the appreciation.

Afterward, Chase watched Cara as she moved about to thank parents for their support and congratulate her young thespians. When she seemed to be finished with those duties, he eased toward her through the crowd. "Excellent performance, Miss Henson."

Cara turned. "Did you like it?"

"I did. And so did my men. Talking instead of fighting saves lives. Maybe we should send the children to Washington."

"Not a bad idea," she said, smiling.

The assemblage broke up not long after punch and cake were served. The children, some walking on sleep-weakened legs, and others already asleep and carried by a parent, were being taken over to Sophie's. She'd generously offered the beds in her big attic to the children of folks who lived outside the town. Her staff would keep an eye on them while those parents invited by Virginia Sutton went on to the dinner.

With Chase handling the reins, the buckboard rattled down the road toward the Sutton spread. Sophie took up most of the seat, Cara, squeezed in between the two larger people, could not avoid having her thigh pressed hard against Chase's. His muscles felt rocklike. She told herself the pressure didn't bother her, but her body called the lie. Every time the wheels hit a rut, which was often, the upward motion threw her solidly against him, and the shocking result of her breast boldly meeting the side of his well-developed upper arm shortened her breath.

"Chase, for heaven's sake, rein more to the right, you're about to kill me," Sophie ordered after a particularly violent jolt.

"Sorry, ladies," he offered apologetically.

He expertly reined the team more in the direction Sophie requested, but his movements only increased his closeness to Cara. His hard arm slid against her nipple every time he adjusted the leads. Each pass was shattering and intimate. Cara didn't know if it was accidental or not, but she prayed they reached Virginia's before she swooned.

"Comfortable, ma'am?" he asked innocently, turning in her direction.

She glared at him. "Quite comfortable, Sergeant. Thank you."

Chase, an experienced member of his gender, knew her detached manner was a pose. His accidental brushing against her breast had been just that: accidental. But, had Sophie not voiced a complaint, he would have been content to drive the rutted side of the road just so he could hear the soft, shaky breaths Cara drew each time he inadvertently stroked her.

Too soon, the lights of the Sutton house came into view. Moments later, Chase extended a hand to help Sophie alight. While she moved off toward the house, he turned his attention to Cara. He placed his large, strong hands upon her waist and effortlessly lifted her clear of the buckboard. Her skirt billowed a second before settling back into place, and then he brought her down slowly, so slowly the heat of their bodies seemed to mingle.

When the earth became solid beneath Cara's feet, she scarcely noticed. The raised voices of the people celebrating inside faded away. She stood there, her heart doing flip-flops, her throat clogged. Only the raw power emanating from him and the directness of his gaze touched her. She felt torn between wanting to flee from the wild magic she sensed in him and wanting to stroke the dark planes of his face. Why hadn't she ever experienced this sweet fear with any other man? The feelings and desires he'd awakened were as wondrous as they were disturbing.

Sophie's call from the porch broke the spell, and Cara backed away, hoping the darkness of the night would mask her trembling unease.

Chase smiled, and reluctantly let her go. His gaze followed her as she moved quickly to the house and then inside. Patience, he reminded himself. Patience.

Chapter 4

As usual, Virginia Sutton was the most elegantly dressed woman in the room. Her son, Miles, born to her at an early age, was not yet twenty and she was still a stunning woman at thirty-five. Her gown, low-cut and created out of gold brocade with satin trim, displayed her curvaceous figure to best advantage. Any other woman would have looked overdressed in this room full of women clad in mostly homespun and gingham, but not Virginia. The jewelry and fancy gown declared her position and prestige in the town she all but owned, and she wore her expensive finery with dash and without guilt.

The atmosphere was more subdued than at Sophie's gathering, undoubtedly because no one wanted to break any of the imported treasures or spill anything on the fine Spanish rugs in Virginia's magnificent home. Everyone was on his best behavior.

Still, people seemed to be having a good time, Cara saw as she looked around. The food was plentiful, the music lively, and Virginia's fabled liquor flowed freely.

Cara tensed as she spotted Virginia making her way through the crowd in her direction. Although Virginia stopped here and there to chat and smile with the most distinguished of her guests, her gaze was riveted on Chase. Cara turned away, hoping the woman would look for prey elsewhere, but knew there was little chance. There wasn't a man in the room who could match Chase. Every female had turned his way when he'd entered. The snug-fitting uniform showed the power in his tall, trim body and the mustache perched so spicily above the glorious-looking mouth made him all the more dazzling. Virginia would want him, and Virginia always got what she wanted.

"Cara," Sophie said, "you take care of Chase for a few minutes. I need to speak to Sybil over there. I'll find you later."

Sophie moved away quickly.

Take care of Chase, Cara thought. She looked up at him and found him smiling down at her.

"Well?" he said. "You heard what the lady said."

But before Cara could respond, the voice of the Black Widow sounded at her back. "Ah, Miss Henson, and who is this handsome man?"

Cara turned to Virginia and made the introductions.

"Pleasure, ma'am," she heard Chase say.

"No, Sergeant Jefferson, the pleasure's all mine . . . You know, I was a bit skeptical about having this soirée. You and your men are very famous but I had visions of trampled rugs and broken crystal. I'm glad to see I was wrong. Your men are quite well-mannered and, in fact, a few are most handsome. Wouldn't you agree, Miss Henson?"

"Yes, the men are well-mannered, very clean."

Virginia laughed softly. "Ah, Miss Henson, you would concentrate on their manners. Sergeant, our Miss Henson is a most competent educator, but I'm certain she wouldn't know what to do with a handsome man if he fell facefirst into her . . . lap."

Cara's eyes blazed, but she held her tongue.

"Come dance with me, Sergeant," Virginia invited.

Chase heard the velvet-sheathed order, but since he took orders only from the United States Army, he said, "I'd like that, but I promised the first dance to Miss Henson."

Cara could have kissed him. But she forced herself to recall that after he was gone, Virginia would still be there. She decided it was best to be gracious. "I don't mind, Sergeant. Besides, I'm not much of a dancer. You go ahead. We can dance later or another time."

"Are you sure?"

She nodded. "I'm going to get some punch."

"Excellent idea, Miss Henson," Virginia said.

"Well, don't go far, Miss Henson," Chase cautioned in a voice that made her heart start doing those crazy flip-flops again. "Wouldn't want to lose you in this crowd."

"I won't get lost," Cara replied and went off to find the punch table.

From across the room, Cara watched Chase and Virginia dance to the slow sweet strains of a Spanish guitar. Virginia's smile was her dazzling best. It was easy for Cara to see why so many people considered the Black Widow one of the loveliest women in all of Graham

County. Few women possessed such flawless golden skin, such big sherry-colored eyes as she or such hair the color of dark wine. No wonder that few men could resist her beauty, Cara thought. As much as she disliked Virginia, she realized that the older woman knew much more about handling a man like Chase than she ever would.

Not wishing to watch them together for another moment, Cara stepped back into the crowd, then made her way to the back door. Sophie's gently restraining hand suddenly stopped her.

"Have you seen Chase, dear?"

"He's dancing with Virginia."

"Is that why you're running off?"

"I'm not running. I—I need some fresh air."

"Ah, I see," Sophie said, then added, "don't let that woman run you out of here."

"This has nothing to do with Virginia. It's warm in here is all."

They both knew it was a lie, but Sophie let it go.

Near the back door, Cara passed Miles Sutton, leaning against a wall with a drink in his hand. He leered and toasted her with the glass. She ignored him.

Once outside, pulling in deep lungfuls of the cool night air, Cara felt much better. From her spot on the long wide porch, she saw others who'd come out to escape the crush inside. Under the lights of the moon and of lanterns stuck on poles, several men were pitching horse-shoes, laughing, talking, and passing jugs.

"Well, hello, Miss Cara."

She turned to see the sheriff stepping up onto the porch and nodded at him. "Sheriff."

"What are you doing out here all alone?" he asked with a smile. "Young, pretty woman like yourself should be in the middle of all that dancing in there."

The music had changed. Lively strains of fiddle music were drifting out to them now. When Cara did not reply, his voice became tinged with concern. "You feeling poorly, Miss Cara?"

"I'm fine, Sheriff Polk. Just came out to get some air."

There was a shared silence, then he said, "I went ahead and talked to Jefferson. Hope that was all right?"

"I appreciate your concern, Sheriff. But I do believe Virginia is going to fix my troubles with the sergeant."

"Virginia?"

"Yep. Take a look inside."

He turned to the window behind them, and Cara knew that even with all the people in the way, the laughing widow and the handsome soldier wouldn't be hard to spot.

"Oh," the sheriff uttered in understanding.

"Yes, oh," Cara echoed, looking out into the night. "If you had a daughter, Sheriff, what would you tell her about a man like Chase Jefferson?"

"Well, I'd tell her that he's a fine man, but probably not for her. He's a soldier, and many of them don't like putting down roots. But I'd also tell her to look in her heart. It is, after all, her life."

For a moment she mused on his words, then said, "That's sound advice, Sheriff."

The sheriff smiled wryly and ambled off, leaving Cara alone with the night and her thoughts.

Chase excused himself from Virginia's side as quickly as politeness allowed. She was indeed a very beautiful woman and he hadn't missed her slyly couched hints about her availability. In the days before meeting Cara, more than likely he would have taken Virginia up on her offer, but the whole time he was dancing he'd had no other woman on his mind than the schoolteacher.

He'd witnessed her exit and the tightness in her small face when he'd led Virginia out onto the dance floor. Where had she gone? he wondered.

Cara didn't even have to turn to know he stood behind her. She could feel his presence like the stroke of the night breeze against her cheeks. "Is Sophie ready to leave? She said she didn't plan to stay long."

"Almost."

"So, what do you think of the Widow Sutton?" Cara asked softly.

"I expected her to be older."

After a long silence Cara said, "She's very beautiful, isn't she?"

"Yes, she is, but then so are you."

Cara turned to him then. "Even if it isn't true, it's a nice thing to say."

"You doubt my veracity?"

"Veracity? That's a pretty big word for a lowly soldier who tramples carpets and breaks crystal, wouldn't you say, Sergeant?"

He laughed. "Is she always so predatory?"

"With me, yes, and I have no notion why. After all, I wouldn't know what to do with a man if he fell facefirst into my lap."

"Ah, schoolmarm, don't tempt me . . . Never mind," he said softly. "So how was my behavior?"

"Stellar, Sergeant. I haven't wanted to succumb to your talents once."

"Then dance with me."

His offer made her sense leap. "Out here?"

"Here and now. You promised me a dance, remember?"

She took a hasty look around to see who might be near. Recklessness overcame her again. "I'd like that very much."

She placed her small, trembling hand in his large, sure one. His other lightly graced her waist. He began to glide her around the dark porch. The music flowed gently from inside. Cara could not tear her eyes away from his shadowed gaze. The hand on her waist burned through the fabric. Her feet were keeping excellent pace with his polished steps, and she felt as if they were dancing on air. He moved her onto the darkest part of the porch, and after a few more charged moments, their steps slowed, then stopped, and their gazes locked. He released the hand holding hers and reached up to stroke her cheek. Her eyes closed. He tenderly tilted her chin and lowered his mouth to cover hers, brushing her lips until they opened for the temptations offered by his tongue, and he licked their sensitive corners.

"Now who's succumbing?" she whispered.

"Sassy woman . . ." He pulled her against the hard, long length of him, and she caught fire. She gave no thoughts to morality clauses, Virginia Sutton, or the men pitching horseshoes who might be able to see them. Her whole being was enthralled by him and the realization that she'd been wanting this . . . wanting him, all night. She slid her hands up his muscled arms and thrilled to the pressure of her lips on his. Taking a lesson from him, she slid her tongue against the opened corners of his mouth. He groaned at her boldness and pushed her gently back against the porch post. His hard thighs moved against her in a slow rhythm that, unaware, she began to mimic. She sighed with pleasure as his lips left hers to sample the side of her jaw, her neck, while his strong hands made slow, hot circles up and down the sides of her white blouse. When his right hand began to explore the shape of her skirt-draped hip and thigh, Cara came up for air, and clamped her hand on his wrist. "We have to stop. . . ." she murmured.

He did so, but with great reluctance that equaled her own. They shared several more soft, sweet tastes of each other before he finally withdrew.

Cara's breathing took a moment to quiet, and while it did, she filled her eyes with him. "You are determined to ruin me, aren't you?"

"Only if you want me to, darlin'."

She smiled, passion blazing in her eyes. "Sophie's probably ready. . . ."

"One more kiss."

He reclaimed her mouth, and his lips moved over hers for a few endless seconds. Only after he heard her soft moan did he let her go.

"Now we can leave," he whispered. "You go and find Sophie. I'll meet you out front with the board."

Cara quickly found Sophie. On their way to the door, Cara's gaze locked with Virginia's. Even from across the room, Cara could read the anger in those eyes. She nodded politely and followed Sophie outside.

As they rode home, Cara wondered when the passion would subside. Every inch of her body throbbed. Being squeezed against Chase made it impossible to forget the interlude on the porch. She stopped trying. She'd enjoyed it. She would probably be appalled at her actions in the morning, but not now. Now the feeling of him so solidly against her made her senses sing.

Chase pulled the horse to a halt up in front of Sophie's place and waited for the women to get out. "I'll take this on over to the livery."

"Thanks, Chase."

"Good night, Miss Henson."

"Good night, Sergeant," she returned softly.

"Tell me about Cara," Chase asked Sophie as they sat in her office. He'd stopped in after taking the buckboard over to the livery, hoping Cara hadn't gone up to her room yet, but she had.

"She's a lot like me, knows her own mind, independent."

"She says she's been on her own since she was nine."

"Yep. Her grandfather was killed by Union soldiers in '64."

"*Union* soldiers?"

"Union soldiers. Her grandfather was a free man. Some of Sherman's troops lynched him when he wouldn't tell them where his master had gone."

"Lord," Chase whispered.

"I know. Some other troops, Black troops I think she said, found her a few days later in the root cellar, delirious and in shock. She lived in a contraband camp for a while and then went to an orphanage."

Chase's heart broke for Cara. He remembered how solemn she had become when he first asked after her kin. No wonder. "What happened to her parents?"

"Mother died in childbirth, father in one of the late battles of the war. He was with a Black regiment."

"She's had a hard life."

"Yes, she has, but then so have you."

He didn't speak of his own past. "Tell me why she hasn't been snatched up by one of these farmers around here."

"She's real smart, and some men are put off by that. And she's not easily impressed. When the Black Widow's son came to town six months ago, he was just sure she'd be bowled over because he'd attended Howard College. Well, she wasn't. He runs a saloon for heaven's sake. I guess he thought that wouldn't matter."

"Virginia Sutton has a son?"

"Yes. Showed up one day out of the blue. He and his ma don't get along very well though, according to what I've heard. He told Cara she's fated to be with him."

"Fated?" He'd never met the son, but already he didn't like him.

"Fated. But she is a fine woman. Make some man a good wife."

"Don't look at me that way. I don't know a damn thing about marriage—and I plan to keep it that way."

"Then why all the questions?"

"Curious, that's all."

"Your curiosity could cost her her job. I heard about you kissing her over at the school."

Chase stood. "Well, that's between me and her."

"And between you and me. I have to tell you I'll shoot you with your own Winchester if you break her heart. She's a schoolteacher, not some woman in a cathouse."

It was the second time he'd been warned off Cara, and it didn't sound any better coming from Sophie than it had from the sheriff. "I do know the difference, Sophie," he replied tightly.

"I'm not trying to make you mad, Chase Jefferson," she scolded. "But you remember that she is as inexperienced as she looks."

"Yes, ma'am." He walked toward the door. As he reached for the knob, he looked back. "Any more advice?"

"Yes, as a matter of fact. I was in the man-and-woman business for a long time, and one of the things I learned is this—for every man in this world, there is a woman somewhere who will make him sell his soul for just one of her smiles. Be careful where your curiosity takes you."

He nodded and left.

* * *

In her room, Cara undressed and slipped into her nightgown. As she walked past the mirror, she caught a glimpse of herself. She touched her mouth hesitantly. The memory of Chase's kiss still burned, and she relived the trembling wonder of it all. She'd never been called beautiful before. She'd been called stubborn, opinionated, and, by a few people, unladylike, for her penchant for playing baseball with the children every Friday, but beautiful? She stared at her reflection. The glass confirmed what she already knew; her features would not stop a clock, but they didn't qualify her as a great beauty, either. She shook herself free. Then, musing that the man probably called every woman he met beautiful, she picked up the hairbrush.

The light offered by the turned-down wick of the small lamp beside her bed barely pierced the soft shadows. Seated on the edge of the mattress, Cara brushed, then braided her hair. A soft knock on the door startled her. She slid off the bed and walked the short distance, pulling on her robe as she did. "Who's there?" she called quietly.

"Chase."

Cara went weak against the door. "Sergeant, go away, please. Unless the house is on fire, it will have to wait until morning."

"It can't," he called back.

Oh, dear heaven, Cara thought. What could he possibly want at this late hour? Surely, he didn't think the kisses they shared were an invitation for a midnight tryst in her bedroom? "Go away."

"Cara, if you don't hurry up, somebody's bound to see me out here."

Cara hesitated. Did she dare let him in?

"Either open up," he said, "or everybody's going to know the schoolteacher's having a midnight visitor."

She thought about the other boarders and the children sleeping upstairs in the attic room while their parents were at Virginia's. "You wouldn't dare!"

"I'll pound on this door so hard, they'll hear it in Houston."

Cara quickly undid the bolt, but only opened the door wide enough to see out, hiding behind it. "What do you want?"

"Can I come in?"

Looking at him, Cara could think only about his kisses—and someone seeing him in the hallway.

"Well?" he prompted. "The longer I stand out here, the better the chances I'll be seen. Please, Cara, this will only take a minute."

He was right about the percentages, of course, Cara realized. She stepped back and he slipped in.

It took Chase's eyes a moment to adjust to the dimness. Once they did, he drank in the sight of her. Just looking at her made him hard as granite.

"What do you want?" she asked, already feeling drawn to his mustached lips.

"A truthful answer to your questions involves my seducing you, schoolmarm . . . and I've promised myself that won't happen."

Cara swallowed hard and pulled her robe more tightly about her.

"I really came to make a date to see your students. How about day after tomorrow?"

"That sounds fine." She couldn't take her eyes off his mouth. Her hands itched to slide up the muscles of his arms and to feel his touch in return. She turned away from temptation and moved across the small room, hoping it would help them both to keep from falling into each other's arms.

Chase grinned, mentally applauding her perceptiveness. Yes, he wanted her. He wanted her very badly, especially after tasting her sweetness earlier. "Scared of succumbing to my talents, Cara?"

"Frankly, yes!"

Her answer pleased him. "Well, then, I'll try to be good. Have you read all of these books?"

"Yes, I have." She still felt the wild magic and was valiantly trying to set it aside.

The books were stacked and piled everywhere: on the two needlepoint chairs, on the shelves that took up one wall, beside and under the dresser and its companion table. She watched as he picked a book from one of the two-foot-high stacks atop the trunk at the foot of her bed. He glanced at the title, flipped through the pages a moment, then set it back before choosing another.

Cara wished she'd turned up the lamp. She'd toyed with the idea upon his entrance but had chosen not to. She hadn't wanted the action to be misconstrued as an invitation to prolong his stay.

Only now did she realize her mistake. She couldn't handle the man in full light, and tonight proved she couldn't handle him in the dark. How could she have ever thought softly lit shadows would offer her any better control? At that moment, he looked up from the book in his hand and his gaze was so bold her heart seemed to lodge in her throat. "How much longer do you plan on staying?" Her voice came out in a nervous croak instead of the nonchalant tone she intended.

"Long enough to kiss you again."

The frankly spoken statement, coupled with the husky, bold tone, put a trembling in Cara's knees and a shuddering in her soul. "I think you should—should go," she stammered.

The wavering light of the lamp directly behind her turned her thin nightgown and robe nearly transparent. The peaked curves and inviting hollows of the bare body beneath were displayed in a startling silhouette that Chase found highly arousing. His eyes were taunted by the dark, shadowy circles of her nipples, and the equally tempting dark patch above her slightly parted thighs. Her positioning was an age-old female trick, but he felt certain Cara did not know. Her innocence made the tableau that much more erotic.

"I can't go anywhere as long as you're standing in front of that lamp. . . ."

It took Cara a moment to grasp his meaning, but his vivid look, accompanied by the thoroughly male smile playing beneath his mustache, set off an inner warning that caused her to glance down at herself.

The sight widened her eyes. Scandalized, she jumped away from the light like a surprised jackrabbit.

"Much better."

Cara did not think it better at all! Her breathing could barely keep pace with her furiously pounding heart. "Sergeant, please leave." He had her shimmering like heat on the horizon.

He set the book down and walked to the door. Cara sighed with relief. In truth, however, her feelings were divided. A part of her wanted his kiss, wanted him to stay, to talk. She realized she wanted to know this man—could know that man, if she let herself go. But he would be riding away soon and she would probably never see him again. All the more reason to hold back.

"Good night, *mariposa.*"

The unexpected and huskily spoken word rolled over Cara with a trembling warmth. She had no idea what it meant, but she was determined not to succumb. "That a standard good night for the women who let you into their bedrooms at night?"

"No, but it will be for you, sassy woman. Do you know what *mariposa* means?"

"No."

"It's Spanish for butterfly. That's how your lips feel when I kiss you. Soft, fluttering butterfly wings."

A second later he was gone.

It took Cara much longer to recover, and even longer to get to sleep.

Chapter 5

Twelve-year-old Issac Brock, the Goliath of the Free Public School of Henry Adams, and bane of those smaller than he, chose eight-year-old Frankie Cooper as his victim of the day. The saber Frankie had worn the night before in his role as buffalo soldier mysteriously had disappeared after the performance. Frankie, proud of the saber he'd cut and sanded himself, had been devastated by the loss. He'd lain awake most of the night up in Sophie's attic room worrying over its fate.

This morning, as the children were filing into the schoolroom, Issac Brock slyly let on where the saber might be found. Frankie and his best friend, Willie Franklin, ran out of the school ignoring Cara's repeated calls to return. When she asked the other students if they knew what the boys were up to, no one offered an explanation.

Twenty minutes later, Cara, reciting the lesson, looked up to see Frankie and Willie reenter the room. Their faces were the angriest eight-year-old faces she'd ever seen. Their fists were balled tightly at their sides. Frankie had tears in his eyes. In moments it became apparent the two friends where advancing on Issac Brock. Upon reaching his target, Frankie attacked like an enraged terrier. The startled Issac yelled and tried to shake free of the punching, kicking, and crying dervish Frankie had become. Willie jumped on him, too, adding more weight to the fight. Issac, pummeled high and low, began spinning in an effort to break free. He probably would have succeeded had not Frankie's nine-year-old sister, Faye June, launched herself across the room to aid her baby brother. All hell broke loose then. Child after child threw himself into the fray—on the side of Frankie and Faye June. Issac had played nasty pranks on nearly every child in the school over the past two years, and Cara knew he deserved what he was getting, but she was the teacher and had to act as peacemaker.

She waded into the tornado that had spilled out of the small class and into the dust in front of the school. She pulled off a child here, grabbed one around the waist there, and peeled away the top layers. She sifted through the middle layer. Some pretty serious fighting was going on at the eye of the storm, and Cara caught a small fist in the eye. She instantly curled up, hand to her tearing eye. When the stars finally ceased whirling in her head, she shouted, "All right, stop this *now!*"

The children had heard her use what they called "The Voice" only a few times during the two years she'd been their teacher, but they recognized it, and every one of them froze. She peered through the watery eye and saw that they were now lined up and waiting, all thirty-five of them. She heard a deep male chuckle, and turned slowly. A mounted Chase Jefferson and a few of his men were watching from the street. Her glare dared him to laugh again, and he quickly composed himself.

"Do you need some help, Miss Henson?"

She ignored him. She also ignored the other townspeople who'd stopped running errands to watch. But she didn't ignore the children who looked as if they wished she would. "Now," she said softly, "Frankie Cooper, you may begin."

He told her about his saber.

"Where's the saber?" she asked crisply.

Willie Franklin, holding a hand to his bleeding lip, went over to the grass next to the school's outer wall and brought it to her. She took the hilt but wanted to drop it when she noticed the saber's filthy condition.

"He threw it in the church privy!" Frankie Cooper screamed, enraged all over again. He lunged at Issac. Cara grabbed him by the shirt and glared at Issac.

To Willie she said, "Go around to the pump and put some water on your lip." She sent one of the children who hadn't been involved in the brawl to get some rags to help clean up Willie and the others with cuts and scrapes. Out of the corner of her eye she saw one of Chase's men dismount, grab a small bag from his saddle, and head around to the back of school. She assumed he'd gone to help, and she gave thanks for somebody who seemed to have a little sense.

She returned her attention to the slime-covered saber. It had a note tied to it with a gnarled piece of wire. Cara read: "I got yu good Franke Koopr an if yu tel mis hisen or enybody els yu r a babe."

"Issac did you write this?" She had no doubts he had. His spelling had always been . . . distinctive.

"Yeah."

"Detention for two weeks."

"Aw, it was just a joke!"

"Frankie Cooper, Faye June, one week. The rest of you, detention, one day. Now, everybody inside!"

Chase dismounted and was standing a little ways off, legs slightly spread, arms resting behind him. An army stance, Cara supposed. She hadn't forgotten his snickers. "Yes, Sergeant?"

"Sorry I laughed. Let me buy you a steak."

"No, thank you. We'll be eating with the ladies of the A.M.E. Church tonight, or didn't Sophie tell you?"

"Not to eat, schoolmarm. For your eye."

In full view of everybody on the street, he tilted up her chin and peered at her hurt eye. It was nearly shut. "It's going to be a beauty."

She backed away from his hand. "I'll see if Sophie has a steak."

"You should probably go lie down."

"Have you ever been told to lie down because of a black eye?"

"No."

"Then why are you suggesting I should?"

"What are you so mad about all of a sudden?"

"I'm not a hothouse plant, Chase Jefferson, and I do not like being laughed at."

"I did apologize, remember?" Chase found it difficult to keep his mustache from giving away his mirth. If she could only have seen herself wading through the children. He would never laugh at the sight of her being hit deliberately by anyone, even a child. But seeing the battling children tumble out of the door, then watching her emerge from the school like an angry mother hen to pull children off the pile, yelling the whole time, had been too comic. She'd looked so startled by the accidental blow that he'd chuckled in spite of himself. Thinking about it now brought another round of chuckles—a very unwise slip, judging by the angry expression on Cara's face. She strode away, and he was hardpressed to stifle his laughter.

Cara walked over to thank the soldier who'd gone around back to help the children, then turned to Chase and his men. "I'm glad I could provide you Yankees with some entertainment," Cara said coolly before turning sharply and marching back to the school.

"Looking forward to this evening, Miss Henson," Chase called.

Cara gave him her back and went inside. Only the presence of the children kept her from slamming the door behind her.

* * *

After spending the balance of the day in the saddle, Chase used the long ride back to Henry Adams to rid himself of some of his anger. Of the five ranchers the colonel's aide at Fort Wallace had asked him to contact, only one had stuck by the agreed upon price for the horses the cavalry wanted to buy. Two of the ranchers on the list had only nags for sale; the other two—well, the other two wanted absolutely nothing to do with "nigger soldiers," and at gunpoint ordered them off his land.

Chase's smoldering ire flared back into full flame as he replayed the incident. More than a few Black troopers had lost their lives to short-sighted, narrow-minded individuals like the two he and his men had encountered this day, while the army, fettered by the times and its own outdated policies, offered little in the way of support. An incident at Fort Concho, Texas, in '78 stood as a grim example. The army command had received reports concerning clashes between the troops and townspeople of neighboring San Angelo. For sport, Black soldiers were being shot on sight. On the day Orderly Peter Jackson was killed while bringing to town a message from the fort's commanding officer, the Black troopers had had enough.

Officers at the fort tried to have the perpetrators, patrons of Bill Powell's saloon, arrested for the young soldier's murder, but the lawmen sided with the townsfolk.

That night, twenty Black soldiers, led by Sergeant Gadsby, armed themselves with two six-shooters apiece, slipped past the fort guards, and walked the three miles to town. When they entered the saloon, the soldiers each ordered a drink. As soon as they'd downed the whiskey the men spun in unison and opened fire. Only seven troopers survived the subsequent shootout, but when the smoke cleared there were also thirty-five dead Texicans on the saloon floor. The surviving soldiers, certain the army would turn them over to the town's lawmen, left that night for territories where there was no law.

Extreme measures, some would say, but these soldiers were part of the United States Colored Troops, which comprised twenty percent of all the cavalry in the West. They rode from the Mississippi to the Rockies, from the Canadian border to the Rio Grande, protecting stages, wagon trains, and survey parties. They chased renegades and outlaws, working often for less pay than their white counterparts.

And to what end? It was a question Chase asked himself with increasing frequency lately. He'd been with the army most of his adult life. As a younger man filled with the fire of freedom during the Civil War, the enthusiasm and euphoria of victory made the rigors of Black soldiering a cross he, and many like him, had been more than willing to bear. For freedom, especially to a race who'd tasted very little, it seemed a small price to pay.

But the years passed, and now an older man—too old, maybe, he thought—rode the buffalo soldiers' trail. Watching his men make do with the used mounts and broken equipment handed down from other, more traditional units had always been offensive, especially in the light of the Tenth's distinguished record. But to be told continually by the generals and politicians in Washington that these same men, no matter how brave or resourceful, no matter the honors and medals bestowed upon them, did not have the genetic competence to be commissioned officers played hell with Chase's morale—especially when rifle-toting civilians were allowed to cheapen and demean not only the uniform but also the men inside.

And he could see no solution, at least not in the near future. For a while the equality promised after Lee's surrender at Appomattox had come to pass. Blacks began to achieve levels in society unprecedented in the country's history. Mississippi native B. K. Bruce, a highly intelligent man and a former slave, was elected to the United States Senate. Other elected Blacks from the South sat in the United States House of Representatives, in statehouses, and as state officers. Former slaves were able to work their own land. Those who'd served masters as artisans, tanners, bricklayers, and in other skilled capacities now could ply their trades. Radical Reconstruction, as the times came to be called, lasted fifteen years in some places and barely five in others.

Now the clock had swung back. After pardoning those who'd split the country, the Federal government had begun to allow those same individuals to retake the land. In the South Sea Islands off the coast of South Carolina where Chase had worked with General Tubman after the war, ex-slaves had been granted confiscated land by the Federal government. The people had worked, planted, formed township societies, and lived within the law for nearly a decade, only to find themselves confronted suddenly not only by returning planters demanding the Blacks submit to a modified system of bondage, but also by Federal troops sent to back up the planters. The long-fought-for right to vote had been repealed in many places. The nightriding Ku Klux Klan, spreading terror, continued to gain members. And throughout all of this, one could count the Black graduates from the army's West Point on the digits of a three-fingered man.

Chase loved his country. The debates being waged by the societies promoting emigration to Sierra Leone and other foreign countries held little appeal for him. As a member of the army, he felt a great obligation to carry forward the hopes and traditions of those Black soldiers who'd gone before, for the benefit of those who'd come in the future.

Chase knew, though, that a man could take only so much. The sneers and slurs from homesteaders and the threats of Reb ranchers were taking their toll. He'd been soldiering a long time—and he wasn't sure how much longer he could endure.

"Cara, maybe you should go home. That eye's pretty bad," Sophie said from across the church kitchen where she was uncovering the baked goods brought in by the ladies of the church for the night's dinner.

"Sophie's right, Cara," Sybil Whitfield chimed in. "Doesn't it hurt?"

"Yes, it hurts, but the steak helped. Thank you, Sophie," Cara said, "but I'll be fine. Even a one-eyed woman can cut potatoes. And you need the help."

They did, of course. The parishioners numbered nearly one hundred strong, and all were coming tonight to break bread with the Tenth. Many more women would be arriving shortly to set up tables and the like, but Sophie and Cara had volunteered to come early to help Sybil get the meal started. Since it was Thursday night, the weekly choir rehearsal would be held after dinner, as would the monthly Men's Club meeting. Cara, who had the singing voice of a bullfrog, would take herself home directly after the clean-up.

"I haven't seen your sergeant all day, Cara," Sybil said playfully.

Sophie laughed. "Better not let the Black Widow hear you call him that. I thought the woman was going to have him right there in the middle of the dance floor last night."

"He's not my sergeant," Cara pointed out.

"Well, he should be. What do you think, Sophie?"

Sophie looked over at Cara and said sagely, "I'll hold my vote a while longer."

"Now that Sybil, is a smart woman," Cara said, and went back to cutting potatoes.

Later, as she moved about the room with the other women, laying out silver and china, Cara saw that some members of the Tenth were already arriving. She'd not seen Chase so far, however. She told herself she wasn't looking for him, but she'd been telling herself a lot of things about him lately that weren't true, such as, she wasn't attracted to him, and his mustached smile was as ordinary as any other man's. On Cara's walk back to the kitchen to get more plates, not even her swollen eye kept her from seeing Virginia Sutton and her son, Miles, enter the church hall. Dressed in a midnight-blue taffeta dress that showed her curves, Virginia smiled like royalty at the soldiers and townspeople milling about. Virginia was looking for someone, that was clear. "Now I wonder who that could be?" Cara said sarcastically under her breath as she went into the kitchen.

When people began to go through the line to help themselves from the buffet set up on the far side of the room, Virginia chose to sit with Cara, Sophie, and Sybil.

"And how is everyone tonight?" Virginia asked, taking a seat. "I thought I'd come join you over here. Good heavens, Miss Henson, what on earth happened to your eye?"

"Two of the students were fighting this morning. I inadvertently got hit trying to stop it."

"Are you having trouble controlling the children, Miss Henson?"

"No, I'm not."

Virginia looked doubtful. "Well, that's something to discuss when your term expires next time. You'd agree with that, wouldn't you, Mrs. Whitfield?"

Sybil answered in a cool voice. "I would think Cara's renewal would be a foregone conclusion. The reverend and I believe she's done more than a commendable job."

"Well, it won't hurt to take a look at this issue. We can't have our schoolteacher brawling with the students."

Cara's prospects for a pleasant evening plunged further when Virginia waved her son over to the table. Miles pulled out one of the two remaining chairs and sat. "Evenin', everybody. Miss Cara, what happened to your eye?"

Virginia answered for her. "She was in a fight with the students. Can you believe that?"

"Certainly not," he said, grinning. "When you going to visit me at the Lady again, Miss Cara?"

"The next time you serve alcohol to one of my students."

Virginia's eyes riveted on her son. "You sold liquor to a child?"

"Mother, I already explained to Miss Cara: Fess Brock's kid is no child."

"The boy's twelve, Mrs. Sutton," Cara said.

"Twelve! What were you thinking of, Miles?" Virginia asked.

Cara had never expected to find herself on the same side of an issue as Virginia Sutton, who then added, "If it happens again, you won't have to worry whether Miss Henson will be visiting you, because it will be me, with the sheriff. Do you understand me?"

"The way I run my business is my affair, Mother, not yours."

"It's my affair if you serve a child ever again. Do not let that happen."

Miles's cheeks had reddened with his mother's chastisements, and his gray eyes blazed. No one at the table said a word, but everyone's face mirrored the expression of disgust on Cara's.

Chase did not arrive until midway through the meal. When he walked up behind her at the table and placed his hands on the back of her chair, Cara experienced the same kind of knowing she'd experienced the night before on Virginia's back porch. She felt his presence as distinctly as she felt her own beating heart.

"Good evening, everyone."

"Have a seat, Chase," Sophie said. "I'll get you a plate."

"No, sit and finish your meal. I see the food over there. I can get a plate in a minute. How are you, Mrs. Sutton?"

"Very good, Sergeant. And you?"

"Fine. I apologize for being late, Sophie. We didn't get back to town until a little while ago."

"Well, we're glad you can join us," Virginia veritably purred. "Sergeant, this is my son, Miles."

"Ah, the saloon owner. Hello."

Miles, still angry, nodded curtly.

Only after those pleasantries did Chase address Cara. "How's the eye, Miss Henson?"

"Fine, Sergeant, thank you," she answered. To her surprise and embarrassment he gently titled her chin and peered at her face. She was acutely aware of Virginia's presence and wanted to pull away, but couldn't.

Chase was concerned about her eye. It had swollen closed, and dark green stains of bruising ringed it. Uncharacteristically, he wanted to kiss the hurt away as if she were a child. "Did you give her a steak for it, Sophie?" he asked, still holding her chin, slowly turning Cara's face this way and that as he evaluated the damage.

Before Sophie could reply, Virginia asked suspiciously, "You knew about her eye, Sergeant?"

Chase ignored her to hear Sophie's answer.

"Yes, Chase, Dulcie got her the biggest one she could find."

Only then did he respond to Virginia. "My men and I were headed out of town this morning when we passed the school yard and saw Miss Henson and the children."

"And how do you think she conducted herself?"

"Considering the blow she received, I thought she showed remarkable patience."

"I see," Virginia replied.

Chase quickly excused himself then to get some food, and Cara went back to eating, purposely avoiding the Black Widow's venomous gaze.

At the end of the meal, two men, one Black, the other white, walked into the church hall. The strangers were dressed in the fancy suits and ruffled shirts associated with gamblers and drew the attention of most everyone in the room. Cara watched as Sheriff Polk approached them. The three conversed for a moment; the two men smiled, nodded, as if thanking the lawman, then started toward the back of the room.

The men walked briskly to Miles's side.

"Well, boy," the Black man said. "You got our money?"

Miles stiffened. Cara watched him turn to the man and saw his eyes go as big as plates.

"Bet you thought you'd never see us again, eh, Reverend?" the white one asked, smiling.

Reverend? Cara shared quizzical looks with Sophie and Sybil.

"Miles, you know these men?" Virginia asked.

"They're . . . business acquaintances, Mother."

"Business acquaintances. That's a polite way of putting it. This your ma?" the Black man asked.

Miles nodded his head.

"Well, ma'am, me and my partner here beg your pardons for interrupting your meal, but your son owes us some money."

"Quite a large sum of money, ma'am," the other interjected.

Virginia drew herself up. "How much?" she asked coldly.

"Mother, it's not your concern."

"It most certainly is, because I'm the one who's going to end up paying. Wasn't being dismissed from Howard for gambling disgrace enough for you?"

"Evidently not. And why don't you say it louder? I'm sure the people in the front didn't hear you, Mother."

"My, my," the Black gambler said. "I ever sass my ma like that, I'd be picking buckshot out of my hide."

His partner laughed and added, "You know, I'm of a mind not to accept his lovely ma's money. He acts like a man, let him pay his debts like a man."

Cara looked around the room and saw every eye trained on the drama unfolding at her table. It would be weeks before the gossip died down.

"Where did you meet my son?" Virginia asked.

"St. Louis, eight months ago."

"Why did you refer to him as Reverend?"

"Because that's what he said he was. Course he don't have on the spectacle and he don't have his holy book, but he's the one we're looking for. No doubt."

Virginia had come to a decision. She rose, smiled regally, then said, "Gentlemen, I'm going to take your advice. He's a man. He can pay his own debts. Good night." She turned to Chase. "Oh, Sergeant, I'm celebrating my birthday in a few days. I'd be honored if you and your men would attend the party." After Chase inclined his head in acknowledgment, she nodded frostily to her son, saying only, "Miles." And she walked across the silent hall and out the door.

The Black gambler looked at Miles and said pleasantly, "Well, Reverend, we'll give you one month to come up with our money."

"I'll . . . need more time. I—"

"One month."

The two men tipped their hats to Cara and the other women at the table and departed.

That night, Cara continued her search for the missing book she'd promised her student. There were still a few crates to go through on the upper shelves, so ignoring the painful throb in her eye, she dragged the sawhorse over to the shelves, hiked up her skirts, and climbed. The changes in the orientation of her head caused greater pain in her eye. She placed her hand against the row of books to maintain her balance, deciding to be wise for once and get down. But being one-eyed threw off her depth perception. She took a side step and slipped. Frantically clawing books and air, she fell to the floor, bringing down an avalanche of books and paper on top of herself.

On the other side of the wall, Chase, working on reports, heard Cara's scream, followed by the heavy thumps of things hitting the floor. Alarmed, he snatched up a shirt and ran to her door. He rapped loudly. "Are you all right, Cara?" He slid his arms into his shirt.

"No," he heard her call back grumpily. Then she asked, "Can you break your ankle falling off a sawhorse?"

"Depends." He chuckled, shaking his head at her spirit. "Let me in, and I'll take a look."

For a moment there was silence. Then came her loud pain-filled groan. "I can't walk over there. Just come on in. The door isn't bolted."

Chase found her sitting on the bed, trying to take off her shoe. The buttons were giving her problems because of her limited vision.

"Need some help?"

"If you would . . ."

Chase closed the door and picked his way to the bed through the books littering the floor. He took her small foot in his hand and began to unlace the shoes. "This another of your gifts?"

"Don't start with me, Sergeant. It has not been a good day."

"I'm sorry," he apologized, smiling. He eased off her shoe, apologized sincerely again when she winced, and set the shoe aside. "You're going to have to take the stocking off."

"Turn around."

When he looked confused, she said, "Sergeant, your talents may be many, but they do not entitle you to see me taking off my stockings. Now stand up and turn away."

He complied and she quickly lifted her skirt, pulled off the black stocking, then readjusted the skirt. "Now you can turn back," she said and held out her bare foot for his inspection. "Do you think it's really broken?"

Chase moved her foot and ankle gingerly, noting which movements gave her the most pain. "It doesn't seem to be broken, but it does look as though you have a very bad sprain."

"That's a relief."

"Maybe not," Chase said, rising. "You're going to have to stay off it for a few days."

"I can't do that," she gritted out, trying to put some weight on the ankle. "I have school—oh!" The sharp pain put her right back on the bed.

"See? You are so hardheaded."

"I think I hurt my hip, too," she said, wishing she could rub it, but he was standing right next to her.

"I'd offer to kiss it and make it feel better, but that isn't something a gentleman suggests to a lady."

She shot him a look that should have singed the skin off his magnificent chest, visible where his hastily donned shirt remained unbuttoned. He simply smiled at her.

"Didn't I say a woman can be kissed in a thousand places?"

It was her turn to be singed.

"However," he continued, "right now you should soak your ankle and maybe that hip as well in some warm water. I'll go down to the kitchen and bring up a few buckets."

"I'll be fine."

"Do you want to walk tomorrow, stubborn woman?"

"Well, yes, but—"

"Then do this. You need help, schoolmarm, and the U.S. Cavalry is more than willing to assist."

Cara reluctantly nodded agreement.

He returned from the kitchen a few minutes later. "Couldn't find Dulcie. Is everyone still at the church?"

"There and at the Men's Club monthly meeting."

"Well, I put some water on the stove." He looked around her cluttered room. "You're going to need a tub in here, but I can't imagine where we'd put it."

"Usually I have to rearrange things to bring in a tub."

"How long does it take?"

"A day or so."

Amazed, he shook his head. "Personally, I don't see how you can get another book in here, let alone a tub."

"Well, just bring water for the ankle. I'll take care of the hip tomorrow."

Chase could see the difficulty she seemed to be having in trying to sit up. "Leg getting stiff?"

"A little bit. It's sore mostly." She sighed. "Lord, what a day. First my eye, now this. Maybe I should be locked away for my own safety."

He grinned.

"Not funny. I can barely see you out of this eye. I'm a sight, I'll bet."

"The eye will heal," he said softly. "It makes your face even more interesting."

"You're so kind, Sergeant," she drawled.

Cara could feel herself succumbing to his magnetism. She hoped he hadn't noticed her staring at his chest. His strength drew her, made her want to feel the warmth of his skin beneath her palms. She shuddered and looked away. "Do you think the water's hot now?"

"I'd better go and see."

Chapter 6

Cara was growing testy because of her aches and pains. Chase had been gone for such a long time. In a few moments she would go after the water herself, despite her bad ankle.

She was about to try to climb off the bed and hobble down to the kitchen when she heard noises coming from Chase's room. What in the world could he be doing in there? He appeared within seconds, but without buckets.

"Is the water still heating?" Cara asked.

"Nope. All set. Nice hot bath waiting for you in my room."

"Your room? Oh, Chase, you know I can't possibly—"

"I set up a screen next to the tub, and you'll be safe." He grinned. "No fun chasing somebody who can't even run, much less chase back." Before she could protest again, he moved to her side and gently scooped her into his arms.

Suddenly Cara felt wonderful. Her ankle might throb and her hip might ache, but she couldn't care less. She felt Chase's warmth, his strength. Never had she been so cared for, so cherished. She couldn't repress a sigh.

"If you want me to leave you, Cara, I will," he murmured. "But I'm concerned about you, and I'd like to stay nearby in case you need me. I'm worried you might slip or have trouble getting in or out of the tub."

His low voice was a caress, his words an embrace.

"Thank you," she whispered.

His room was dark. Conscious of Cara's modesty, Chase had doused the lamps. The only light came through the opened curtains at the big front window from a moon that was round and exceptionally bright this warm May night. He carefully made his way across the room and deposited Cara on the bed; the tub sat next to it, the screen behind it.

"I'll just get out of your way, schoolmarm. You let me know when you're ready for me to lift you into the tub."

Emotion filled Cara as she watched Chase disappear around the screen. She guessed he was standing in front of the window, looking out on the street. She was so moved by his tenderness that it took her several minutes to compose herself and strip down to her chemise and slip. The moment she called out to him to help her into the tub, she felt transformed. Barely dressed and alone in a moonlit room with the strapping, handsome, virile Chase Jefferson, she felt brazen . . . and reckless.

It was Chase who was in control and banked the fires within Cara that were threatening to flare into flames. He seemed to her to be very businesslike about the whole matter of lifting her and depositing her in the tub. And he was downright quick at getting himself back around that screen. She couldn't help but feel disappointed.

Damn, Chase thought, this was going to be more difficult than he'd anticipated. Lord, just one look at the moonlight shining on the skin of Cara's neck and the swell of her bosom had made him hard as a rock. How he wanted this woman . . . wanted her physically, of course, but wanted her, too, in every other way a man could want a woman. He was shaking and took deep gulps of air to help get himself back under control.

The water had cooled but still held enough warmth for Cara to sigh pleasurably after he eased her in. It seemed to welcome her sore, aching body with soothing open arms. She didn't think about being half dressed in Chase's room. All thoughts and fears, real and imagined, fled as she luxuriated in the warm water and let its blissfully, lulling peace enfold her.

Still, she was acutely conscious of Chase's presence across the room, especially when his voice came out of the darkness. "Mind if I smoke, schoolmarm?"

She didn't and told him so, compelled to turn in the tub and look over her shoulder. He stood as a tall, dark shadow at the window. He'd opened the curtains and the hems flapped lazily in the May breeze. He was reaching into his shirt pocket.

"Something wrong?" he asked softly.

"No," she answered, quickly looking away. She heard the match strike, then imagined the flare illuminating his face.

In the silence, crickets and other night songs could be heard through the opened windows. A dog barked in the distance, and every now and then, Cara heard the faint strain of the organ and voices of the choir emanating from the church. To fight her rising awareness she was determined to start an innocuous conversation with Chase. She said the first thing that came to mind. "Sophie says she and Asa have known you a long time."

"A very long time. I've known Asa even a little longer, though." Chase was usually very closemouthed about his past, not because he felt ashamed, but because of the dangers that had schooled him to silence. Suddenly, with Cara, all that changed. He wanted to tell her everything about himself. He also liked the sound of her husky Georgia voice. If he couldn't touch her, he could at least enjoy the pleasure of hearing her voice in conversation.

"Sergeant?" Cara prompted.

"I'm sorry, what did you ask?"

"Where was it you met Asa?"

"Stealin' away."

Cara went still. "You were a slave?"

"Yes. That bother you?"

"No. Should it?"

"It bothers some women."

"That's ridiculous. You didn't ask to be a captive."

"I know, but back East things like that matter to quite a few folks." Cara sensed his bitterness. "How old were you when you ran?"

"Two days past twelve."

"You ran alone?"

"No, there were other men and women who left with me. Asa and I got from Mississippi to Louisiana. Knocked on Sophie's back door looking for work one day, and she took us in. Stayed with her until she and Asa shipped me back East to Asa's sister in Philadelphia. She fed me, saw to it that I got proper schooling, and at eighteen, she shipped me back to New Orleans."

Cara realized that in ways, their pasts were similar. "Did you get to know either of your parents?" It took Chase so long to reply that she thought he might not.

"My father was hanged a few hours after I was born. He never saw me. I was told my mother died two weeks later. Asa knew them both and said she died of a broken heart."

Cara wondered if the world had scared him as much as it had her when she first realized she'd have to go through life alone. "What made you decide to run?"

"All the talk in the quarters at night about freedom and the drinking gourd."

Cara knew about the drinking gourd. It was another name for the North Star. Some also called it the Freedom Star, and many runaways used its positioning in the sky to guide the way North.

"The adults would tell stories of going North where they'd be free to name themselves and work their own land," he continued. "For many years, I was too young to really understand what it all meant, but they spoke of it with such reverence and awe that I think the tone of their voices when they talked about their dreams grabbed me more than anything. As I got older, I knew life had to be better somewhere."

"Did you leave any family behind—brothers, sisters, grandparents?"

"No brothers, no sisters. My mother's mother lived on a place a few miles down county. I saw her only once, about a year before I left. She said my father ruined her daughter. Called him a dirty black African, and me a dirty black African bastard. Said she didn't have any grandchildren."

Cara's heart broke for him. Even though she'd had her grandfather only a short while, he'd loved her very much. How awful it must have been for Chase to have that sole family member toss his heritage back into his face like so much offal. "How could anyone say such hateful things to a child?"

"Didn't seem to bother her. Asa told me later she'd gone a little mad after my mother's death. My grandmother was the mistress of a white planter who got her pregnant. That child was my mother. Some said my mother was the most beautiful woman in the state, Black or white. The planter who owned her planned on selling her to another planter a couple counties away, but her relationship with my father and her pregnancy made the sale impossible."

"Surely your grandmother didn't approve of her daughter being sold?"

"According to Asa, it had been her idea."

Cara gasped.

"It's not so surprising. My grandmother belonged to that small percentage of slave women who felt that being the master's mistress gave her importance and some little bit of power over her life. A mistress might get her own little house away from the quarters; she'd eat better, dress better. When the master got her with child, she might not have to see her son or daughter put on the block. Instead, if female, she often became the companion of a planter or was given to one of the legitimate white children as a birthday or wedding gift. If male, he might be given his freedom when his father, the master, died."

"So your grandmother thought she was securing her daughter's future."

"I'm sure she did. After all, the women in her line had lived that way for generations. She probably did go mad when she discovered her beautiful mulatto daughter had lain with a troublemaking field slave. His name was Branch."

"Branch?"

"Yes, for the size of his arms. Asa described him as being as tall as an oak and able to do the work of two men. The master had him on the books as Toby, but he would only answer to Branch."

"How'd your parents meet?"

"Long story. My daddy was not a model captive. The overseer was mad at a slave woman he said wasn't pulling her weight in the field. She'd been sick for a time, but the overseer didn't believe that and accused her of slacking. To teach her a lesson and to discourage others from trying it, he took her to the barn, tied her hands, then hung her up by her bound hands to a hook in the ceiling. When he raised the whip to give her the first cut, my father, who like the other slaves had been brought in to watch, stepped between her and the lash. The overseer obliged my daddy, who offered to take the woman's place. It took four men to raise Branch to the hook in the ceiling, and they didn't cut him down until the blood ran down his heels."

Cara tasted bile on her tongue.

"They rubbed salt into the welts on his back, flung him into a four-by-four pit, and left him there. At the end of three days, they hauled him out barely alive, and the master sent Pretty Sally, my mother, down from the big house to see about him. She was a root woman and the healer for the quarters."

"She was able to help him?"

"Quite a bit, it seems." He guffawed. "She found out she was breeding his child just a couple months after she first started treating his wounds."

"And her mother didn't approve."

"I heard no one but Branch and Pretty Sally approved. The master was so furious he sent her to the quarters until she gave birth. Before then she'd lived with the servants in a small wing of the main house. She worked a loom."

"So what happened to you? Who raised you?"

"Everyone and no one. How much do you know about a slave's child-hood?"

"Not very much."

"Well, every baby started out in the nurse house. Usually there was an older woman looking after anywhere from twenty to a hundred ba-bies, depending upon the size of the place. Then when you got to be about five or six, you went to work, either in the house doing something like fanning flies away from the table while the master and family ate, or out in the fields where you got to pick weevils off cotton or worms off tobacco. At eight or nine you pulled your weight like any other adult."

"Did you live with a family?"

"At first, but they were sold when I was about ten. The master kept me because of the good price he'd be able to get for me once I was full-grown."

Cara could give no name to the emotions rising within her. They'd both had great tragedy in their lives, but while she'd been rescued and nurtured by Rosetta and Harriet not long after she'd lost her grandfa-ther, he'd gone most of his childhood with no one. She knew with certainty that it must have been terrible to be a child under slavery, but also to be a child alone, without family . . . What a testament to his strength of character that he'd gone beyond mere survival to make so much of his life!

"You're a very brave woman, Cara Lee Henson. Sophie told me about your grandfather."

Grief, sadness, acceptance for herself mingled with all the emotions Chase's story had evoked. "We're both survivors, you and I."

"Does it bother you, me wearing the uniform of the Union Army?"

"I tell myself no, but deep down inside I'm sure it does. I—I have nightmares sometimes about Bluecoats."

"Then I won't wear it when we're together."

The sincerity in his offer touched her deeply. "No, please. It's my problem, not yours." Silence resettled and then Cara added, "Silly, isn't it? A grown woman still scared of something from her childhood?"

"No," he answered. "We can't always control the things that haunt us."

"Since I left the orphanage, I've never told anyone about my night-mares."

"Then I'll hold the confidence close to my heart," he pledged softly.

The water had cooled, and Cara wanted to get out of the tub.

Chase had turned to her to ask about her years at Oberlin, but forgot the question as he watched her rise, moonlight and water streaming off her scantily clothed body. The wet chemise and slip, molded against her curves, were so provocative he couldn't catch his breath. She lifted her leg to step out of the tub, and he cried out a warning for her not to put weight on the ankle. He didn't trust himself to get any nearer, but knew she needed his help. "Hold on. Let me lift you."

"No. I can manage on my own. If you'd just hand me my skirt and blouse, then bring the screen, I'll get out of this wet slip. Sophie will shoot me if I drip water all over the floor."

He did, then returned to his spot by the window.

Behind the screen, Cara balanced on her good leg, carefully rid herself of her dripping garments, and dried herself with the towel he'd hung atop the screen. After cautiously getting out of the tub she put on her skirt and blouse before wringing water from the wet things into the tub.

"Sergeant, I—I thank you. You've been so kind. My ankle is still sore, but not so tender as it was, and my hip feels less stiff."

"Good." He looked up then as she hopped out from behind the screen. "You shouldn't be on that ankle, schoolmarm." He hurried to her side and picked her up.

She smiled. "This carrying business is not too bad."

"Glad you like it. Want to go back to your room now, Your Majesty?"

"Yes," she said in a royal manner.

He carried her to her room and carefully set her down on the bed. "Are you going to be all right now?"

"I think so."

Cara couldn't bear the thought of Chase parting from her yet. She learned a lot about him and been moved by his disclosures. She felt a closeness she wasn't certain he returned, but he'd been so tender with her tonight . . . "Were you busy—before you heard me fall?" she asked. "I mean, I hope I didn't take you away from anything important."

"Nope. I was just looking over some reports I'll be filing next week. Why'd you ask?"

"Just curious."

He nodded his understanding. Chase didn't want to leave, especially after the confidences they'd shared. He found Cara fascinating and didn't want their time together to end. He wanted to kiss her, very badly, but he'd promised her and himself he'd behave. "How long does choir rehearsal usually last?"

"Sometimes two hours, sometimes three. If the spirit gets going they could be down there until sunup. It's happened before. If you're not busy, I'd be pleased if you'd stay and talk a little more with me."

Those were the sweetest words Chase had heard all day. "I'd like that."

They talked for hours about army life, politics, and the state of the race. He regaled her with tales of his journeys throughout the West and the places he'd seen and the people he'd met, and listened to her stories of life in the orphanage. Her interests surprised him, though knowing her as he did now, they shouldn't have. Out of the blue he asked, "You like to fish?"

"Sure," she replied. "I'm a country girl. We always did our own hunting and fishing."

He laughed and she enjoyed the sound. "What did you do after you left Oberlin?"

"Tried to find a school board I could work for longer than a month."

She looked at his confused expression and smiled. "This is my third teaching position."

"What happened with the other two?"

"My first one lasted almost two weeks. The president of the school board wanted to 'teach' me some things I didn't want to learn . . . at least from him." Cara couldn't believe she'd said that! She hastily took up the story again, trying to ignore the amusement Chase made no effort to hide. "The last job was in a place called Blessed, Ohio. Stayed there just long enough to get thrown in jail."

"What?"

"I went to jail."

"Why?"

"The school board told me that educating girls was a waste of the town's money. Girls were banned from the schoolroom. I thought otherwise."

"So they put you in jail?"

"Actually, I chose jail. They called it a choice: teach only boys or go to jail."

"And of course, you chose jail. In other words you went to Blessed, Ohio, and caused a ruckus."

"Not intentionally, no, but I suppose I did."

"How long were you there?"

"A day and a half."

Chase's laughter exploded. Cara, unable to contain herself, joined in. Placing a finger to her lips to caution him to be more quiet lest someone hear, she thought how wondrous it was to make Chase laugh. They both had tears in their eyes when the laughter subsided.

"Less than forty-eight hours. You are gifted, aren't you?" Chase rose stiffly. His back complained from the prolonged sitting, and he stretched to get the circulation going in his limbs. He looked out the window and saw the first red fingers of dawn on the horizon. Was it really that late? "Sun's coming up."

"That's not possible," Cara said in surprise.

He walked over and pulled back her curtains so she could get a better view from her spot on the bed. "Good Lord, I have to teach school today."

At that moment, a knock on the door made them freeze in shock. "Cara?" called Sophie's voice in a loud whisper. Cara shot Chase a look of panic, then had an idea. She placed her finger to her lips, signaling him to silence, then called back in a sleepy voice, "Sophie, is that you? Is something wrong?"

"No, dear. Sybil canceled school today because of your eye. So go on back to sleep. Dulcie says she'll bring you some breakfast later on."

"Thank you . . ." she replied as if in the throes of sleep.

Chase and Cara waited until they heard Sophie's steps fade away down the hall before releasing their pent-up laughter.

"You are good, schoolmarm, damn good," Chase said, grinning. "I can't remember ever having this much fun with a woman sitting down and fully dressed."

"I'll take that as a compliment." Chase was still chuckling, and Cara kept smiling in response.

"Thanks for a memorable night," he told her.

"Thank you."

He walked over to his door and Cara remembered something, "I left those wet clothes wrapped in the towel on the side of the tub. Can you bring them, please?"

He nodded, disappeared, and returned with the bundle. She had him set it on the seat of an old chair whose finish wouldn't be marred by the moisture. "Thank you." She watched him walk to the door again. "Good night, Sergeant. . . ."

He looked back and said just as softly, "Good morning, Cara Lee. . . ."

He stood there then, unmoving, looking at her, and she could feel his "talents" calling. He walked slowly back to her side. "I can't leave without this. . . ."

He bent and kissed her slowly, very slowly until her breathing was ragged and her body burned. And then he was gone.

"Sophie, when did you first know you were in love with Asa?" Cara asked.

Sophie and Dulcie both looked up from the peas they were shelling and studied her face.

"Is that so improper a thing to ask?"

"No, you just took me by surprise is all," Sophie said. "I guess I first knew when I was in love when I couldn't go a day without wanting to see him. And when I did see him, all I could do was grin. Scariest experience of my life."

Dulcie piped in, "You should have seen her, Cara. Asa hadn't been in the house two days before she started throwing herself at him."

"I did not!" Sophie gasped. "Well, maybe a little. He was so handsome, just looking at him made my teeth ache. Still does."

Cara noted the satisfied smile on Sophie's face. "Is that the grin, you meant, Dulcie?"

Dulcie looked at her friend and nodded. "Yep. Finish the peas, Sophie, we'll never get done if you don't quit daydreaming about that man of yours." She winked at Cara. "You'd think she'd act her age, old as she is."

"Age has nothing to do with it," Sophie retorted. "The wood may be aged, but it still kindles."

Dulcie howled gleefully.

"And besides, Dulcie," Sophie continued, "you are the last female fit to be discussing age and men. How old is the new apprentice over at the livery I saw you sitting with in church yesterday? He can't be a year over thirty-five."

Dulcie grinned but didn't respond.

"You're awfully quiet now, Miss Dulcie Fontaine."

Dulcie chuckled. "Pax, Soph." She whispered, "He's thirty-six."

Cara shook her head at their play.

"So, Cara," Sophie said, "why the questions about me and Asa? You grinning more than usual lately?"

She dropped her head but couldn't stifle the grin. "Not really."

"Liar," Dulcie chirped. "It's all over town. The Black Widow's going to be real ornery when she hears about him dancing with you on her porch, in the dark."

"That's another symptom you know, Cara," Sophie pointed out.

"What?"

"Losing your mind and doing things you wouldn't have two weeks before."

"Listen to her, Cara, she's an expert."

"Will you stop, Dulcie. I'm trying to be serious here." But they all saw her smile.

"So you're telling me this is normal?" Cara asked.

"No, dear. We're telling you you're in love."

As Cara dressed that evening for Virginia's birthday party she thought about the talk with Dulcie and Sophie. Was she really in love? She found the idea disconcerting because she was sure Jefferson wasn't. A harmless flirtation was all it was for him, and in just a few days he'd saddle up and ride out of her life. Still, she was afraid Dulcie and Sophie were right. She was in love with Jefferson, and didn't know what to do with the feelings or how to proceed.

Cara rode over to the party with Asa and Sophie. Cara had chosen to sit on the end of the bench so Sophie could sit next to her love. Cara viewed the relationship between them with fresh eyes. She noticed how content they seemed with each other's company—the way Sophie's arm laced with Asa's as he held the reins; the softness in their gazes as they shared a word or two. They appeared so peaceful, so complete. She was envious, and for the first time wondered if maybe there was more to life than the joy found in being a teacher.

Virginia's guest list included the cream of the region's Black society, Cara saw as she, Sophie, and Asa made their entrance. Uniformed members of the Tenth were sprinkled among bankers and hoteliers, elected officials, and land wealthy cattlemen. Tonight's guest list didn't at all resemble the one for the affair last week. There wasn't a dress of muslim or gingham in sight. Cara had worn her "good" blouse and a fairly new black skirt, but she knew she still looked slightly out of place alongside the women in their finery and with her wounded eye. It had healed somewhat in the past three days, the bruises beginning to fade and the puffiness going down considerably. Yet, still, she felt pretty. Pretty and younger than her twenty-six years . . . all because of Chase, of course.

And then Chase appeared next to her—and the evening turned from delicious anticipation to disaster. She'd been speaking with Delbert Johnson, the doctor from Nicodemus. He'd courted her during the first year she'd been in the Valley, but they hadn't suited and had ended up friends rather than husband and wife. Chase and Delbert just seemed to hate each other on sight and snarled dreadfully at each other.

Cara had no idea why Delbert was being so cold. "You act as if the sergeant has wronged you in some manner, Delbert. Has he?"

"It's you I'm worried about Cara," he said. "People are talking about this torrid affair you're having with him."

Cara almost laughed. "I'm not having an affair, Delbert."

Chase *did* laugh, which made Delbert purse his lips and say angrily, "Sergeant, you may not take this woman's reputation seriously, but we in the Valley do."

Chase was tired of people telling him how to treat Cara. "Doc, if I weren't worried about her reputation, believe me, she wouldn't have one left by now." His smile made Cara shyly drop her eyes for a moment. "So, Doc, if you're really worried about Miss Henson's reputation, you tell your neighbors that as much as I wish the word 'torrid' described our activities, it doesn't apply."

Delbert raised his chin but looked uncomfortable with the slight setdown. "I apologize, Sergeant."

Chase answered coolly, "She's the one you should be apologizing to. Not me."

Cara realized Jefferson was angry. She hadn't seen the hard jaw and brittle eyes since that first night back in Topeka.

Delbert looked damn uncomfortable now. "Cara, I'm sorry. You know I'm not one to spread gossip. I apologize."

"Apology accepted. And gossip or not, you're a true friend because you were concerned enough to confront me with what you'd heard."

He took himself off after that and Chase drawled. "You've been here five minutes and already you're causing a ruckus."

"Me?!" she whispered, then she realized he was teasing, so she teased back, saying saucily, "You just wait till later. I'll show you a real ruckus."

She left him standing there openmouthed as she moved off into the crowd.

Every time Cara glanced up from the many conversations she had while awaiting the call to dinner, she found his eyes waiting. Sometimes he simply smiled, other times his gaze held so much heat, she seriously expected her skirt to go up in flames. It was the most sensual experience of her life, and by the time dinner arrived she was hungry only for him.

Dulcie had been contracted to do tonight's dinner, and the lavish affair did honor to both hostess and chef. Cara picked at her food. Seated at the table with her were the Three Spinsters: Daisy Miller, the A.M.E. Church secretary; Rachel Eddings, the town's telegraph clerk;

and Lucretia Potter, the town milliner. Usually Cara enjoyed their company. All three women were intelligent and opinionated.

"Cara Lee Henson, what are you moping so about?" Rachel asked.

Daisy offered her own explanation between bites. "It's that soldier, isn't it?"

Cara shook her head in wonder at small-town living, then asked, "Is there anyone in town who isn't talking about me and 'the soldier'?"

"Everybody I know is," Lucretia said.

"I loved a soldier once," Rachel said. "He was a redhead just like me and he looked so handsome in his uniform the day he left with the troops from Louisiana."

"What happened to him?" Cara asked, because she knew Rachel had never married.

"He was killed at Milliken's Bend, Virginia, in June of '63. I'll never forget him. . . ."

The table quieted for a moment, then Rachel said, "Cara Lee, if you have even a tiny hope for happiness with Sergeant Jefferson, seize it. Life very rarely gives out second helpings."

"She's right, Cara," Daisy said. "If I had it to do over, I would take more chances in life. Now that I'm old and gray, I don't even have memories, just dreams of what might have been."

Cara looked at the three and said, "Ladies, I dearly appreciate your advice and your concern, but I can't have everyone thinking like Delbert Johnson. He thinks I'm having a torrid affair."

"Delbert Johnson is still sweet on you, Cara, and is just looking to stir the pot," Daisy pointed out. "Some folks are talking crazy, yes, but most of us are just sitting back enjoying the romantic gossip and hoping Jefferson's the one."

"The one for what?" Cara asked.

"The one for you," Lucretia said in mock testiness. "Haven't you been listening, dear?"

After dinner, Cara excused herself from the ladies to seek out Sophie. On her way out of the dining room, Miles Sutton called to her.

She turned back.

"Can you and I go someplace and talk? It's about the night at the church dinner."

From the humble look on his face Cara gathered that he wanted to apologize. "Where can we go?"

"How about we just step outdoors for a moment?"

Cara took in the fresh air and glanced up at the stars. Miles stood beside her and did the same. "You know," he began, "I didn't appreciate you bringing up that incident with the kid to my mother."

So he hadn't wanted to beg her pardon. "If you think back, you brought up the subject," she said tartly. "Is this all you wanted to speak with me about? Because if it is, I'm going back inside."

"And if it's not?"

"I'm still going back inside." She turned to walk away.

He grabbed her arm. "Hey, don't walk away from me when I'm talking to you."

"Miles," she said, "in the last week, I have had my eye blackened and my ankle sprained. I've had enough bruises to last a lifetime. I do not need another one on my arm. Let me go."

"Why don't you like me? Other women do."

"It's because I have terrible taste in men, everyone knows that. Now let me go."

"I'm not good enough for you." He shook her. "Is that it?"

"Let go!"

Chase stepped out of the shadow of the house. "You heard the lady. Let her go."

Miles released her instantly.

"Are you all right?" Chase asked, watching Cara rub her upper arm.

"Yes, Sergeant. Thank you."

Chase turned his attention back to Miles, and when he spoke his tone was wintry. "Don't ever put your hands on her again. Do you hear me? Now apologize."

Miles opened his mouth as if to protest, only to have Chase bark, "Do it!"

Miles mumbled an apology, then looked at Chase with cold eyes. "You're going to be gone in a few days, soldier, and then the field will be wide open again."

Before the words had died on the night air, Chase had Miles by his shirtfront and lifted him up on his toes. "I know that wasn't a threat I heard, was it, boy?"

In the moonlight Miles's face looked pale with fright. He shook his head.

"That's what I thought. Because if I had heard a threat I'd have to ask the lady to step back inside so she'd be spared the sight of me whipping your ass." Chase let him go. "Now you stay away from her after I ride out, and you'll live a long life. The problems you have with those gamblers will seem like child's play if you have to tangle with me. Say good night."

Miles did so quickly and stiffly walked back into the house.

"You sure you're not hurt?" Chase asked, moving to Cara's side.

"No, I'm fine. Angry but fine. How'd you know I was out here?"

"I saw you step out with him. You want to go back in?"

"In a minute. Let me calm down first. I actually believed he wanted to apologize to me. He looked so innocent. What a snake."

"Who rescues you when I'm not around?" Chase asked, brushing back one of the delicate curls framing her face.

"I usually rescue myself."

"That's right. I'd forgotten."

"And I was doing fine until you came into my life."

"Well, we can't have that. A man likes to have something to do."

"Then maybe I should advertise after you leave . . . What are you doing?"

He was sliding the pins out of her hair. "I want to see you with your hair down."

Cara rippled in response to the whispered touch of his hands. "There's a houseful of people inside. If I let my hair down it'll just give them more to talk about."

But she did let him. Very slowly, one by one, he took the pins from her hair. Its full weight unfurled and she shuddered with the intimacy of the deed.

"Well"—he eased her hair away and kissed the side of her neck—"you should fix your hair again. We don't want this to get torrid. . . ."

Cara lifted a hand for her pins. He put them in her upturned palm, while placing delicate whispers of kisses along her jaw. She could feel herself sway on legs that suddenly had gone weak. She was glad his big body sheltered her from any prying eyes so that for just a moment she could lean back against him and savor the feel of his strong chest and legs pressed against her.

"I'm calling off the competition we've been having."

"Why?" she asked, her breathing increasing in proportion to her rising desire.

"Because if I wait for you to ask for my kisses, I'll still be waiting when I ride out." He leaned down and kissed her with a fierce gentleness.

When he released her, she stared up through the haze of passion and asked, "So that means I'm the winner. Correct?"

"Don't gloat."

She grinned. "Admit it, there is one woman on this earth who can resist your talents."

He winked. "We'll see. I'm still waiting for this ruckus you promised me."

Cara hadn't forgotten her bold challenge. "Well, I'm glad I won. Now I can succumb willingly. Kiss me, Sergeant."

He did. Slowly, sweetly, thoroughly.

"Everybody's going to notice my hair's different," Cara said, repinning her hair once they called a mutual halt to the kissing.

Chase laughed. "It's a little late to think about that now."

"Yes, it is. Sophie said doing something like this is a sign that—" She closed her mouth and concentrated on her hair. "How's this?"

"I liked it the way it was. But you didn't finish. Sophie said it's a sign of what?"

"Nothing." She had no intention of telling him of her love. "We should probably go back in."

He stopped her and tilted up her chin. "What's the matter?"

"Nothing. I'm fine."

"You sure?"

"Yes." She smiled up and beckoned him with a finger. He leaned down, and she stood on tiptoe and kissed his mouth gently. "Thanks for the rescue . . . again."

Back inside Cara found Sophie in the library playing poker. Cara was really ready to return to town, but knew Sophie rarely liked leaving a table when her cards were hot. Cara took one look at the despondent faces of the men at the table and knew her landlady was winning big.

When Cara came over and whispered her desire to return home, Sophie looked up from her hand and instructed, "Tell Chase to take you in the buckboard. Asa and I can hitch a ride home with someone later."

"Are you sure?"

"Yes, dear. Now run along. These gentlemen still have money in their clips with my initials embroidered on it, and I plan on taking it all before I leave."

On the buckboard ride back to town Cara sat beside Chase thinking about their departure. Virginia had been visibly upset at Chase's leaving. She made it clear by her icy manner at the door that the best birthday gift of the evening had been the tall, mustached cavalry soldier in Union blue, and she had planned on unwrapping that present at her leisure. However, Chase had politely declined the Black Widow's invitation to return for dessert after escorting Cara back to town. Virginia's look of outrage was a memory Cara would cherish for some time to come. "You made Virginia very angry by leaving."

"Woman like her needs to be humbled sometimes. She'll get over it. You know, schoolmarm, you don't have to sit way over there."

She smiled shyly and scooted down the bench to his side. "Better?"

"Somewhat."

She slid over again until their bodies touched and linked her arm into his as he played the reins.

"Perfect," he pronounced and kissed her on the brow. He drew the horse to a halt. "Is there someplace we can go?" He kissed her sweetly on the lips.

When he withdrew, Cara tried to think, but she never got the chance to gather her thoughts because he kissed her again, this time deeper, longer, inflaming her with the tiny thrusts of his tongue. "You are so lovely . . ."

The potency of his kiss overwhelmed her once more. Cara slid her hands up the strong muscles of his arms and shoulders, her palms tingling from the contact. He dropped his burning mouth to the trembling column of her throat, and she sighed weakly as his hands came up and slid over the softness of her breasts. She arched as her nipples tightened in response.

"I've been wanting to do this all evening," he said. Fitting actions to words, he undid the top two buttons of her blouse. His hands teased, seduced, and then moved to undo more buttons. He brought his palm up to cup the soft weight, and her gasps rose into the darkness like passion-filled notes as he rubbed at the berry-hard nipple with the flat of his thumb.

Chase couldn't help himself. Touching her, tasting her, having her scent fill his senses, were drawing him further into the storm. He knew she'd be sweet, but not this sweet. Her mouth was as ripe as a desert bloom, and her lush breasts . . .

Cara felt his hand push the delicate, cream-colored camisole aside, and transfer that potent mustached mouth to one bared nipple. His tongue boldly circled the straining peak, making the moment flash red-hot behind her eyes. She almost screamed. Lightning pierced her in response to the passionate sucking. She knew now why she'd never let another man do this before—she'd been waiting for Chase Jefferson.

"A thousand places, *mariposa,*" she heard him whisper as he shifted his attention to the other bared breast. "A thousand places."

He kissed his way back to her mouth, his fingers keeping her nipples hard. He pulled her into his lap, branding her with each passion-filled caress. Her hairpins tumbled into the dark recesses of the buckboard as he removed them one by one. When the weight of her hair fell free, he combed his fingers through the thick dark riches, then filled his hands with it as he brought her mouth back to his.

Chase wanted to spend the rest of his life kissing her, hearing her soft sighs, feeling her nipples ripen beneath his touch. Her trembling response had produced a very large commotion in his trousers, so much so he wanted to lift her dress and take her there and then. He held himself in check, however, remembering she deserved better than to be deflowered on the seat of a buckboard. "Cara, we have to stop."

She didn't want to stop. The newness of what she was feeling made her want more. She kissed the mahogany column of his throat and the strong line of his chin. Imitating him, she gave tiny licks to the corners of his mouth, and when he opened to her soft command she boldly slipped the tip of her tongue inside, savoring the moan she elicited along with the taste of him. He responded with a growl and brought her closer, brazenly rubbing his big palms over her hips, setting off a rhythm that kept slow pace with her rising desire. Her breathing increased at the feel of his hand sliding her dress up her thighs. He squeezed the soft flesh, making Cara aware of the liquid heat at her core. He boldly circled his hand up inside her loose-fitting drawers and over the surface of her hips. He squeezed there also, and she felt herself tighten with erotic sensations.

"You're supposed to be stopping me," he whispered, bending her back over his arm so he could feast on the sweetness of her dark nipples again. He lingered there, sucking, nibbling, and circling the buds with his tongue until her breath came out in ragged gasps. The hand in her drawers moved over her, touching, stroking, priming her for what, Cara did not know. She only knew that she didn't want him to stop, not the kisses, not the wanton hand—Cara stiffened with the explosion that immediately followed. She felt as if she'd been flung up into the stars. She clutched his arm as she rode the wave and hoarsely called his name.

When she finally came back to herself, she focused and found him looking down at her with both tenderness and amusement. "You are a very passionate woman," he whispered, then bent and kissed her once more. "I can't be alone with you . . . ever again."

Cara sat up straighter. The fact that he did not appear to be teasing made her go still. "What are you saying?" Her breasts seemed to be throbbing with a life all their own, and she couldn't stop the spiraling heat between her thighs.

"I'm saying I'm about a half second away from putting you in the back of this wagon and taking you right here in the middle of the road." Their eyes held, and she spoke softly. "And that's bad?"

Chase looked away from the sight of her still budded nipples and off into the less arousing black of the prairie. "Yes."

"Why?"

"Because it's dangerous—for you and me. Had I known that you'd be as passionate in my arms as you are in life, I never would have started this. It isn't a game anymore."

"So your honor is getting in the way?"

"Among other things, yes."

"What are the other things?"

"The fact that you deserve better." God, he was hard! He deliberately set her off his lap. "Too dangerous, schoolmarm," he said in response to her look at being set aside.

Cara, hastily readjusting her clothing, didn't know whether to be angry or sad. She felt a little of both. "So, now that you've gotten what you wanted, you're done, gone?"

"I haven't gotten what I wanted, darlin', not by a long shot. I can't have what I want, is what I'm trying to explain. A woman like you deserves a man who can offer more than I have. I'm not husband cloth, Cara Lee. I don't know anything about cleaving unto a woman."

"Sergeant, I don't remember asking you to marry me."

"Don't get smart. If you come near me again and offer me what you did tonight, you're going to need a husband."

Cara understood. "So, for my own good and the good of any potential babes you may plant, I should keep my distance."

"Exactly."

Cara wondered if he'd been born this arrogant. "Take me home."

"Look, maybe I'm not explaining myself well, Cara Lee."

"Sergeant, take me home. Now, please."

Chase looked into her eyes. He wanted her so badly that he ached, but he'd hurt her with his clumsy explanation of his own deficiencies, and this was not the way he wanted the evening to end. "Cara—"

"Please, Sergeant. You've said more than enough already. I will keep my distance."

A frustrated and still aching Chase picked up the reins and headed the team home.

When he stopped in front of Sophie's house, Chase put on the brake and turned to her. "I'm going to be gone tomorrow to help your sheriff round up some rustlers. I'll be back on Friday."

"I'll try not to throw myself at you *if* I happen to see you."

"You're determined to be mad about this, aren't you?"

"No, Sergeant, I am determined to stay away from you, so you won't have to marry me. Good night."

An angry Chase waited for his angry schoolmarm to get safely inside. When the door closed behind her, he turned the board around and headed for the livery.

About an hour later, Cara, now in her nightgown, lay in bed staring up at the dark. Not even her anger could mask the singing in her senses. He had turned her into an absolute wanton and she did not regret one glorious moment. He'd split the world in half right before her eyes and all she'd been able to see were stars. But how like a man to presume to decide what's best for a woman, she thought testily. She'd been doing fine taking care of her own honor. She also had never felt the need for a man in her life, but now that he'd made her experience the first lust-filled strains of a lover's tune, could she really resume her celibate spinsterish existence? Could she honestly continue to believe that her committee work, books, and devotion to teaching were enough to fill her life? And suppose sometime in the future she did meet a man she could term "right"? Would the lovemaking be as hot and powerful as the moments in the buckboard? Could this unmet man purge the memories of Chase Jefferson from her blood? More importantly, after tonight's dalliance, did she even want another man?

Cara had no answers. For a woman who'd survived very well up until then on the strength of her character and the sturdy quickness of her mind, she found herself grappling with questions neither could solve.

In the end, though, she decided to take Chase's advice. She would simply avoid him and hope that after he rode out of town her love would fade away.

Chapter 7

Chase had gone to bed the night before aroused and hard as iron. He'd awakened that morning in the same condition. Lying in bed, he could hear her moving around on her side of the wall as she prepared for another day's schoolteaching. He ached for her. This playful flirtation with Miss Cara Lee Henson had exploded into a situation that had taken on a life of its own. Torrid. That was the word. It sure summed up the desire he felt. God, he wanted her. He'd hurt her feelings last night, and he hadn't intended to. He'd been trying to relate the seriousness of taking their relationship further. He was certain Cara knew nothing about casual relationships, and his life did not jibe with anything more permanent, at least not at this time. Would it ever? He didn't know.

He heard her door close; she was leaving for school. He tossed off the covers, got up, and padded naked over to the window. He pulled back the curtain and waited for her to appear below. He saw her stop to talk to Asa, who was loading a wagon out front. They shared a few brief words, then she blessed Asa with one of her beautiful smiles and set off up the street in the direction of the school. Chase dropped the curtain back into place. He'd told her to stay away from him, but could he stay away from her? When he and his men first came to town he'd cautioned everyone to keep away from the women. He hadn't taken his own advice. He'd lain awake most of the night recalling the scent, taste, and feel of her. The sensual memories made him want to see her today, his vows be damned, but she'd probably take a Winchester to him if he approached her too soon. He thought on the dilemma a moment, trying to work out a scenario that would bring the two of them together in a way that would not seem contrived. He smiled then, remembering he had a legitimate excuse to see her. The night of the children's play he'd promised to pay the school a visit, a promise he'd been unable to honor as of yet because of the rustlers he and his men were tracking with Sheriff Polk. Grinning now, thinking about how absolutely furious Cara would probably be, Chase prepared to wash up and go meet Polk.

After their last parting, Cara wanted to fly into a rage when Chase showed up at the school Friday morning. How could she stay away from him if he wouldn't keep his distance? The children were delighted, of course, barely letting him in the door before peppering him with questions. Cara restored order and offered Chase the chair at her desk while she took a seat in the back.

He talked to the children of uniforms, and soldiering, and Indians. Though she tried to remain unmoved by him, the cadence of his voice captivated her in spite of the vows she had made. When she glanced to the front of the room, his eyes were waiting. He continued the explanation he was giving but did not break the contact. Once again she was struck by how devastatingly handsome he was, how sensually the mustache framed his mouth, and how brilliantly his eyes shone.

He turned from her and answered another question. Cara let out her breath, not realizing she'd been holding it. Knowing he could mesmerize her with the sound of his voice or with a simple look across a room only added to her distress. His presence unnerved her enough; she did not need to be exposed to the other weapons in his arsenal.

But he obviously came fully armed. His eyes alternately seduced and ignored her. He had her so off-balance answering the pull in his gaze, she had to mentally shake herself, dampen down her outrageous longings, and remember who and where she was.

The children were oblivious to the undercurrents between Cara and their visitor. All they cared about were his adventures.

And he had plenty. Cara found herself hanging on every word as he described a deadly trek across the Staked Plains, chasing outlaws, and the many places he'd seen.

The children's favorite subject, however, seemed to be the Indians. Not only was Chase knowledgeable, but he spoke of the culture, customs, and beliefs with a respect she'd rarely heard. He described their games, myths, and to everyone's further awe, the special friendship he had with a Sioux brave named Dreamer of Eagles. Chase taught Cara's students more about America's native race than she could have in a lifetime. By the time he finished speaking, the class knew that the Apache and the Ponca were as different in some customs and beliefs as

Irish were different from Germans; that the Sioux Nation had three families, the Lakota, Nakota, and Dakota; and that one of the most solemn of all Plains rituals was the Sun Dance. Once again Chase revealed to her a different facet of himself, this one as fascinating as those she'd observed previously.

She returned her attention to the tall soldier seated so casually on the edge of her desk. He was winding up, answering a few last questions, and relating bits of information about his brethren Sioux. He reached behind him to a long, oilskin-wrapped parcel he'd placed on Cara's desk when the visit began. At the time, she'd been so upset by his arrival that she'd paid little attention to the long package. Now, as he brought it around to rest on his lap, she became as intrigued as the children.

"I want to show you a *siyotanka*," he told them. "Can you pronounce that for me?"

While the children complied, he untied the three small lengths of twine holding it closed: one at each end, and one in the middle. "Does anyone want to guess what a *siyotanka* is?"

The audience guessed everything from a gun to food as he removed the oilcloth. None of them was correct.

He looked to Cara. "Miss Henson, do you have a guess?"

The children turned to her expectantly, but she shook her head in denial.

"All right then, let's see if we can figure it out."

He then placed the package flat on the desk and slowly unfolded the soft cloth of inner wrapping. After very carefully lifting out the treasure, he held it up for them to see.

The *siyotanka* was fashioned from gleaming, polished wood. It looked to be about the length of a man's forearm. "What's this look like?"

He held it up horizontally.

"A long bird with no wings," somebody sang out.

"Yeah, with its mouth open," came another young voice.

Everyone laughed at the description, including Cara and Chase, yet the longer Cara looked at it the more she tended to agree. It did resemble a long featherless bird, especially with the red paint across the top of its head. Jefferson called the paint *washasha,* the sacred red color.

"Any guesses now as to what this is used for?" He looked around the room, but no one had any new theories. "It's a flute," he explained, smiling. He played a few notes, and the children responded excitedly.

"But it's a very special flute. Sioux braves only use it to play music to someone they love."

Cara's attention shot up, but he seemed not to notice.

Chase continued by telling the class the legend of how the Lakota acquired the flute with the help of the *wagnuka,* the redheaded wood-pecker who came to a lost hunter in a dream. At the end of the tale he looked out over the rapt brown faces of the children to Cara. "Suppose we pretend that Miss Henson is my *winchinchala?*"

The students all giggled. They knew from the telling of the legend that the *winchinchala* was a pretty girl.

"Is that all right with you, Miss Henson?"

That he could ask such a thing with such an innocent, disarming face made all manner of retribution flash through Cara's mind. Damn him, damn him, damn him. But she kept her composure. "That's fine, Ser-geant, go ahead."

"Thank you, Miss Henson. Now, Indians are pretty shy, and some-times the flute can say the things a brave cannot. . . ."

He began to play. His outstanding talent revealed itself in the first few notes. His fingers moved over the holes with both precision and grace.

Cara's surprise at his adeptness soon faded as she became caught up in the sound of the song. The slow, pure notes, so hauntingly filled with yearning and desire, floated in the room like a rising, melodic breeze.

His dark eyes above the instrument were for her only. Those twin dark jewels of heat, coupled with the fluid, oscillating music, touched, stroked, and seduced, making her body come alive and her lips part as the notes flowed sweetly into her core. There was no pretense in this, Cara noted. This was real. Eventually the music slowed, then stopped.

The children clapped in enthusiastic approval; for them it had been merely a pretty song. Cara used the moment to escape Chase's scrutiny and regather her scattered senses. When she had, she stood. "Children, let's thank the sergeant for visiting with us today."

He received another rousing round of applause.

"Can he stay and have lunch with us, too?" asked little Rilla Walker.

"Yeah," said someone else, "can he stay and play baseball?"

Suddenly, the small classroom echoed with competing, pleading re-quests that their hero remain. Cara silenced the din with one teacherly clap of her hands. She wanted Chase here no longer than absolutely necessary. The students had other hopes, however. One look around the room showed tensely waiting faces. Cara's only hope lay in Chase's refusing. "Children, maybe the sergeant has other plans for this after-noon. He's been kind enough to share most of the morning with us. We really shouldn't impose any more on his time."

They turned away, their disappointment obvious. The resulting silence pulled at her heart. She felt like an ogre. "All right," she said in surrender. "If the sergeant has the time, he'd be more than welcome to stay for lunch and baseball."

All eyes turned to the soldier. When he accepted with a smile, their joy rang to the roof.

Lunch was taken on the grassy knoll behind the school. Sophie's staff always provided a picnic lunch on Fridays, and today's basket held slices of succulent ham, thick edges of freshly baked bread, an assortment of fruit, and a large, cold container of Asa's famous lemonade. Most of the children took their portions of the meal over to where Chase sat, eager for more of his stories.

After lunch had been consumed and the clean-up finished, the children ran off for a game of tag. Cara repacked Sophie's basket.

"Need some help?"

Cara looked up from her task. "You know, Sergeant, I can hardly avoid you if you show up at my door."

"That is a problem, isn't it?"

"Yes, it is."

With easy grace he lowered himself to the grass beside her and lay flat on his back, letting the sun warm his face. "I'm here for the students, not for you, schoolmarm. . . ."

"And stop calling me that." She'd never heard the word spoken so . . . so sensually. Every time he called her that, his voice did strange things to her insides.

He turned over on one elbow. "What's wrong with you?"

"Nothing that seeing you ride out of town wouldn't cure."

He sat up, and when she made a move to straighten, he stayed her with a gentle hand on her arm. "You really are upset."

"Yes, I am. First you tell me to keep my distance, lest you be forced to marry me, and today you show up here and seduce me in front of my students."

Chase hid his smile. "Is that what I did, seduce you?"

"Yes—I mean, no!"

Again she tried to rise, but he kept her near. "You and your damn *siyotanka*," she added accusingly.

"Would it make a difference if I told you I've never played it for any other woman before?"

"No," she lied.

Chase smiled. Lord, she was tough. When he left the day after tomorrow, he'd miss her a great deal.

"I have to see about the children," she told him. He didn't try and stop her this time, so she wasted little effort putting a fair amount of distance between them.

Friday afternoons were reserved for baseball, a game Cara loved as much as the students did. Usually she made sure the teams were evenly divided by ability, with Cara pitching for both teams. Today the teams were split up by gender, boys and girls. Cara played on the girls' side, boys on Chase's team. Cara stood with the rag-and twine-wrapped ball in hand waiting for the striker to get ready for the pitch. It was the last inning, with the girls ahead by two runs. The boys' team had two outs but all three bases had a screaming, cheering boy chomping at the bit to score. And Chase was up to bat.

Preparing to pitch, Cara looked back at her girls. They seemed ready, their faces a study in concentration. One more out and they'd win. She slowly swung her attention back to the waiting striker. He, too, had a face serious with concentration. She'd made him strike out twice already today. Did she have the skill to do it one final time? "Are you going to be able to hit one this time, Sergeant?" she called to him sweetly.

"Just throw the ball, schoolmarm," he growled.

So she did. The pitch came in belt-high and blazing. Chase swung, and this time the force of the wood slat meeting the ball echoed loudly and sent the ball sailing over the heads of the girls in the field. Chase took off for a tour of the bases, while the girls took off to find the ball. Retrieval came too late. First the other boys scored, then Chase touched home. The grin he shot her made her laugh. She held no grudges. His team had beaten hers fair and square.

After the game Cara rounded up her students and their honored guest for the return to the school. The day was over.

Cara's assignment homework drew groans, but the students gathered up their belongings, then lined up to share a final farewell handshake with Chase. Five minutes later, they ran out of school, yelling into the freedom of the sunshine.

When the last one disappeared, Cara turned to Chase. "Today meant a lot to them. Thank you for keeping your promise."

"They're a good bunch," he replied. "Where in the world did you learn to pitch such a wicked ball?"

"Not wicked enough," she corrected, remembering how he'd won the game. "My friend William taught me at Oberlin. It's quite the pastime back East." She noticed the rewrapped *siyotanka* on the desk. "Where did you learn to play the flute?"

"I played fife for a unit back in Philadelphia when I was young. The transition to Sioux flute was simple after Dreamer showed me the fingering."

"Dreamer is the Sioux brave you told us about today?"

"Yes, I met him during those years in Philadelphia."

"There are Indians in Philadelphia?"

"Probably. But he lives in Dakota Territory. His father sent Dreamer and his sister, Eyes Black As Raven, back East for schooling."

"How'd you meet him?"

"In a fight one day on the street."

Cara looked up, surprised.

"You remind me of him in some ways. He likes to cause a ruckus wherever he goes also."

"Get on with the story," Cara cracked.

He chuckled. "I came around a corner one day and saw Dreamer getting the tar beat out of him by four locals. I stepped in to even the odds. We've been friends ever since."

"Did you know him before that?"

"Nope."

"Then why did you join in?"

"He needed the help."

"What were they fighting about?"

"Whether the locals were going to continue to call his sister 'dirty squaw.' "

Cara nodded her understanding. She thought Chase would be a good friend: loyal, fearless. She remembered the way he'd taken on that brute with the horses back in Topeka. A better friend than lover, she thought regretfully. "You seem to know a lot about Indians."

"Dreamer's fault. He said a soldier posted in the West had an obligation to learn, and he's right. The government doesn't agree, however. If they feign ignorance, they don't have to acknowledge land claims or honor treaties or see to it that those captive in reservations are provided the basics like food and shelter. After all, they're just savages. But we owe the native peoples a lot. Most of the roads in the country are based on trails they blazed hundreds of years ago. All those so-called explorers who were going around discovering everything would still be standing on the dock if the Indians hadn't shown them around. Canoes. Corn. Dreamer says his brethren on the East Coast should have let those first Pilgrims starve. Would've saved everyone a lot of grief."

"Are his people suffering very much?"

"Yes. We're seeing the end of an era. A way of life is being wiped out right before your eyes, and no one cares because, after all, they're just savages."

Cara could almost touch the bitterness in his voice. No one she knew spoke of Indians with such passion. She glanced over to the now rewrapped *siyotanka* on her desk. She could still feel and hear its compelling tones. "Despite what I said outside, it's very beautiful. How long have you had it?"

"Let's see, probably, nine, ten years. It was a gift from Dreamer's father. Told me I might need it someday."

Their eyes held for a long spark-filled moment. Cara's attractions to him seemed to be growing stronger, and she had no idea how much longer her defenses would hold. She wanted to share all with this man because no other like him would ever cross her life's path again. That shocking admission made her turn away and direct her attention to something less volatile. She busied herself with rearranging the array of papers crowding the desktop.

Chase was finding that no matter the moment, location, or circumstance, every time he came near her he wanted to touch her, kiss her. Considering that their futures would never intertwine because of the career he'd chosen, he found the depth of his urge not only irrational but also a bit frightening. Why couldn't he simply walk away, forget her? No woman before had ever sent him through such a maze of uncharted territory.

Still fussing over the desk to keep from throwing herself into his arms, Cara gave him a quick glance and met the inferno burning deep in his eyes. She shimmered in the heat, swallowing in a suddenly dry throat, while *mariposas* took flight in her blood.

"Cara, you're a teacher. Explain to me why I want to make love to you whenever we're together. I've been trying to be a gentleman about this, but it's hard . . . damn hard."

Cara rippled in response, the heat of him beginning to weaken her will. She tried to deny herself and him. "Chase, it's getting late. . . ."

He slid from the desk and came over to where she stood behind the desk. He stopped less than a breath away, and lifted her silent face to his eyes. "Never in my life have I ever met a woman like you."

In the charged seconds following his murmured declaration, Cara trembled as he continued to view her with a brilliant hunger. Their last interlude came back in a rush, and though she tried to thrust the images away, just the warm, firm pressure of his hand beneath her chin made her pulse beat loud in her throat. He lowered his head to brush his lips oh so fleetingly against her own before pleasuring her with a kiss that put a sweet weakness in her knees.

"I want to see you tonight."

"You wanted me to stay away."

"I lied."

He gathered her in and the kiss deepened, plunging her into a dazed and hazy state of being. The world and reality could not compete with the intoxicating pressure of his lips or the heat of his palms roaming slow patterns over her back and waist. Cara felt drunk, disembodied. She shuddered as he left her mouth to trail caresses down the fevered skin of her neck and slid his hands boldly over her hips, instilling a blissful ache.

"Say you'll have dinner with me, Cara, and I'll go."

She didn't want him to go. Last night she'd been unaware of just how powerful desire could be. Today she embraced it gladly, openly. She didn't protest when he undid the first few buttons of her shirtwaist and kissed the skin he bared with a tenderness that made her moan. His hands caressed her breasts, plying the nipples until they tightened with begging response. He moved aside the flimsy cotton camisole and flicked his tongue against the bud he'd already prepared. He feasted then, gently, passionately, and Cara's world began to soar.

The rumbling sounds of a buckboard passing by outside reawakened reality and Cara pulled back, breathless and shaken with wanting. His brilliant gaze held such burning passion she had to look away, her hand moving to still the wildly throbbing pulse at the base of her bared throat. Turning away did not help. The exposed skin over the pulse point still held traces of the dew left by his tongue. The dampness reignited her flaming senses. She closed her eyes as wanton response spiraled anew. No man had the right to wield such power over a woman, she thought. No man. Especially one riding out of her life in less than forty-eight hours.

The sounds of the buckboard faded off into the distance, leaving the classroom silent.

"So," Chase said, smiling at the passion darkening her feline eyes, "will you have dinner with me? Or do you need to be . . . asked again?"

"No!" she cried more hastily than she intended. "I mean—yes, I'll have dinner with you."

He grinned, and once again Cara had to look away from the wicked magic in his dark eyes lest she agree to something else entirely, right there and then.

After a short discussion they agreed to a time and place, though neither of them was concerned with anything so mundane.

"I'll see you tonight, schoolmarm. . . ."

Cara nodded. Still shaken, she watched him stride to the door and out.

They met at the Sutton Hotel. Cara arrived first, nodding greetings to the familiar faces in the dining room. Chase came in moments later and drew the curious gazes of almost everyone as he crossed to the small table where Cara waited. Cara ignored the knowing looks and speculative glances of her neighbors and greeted Chase with a broad smile. "Good evening, Sergeant."

He grinned. "Evening, schoolmarm." He took the chair across from her.

They shared a few moments of small talk, then halted as Mae Dexter came over to take their order. "Hello, Miss Henson, Sergeant Jefferson."

Cara was a bit surprised to see Mae. Cara knew she worked for Virginia Sutton at the bank, but Cara had never seen her at the hotel. When she expressed this, Mae responded, "I just started today. Papa says if I'm to go to Oberlin in the fall, I need to help with the expenses."

Cara was pleased to hear Mae would be attending her alma mater. They spent a few more moments discussing the housing offered there, classes, and the like, then Mae took their orders and headed to the kitchen.

"So, Sergeant," Cara said, "have you and your men enjoyed your stay here?"

"Yes. The tributes, the dinners—we're going to have to go back out on the trail to get some rest."

Cara smiled. "The elders will be pleased."

"They have our thanks."

Cara wondered why she'd been fated to love a man she'd never see again. Life had played her some cruel tricks, but this had to be one of the worst. "Where are you headed next?"

"Fort Davis, Texas."

"And that is where?"

"Chihuahuan Desert. Southwest Texas."

"Sounds far away."

"Yes, it does," he replied, looking into her eyes.

Cara tried to dampen the wave of sadness welling up at the thought of his leaving.

"Something wrong?" he asked.

She told him the truth. "Just thinking I'll probably never see you again."

Chase wanted to reach across the table and take her small hands in his, but he was conscious of the other people in the room. "I'll miss our play, too, schoolmarm," he said softly.

Cara read the solemnness in his face and stiffened her lip against the sharp sting in her eyes. Lord, she hoped she wasn't going to start to cry. Luckily Mae chose that moment to appear with their meals, giving Cara the needed opportunity to think about something else.

When the meal was finished, he walked her home. Cara had decided not to dwell on the sadness. She had another day with him to savor, and she wanted to make the most of the time they had left. Besides, being sad would not prevent his departure.

"You've been awfully quiet this evening, schoolmarm," Chase said, walking beside her.

"I have, haven't I? Well, that's going to change."

He chuckled. "I don't know if that's good or bad."

"Of course it's good. And when we get to Sophie's, I'll prove it."

He stayed her with a hand on her arm. He looked down at her. "Prove it—how?"

"Not in the way you're thinking, Sergeant," she said, grinning, though she would dearly love to experience his magical lovemaking again.

"How do you know what I'm thinking?"

"It's the look in your eyes. Sometimes I think my clothes are going to catch fire when you look at me that way. . . . But we're not supposed to be talking about that, are we?"

"No, darlin', we're not. . . ."

The huskily spoken endearment fired her as much as his eyes. "Well, will you settle for something that's almost as sweet?"

The mustache flashed his pleasure. "You're playing with fire, you know that don't you?"

"Who, me? I wouldn't know what to do with a man like you . . . if you fell facefirst into my lap."

Chase could feel his manhood stir. His eyes sparkled as he replied, "Keep it up, and I'm going to rectify that problem."

Cara smiled with challenge. "Do you want what I'm offering as proof or not, Sergeant?"

"Yes," he said, wondering how he was going to keep his hands off her until he rode out the day after tomorrow. "Now march, before I show some proof of my own."

In the kitchen at Sophie's, Dulcie looked up at their entrance and smiled warmly. "Well, how was the Black Widow's food? Hope you have an antidote for spider venom. I hear she puts it in the potatoes."

Cara shook her head and smiled. "The food was fine, so stop. We came for our dessert."

"It's right here," Dulcie replied. "Just took it out of the oven, so be careful when you're handling it." She handed Cara a basket.

"Thank you, Dulcie. Follow me, Sergeant."

Outside, behind the house, Cara led him to the waiting buggy. "Get in," she told him as she climbed in on the left. She turned to put the basket on the buggy's floor and picked up the reins. Only then did she notice he hadn't moved. "What's the matter?"

"Where are we going?"

"On a picnic."

"At this time of day? It's going to be dark soon."

Cara looked out at the beautiful red of the setting sun. "So it is. Get in."

He did.

Once they'd cleared town he turned to her. "You know, you're pretty good with the horses."

"I've been driving teams all my life."

"Answer me this. How're you going to explain us leaving town together? Quite a few of your neighbors saw us."

"I always go out to visit students and their families on Friday evening. Asa usually goes with me, but he's down in Rice County. I'm hoping everyone will think you're escorting me in his place."

"This is how you usually spend Friday nights?"

"Most times. Why?"

"You're a beautiful woman, Cara. You should have a beau taking you dancing on Friday nights."

"But I don't, Sergeant. Besides, this gives me an opportunity to talk with the parents about their children's progress. We've only one stop to make tonight, then we'll have our picnic."

Cara pulled the buggy up to the soddy that housed the family of a little girl who'd missed school for several days due to a terrible cough. She was doing much better, the mother assured Cara, and Cara gave the woman the work her daughter could review while recovering. The mother thanked Cara and waved until the buggy pulled out of view.

"Now," Cara said. "Our picnic."

When Cara halted the buggy behind an old broken-down soddy in the middle of a field of just greening sunflowers, Chase stared around. "Where are we?"

"We are here."

Cara hopped down and grabbed the basket Dulcie had prepared. "Come on." She laughed, looking at his skeptical face. She snatched him by the hand and pulled him in her wake.

About fifty yards from the soddy Cara stopped. "Now I need your brawn. Can you open this door?"

Chase looked down at the plank door set in the earth at their feet. "Is this a dugout?"

"Yep."

Chase eased up the heavy door and peered down into the blackness. "This is where you want to have a picnic?"

"Yes. See that rope nailed into the door? Pull it up, please."

Chase hauled up a lantern. Cara took some matches from her skirt pocket and lit up. "Now ease it back down so we can see our way along the stairs."

Again Chase followed her instructions and slowly sent the light on a return descent.

"Now we can go down."

Once they were both on the floor of the underground dwelling, Chase stood in the gloom while she lit a few more lamps positioned around the earthen walls. The lights banished the shadows, and he looked around. The place was surprisingly clean. There were no animal droppings or standing water usually associated with such deserted places. "I haven't been in a dugout in I don't know how long."

"They aren't used much anymore, at least not around here. The post office in Nicodemus is still housed in one. Sophie said during the first winter, the whole town was underground."

Cara spread out a large tarp on the earthen floor and then began to unpack the basket Dulcie had provided.

"How did you find this place?" Chase asked, joining her on the floor.

"It belongs to the children."

Chase chuckled. "Really?"

"Yes, this is their secret place. I was let in on the location only after signing my name in blood." The surprise on his face made her smile and add, "I'm serious. I signed an oath saying I would not reveal the location of the secret dugout to any other adult unless it was an extreme emergency. Do you have any idea how much blood it takes to write 'C. Henson'?"

He laughed. "A teacher who signs her name in blood. No wonder they adore you."

"Not always," Cara corrected, handing him a fork and a napkin. "Sometimes I'm Henson the Hag, or Henson the Horrible."

"Never," he contradicted in whispered response.

The tenor of his low voice made her senses rise. She dampened them and concentrated on cutting the pie she'd taken from the basket. "I asked Dulcie and Sophie, and they said this was your favorite when you lived with them in Louisiana."

With wonder all over his face, Chase took the offered plate on which sat a still warm piece of . . . "Peach cobbler?"

"Yep," Cara replied, cutting herself a piece. "I hope they were right."

"They're right. I haven't had any in years. This is why you wouldn't let me order dessert at the hotel?"

"I thought it would be a nice surprise."

Chase ate his first bite, and the glorious taste brought forth a groan of pleasure. Cara smiled at his reaction. They ate in silence a moment, then Chase said, "Thank you very much for this, Cara Lee."

"You're very welcome."

While they ate, Chase looked around the room and spied an old broken-down stove in the corner. "That thing doesn't still work, does it?"

Cara nodded and politely tried to talk around the pie in her mouth. "Not anymore. It might if it had the stovepipe. All of the old dugouts had one of those stoves. Sophie said that's how you found Nicodemus and Henry Adams back then, by the stovepipes. They were the only structures in the towns above ground."

"I couldn't imagine living below ground," Chase observed, running his gaze over the earthen walls and floor.

"You do what you have to sometimes. That first winter people didn't have time to build homes or soddies, so they carved these places out of hillsides or dug them out of the earth. Some of the original 'dusters will tell you they preferred living below ground in Kansas to living above ground with the Redemptionists."

"You have a point there, schoolmarm."

"Do you want more?" she asked, noticing he'd devoured the first piece.

"Yes, and give me a man's portion this time."

Cara saluted him crisply and barked, "Sir, yes sir, sir."

Chase laughed at her application of the Tenth's well-known three-sir response to an order. "How'd you know about that?"

"Just by being around you and the men. It's very distinctive, hearing them say 'sir' three times every time they're asked to do something."

"It's a tradition," he responded, taking the newly cut piece of cobbler. He smiled at the slab of pastry she'd given him. "Now this, Miss Henson, is a man's portion."

Cara cut herself a small second piece and joined him.

When they'd polished off a good portion of the pie and neither of them could eat another bite, Cara rewrapped it in the cloth and placed it back in the basket. She could tell by the blackness of the sky above their heads that the evening was coming to a close. "We should be getting back, I suppose . . ."

"Probably," he replied, but made no move to stand. He seemed content to sit and watch her, making her desire heat up the longer his gaze caressed her. And when he did finally stand, it was not to lend her a hand in gathering up the tarp or basket contents. Rather, he slowly climbed the earthen stairs and pulled down the until now open dugout door. He made his descent and Cara could feel her clothing ignite from the blaze in his smoldering eyes. He came back to the tarp and sat down. For a moment he said nothing, touching her only with her gaze. She stood, locked by the passion he'd unleashed, until he said softly, "Come here, schoolmarm . . ."

Cara set the basket aside and came over to where he sat. He held out his hand. Trembling, she slipped her hand into his and let him slowly guide her down to a kneeling position at his side. He leaned over, and with a hand in her hair brought her mouth to his.

The kiss moved over her like the faintest of moonlight and she drank it in like a night-blooming flower. As it deepened, she ran her hands up his arms, savoring his strength for what she knew would be the last time.

Chase knew he shouldn't be tempting fate by having her near, but to deny himself was something he could not do. Her mouth, still bearing the sweetness of the cobbler, opened to the tasting of his tongue, and he enjoyed her as if she were the ripest of peaches. Groaning with the pleasure of her, he moved her to sit atop his lap. He left her mouth to kiss the faint bruising around her eye, the edges of her hair, the shell of her ear, his manhood hardening beneath her soft hips. "Cara, I want to open your shirt . . ."

Cara didn't protest. Feeling him undo her buttons and kiss each inch of bared skin made the heat between her thighs flow in sweet response. His mouth teased her nipples through her camisole while his hands roamed languidly. She parted her legs to let him slide his hot hand into the throbbing warmth they sheltered, then moaned softly as he dallied lazily through the fabric of her skirt. He pushed the bodice of her camisole down below her breasts and took one dark nipple into his mouth.

"Cara Lee . . ." He breathed, moving his lips to fire her other nipple. He slipped his hand beneath her skirt and squeezed her thigh lovingly. He pushed her dark stocking down her leg, then ran his trembling hand back up the bare limb until he reached the warm curve of her soft hip. He repeated the process on the other leg, then pushed her skirt to her waist and explored until her breath rose against the silence. "Can I?" he asked raggedly, already tugging her drawers down her hips, knowing he'd die if she denied him, but she whispered, "Yes . . ."

Cara rippled in response to being bare to him. The first touch set off such a joyful response, her senses began to spin and feed on the whirlpool that spread from his splendidly wicked hands to her shuddering core.

When he withdrew his hand, Cara groaned in protest. He smiled with hot eyes and kissed her. "Such an eager little Cara Lee . . ." he whispered, then wordlessly removed her shirt and helped her out of the camisole. "Now . . . put your shirt back on. Don't want you to catch a chill . . ."

Once she'd done that, he had her lie with him on the tarp so he could slide kisses slowly down the golden plane of her body. He pushed at the open halves of her shirt, lingering over the beauty of her breasts until they were hard and pleading. His mustached lips brushed over the flatness of her belly beneath her rucked-up skirt, and his tongue set fire to the recessed nook of her navel. When his lips brushed the swollen place between her open legs, a cry broke from her and filled the silence. "No . . ." she protested, trying to back away, but his large, gentle hand on her small waist kept her there.

"Hold still, darlin' . . ." he whispered hotly.

A soft lick made her stiffen in both disbelief and delight. Everything melted into fire. Boldly, yet gently, his fingers parted the blackberry forest, giving him intimate access to the hidden shrine within. As he enjoyed her, Cara's hips rose shamelessly for more. Never in her life had she thought such pleasure possible. He tasted, nibbled. Her head upon the tarp moved back and forth like that of a person insane. Release shattered her almost instantaneously. Her shout of elation pierced the quiet.

"Next time you'll have more stamina," he promised, leaning down to give her one more scalding lick, and Cara buckled with a strangled scream.

Chase was harder than he'd ever been in his life. His raging manhood demanded release, and as he eased her back to herself with soft kisses on her lips and butterfly touches between her honey-filled thighs, he had to exert a lot of control not to continue. All he could think about was settling himself between her soft thighs and taking her until she climaxed calling his name. However, he'd vowed not to compromise her and he would not.

A totally dazed Cara sat up. The warm amusement she met in his gaze made her smile shyly and turn away; she had enjoyed herself entirely too much under this man's spell and he knew it. "I take it all back, Sergeant," she said. "You are *very* talented."

The mustache curled over his smile. "You're welcome . . ."

Cara rose to her knees and kissed him. "Are we going to continue now?" she asked, nibbling on his bottom lip, running her hand over his chest.

"No, we are not," he responded, drawing on her lips. "Now stop, before I explode . . ."

"Chase . . ." she coaxed against his ear.

"No . . . Close your shirt . . ."

But before she could, he bent to her breasts and his warm mouth pleasured them until they were begging, damp and hard once again. He then raised his head, pulled the halves of her shirt closed, and began buttoning her up.

"But what about your pleasure?" Cara asked, keeping still while he completed the task. When he didn't speak, she peered at him. "Chase?"

"Cara Lee . . . my pleasure's fine," he lied. "Now do me a favor, darlin' . . . go sit over there a moment." To allay the concern in her face he gave her one more kiss. "Go on . . . or we'll never get back."

Cara complied but with great reluctance. "Are you okay?"

"I'm fine, schoolmarm, just need to . . . catch my breath."

Cara didn't believe him for a minute. He'd been as aroused as she, yet he'd gotten no release. Even someone with her limited experience knew lovemaking involved a joining. "Chase—"

"Pack up the basket, please, and no more talk about this." He wondered how it would feel to spend the night in a dugout. He'd be finding out if he couldn't bring his desire under control; right now he was still so hard he couldn't walk, let alone climb the stairs to the surface.

"You know something, Sergeant?" Cara said, placing the dishes and napkins back in the basket. She then retrieved her underwear. "You are too damn noble for your own good. Has it ever occurred to you that I might have wanted you to continue?" There, she'd said it.

He sat with his back to her so she did not see him smile as he replied, "You know something, schoolmarm? You wouldn't last a minute in the army because you don't take orders worth a damn."

"I'll accept that as a compliment," she said, pulling her drawers back on, trying to decide if she was mad or not. She decided she wasn't because deep down inside she loved this man. The fact that he continued to treat her with such unfailing respect made the love stronger, even if she found it frustrating.

As it turned out, Chase did not have to experience a night in a dugout. Cara kept quiet long enough to let the memories of his arousal fade to a dull roar, and they left. Outside, he gingerly climbed into the buggy, thankful for the first time in his life not to be on horseback. He sat back, eyes closed, as she guided the team to town.

"Chase, I wish you would let me help you."

"Cara Lee, I don't want to talk about this."

"But I do. You look like you're in pain."

"Darlin', you're just making it worse."

"I'm sorry," she apologized. Cara kept her mouth closed for the duration of the trip.

In bed that night, aching and hard, Chase told himself he'd done the noble and honorable thing by denying himself that which he wanted most. However, his body disagreed. Every time he thought of Cara half-naked and twisting under his pleasuring, the ruckus started up again. She had him so in knots he'd actually thought of seeking out Virginia, a thought that indicated just how desperate the situation had become. He'd banished the plan just as quickly, however, because no other woman would do. He wanted Cara.

If he could hold out for only one more day, he could leave the school-teacher just as he'd found her, intact. But he also knew that if the situation presented itself, he would not be so noble again; he would take her with all the tenderness and vigor he possessed.

Chapter 8

As Cara drifted off to sleep, her final thoughts were of Chase. When she awakened Saturday morning, her mind picked up the same thread. Who would have thought she'd fall in love with a Union soldier? She corrected herself: He'd ceased being defined so simply for quite some time now. It was as if he'd been sent to counter the tragedy and death of her grandfather. In her nightmares the demons wore Union uniforms. In this new reality a flesh and blood man was in that uniform. And he was a fine man who had his own demons from the past; a man who'd taught her passion; more importantly, a man who cared.

And she cared for him in return. She knew a good portion of his interest in her lay in the physical realm, and last night had been a vivid demonstration. But tomorrow morning he'd ride out of her life, never knowing he'd be carrying a piece of her heart.

Cara got up. She had cleaning to do at the school. She hoped the chores would give her something else to think about.

They didn't.

She thought about Chase with every swipe of her mop and every rub of polish on the desks. She thought about him as she washed the windows and as she cleaned out the storm cellar and reclosted the supplies. To keep from going back to Sophie's and possibly running into him, she inventoried the school's supplies, made lists of items she needed to order and those she'd have to beg for in letters to the aid societies back East. Lesson plans came next, six weeks' worth.

As the afternoon waned, she spent the early evening hours catching up on her correspondence and penning a letter to her friend William Boyd. When night fell, she could find nothing else to detain her. Her stomach was also reminding her that she hadn't eaten since breakfast, so she doused the lanterns and left the school.

Back at the boardinghouse, she got a plate of food from Dulcie and took it up to her room. Cara thought the ideal situation would be to avoid Chase until he left. By doing so, she hoped to lessen her heartbreak.

After her meal she sought out Sophie for permission to use the big claw-footed tub in the rooms Sophie shared with Asa. Cara usually took her baths in her own room, but every now and then she needed the luxury Sophie's big tub provided, and tonight was one of those times. Sophie was more than agreeable, telling Cara to help herself, so she did.

When Cara returned to her room after the bath she felt like a new woman. The warm water and the aromatic salts she'd added to it had eased a lot of her inner tension. She read for a little while, then crawled into bed. She tried not to think about Chase, but she lost the battle, just as she had all day.

And now to make things worse, she heard the door close next door and then sounds of him moving around. The more she attempted to shield her mind, the stronger his presence seemed to intrude. Why him? she asked herself again for the hundredth time. Why this man when there were so many thousands of others in the world? She pounded her pillow and turned over on her side. No amount of shifting positions freed her from the memories of his kiss, the delicious curve of his smile, or the vibrant, yearning notes of the *siyotanka.*

When the sounds of sloshing water came through the wall, Cara tried to close her ears with little success. He was bathing; smoking, too, she realized as the first tantalizing whiffs of tobacco began to slide into the room from under the door. The scents played gently with her nose and havoc with her senses. Cara let her imagination soar over how he must look naked in the tub: the sculpted muscles of his arms and chest, the firm hardness of mahogany-colored thighs. She wondered how it would be to have him sharing her tub. She could almost feel his hands sliding the soap across her skin, the way her breasts would tighten . . . She shook off the fantasy and hastily brought her thoughts back to saner realms.

Through the door came the sound of his singing. His voice was passable. The song, one she did not recognize, praised the qualities of some unknown Spanish beauty named Maria. He sung with a lusty boisterousness that made her think he sang it on the trail. Well, this wasn't the trail and it was late. She wanted to sleep.

When the sloshing finally subsided, the singing didn't, so Cara grabbed her robe and went to his door. She knocked hard to be heard over the refrain.

The song stopped. A second later she heard him undoing the bolt and waited for him to open the door.

Chase wore only a pair of pants. One of Sophie's big towels lay draped over a magnificent dark shoulder, and his hair was still wet. The beauty of him blinded her.

"Let me get my shirt." He chuckled. "I'm liable to melt with you looking at me like that."

His remark shocked her into the realization that she was staring. He crossed back into the room, slipped on a shirt, but left it unbuttoned.

"Now," he said, looking down at her with eyes that made her remember last night, "what can I do for you?"

"The caterwauling. I'm trying to sleep."

"I've been told I have a pretty fair voice."

"Was this person living or dead?"

"Oh, Miss Henson, you wound me to the quick," he cried, placing a hand over his heart.

Cara could not hide her smile.

"I like making you smile."

Cara went all strange inside. "Your singing was . . . disturbing me. I have to go now."

"Wait. If I kept you awake, please accept my apology."

"Accepted."

"Was there anything else?" he asked, unwilling to let her go.

For a moment, Cara could not say. There were so many things she wanted to ask, so many things going on inside herself that she could not define, never mind find the words to express. How did one tell a man who'd blazed a comet's trail across the staidness of her life that she wanted his love? That she wanted whatever the night would bring so she could look back and say she'd loved once and loved well? When she looked into his face again, she saw serious concern reflected there. "No," she answered softly. "Nothing else."

With a gentle finger he lifted her chin so he could better see the truth that might shine in her eyes. "Are you sure?"

"No, I'm not," she replied with a touch of irritation. "What is wrong with me?"

He answered quietly, "Nothing. Come here." Taking her by the hand, he pulled her into the room. "You and I should talk."

Still holding her hand, he led her past the tub and over to a chair beside the bed. He motioned her to take the chair while he sat on the big four-poster bed. "Now, first of all, there's nothing wrong with you. What you're feeling is desire, that's all."

"That's all?"

"That's all."

"And is there a cure?"

"Sometimes . . ."

Cara found the courage to look directly into his eyes, instantly regretting it when the heat they harbored singed her.

"You're a very passionate woman, Cara Lee. When you find a man worthy of you, don't be afraid to show him that side of yourself."

Why was he telling her this? *His* lips were the ones that had set her afire. "I don't think there'll be other men."

"Why not?"

It made Cara a bit uncomfortable speaking of this, especially with him, but she'd faced the future long ago. "No man will want me for a wife. Men out here need a woman young enough to bear children and strong enough to help them carve out a home. They see a schoolteacher as neither. When I first came to the Valley, some of the men who courted me said they couldn't see me behind a plow, even though I've been behind a plow many times in my life."

Truth be known, Chase couldn't see her behind a plow, either, although he didn't doubt her ability to handle one. He could readily imagine her in his bed, however. More than likely, the others had, too. "You're too hard on yourself," he said.

Cara answered wistfully, "Truth is hard."

He picked up her hand and tugged gently. "Come here." When she settled on the bed, he said seriously, "Yes, some truths are hard, but this is a truth you've erected, schoolmarm. It isn't reality. If you could see yourself as I do, or as any man with half a brain does, you'd know how wrong you are. You're a very beautiful woman. You're passionate, caring, smart. Some men probably find you a bit intimidating and a lot opinionated, but that's part of your charm."

Her eyes narrowed at that last comment, and he grinned and brought her fingers to his lips. "When the right man comes along, you'll know."

That's the problem, Cara thought. "Suppose he doesn't?" she asked, freeing her hand from his. "Do I spend the rest of my life wondering what it feels like to know a man's love?"

Chase had no ready response. "Only you can answer that."

Cara looked away. She knew he was right, and she came to a decision. She refused to spend the rest of her life wondering what might have been. "Will you make love to me?"

For a moment, Chase did not reply, and she steeled herself for rejection. Finally, he reached over and raised her chin. "Cara Lee, I have spent ten long days doing my best to keep my hands off you. Don't tease with me now, darlin'."

"I'm not teasing, Chase."

And she wasn't, Chase realized. Her eyes were as serious as he'd ever seen them. "You sure about this? I promised myself after the ride home last night that I would not turn you down again if you asked."

"I'm sure."

He searched her face again. Seemingly satisfied, he spoke. "Then let's close the door."

When that was done, Cara waited as he walked around turning down the lamps. He left only the small lamp beside the bed lit. The full light had fed her confidence, but the flickering shadows, coupled with his tall, assessing presence, brought on trembles of uncertainty. She looked up as he came and stood before her. He held out a hand. She took it and rose to her feet. He ran a worshipping finger over the delicate curve of her cheekbone, then in a velvet voice asked, "What are you thinking?"

"How very scared I am . . ."

Her guileless reply lifted his mustached lips into a smile. "Don't be," he whispered. "The first time should always be special, and it will be. I promise."

He lowered his head and kissed her with such welcoming tenderness, Cara's soul cried out from the beauty of it. Her arms wound around him, and in turn he gathered her in closer, letting her experience for the first time the full blaze of his passion. They fed on each other with mating tongues and roving hands, knowing they had only that night.

She felt the warmth of his fingers grazing her back above her night-gown as he moved her thick braid aside, then came the gentle brush of his lips across the tender skin of her neck. The slender bones felt as if they were melting beneath the sensual assault.

When he eased down the thin shoulder straps of her gown just enough to tease the fiery tip of his tongue against the silken nook of her collarbone, Cara sighed in vibrant response. His big hands roamed lazily up and down her bare arms, gliding over the tense muscles with a penetrating magic all their own until her fears fell away like rain. Every thrilling touch of his lips, and every flute-inspiring pass of his hands, branded her soul. In that instant, she knew that for as long as she lived, there would never be another man able to purge Chase Jefferson from her blood. Never.

Chase had to caution himself. Having her to enjoy at his leisure built a fire in his blood he found hard to control. His lips teased her ear, her throat. His sure hands slipped down to the fullness of her breasts, rolling the nipples through the thin gown until they gave up their own sweet song. If he didn't slow down, this whole thing would be over in a few quick thrusts right here. But even as the thought surfaced, he slid one bold hand into her still laced-up bodice and filled his palm with the warm nippled treasure within. Behind her, the other hand seductively circled the gown over the rounded curve of her hips.

Cara's head dropped back under the heat of his lips on her breasts, then her whole world spun from the feel of his hands slowly undoing the laces between them. She trembled as he slid the ribbons from their stitch-worked holes.

He tugged the last length free. Her bodice opened with a flutter, and he moved the unjoined halves aside, palms brushing her hardness. He lowered his head and placed an achingly slow lick against one ripe crest, then the other. Cara pleaded soundlessly for mercy as he began to love her with his masterful mouth. He sucked her like a piece of rock candy, the sensations hitting her like strikes of lightning. She could barely stand. When her breasts were damp, he left them for a moment to nibble on the lush fullness of her bottom lip, then to brush his hand longingly against the apex of her thighs.

Her legs parted in shuddering response. His first precious strokes against her woman's heat made her close her eyes. Chase reveled in the gifting of pleasure. Her response, so pure and flowing, emboldened his need to seek and lay claim to all she would willingly offer. "Take this gown off."

His eyes glittered. Cara's own breathing roared in her ears. "Is . . . that necessary?"

Chase smiled at her reticence, then bent to once more pleasure a bared, sable-tipped nipple. He lingered until moans slipped from her lips, then ran an adoring finger over the succulent golden undercurve. "Who's the teacher here, schoolmarm?" His teeth played expertly. Desire surged. Her hand moved to his head and felt the soft, black lamb-like curls at the back of his neck as he transferred his kisses to the twin.

"I'll take off the gown, but you'll have to turn around."

Chase smiled. "Cara, that doesn't make sense. Besides, a man likes to see his woman undress."

He'd never referred to her as "his woman" before. The claiming set her pulses to throbbing. But she was still hesitant. "I can't just . . . It isn't—"

"Isn't what?"

"Proper."

Her shyness invoked his tender humor. "Darlin', nothing I plan on doing to you tonight is proper."

The lusty heat in his tone touched her like a brush of his hands. In the end though, it was he who surrendered.

With his back to her, Cara removed the thin nightdress. She could not part with it fully, and when he faced her once again, she was holding it against her body like a delicate shield.

"Oh, schoolmarm," he chided with a humorous sigh.

She looked so fetching. Just enough of the coppery body was left visible to tantalize. His gaze swept up the sides of her rounded hip to the barely concealed breasts, and his desire pounded to a familiar beat.

"Are you going to put out that last light?" she asked, needing the darkness to bolster her courage.

"Nope." He discarded his shirt and the light played over the rippling dark beauty of his arms and broad chest. He kissed her, then whispered, "Visual memories are the best." He nibbled at the sultry petal of her bottom lip. He pulled her back into the claiming circle of his bare arms, paying no attention to the gown she continued to clutch, letting her keep it until she became more comfortable with her nudity.

Cara had had no idea that being naked with a man could be so staggering, so exciting. His warm palms, although callused by the ruggedness of trail life, wandered over her skin like silk. They mapped the thin structure of her neck and the rounded measure of her shoulders before descending down her back to the firm bare flare of her hips. The languid wildfire in his touch spread to the blossom already stroked to full bloom between her legs, and she gave herself up to its tingling heat.

Chase realized he hadn't even come close to imagining how good she would feel half-naked in his arms, her head thrown back under his impassioned sucking. The reality of her hard little nipples, and the stain texture of her hips filling his cupping, exploring hands, made him harder than any dream.

Cara was barely aware of his lifting her to the bed, but very aware that his lips never left hers. The mattress gave under their combined weight, then supported them as Chase pulled her in against him.

His bare upper body was hard and warm. Even though he still wore his trousers, Cara could feel every breathing inch of him, especially that hard promise that was a virgin's forbidden fruit. She basked in the feeling of being naked against him as his caresses roamed freely. The gown lay between them twisted and forgotten until his exploring hand discovered it down by her knees. When he began to move it over her shimmering skin, Cara stretched and moaned. Slow, circling invitations transformed the practical garment into a provocative instrument of seduction. He rubbed it over the flat plane of her belly and the sleek structure of her hip, followed by lazy erotic tracings up to her bursting nipples, then down to the blackberry curls at the apex of her thighs. As he purposefully brought it up against the heat sheltered there, Cara gasped. He lingered, dallied, tempting her to open to him. Under his hand the gown stroked that aching, straining part of herself, coercing her legs to spread wide, then wider still.

Chase kissed her mouth in reward for her exquisite offering and, despite the urgent hardness roaring to be released from the crotch of his trousers, took his time with her pleasuring. For a man who'd always taken his lovemaking lightly, he was very serious this night. He wanted her ready, as ready as a man would want his virgin wife on their wedding night, ready to receive him and the mysteries of pleasure—all without pain and without fear. This beautiful woman was offering the most precious thing a woman could offer a man. In return, he could give no less.

So he continued to stroke her with feathery, circling promises; promises so wistfully piercing, Cara could not help but cry out. Chase, eyes glowing, watched her body arch to the scandalous manipulations of the cloth, and then, as he moved the garment aside, to the warm surprise of his bare hand.

He leaned down, placed a kiss against her heat and spent a few fire-filled moments loving her as he had the previous night in the dugout. Only when completion tore his name from her lips did he withdraw.

Leaning back, Chase smiled into her eyes. In the soft light she looked highly seductive. Her nakedness coupled with the tastes he'd had of the firm high breasts, the flat satin plane of her belly, and the sweet fragrant honey flowing from the font of cinnamon-gold thighs added up to a desire both hard and true. He stood and began on the buttons of his pants. His manhood would be denied no longer. His black eyes blazed into hers as his fingers worked their way down the placket. When he freed the last one, she hastily turned away.

"Turn around and look at me, Cara Lee," he instructed softly. The tone, so hushed and gruff with passion, stroked her in all the places still throbbing from the vivid tutoring just moments before. "Men and women are just built different, that's all."

Summoning courage, Cara turned back, but her gaze settled high, on his face. His mustache twitched. "Where's your thirst for knowledge?"

She smiled. "Do you have any idea what the school board members would say if they could see me like this?"

"Probably the same thing I'm saying, see?"

Innocently, her eyes followed his lead, only to find themselves settling on the magnificence she'd been trying to avoid. Startled and breathless, she looked back up into his smiling eyes. When he came around the bed, moving as fluidly as a cat, she watched him without shame. The light played over his beautifully sculpted strength, while his manhood boldly teased her eyes. He stood with all the arrogant radiance of a Dahomey king and let her look her fill. Even as his presence overpowered her, even as she felt passion renew and build, she suddenly felt inadequate, inexperienced. How could she ever think to please a man as potent and knowing as he?

His soft voice cut into her thoughts. "Thinking again, I'll bet."

Guiltily, Cara dropped her eyes.

"If that mind of yours is still going full throttle, I obviously haven't distracted you enough."

He climbed onto the bed, placed his large hands on her waist, and drew her to sit before him atop his lap until she was settled in and surrounded by his velvet warmth. His skin seemed to scald her everywhere. His manhood, pressing commandingly against her hips and spine, exuded sensations so unnerving that it reduced her mind to a crawl.

While his mouth whispered passionately over the outline of her jaw, his hands moved wantonly over curves, peaks, and valleys. The kisses descended to the crook of her shoulder and Cara sighed, trembled, and melted against the strong chest at her back, letting him work his magic.

"Open your legs . . ." Chase slid his hand over her damp warmth, and using his long-boned fingers, gave her a splendid, breath-stealing preview of the bliss to come. "Now," he murmured. The rhythm tempted her hips and caused them to move in slow seeking circles. Her passion infected him. Her hot little body pressed so intimately against him made his manhood pulse with power.

Cara felt the passion building like a gathering storm, and this time when the waves burst over her she turned her face into the steadying strength of his shoulder as her body splintered into a million brilliant pieces.

Kissing her passionately, Chase laid her down, then, looking into her eyes, eased her thighs apart. He entered her gently, and only slightly.

The partial gaining brought on such a rush of roaring emotion he almost succumbed to the urge to thrust himself fully into the silk passage. Biting his lip, he held back. Hands filled with her luscious hips, he waited, pulsing. He had not brought her this far only to inflict hurt now. He'd promised it would be special; the vow would be kept.

So he teased her with the promise of it, sliding first in and then out, gaining entry bit by bit, little by little; feeling himself almost shatter with the desire for more, telling himself he could hold on until she could come with him. His hands then left her hips and moved over her tense, flat belly and the hard crests of jutting curves like the fluttering notes of his flute. He toyed with the portions of herself already attuned to his hands, making her open to receive him, cupping her hips as he convinced her to take in one more tantalizing inch, then another and another. The sweat dampening his forehead, brow, and back were a testament to granite-hard need and the control he fought to maintain. He bent down and kissed her mouth, savoring the double possession. "It may hurt, darlin' . . . but just this once . . ."

The last thrust pushed him past her maidenhead, and she stiffened.

Chase kissed her lips softly. "That's the only time it will hurt. It goes much better from here . . ."

Cara gave herself over to his kisses and soothing hands, hoping they would distract her from the hurt. Initially they did not; too much of herself was centered on the fiery tenderness enveloping him. A moment later, he resumed his sultry stroking. Gradually, the sweet invasion, aided by the hands guiding her hips, overrode all; she knew no pain, time, or place. The deliciously slow circles he tempted her to join became her whole world.

Then it began, that glowing, reaching brilliance; rising this time not from his hands or mouth but from the hard perfection moving like bliss between her thighs. The pleasure rose and spread, radiating over her in much the same way as the light of the lamp pulsed over the tautened lines of his face. More strokes stoked inner fires even higher, making her hips rise to seek and accept all he had to give.

Caught up in the rhythm and feel of her, Chase ground out, "Oh, Cara . . ." She was so hot and soft, her body so beautifully responsive, he could hold back no longer. His hands tightened on her hips and he boldly gifted her with memories guaranteed to last a lifetime.

Later, much later, a half-asleep but fully sated Cara had no idea of the time when he finally carried her back to her room and put her to bed. She returned the poignant farewell of his parting kiss, heard the last whispered voicing of her name, followed by the faint, dull sound of his door as it closed. Then she slept.

But Chase did not. He had only a few hours before he and his men would depart, and sleep at this point was out of the question. More than anything he wanted to slide into bed with Cara and kiss her until she awakened, but he had gear to pack and horses and men to round up.

It didn't take him long. Being cavalry, he traveled light. As he looked around the room to ensure he hadn't left anything in the drawers or beneath the bed, his eyes grazed the mattress. In the center of the rumpled sheets lay the proof of her virginity. The vividness of her passion made him want to see her one last time.

He soundlessly reopened her door and stepped inside. Over in the bed she slept peacefully, her breathing rising and falling in the silence. The pain of leaving her overcame him, as did the realization that he'd probably never see her again. He bent and tenderly kissed her soft cheek. "Goodbye, schoolmarm," he whispered thickly.

He gave her cheek one last parting stroke with his hand, bent to kiss her again, then quietly slipped away.

When Cara awakened, she looked at the clock beside her bed and panicked, realizing she'd overslept. Then came the memory of how she'd spent the previous night and she could only smile. She got up, padded over to Chase's door, and knocked softly. She heard movement, then the door opened, but to her surprise, Sophie stood on the other side.

"Oh! Good morning," Cara stuttered.

"And good morning to you," Sophie replied. "You overslept."

Cara did not say a word.

"I'm not judging," Sophie told her softly. "By the way, Chase said to tell you that he'll be at Fort Davis if you need to contact him."

Cara looked past Sophie and into the room. "He's gone?"

"Yes," she said gently. "He and his men rode out a little after dawn."

Cara's heart shattered.

"Dulcie saved you some breakfast," Sophie said.

"Thank you."

"Well, I need to finish cleaning up in here. Cara, if you need to talk to someone, Dulcie and I are here."

"I appreciate that, but I'm fine. I'll . . . be down to eat in a while."

Stunned, Cara closed the door. Of course, she'd known he'd be leaving this morning, but she hadn't counted on his not saying goodbye.

Chapter 9

After receiving his new orders Chase had saluted the colonel at Fort Supply, and left the commander's office. Two hours later Chase mounted Carolina, and rider and horse headed north out of Oklahoma Territory. Chase hadn't wanted this assignment. He and the colonel had agreed this investigation should have been handled by the local U.S. marshal; what with all the demands placed on the soldiers in the area from renegades, lawbeaking survey parties, and homesteaders clamoring for protection, tracking mail coach bandits rated very low on the army's list of priorities.

But a growing number of the express line's men had been killed. Bank officials all over the region were screaming for the army's intervention. Chase's orders were to go into the area where the robberies had been concentrated and investigate. He was to pose as a civilian, conduct his investigation as a spy.

Had Chase not served with General Tubman during the Civil War, he might not have been tapped for this assignment. Playing the part of a drifter would give him access to ordinary people, and as General Tubman had proved to the Union brass during the war, cooks, stablehands, laundry workers and the like were invaluable sources of information. More likely than not, they knew more about what went on than the town officials did. As long as Chase didn't draw unnecessary attention to himself by acting outside the bounds usual for a man of his race, the operations generally went smoothly.

This was not a role Chase relished. On several occasions, no matter how invisible he tried to be, he found himself in conflict with individuals who still harbored the hatred and bitterness of the war. One such incident in Texas, three years before, had resulted in a ten-day jail stay for him and three broken ribs. He'd gone into the small town after information on some horse thieves. The Reb sheriff accused Chase of breaking the law. He beat Chase, charged him, and threw him in jail. Chase believed he still might be in that jail if a guard on one of the overland coaches hadn't recognized him and wired Colonel Grierson at Fort Davis. Even after being contacted by the colonel, the sheriff, convinced Chase needed to be taught his "place," refused to release him until the army's threats forced him to do so.

There had been no such incident on this trip. Over the past month, he and Carolina had visited all the towns on the colonel's list except one that he'd deliberately left for last. Although Chase hadn't run into any trouble, he also hadn't turned up any information about the robberies.

The latest coach ambush had taken place two weeks before on a trail between Dodge and Wichita, Kansas. Again, the driver and guard had been killed, their deaths bringing the count to nine victims.

The town Chase had to visit now was Henry Adams. He was due to give his report at Fort Wallace, Kansas, in less than a week. There would be enough time to find out if Sophie or Asa could shed any light on the robberies and to visit Virginia Sutton. Funds from the Sutton Merchant Exchange were among those stolen in the first outlaw attack. He'd been asked to relay the army's reassurances that a thorough investigation was under way.

By operating within such a tight time limit, Chase hoped he'd be less inclined to seek out the real draw in the small town—Cara Lee Henson. Leaving Cara that May morning, Chase had assumed the memories of her would fade. He and his men went back to guarding roads, fighting renegades, and mapping water holes. In the unforgiving climate of the Southwest Territories, Chase defied any man to linger over the memories of any woman.

Yet he had.

Neither heat nor sun, nor long patrols across the harsh desert landscape kept memories of one small schoolteacher at bay. And on days when safety and survival wiped her from his thoughts, she visited his dreams, lingering, waiting.

He began to see Cara in the face of every woman he encountered. He imagined her hips swaying beneath each skirt, and her eyes . . . those copper eyes shimmered no matter where he looked, effectively killing any desire he might have had for anyone else.

He'd finally come to admit to himself that she haunted him. He also had to admit now, as he fished in the pocket of his double-breasted shirt for a smoke, that his feelings for Cara Lee Henson went way beyond attraction . . . way beyond.

In keeping with the tradition originated in the 1830s by the Black abolitionists of the North, the people of the Valley busily prepared for the annual celebration of August First.

When the British Parliament decreed an end to slavery in the British West Indies on August 1, 1834, America's Northern Blacks embraced the day for the hope it held for those still in bondage in the United States.

Since Blacks found little reason to honor July Fourth, they embraced August First instead. It became a day of celebration, a day for antislavery rallies and speeches; picnics and parades; and in Black churches from Cincinnati to New Bedford, Massachusetts, midnight services, known then as night watches, were held in solemn commemoration.

Those celebrations in the thirties and forties were usually joint town affairs and were well-attended. Seven thousand people participated in one such gathering in New Bedford, Massachusetts, and in 1849, August First in Harrisburg, Ohio, drew an interracial crowd of two thousand, the largest coming together for any event in the town's history. Now, nearly fifty years later August First continued to be a date for gathering to honor the past and to look forward to the future. The Black colonies of Kansas took turns hosting the main activities, and this year the task fell to Henry Adams.

The town was a hubbub of activity. The flag of the United States flew beside flags of Liberia and Haiti, and the standard of the Nicodemus Town Company. Food was cooking, kinfolk were gathering, and desserts, baked to garner prizes in a contest, were set on sills and porches to cool.

Some folks had already ridden the thirty miles to Ellis to bring back relatives arriving by train, and there was not a room to let for miles around.

The people of the Valley first attended church on the morning of August First. The traditional sunrise service commenced at six A.M. with prayers, hymns, and thanksgiving. Everyone in attendance under the big tent knew of the violence spreading like a plague across the South—the lynchings, the burnings, and the disenfranchisement—but Reverend Whitfield spoke of the need to persevere. When he vowed "to let nobody turn us around," the responsive "amens" rang to the rafters. He reminded the celebrants of the Black colleges being built; of the vision of people like Henry Adams, Martin Delaney, and Mary Jane Garrett;

and of the Homestead Associations all over the territories fostering the continuing migration of thousands of Blacks to the newly opening West. Progress would come, he promised, and whether it came with the swiftness of a railroad train or the crawling pace of a snail, destiny would not be denied.

The traditional after-service breakfast followed the last hymn. There was not enough space beneath the tent for all the people, but the food never ran out, and on the acreage cleared just a few days ago by the Men's Club, there was more than ample room to spread a blanket or tarp to sit upon.

While the clean-up committee stayed behind, the majority of the people headed over to Henry Adams's Main Street to view the parade.

As always the Civil War veterans marched first with Mr. Deerfield, the oldest surviving combatant, leading the way. The people lining the street cheered loudly as the men representing state companies from all over the nation filed smartly by. But the crowd saved its most boisterous appreciation for the two largest contingents of veterans: the men of the six companies of the First Regiment Kansas Colored Volunteers, one of the first Black regiments organized during the war, and the soldiers who'd served in Major George L. Stearns's Tennessee regiment, the Twelfth Colored Troops.

After the veterans came the Free Masons and their nine-member band, followed by the Knights of Labor and college students carrying banners from Oberlin, Howard, and Prairie View.

For the first time, thanks to Cara's prodding, the children were allowed to participate in the parade, and more than a few parents had tears in their eyes as they watched their offspring march past.

Trailing the children were members of the political societies. Republicans and local and national Independents marched with representatives of the nearly extinct Greenbacks. The people cheered all. However, the three Black men marching under the banner of the Democrats were given a different kind of greeting. They were met with eerie silence. For the majority of the celebrants, the Democrats were synonymous with Black Codes, lynchings, and the Kluxers. The people wanted nothing to do with the call of East Coast Blacks for the race to align with the Democrats to keep the increasingly distant Republican party from taking the Black vote for granted. The Democrats were the reason the Valley residents had joined the Exodus in the first place.

When the three Black Democrats moved on, the air seemed to clear and the festive atmosphere returned. Soon everyone was cheering again at the passing of church societies, merchant associations, draymen unions, colonization organizations, and the robed and singing visiting choirs that had come for the annual August First choir competition.

The rest of the morning and afternoon were devoted to horseshoe tosses, greased hog races, and hay bale rolling. Cara presided over the children's fastest-pet contest, and awarded first prize to Frankie Cooper, who'd been training the family rooster for months.

Cara, her name on so many committees, had hardly a moment to catch her breath as the afternoon waned. She went from the baseball competition to helping Sybil with the choirs. From there she hurried over to the schoolhouse where the Graham County Debate Society would be holding one of the more serious undertakings of the celebration. The topics the society chose were always controversial. The year before a representative from Bishop Henry M. Turner's American Colonization Society had come to town beating the drum for emigration to Africa. The speech drew over two hundred people and press coverage from around the state. This year's debate—"Frederick Douglass— Whom Does He Really Represent?"—promised to be fiery. Many people had never forgiven Douglass for not supporting the Exodus.

By the time Cara finally made it back to Sophie's she was exhausted. She grabbed a plate of dinner from Dulcie in the kitchen and retreated to the quiet of her room to eat before going back out to listen to the choir competition.

When Cara left the singing around eleven that night, the voices were still going strong. It was not unusual for the dawn of August second to be greeted by still rising hymns. If they were singing when she awakened she'd come back. But right now, she wanted nothing but her bed.

She wasted no time lighting a lamp, stripped off her dress and tossed it into the basket with other clothes ready for the laundry. Heading to bed, she froze at the sight of a man standing in the shadows.

"Evenin', Cara Lee . . ."

Cara stared, absolutely stunned.

"Never knew you to be at a loss for words," he said, stepping out of the shadows.

Cara instinctively backed up. "How'd you get in here?"

"Your door was unlocked. How are you?"

"I'm fine," she whispered. She couldn't believe her eyes. She'd never expected to see him again. She'd written to him a few weeks after he'd left in May, received no answer, and had come to believe that Chase was done with her.

As he stood in front of her now she had to fight to bring the trembling in her limbs under control. The stubble on his face appeared to be weeks old, giving the already handsome features a hard, dangerous edge. "Let me light a lamp . . ."

Her hands shook as she lit the lamp and replaced the globe. In the light she could see he was not in uniform but dressed in a faded blue double-breasted shirt and snug-fitting leather trousers. With the stubble on his face and the gun strapped to his thigh, he looked like an outlaw. His power, his all-knowing, born-to-seduce gaze, made it difficult for her to breathe. "Does Sophie know you're here?"

"Yes, I talked to Sophie and Dulcie earlier. Asa, too. No one else needs to know I'm in town, Cara."

"Are you on army business?"

"Yes, I've been assigned to look into the mail coach robberies."

"Oh. We've been hearing a lot about those robberies. The outlaws seem meaner than most . . . almost like they're eager to kill. Be careful, Chase." She paused. "Have you eaten?"

"Dulcie fixed something for me earlier."

Chase wanted nothing more than to pull her into his arms but sensed her reticence. "What's wrong, schoolmarm?"

Hearing him call her that was almost her undoing. The memories that flooded back were searing. "Nothing's wrong, Sergeant."

"You're lying, Cara Lee."

He was right, of course. "I know I said no ties and no commitments, but I thought you'd at least answer my letter."

"What letter?"

"The letter I wrote after you left."

"Cara, I swear, I never received a letter from you. Where did you send it?"

"Fort Davis, Texas."

"That explains it. I was in Texas only a couple of weeks before Colonel Grierson sent me to the Indian Territories in Oklahoma. Your letter's probably still with my mail back there."

Cara's heart sang. He hadn't dismissed her like a piece of fluff in a cathouse.

"Better?" he asked, dazzling her with that smile.

"Very much so."

"Then can I get my kisses now?"

Cara went straight into his arms.

Chase swung her off the floor, kissing her passionately. For the first few moments they did nothing but enjoy the sensations of each other. Cara fed on his welcoming kiss and refamiliarized her hands with the hard strength in his arms and back, while he did the same with her back, waist, and hips. And the longer they stood, the deeper the kisses became. The caresses took on an urgency that infected them both, the silence broken only by the harsh sounds of their breathing. Chase blazed a hot trail of kisses down her throat and wasted little time undoing the laces on the bodice of her nightgown. Cara, trying not to lose a moment of his kisses, pulled the buttons off his shirt. She lost the sensual race, but when his mouth closed over her breast, she felt as if she'd won.

"Lord . . . Cara Lee . . ."

He nibbled her until she thought her nipples might moan. The feel of him, the feel of his mouth . . . She welcomed his hands when they pushed her gown off her shoulders. He planted kisses against her bare shoulders, her throat, her hairline. She wanted this. Lord have mercy on her soul.

He carried her to the bed. While he discarded his shirt and trousers, his eyes glittered. She pulled the gown over her head and off.

"How can you be more beautiful than I remembered?"

He lay down beside her and pulled her close. Cara kissed him and ran her hands over his chest. "How can you be more handsome than I remembered?"

He groaned and pulled her atop him. They came together with a swiftness that declared a burning mutual need. Cara met his strong strokes with a strength of her own, and moments later they were both soaring on wings of shuddering completion.

Cara lay on his chest, fulfilled for the moment. Only after she came back to herself did she realize where she was. She looked down into his eyes, and her smile garnered a smile from him in reply. "How many ways are there to do this?" she asked.

"Hundreds."

Cara snorted. "Hundreds? I don't believe that at all."

He laughed. "You willing to call my bluff?"

She felt him surge within her and smiled in surprise, using her inner muscles to squeeze him gently. "Hundreds. Really?"

He reached out and ran a finger over her breast, "Would you like to be taught, Miss Henson?"

They began again, more slowly this time, and Cara found she liked being positioned on top. His hands could touch all the places he desired while he sucked her breast until the nipples stood out like sable jewels. Gone was the earlier urgency, and they could indulge in a more leisurely passionate play of lovers. He thrust and she rode, sighing, then keening as he brought her once more to the heights.

Much later, as they lay entwined, Cara said, "Chase, we have to talk."
He rolled over onto his side and kissed her mouth. "About what?"
She let the kiss fill her, then withdrew. "Us."

"What about us?" he asked, sliding his finger over her lush mouth.

"I—we can't do this again. Promise me you won't seek me out if you come to town again."

Chase could see the serious set of her eyes and searched them for her intent. "Why not?"

Cara sighed unhappily. "Because I think I'm a lot more serious about . . . us than you are."

Chase, propped up on his elbow and looking down into her face, was at a loss for words. The ramifications were staggering. "I'm not husband cloth, darlin'. You already know that."

"Yes, I do, but you and your talents are going to make it hard for me to be with someone else should someone else ever come along."

"You told me the last time we were together you didn't think there would be another man. You seeing someone?"

"No, but who would've thought you'd come into my life?"

"I see your point. You're saying I've spoiled you for other men?"

She looked at the mustache curling around his smile and replied, "Don't gloat. But, yes, my arrogant pony soldier, you've spoiled me for other men. It's bad enough that I'll be comparing all kisses in the future against yours."

"Just kisses?"

"Arrogant, arrogant man!" She laughed.

"Talented," he corrected. Chase looked down at her and wondered how in the world he could give her up. He didn't want to. The thought of never kissing her lips again or hearing her keening when he touched her went against every male instinct he possessed, but this was Cara Lee, his Cara Lee, and if she wanted the moon, he'd try his damnedest to grant her wish.

"What are you doing?" Cara asked as he got up and pulled on his shirt.

"Leaving."

"Why?"

"Isn't that what you want?"

"No."

"I thought you said . . ."

"I said next time. This time you're supposed to be giving me lessons in those ninety-eight other ways to make love, remember?"

Her sly gaze made his manhood leap powerfully. "Why, you wicked little schoolmarm," Chase replied in a tone laced with amazement and delight.

And when he rejoined her on the bed, she showed him just how wicked a little schoolmarm could be.

When she awakened the next morning, he was gone. Slamming her fists into the mattress, she swore at herself for still being in love with him.

Cara didn't get her monthly flow in September. Her monthly had never come like clockwork, so she chalked it up to the chaos that accompanied the beginning of the school year. Quite a few families had migrated to the Valley over the summer, and Cara found her small classroom more crowded than ever. She dealt with the lack of space by having the younger students share seats whenever possible, but there weren't enough books and other materials to go around. Cara approached Virginia Sutton about the problems, but the Black Widow did not see it as one the school board should deal with. The board was paying her a salary, Virginia noted, and had also paid for books in January. There was no money for more. The children would just have to make do. The other three members of the board, hand-picked by the Black Widow, went along with the decision. Cara refused to let them have the last word.

Cara began to solicit businesses in the Valley for funding. Sophie was more than happy to contribute, as were other business owners. No one in town had the ability to donate all the money the struggling school needed, but they gave what they could. By the end of the second week of school, Cara had a portion of what she needed, but was still short by a lot. The only business she hadn't approached was the saloon owned by Miles Sutton.

When Cara walked into the Liberian Lady, she vowed not to let Miles's attitude deter her from her mission. She spotted him behind the bar, an easy task since he was the only person inside. He noticed her approach and smiled. "Well hello, love."

Cara snarled inwardly, but kept her expression pleasant. "Miles."

He came out from behind the bar. She looked around the place and noticed he'd made quite a few improvements. The floor was now a real floor, wood having replaced sawdust over dirt. There was wood trim on the walls; the staircase that led up to the quarters of his hostesses resembled something more akin to a grand mansion than a Kansas saloon. He'd even had a tin ceiling put in.

"How do you like my improvements?"

"Very nice," she lied.

"You know it's hard to make a profit on a place like this. People traveling West prefer to spend their money in places like Nicodemus or Wichita. Henry Adams is a town to ride through, not stop in."

"Well, you seem to be doing fairly well."

"With a mind as shrewd as mine, it isn't too hard."

"Well, then you can contribute to the school fund," Cara noted, seizing her opening.

"I heard you've been begging for the school. If I contribute, what's in it for me?"

Cara once again kept her face void of all emotion. "A well-equipped school."

"That all?"

"Yes."

Their eyes held a moment, then he spoke. "I still say we are fated to be together."

Cara chose to ignore that. "Will you contribute or not?"

"Will you at least have dinner with me?"

"No."

"You'd make a good businesswoman, love." He changed the subject. "When was the last time you heard from that soldier, Jefferson?"

"Miles, we are discussing the school."

"Yeah, well, he better be glad he left town. I didn't like the way he tried to make me look bad that night you and I were talking outside my mother's house."

Cara didn't bother reminding him who'd started that confrontation. Miles seemed never to take responsibility for his actions. "Will you be contributing or not?"

He looked her up and down like a buyer. "Yeah, how much do you need?"

"As much as you can afford."

"All right, wait here."

He went up the new staircase and returned a few moments later. He handed her a small canvas bag. Cara looked at him in surprise when she took the bag and felt its weight.

"Open it," he said, looking at her with those mysterious gray eyes of his.

She did and her surprise heightened. "There must be two hundred dollars in here."

"Just about. Is that enough?"

Cara stared at him. "Why, yes."

"Good."

"Thank you," she told him, amazement filling her voice.

"My pleasure. Just remember what I said. Fated."

By the beginning of October the weather had already changed and the people of the Valley began to prepare for winter. Cara had to light the stove in the mornings now, and she and the children had spent one morning a week since school began in September gathering and storing brown stalks of corn and sunflowers to use as fuel for the old black stove.

Cara's sickness began the first week of October. The body-sweating, gut-wrenching nausea gripped her as soon as she left her bed. That first morning, as she raced to the chamber pot, she assumed it had been caused by something she'd eaten the night before. Gasping, she'd crawled back to bed and lain there until the world righted itself again. When the malaise continued each morning for the next week, and a few times in the middle of school's opening lessons, she groaned not only in discomfort but with dread. As horrifying as the knowledge was, she had to admit the truth to herself: She'd gotten herself pregnant with Chase Jefferson's child.

It took all her pride and strength to go and see Delbert Johnson, the doctor over in Nicodemus. He confirmed her suspicions. She also received his pledge of silence for as long as she needed it.

Secrecy didn't matter, however. The townspeople suspected she was pregnant. It began with the frosty stares directed at her by two women on their way out of the mercantile. The two, friends of the Black Widow, had never been overly friendly in the past, but because their children were in Cara's class they had been Christian enough to speak. Not on this occasion.

Shrugging off the snub, Cara went on into the mercantile, puzzled by their attitude. Her purchases made, she walked back in the direction of Sophie's. Approaching her on the wooden walk were two other women, also mothers of students. They were talking quietly as they moved in Cara's direction, but stopped abruptly when they spotted her. Their steps halted, and Cara felt herself burned by their accusing stares. One of the women, the mother of Willie Franklin, looked momentarily embarrassed and opened her mouth as if she intended to speak, but her companion stayed her with a hand on her arm, and Willie's mother simply looked away. Cara, offended because she could not understand the hostility, continued to move forward. To her amazement the women crossed to the other side of the street.

Later, in her room, Cara answered a knock on her door. It was Sophie, and it was easy to see by the grimness on her aging but still beautiful face that she had something pretty serious on her mind. "What's wrong?" Cara asked, looking up from the laundry she was folding.

Sophie asked plainly, "Are you carrying Chase's child?"

Cara's whole body stiffened.

"Are you?" Sophie asked again.

Silence.

"Cara?"

Cara's reply was just as quiet. "Yes, I am. And I don't want him to be told."

"Suppose he wants to know? Chase would never run from a responsibility like this. He wouldn't want you fending for yourself when you are carrying his child."

"I don't want him told, and I mean it, Sophie. This is my problem. Chase has made it very clear how he feels about marriage, and I don't want him forced into doing something he doesn't want to do."

Cara thought back to the afternoon's incidents with the women. "Does the whole town know?"

"Just about. Your children have been telling their parents about you being sick in the mornings."

"Then I suppose it's pretty silly to ask whether they're going to make me resign. It's only a matter of when."

"The Black Widow has called a special town council meeting tomorrow night. The elders want you to attend."

"Then that's that," Cara summed up bitterly. "Virginia will finally get her way."

"Not without a fight from me she won't. A lot of people in this town care for you a great deal."

"I appreciate that, Sophie, but I don't want others dragged into this."

"Well, you know you and the baby can stay here as long as you want. I sort of like the idea of playing grandmere."

Cara smiled sadly. "I can't. A baby shouldn't have to pay for her mother's sins. People can be cruel."

"That's true, but where will you go?"

"Haven't decided yet."

"Don't you believe for one minute that the folks will let you leave without some type of fight. Dulcie was over in Nicodemus this morning, and she said there're a lot of people over there talking about coming to the meeting tomorrow to speak for you. A few here may hold the baby against you, but not everyone is a Virginia Sutton."

Sophie's support and understanding soothed Cara, but she placed little faith in her friend's optimism. Schoolteachers had to be above reproach. Yes, it hurt thinking about leaving her students, but she expected the meeting tomorrow night to be a mere formality. She'd be dismissed. "Lord, what a mess," she whispered, fighting the sting of tears.

Sophie pulled Cara into her arms, and Cara felt strength flow from the hug. Sophie drew back and in a coaxing voice entreated again, "Please, let me wire Texas. Chase will—"

"No, Sophie," Cara said, pulling away. "The first thing he's going to want to do is give me and the baby his name. Not because he loves me, but because he's going to feel obligated. And I won't do that to him."

"But what about you? How are you going to provide for a baby?"

"Sophie, I've been providing for myself for many years. I'll do whatever it takes to feed me and the baby. I'll scrub floors, take in laundry, anything. I'll lie, pass myself off as a widow, if it has to come to that. But this isn't Chase's responsibility. It is mine and mine alone."

"Suppose he comes back?"

"If he does, it won't matter. I won't be here."

"Oh, Cara Lee, let the people who love you help."

"Then help me by not telling Chase. And stop worrying. I'm from strong Georgia stock. My baby will be strong, too. We'll both do fine."

The news of Cara's pregnancy spread like prairie fire. The town council meeting the next night was packed. There were arguments on both sides. Those against, egged on by Virginia's forces, shouted the louder; those in support of Cara sought to instill calm. Her supporters —Sophie, Asa, and the Three Spinsters, primarily—addressed the elders with logic. Where were they going to get another teacher as dedicated and as knowledgeable as Miss Henson? Her wages were hardly substantial enough to draw anyone of equal quality as a replacement. And the children were thriving under her fine tutelage and care.

"But we cannot condone someone with no morals teaching our children," one of the detractors shouted self-righteously. A buzz went up in the crowd. "She has morals, the morals of a cat!" another person pointed out.

The argument grew so fierce at that point, Cara actually expected a fight to break out. Sheriff Polk, always on hand to keep the peace at meetings such as this one, banged his gavel, but it couldn't be heard over the shouting and accusations.

They finally took the vote.

It turned out as Cara predicted. She was stripped of all duties until further notice with formal dismissal to follow.

"Sophie, I'm going to make one last trip over to the school. I think those two books I've been looking for are there."

Sophie glanced up from the newspaper on her desk in answer. Cara was peeking around the door. "Have you packed everything else?"

"Just about. Asa'll take my crates over to Ellis and put them on the train sometime tomorrow. Will you please stop looking so glum?" Cara stepped into the office. "I know you don't think this is a good idea, but I'm going to be fine. And I will write when I get to California. I promise."

"It says here in the paper that the Tenth was in Oklahoma a few months ago. You know anything about this David Payne fellow?"

Cara shook her head.

"Well, according to this, he and his followers, called Boomers, are challenging the government's right to keep white settlers out of Indian Territory. Seems Payne and the Boomers keep trespassing and the Tenth and the Ninth keep escorting them out."

Cara knew Sophie was still trying to make her think about Chase, and it was working. "Has anybody been hurt?"

"Nope. At least not yet. It says Payne's mad at the politicians, not the troops. There's even mention of the soldiers sharing their army rations with Payne's folks. I think that's pretty interesting." She put the paper down.

"Yes, it is."

"Cara—"

"Sophie, don't please." Cara knew exactly what she'd been about to say. They'd been going round and round on this subject since the night of the elders decision two weeks before. "I can make it alone. Please, tell me you understand?"

Sophie sighed. "I do, Cara." Then she added, "Make sure you put on something warm before heading over to the school."

"I will."

Cara's cloak felt good against the chill of the late October night. The wind whipped across her bare cheeks and fingertips, encouraging her to quicken her steps. Inside the schoolhouse she found the missing books with no trouble. Holding them against her chest, she took one last look around. She'd miss this place terribly. She forced herself to go quickly then, lest she break down and cry.

She closed the door and put on the lock. The Reverend Whitfield would resume teaching until a replacement could be found, and Cara reminded herself that she had to leave the keys with Sophie in the morning before departing for Ellis. Cara had no idea what lay ahead in California, but the newspapers down at the mercantile attested to many established Black communities there. She was certain she could carve out a niche for herself and the baby.

A horse and rider moved suddenly out of the shadows, startling her.

Seeing it was only Miles Sutton, she relaxed, but his tone of voice soon roused her anger. "Well, if it isn't the town whore," he sneered.

The animal beneath him danced nervously, tossing its head back and forth, making Miles work to keep it under control. "So, Cara, I hear you're going to wrap the bastard in Union blue after you whelp."

Cara tried to move on, but he guided the stallion up on the walk to block her path. "Didn't I tell you we were fated? And what do you do? You spread your legs for that soldier. You owe me an explanation."

"I owe you nothing, Miles. Now let me pass."

"No."

Cara saw him weaving slightly in the saddle. In the dark she couldn't be certain, but she was willing to bet every book she owned that he was stinking drunk. She took a hasty evaluation of the surroundings, looking for help, but saw no one.

He leaned down into her face, and for a moment she thought he might fall, so precarious was his seat. "I'm celebrating a very profitable business opportunity. Would you like to help me celebrate back at the Lady?"

"No."

"Well, if you can spread your legs for him, you damn well can spread them for me. Now come on!"

His arm clamped onto her waist and, though she fought him, he raised her up to the saddle. She swung her fists, hitting him about the face and the chest desperately attempting to free herself. He was too strong and succeeded in seating her in front of him. Cara continued to fight him. The stallion snorted and reared. When it reared again, she sensed she was about to fall. She clutched at Sutton's shirt but he struck out, and she plummeted to the ground. Her back hit the edge of the walk as the hoof of the terrified horse struck her head. That was the last thing she remembered.

In the hallway outside Colonel Benjamin Grierson's office, Chase pounded his Stetson against the side of his blue-uniformed leg. Three days ago, he'd received the colonel's summons to return to Fort Davis. Chase and a small patrol had been pursuing renegades, and it had been a long hard ride back across the Chihuahuan Desert.

Tiny dervishes of dust took flight under the hat's pounding. He was tired, dirty. He wiped sweat from his face, then retied the damp kerchief around his neck.

The colonel's door opened, and an aide stepped out. "Colonel Grierson will see you now, Sergeant."

Chase entered the office and saluted. "You wanted to see me, sir?"

"Yes, Chase. Have a seat."

Chase availed himself of one of the wooden chairs opposite the desk.

"You catch those renegades?"

"No. We chased them back across the Grande," Chase replied. The renegades would be back soon, no doubt, terrorizing the border towns strung along the banks of the Rio Grande until the army once again chased them back into Mexico. It had become a very frustrating game, in some way as frustrating as the unsuccessful search for the bandits in Kansas the past summer. But Chase had the distinct impression he hadn't been called back to report on the campaign against the bandits. "Has something happened, Colonel?"

"I'm not certain, but we've been receiving telegraph messages for you."

He handed Chase a handful of messages. Puzzled, Chase opened one on top and read: CARA GOING CALIFORNIA. PREGNANT. SOPHIE. Chase's eyes widened.

Before he could digest the news, Grierson handed him another. "This came yesterday."

Chase opened and read the second. CARA HURT. LOST BABY. PLEASE COME. SOPHIE.

Chase's heart stopped. He was numb. There was no other way to describe it. Cara had been pregnant! The enormity of that news alone rendered him speechless. And now to find she'd lost the child, his child. There couldn't be a doubt that the baby had been his. Grief welled in him and he slowly folded the telegrams and placed them in the pocket of his shirt. "Permission to return to Kansas, sir."

"Somebody run down those coach robberies?"

"No, sir, this is personal business. I'm going to marry a woman I met there last spring."

"Well, congratulations are in order," Grierson exclaimed enthusiastically.

"I suppose so, sir."

Their gazes held. Chase had known Ben Grierson a long time. Together they had ridden to hell and back. "Let me be frank, Ben. She was pregnant. She's lost the baby."

"I see," the colonel replied softly. "You have my sympathies, Chase."

"I appreciate that. I just hope she'll appreciate what I'm going to do."

Chase didn't have to debate the issue with himself. Marrying Cara was the honorable thing to do. She was a vibrant and beautiful woman. He refused to let her bear the slurs alone. Had he kept his hands off her, none of this would have happened.

"Chase, are you sure about this marriage? I remember hearing you say a dozen or more times that you weren't the marrying kind."

"She's different, Ben." The image of Cara's laughing face shimmered in Chase's memory, and for a moment he saw nothing else. "So much fire," he added wistfully. "I have to marry her. Only honorable thing to do. And I do care for her, more than I ever have for a woman."

"She'll be happy to see you, I'm sure."

"Don't bet on it. She'll probably fight me all the way to the church."

The colonel's raised eyebrows did not escape Chase's attention. "I told you, she's different."

"Well, take all the time you need. You have enough leave to give everyone in a regiment a long vacation."

Chase stood and saluted, and Grierson returned the salute. Chase headed for the door.

"Oh, and Chase . . ."

His hand on the knob, Chase stopped and turned back. "Yes?"

"Good luck. If there's anything Mrs. Grierson and I can do, please let me know."

"I will, Ben."

Chapter 10

Chase had never been a praying man, but on the long train ride North, he sent more than few a prayers heavenward. Sitting in the cattle car because of the fickle Jim Crow laws, Chase refused to listen to the inner voice that whispered Cara might be dead . . . like the child.

The babe would have been the first in his line since slavery to be born free—free to be educated, free to carry a father's name, free to exercise the right to flourish or fail just like every other American.

He assumed Cara only recently had discovered her pregnancy, and the letter telling him about it was still winding its way to Texas. He would marry her. No question about that. The twin slurs of "slave" and "bastard" would never again be associated with children of the Jefferson lineage. Dwelling on the child's death moved him to a pain-filled numbness. Nothing in his experience prepared him for the emotional upheaval unleashed by Sophie's news. He, who'd ridden into bandit nests, faced death many times over on many campaigns, felt overwhelmed by fear at the prospect of Cara's dying. He hadn't a qualm about breaking his pledge to leave her alone if ever he returned to Kansas. That seemed like foolishness now—maybe madness. He had to help her regain her health; he had to give her his name.

After leaving the train at Ellis, Chase rode Carolina the last thirty miles to Henry Adams under the rising sun. In the distance, light painted the prairie skyline with fiery pinks and reds. He was too bone-tired to appreciate nature's canvas. He could barely sit Carolina. However, his strength seemed to return as soon as he reached the outskirts of town, bringing with it a heartfelt certainty that Cara still lived. He had no idea why he felt so confident, but he did; if she were already dead, he'd know.

Asa answered Chase's summons to the door. They embraced each other, then hurried through to Sophie's office where she was seated behind her desk sipping coffee. She came hastily to him, and the hug they shared was tight with emotion and pain.

"Chase, oh, thank heaven you're here. I'm so glad, so glad," she whispered with tears in her eyes.

"I left Texas as soon as I got word." Chase saw that she looked more tired—old, really, worn-out—than he'd ever seen her. "How is Cara?"

"She didn't have a good night, but Doc Johnson is with her now. You can see her when he's done."

Chase remembered meeting Johnson the night of the Black Widow's birthday. "How'd she lose the baby?"

"Nobody's real sure, but Sheriff Polk says he heard her screaming and when he got to her she was lying"—Sophie's voice cracked—"on the walk, out cold. Miles Sutton was standing over her."

Chase went deathly still. "What was he doing there?"

"He was drunk," Asa said. "He went in to some kind of song and dance about how he'd wanted Miss Cara to help him celebrate a business deal with him, and she fell off his horse."

"She fell? Cara's been around horses all her life. I don't believe that. What's Cara say?"

Sophie shook her head. "Nothing. So far she's still too ill."

"Well, I'm not. He in town?"

"Yes, he is, and the sheriff is handling it," Sophie cautioned. "Cara's our main concern right now. We don't care what you do to him once she's well, but we don't have time to keep your head out of a noose, Chase."

Chase knew she was right. Sheriff Polk had impressed him as a fair man. Sutton wouldn't be allowed to leave town until the investigation was complete. But the thought of Sutton having a part in Cara losing the child made him want to kill the man with his bare hands.

"Chase . . ." Sophie called softly.

Chase came out from behind the veil of rage.

"How long can you stay?" she asked.

"Until she's well enough for me to leave her."

"Well, I'll put you back in the room next door, is that all right?"

He nodded, then fished the telegrams out of his pocket and handed her the one that mentioned California. "Tell me about this."

Sophie read it and looked up at him. "Chase, you have to understand the hell she went through when the people found out she was in a family way."

"Sophie. What does this telegram mean?" he said impatiently.

Sophie and Asa shared a speaking look, then Sophie added, "She was planning to leave for California the morning after the accident."

"Why?"

"She was going to live there," Asa added.

Chase looked to Sophie and then to Asa before asking in a raised voice, "Was she planning on telling me about the baby?"

"Chase, listen, she was—"

"Was she going to tell me about the baby?"

"No," Sophie replied quietly.

He slammed his fist down on the desk, scattering the contents. "That was my child, too! My child! Did she actually believe she'd get away with it?"

"Chase, I don't believe she was thinking—"

"Damn right!" Chase's gut churned with betrayal and pain. Damn her! "Do you think I should have been told?"

"Yes. That's why I sent the first telegram. But Chase, you have to—"

"I rode in a damn cattle car all the way from Texas, worrying the whole way, and you say she wasn't going to tell me about my own child?"

"She didn't want your pity."

"I came back here to marry her! Give her my name!"

"I know, Chase."

"No, you don't Sophie," he whispered icily. He wanted to break something. Rage seemed to be exploding from every pore in his body. He wanted to confront Cara. What would have been her answer to the child's natural curiosity about its missing parent? Had she planned to lie, to say the father was dead? Chase could think of no reason why she would decide to keep quiet, move . . . and, no, they'd never discussed the possibility of a child, but dammit, she should have told him.

The doctor came in then. "Delbert," Sophie asked, "how's she doing?"

"As well as can be expected, I guess." He skewered Chase with an angry, scornful stare. "What are you doing here?"

Chase's jaw tightened at the man's tone. "Just stick to doctoring. How is she?"

Delbert looked into the frigid eyes and said, "If her fever doesn't come down, we may lose her."

"I want to see her."

"She won't know you're there."

"I don't care." Chase paused only a second, then bolted out of the office and up to Cara's room. The familiarity of it swept him up. He walked to where she lay. Stunned and speechless, he knelt beside the bed. He searched the gaunt, terribly still figure smothered beneath piles of quilts for some resemblance to the woman he'd known. The glowing skin and fiery nature were gone. The sickness held her. Chase did not have to be a doctor to know she was gravely ill. He ran his fingers over her delicate brow, saw the ugly gash above her eye, felt the feverish skin. He called her name softly.

Cara heard her name . . . recognized the voice . . . oh, her grandfather had every right to be angry at her for eating all those green plums, and now she was sick, and . . .

"Cara Lee?"

"Papa, it hurts so much . . ."

"I know, darlin', I'm here."

"Are you mad at me?"

"Nobody can stay mad at you for long. Just rest now." He picked up the cloth in the basin beside the bed.

Cara relaxed as something magically cool stroked away the heat on her forehead. "I didn't mean to be a bad girl."

"I know, sweetheart. I know."

Emotions clogged Chase's throat as he gently mopped Cara's fevered brow and cheeks. She was burning up with fever. If it didn't break soon, she would surely die. Setting aside the cloth as she drifted back into a troubled sleep, he placed a fleeting kiss upon the pale brow and tiptoed out of the room.

Downstairs, a somber Chase consulted with the doctor, and the argument that followed had both men shouting at the tops of their lungs. The doctor wanted to hear nothing about an Indian remedy to lower the fever. He didn't care if Chase had seen it used successfully. He didn't care if Chase and his men had administered the cure hundreds of times. He refused to risk killing her with some redskin concoction. The young doctor then challenged Chase's right even to be involved in her care, and Asa had to step between the two to keep Chase from pounding a fist in the physician's face.

All of Asa and Sophie's efforts to calm them down were futile. Chase shouted and the doctor threatened Chase with the law. It was Chase who'd finally had enough. He pushed everyone aside and angrily proceeded back up the stairs. He had no intention of letting the doctor's ignorance and prejudice kill Cara.

When he opened her door and stepped into the silent room, some of his anger drained away. He walked over and, careful not to jostle her unnecessarily, lifted her slight weight, covering and all, into his strong arms. He kissed her forehead tenderly and started walking. He didn't stop to reply to the outraged questions of Sophie and the others. Down the stairs he went, quilts trailing, Sophie, Asa, and the doctor running behind him.

The cold November air bit his cheeks, but he paid it no mind. His concern centered on getting Cara to the Sutton Hotel where he could personally see to her; he knew he could have stayed at Sophie's, but his anger was ruling now.

Chase gave polite nods to the curious townspeople who turned and stared at the small, noisy procession, but he didn't stop. Only when he happened upon Sybil Whitfield, the reverend's wife, did he halt.

"Mrs. Whitfield."

"Sergeant Jefferson."

"I'm on my way to the hotel. Will you and your husband visit me at your earliest convenience?"

He didn't wait for an answer.

People began to gather, and once again events surrounding the ex-schoolteacher put the town in an uproar.

Inside the hotel, Chase barked at the attendant behind the desk to get Virginia. He obeyed, quickly. When Virginia stepped out, Chase didn't wait for her to finish her greeting. "I want your biggest suite, and I want it now."

She took one look at his face and the bundle in his arms, and obeyed without a word.

Inside the suite, Chase placed his light burden down on the bed and made sure she was covered adequately. He then removed from his belt the small rawhide bag he always wore and shook out the pieces of willow bark inside. The bark was one of the many plant medicinals the Indians used. Chase and his men relied heavily on those few roots and herbs the Indians had taught them to find and prepare, especially since the Tenth was not high on the army's list of units receiving medical shipments. Besides, the remedies worked. Had it not been for "redskin concoctions," a lot more of his men would be dead today from wounds, infections, and the parasites that lived in fouled lakes and streams. With a drink made from this bark, Cara would have a fighting chance.

Downstairs, Chase found Asa, Sophie, the irate Dr. Johnson, and the Whitfields talking quietly with Virginia Sutton. He dismissed the doctor, told Virginia to wait, and sent the others up to the suite with Cara. He made Virginia take him to the kitchen. Once there he gave her and her staff specific instructions as to how the tender inner bark should be steeped. He also asked that a thin vegetable broth be kept hot for Cara day and night. He slapped down five gold double eagles, one hundred dollars, on the counter to ensure his wishes would be followed, and walked out.

Chase marched into the suite and declared his intent. "I want to marry her. Now."

"You can't," Sophie said. "Wait until she's well. She can't even speak her vows."

"Now, Sophie. The reverend's wife can say her vows."

Silence fell, broken at last by Sybil. "Sergeant, you can't be serious. I don't even know if what you're proposing is legal."

"I don't care. Either marry us, or what little bit of reputation she has left won't be worth a damn, because I'm going to be staying in this suite with her until she either recovers or dies."

The ceremony did not take long. Sybil did speak Cara's vows, and, when the Reverend closed the Bible and pronounced the deed done, Chase walked them all to the door. Sybil, never one to bite her tongue, had something to say before he ushered them out. "You're very angry now, Sergeant. I hope you won't use this marriage to punish our Cara. She has just lost a child."

"So have I, Mrs. Whitfield. So I really don't need your advice."

Sophie gasped. "Chase!"

Chase turned to Asa. "Take Sophie home, Asa."

For three days Chase spoon-fed Cara the bark tea and thin broth. He'd moved her from the bed to a pallet he'd had the hotel staff place on the floor in front of the room's big fireplace. Having her near the fire made the task of sponging her down safer. In her already weakened state the last thing she needed was to get chilled, maybe contract pneumonia, but he had to sponge her down to lower the fever. On the first night, she put up a feeble, delirium-fed attempt to fight him off when he began to remove her sweat-drenched gown. Moans accented her struggles, but he calmed her by speaking softly and reassuringly, all the while stroking her forehead with a cool cloth. He couldn't be certain she understood, but moments later she drifted back to sleep.

He saw to her every need and wouldn't let another soul touch her. He ignored Sophie's offers to sit with Cara while he got some rest; after the second day she grew tired of arguing and let the matter drop.

At night, when darkness filled the rooms, he watched his wife sleep and played the flute. The mournful, emotion-laced notes of the *siyotanka* said the words he could not. The melancholy beauty of the music floated pure in the after-midnight silence of the hotel, touching all who heard it with its despair, pain, and grief. And each dawn, when light began to fill the room, he put away the flute and gave thanks that Cara had been granted another day.

On the night of the fourth day, the sounds of Cara stirring roused him from half sleep. Every night she'd had nightmares about her grandfather's death, and every night Chase had held her in his arms until the demons passed. Tonight he sensed something different about her fretfulness. Shaking himself to fuller awareness, he took the flute from his lap and made his way over to where she lay before the fire.

Cara decided she must be dreaming. Why else would Chase Jefferson be kneeling beside her? That would also account for the *siyotanka* music she'd heard. She'd dreamed of both many times. Could one dream having a throat as parched as hers felt? As she forced her cottony mind to make sense of it all, she struggled to raise herself to a sitting position, winced with the pain, and heard him say, "Easy now." He sounded so real! "Welcome back to the land of the living," he added.

Cara focused on his eyes, sparkling at her in the dark, and knew this was no dream. She also noted for the first time the absolute unfamiliarity of the room. "Where am I? Oh, water first, please . . ."

He obliged, helping her sit up to sip from the cup he held. "We're at the Sutton Hotel."

After she'd drunk all she could, he took the cup from her lips and eased her back down. She felt as weak as a newborn. "Why are we here?"

"So I can take care of you."

For Cara, it all came back in a rush: Miles, the horse . . . her baby. "I lost the baby, didn't I?"

"Yes."

Even in the faint light he could see the tears start rolling down her cheeks. She turned to the fire. "Why are you here?"

"To make an honest woman of you."

"No, thank you. You aren't husband cloth, remember?"

"Too late. It's already done."

His words made the hair on the back of her neck rise. She swung her head in his direction.

"The Reverend Whitfield married us a few days ago."

"What?" The outburst brought pain. He moved to her aid, but her raised hand stopped him. When the crisis passed, Cara tried again, more calmly, to question him. "Now, what did you say?"

"Maybe we should put this off until you're stronger."

"Chase, tell me."

He told her.

"I don't believe this," she stated flatly. "Sophie put you up to this, I'll bet. Well, we'll just get it annulled. It can't be legal anyway."

"It was my idea."

Cara looked at him as if he'd grown a new head. "Why? You don't want to be married to me, and I don't want to be married to you."

Chase's jaw tightened. "I'm not exactly thrilled about all this, either."

As much as she loved him, she refused to be in a loveless marriage. He'd only hate her in the end. "Then ride out. I can take care of myself."

"You'd like that, wouldn't you?"

"Yes, I would. It would save us both a lot of grief."

Despite the rising tension in the room, a part of Chase could not help but smile. This woman had no intention of dying, not now. It made him happy on another level, too, because when she got strong enough, he planned on strangling her for her treachery.

Chase's prediction about her recovery proved correct. Two days later, Cara was sitting up in bed receiving visitors. She had little or nothing to say to her husband, and her attitude seemed to suit him fine.

Cara began to have second thoughts, however, after listening to Sophie's account of why Cara had awakened here in the hotel instead of in her room back at the boardinghouse. When he came in later that day with a tray of lunch, she viewed him in a different light. He'd saved her life. "Did you really carry me through the center of town?"

He set the tray on her quilt-covered lap, then straightened. He viewed her speculatively, as if trying to discern her true motives, never once dropping the mask he'd taken to wearing since her recovery. "Yes. Why?"

She dropped her head, pretending to fuss with her food. "No reason except that Sophie told me how you took care of me. I'm just trying to say thanks." She looked up. "Thank you, Chase, very much."

"You're welcome. Eat."

He turned and strode out.

After a week of confinement, Cara grew weary of being cooped up. Her strength, although returning, did so slowly, but she wanted very much to go outside and feel the wind on her face, even if it was a cold, November wind.

She begged Chase to take her out.

"No," he replied brusquely. "You can't even make it to the water closet and back without breaking out in a sweat. No."

For the next three days, he kept saying "no." By the fourth day she'd had it.

When he came to bring her afternoon meal, she was sitting on the edge of the bed doing her best to get dressed. She'd already managed to put on a shirtwaist and skirt, and was now trying to roll on her long black cotton stockings. The efforts had cost her, but she ignored the weakness, her labored breathing, and the fine sheen of sweat glistening on her brow.

"What the hell are you doing?" Chase asked coldly.

"I'm going outside!"

Her efforts to don the hose caused her to pant. She felt faint and, angry and frustrated, threw the offending stockings aside. She'd go without them, just as she'd forgone her undergarments.

Ignoring his critical gaze, Cara pulled on her shoes and gingerly pushed herself upright. Her steadying hand against the wooden bedpost was all that kept her from falling flat on her face. Waves of dizziness passed over her. She shut her eyes until she regained her equilibrium and felt able to move.

"You are a little idiot, do you know that?"

"Either help me or leave," she shot back.

Shakily, she made her way from the bed. Her legs felt like pudding beneath her. The door to freedom lay only a short few feet away, but it might as well have been in Texas.

Chase caught her just before she fell. When he lifted her up into his arms, she turned her head into his shoulder to hide her tears.

He placed her gently atop the bed, then began to undo the buttons of her shirt.

"What are you doing?"

"In case you haven't noticed, you're soaking wet," he pointed out. "I'm not going to let you make yourself sick again."

She made no further protests as he methodically stripped off her blouse and skirt.

Chase could feel his loins slowly hardening at the sight of her lush nakedness. She hadn't had a stitch on beneath the skirt and blouse; that fact alone should have garnered her a lecture—it was November outside—though at the moment, lecturing her was the farthest thing from his mind. During the long days he'd nursed her he hadn't looked on her with lust even once. Saving her life had been his only goal. Now, however, all he could see were the ripe globes of her breasts, the curve of her hips that invited his touch, and the blackberry forest at the top of her thighs. "Get under the quilt. I'll get you a dry gown."

It took him a moment to find one in the dresser beside the bed.

Cara caught the old gown he tossed her way, looked at it, and said, "Chase, this gown—"

"Put it on."

Irritated, she complied.

Right away Chase knew he'd made a mistake. It was flannel, yes. It had long sleeves, yes. But it was way too small and didn't have a single button left. The worn fabric of the bodice fit so snugly, her breasts looked ready to spill out, and the tight-fitting halves barely covered the ring of her nipples. He clamped down on his jaw and closed his eyes.

To Cara's surprise, he mumbled something about returning later, then left the room.

With a wealth of pillows at her back, Cara sat propped up in bed looking through the window at the falling rain. The dreary late November day matched her mood. It was almost three weeks, since she had awakened with Chase bending over her, and all efforts to convince him, Sophie, and Sybil to let her walk around fell on deaf ears. She needed rest, they kept repeating. She hated being ill, and for most of her life had avoided it. Her only other serious malady had occurred during her first winter at Oberlin when she got the influenza.

Turning away from the window, she sank back into the softness of the pillows. She resented waking up and discovering she was married. That was a decision a woman was supposed to make for herself. She understood Chase had given Sophie and the others little choice that night. But it was ridiculous for him to argue that she would have been compromised by his staying with her in the suite. She was already compromised, for heaven's sake. Virginia Sutton would not be reoffering the schoolteacher position just because Cara's name was now Mrs. Chase Jefferson. Cara saw leaving town as the only solution to her problem. She was certain that when Chase came to his senses, he would see how absurd it was for them to be married. At that point they could dissolve this questionable union and go their separate ways. Yes, she still loved him, but he did not love her.

Later, she was mildly surprised to see Chase bringing in her evening meal. She hadn't seen him in over a week. It seemed that bringing her back to life had been his only goal. Now her care had been turned over to Sophie and Mrs. Whitfield.

"When you're finished, we need to talk." He set the tray atop her lap and went out to the sitting room to wait.

While he waited he brooded over the events of the last two weeks. Sophie accused him of having lost his mind taking Cara out into the November wind that day of his return, and she was right. His rash actions could easily have made Cara worse. He still couldn't explain it, but knew that given the same set of circumstances, he'd do the exact same thing again.

Sophie called the reaction love; Chase didn't know what to call it. On one hand, he was filled with rage about Cara's plans to keep the baby a secret; on the other hand, he knew he'd battle the devil himself for that woman in there. He'd nearly bitten Sophie's head off when she suggested he simply let Cara go. When he tried to explain his obligation to the memory of the child, Sophie had termed his intentions honorable and offered him nothing but praise for accepting his responsibility, but she cautioned him about trying to build a relationship based on anger, revenge, and honor. She further advised him to look deeper within himself for the other reasons he'd been so adamant about marrying a woman he purportedly didn't love.

"You wanted to talk?" Cara's emotionless voice broke the silence, and he turned from the fire to see her standing just out of the circle of light. She had on an ankle-length bed coat over her nightgown, but he could barely see the coat for the quilt she'd wrapped around herself to ward off the night's draft. He hadn't meant for her to come out here; they could have easily talked in her bedroom. "You shouldn't be out of bed," he chided softly.

Before she could reply, he walked over and effortlessly picked her up.

"I wish people would stop treating me like an invalid."

He didn't answer.

They crossed the room, and she expected him to place her on the settee near the blazing fire. He did, only he sat down first, keeping her atop his lap. "Hold still," he warned when she began to fuss. He adjusted the quilt so she'd stay warm.

Cara could have done without this intimate seating arrangement. She didn't put it past him to have planned this just to put her off-balance. "Is this intended to distract me?"

"Maybe," he acknowledged, but his eyes held no teasing and his mouth was grim.

"You wanted to talk?"

"I do, and what I want to say is this: I married you to give you my name. That's all. I don't want a wife. I'm a soldier, not a farmer. I haven't had roots since I was twelve, and pardon my frankness, I don't plan on growing any now."

His "frankness" was a slap in her face. She knew he'd married her only out of obligation, but to hear him air his displeasure so emotionlessly had not been something she'd anticipated. She felt at once angry and humiliated. "So what are you proposing?"

"I'm working on the arrangements now. I plan on rejoining my unit after the first of the year, but I'll see to your welfare before I leave."

He wouldn't be staying. She'd known it all along, so why did she feel hurt hearing him confirm it? "Will you be returning?" She could be just as distant.

"Probably."

And he looked at her in such a way that she didn't dare ask when. She debated whether to tell him of her own plans and decided she would. "I'm still planning on going to California."

"No, you're not," came the quiet contradiction. "You can either move to Fort Davis, Texas, with me, or you can stay here. Those are your options."

"But—"

"No buts."

"Then I'll get this farcical marriage annulled!"

"Not while I'm alive."

Frustrated, Cara wondered what it would take to get through to him. "Then why do this?"

"Pure selfishness."

Cara frowned in bewilderment.

"Pure selfishness," he restated.

"What's to keep me here once you go running back to play soldier?"

His gaze hardened. "The fact that I'm the best damn tracker you'll ever meet. I'll find you no matter where, no matter what."

"But why? You don't want me!"

"Ah, but I do. That's where the selfish part comes in. I do want you, Mrs. Jefferson, and I'm going to keep you."

His cold voice and eyes brought on an uncontrollable shiver, and now she thought she understood. "Is this your way of punishing me?"

"Maybe."

"You're serious, aren't you?"

"Deadly."

"You'd condemn yourself to a loveless marriage?" she asked quietly. He didn't answer.

Instead, he redirected the conversation. "So decide. Are you living here or at Fort Davis?"

"You can't possibly want an answer now. At least let me think about it before—"

"Now. Here or Davis?"

Cara realized she truly did not know this man. "Here," she stated in dignified surrender. "I'll stay here." As her husband, he had every right to make her follow him back to Texas. He could do whatever he wanted with her future, and no one would care. Besides, she didn't know anyone in Texas.

"Were you intending ever to tell me about the baby, Cara?"

The question caught her off-guard. "Truthfully? I really don't know."

His jaw tightened. "Didn't you think I'd *want* to know? Had a *right* to know?"

How could she explain to him all the turmoil she'd felt about the baby?

"Didn't you think I'd want to know, had a right to know was my question, Mrs. Jefferson."

"No, I didn't," she snapped, temper rising in response to his tone. "I said no ties, no commitments remember?" She then lowered her voice. "The pregnancy was my problem, not yours."

He reminded himself she'd been a virgin and had no other relationship to use as a standard against which to measure what had gone on between them. She'd no way of knowing that the care and tenderness he'd shown her in bed meant something. "Tell me about Miles Sutton and that night you fell."

"Sheriff Polk says it's Miles's word against mine since there weren't any witnesses."

Chase had heard the story by way of the sheriff, but needed to hear her version. He coaxed her to tell it.

When she finished, he was so quiet and still, Cara gave him a hesitant look over her shoulder.

He turned his gaze on her slowly, evaluating, assessing. His attention went to the scar above her eyebrow, a parting gift from the shoe of Miles's horse. It had taken six of Sophie's best stitches to close the gash; three inches lower and she would have lost an eye. He touched the needlework lightly. When it healed, a crescent would remain.

"I'm going to kill him, you know."

She trembled in response to that deadly soft statement. Then, as he brushed his fingertip briefly across her lower lip, she closed her eyes. Cara wondered if this was what it meant to die for love. Because she was dying inside. He was a man literally taking away her life, and all she could think about was how good it would feel to have him hold her while she cried out her grief over losing their child.

Somberly, Chase placed a fleeting kiss on the injury. The scent and warmth of her skin were dizzying.

"I would have wanted to know about the baby, Cara. I never would have let you face something like that alone."

Tears slid down her cheeks.

"Never . . ." he repeated.

She looked at him then. For one long moment she saw in his eyes the man he'd been last summer. The concern rang true, the returning gaze familiar. The pony soldier she'd given her heart to let himself be glimpsed only briefly, then retreated swiftly behind a mask.

Chapter 11

Even though Miles lay beaten on the ground, Chase still hadn't vented all of his rage. He dragged the bloody-faced man to his feet and prepared to let fly another punch, only to have the blow stopped in midair by the restraining hand of someone standing beside him in the darkness. "That's enough, Chase. You'll hang if you kill him."

Chase turned to vent his anger on the newcomer but stopped short upon recognizing an old friend. "What the hell are you doing here?"

"Like you, I'm here to pay a social call on Mr. Sutton. Pretty popular man."

Chase turned Miles loose to slump to the ground like sacked meal. Breathing hard, the cold air turning his breath to frost, Chase took a moment to collect himself. His right hand ached across the knuckles. He'd hit Miles so many times that his skin had cracked. He flexed the injured hand a few times, testing to see if he'd broken a bone. Tomorrow he'd know for sure. Right now it just hurt like hell.

Dreamer of Eagles looked at his friend's bloodied knuckles and said, "Just like you to count coup on my prey."

An exhausted Chase swung his attention to the Indian he'd first encountered on the streets of Philadelphia nearly twenty years before. "You've been after this bastard, too?"

"For a few months now. He and a group of men ambushed a stage carrying some medicine we were expecting at Pine Ridge."

"When?"

"This past summer."

"Are you sure it was him? The army's been looking for some bandits all summer, too, but I can't believe this one's involved." He spoke contemptuously. "He doesn't have the balls to take on a man, only a woman."

Dreamer asked quietly, "Is that why you're out here? Because of a woman?"

"Yes. He injured my wife. She lost our baby."

"She's recovering?"

Chase nodded affirmation.

Dreamer and Chase had not communicated for more than half a year. "News shared by old friends should never be sad. I'm sorry, Chase. However, I must ask, is this woman deaf and blind to want an old army dog like you?"

Chase gave a bitter chuckle. "No, and right now she doesn't want me at all." In answer to the query posed by Dreamer's raised eyebrow, he offered, "I'll explain it some other time. Right now things are just too complicated."

"Chase Jefferson married. Amazing."

Chase steered the conversation back to the ambushed stage. "Why would Sutton and his friends ambush a stage carrying medicine?"

"Because it also carried gold."

Incredulous, Chase stared at him. "Gold? Wait a minute, start over."

When Dreamer finished his tale, Chase realized the puzzle the banks and the army had been trying to put together all summer now had a few more pieces. Dreamer had seen Miles Sutton with the men who'd robbed the stage. But how had they gotten hold of the route itinerary in the first place? Had Virginia been in on the plot? Chase tended to discount that theory; he couldn't imagine Virginia robbing herself. Her outrage over the missing funds had seemed genuine when he'd spoken to her last August. Well, well, well, he thought, looking down at the prone and pummeled Miles. He then looked back to Dreamer. "So you saw them rob the coach?"

"Yes. You see, the first shipment of vaccine we requested never arrived. When the agent told us the stage carrying it had been ambushed and that the bureau back East had arranged for more, I asked if he could find out the route it would be taking."

"Did he?" Chase began to feel the coldness of the wind swirling around him now that he no longer had the fire of vengeance to keep him warm. He looked around for the coat he had discarded upon challenging Sutton and found it lying on the ground nearby. Teeth chattering, he pulled it on.

Dreamer, comfortable in the buffalo robe given to him by his wife, smiled at Chase's attempt to warm himself.

"What are you smiling about?"

"Watching you trying to get warm in something made from a sheep."

When Chase told him to get on with his story, Dreamer did. The seriousness returned to his voice as he continued. "The agent balked at first—he didn't want to give us the route information. Your government is always better at solving Indian problems than Indians," he pointed out sarcastically, "but children were dying, old people were dying, and we refused to let the sickness run its course, as he suggested."

Chase shook his head sadly. The bitterness in the brave's tone was truly justified. The government's treatment of the native population had destroyed an entire way of life. Dreamer's generation would probably be the last true Sioux. "Did he eventually give in?"

"Only after much arguing. We took the information about the route and sent braves to position themselves near possible ambush spots along the way. We were lucky. My riding party came across them down near the Kansas-Colorado border."

"And you *saw* Sutton there?"

"I didn't know his name at the time, but, yes, he was there. In fact, he divided the strongboxes among the others as if he were the head man."

Chase looked down at Sutton, then back to the Indian painted for war. "Too bad that agent didn't go along with you," Chase said solemnly. The agent's testimony could have given the U.S. marshal more than enough information to make sure Miles Sutton woke up in a jail cell in the morning. But because Dreamer's eyewitness testimony would be viewed skeptically in a court of law, if viewed at all, due to his race, Chase could do nothing now except wire Colonel Grierson about Dreamer's account and wait.

"I'll wire Fort Davis and see if Colonel Grierson has any ideas," Chase said. "I'd love to see this yellow belly rot in territorial prison, but we're going to need more proof to put him there. I just know it."

Chase felt no remorse for the beating he'd given Sutton; territorial prison wouldn't even begin to compensate for the grief Sutton had caused. The rage began rising all over again. Dreamer obviously sensed it because he took Chase firmly by the arm.

"Go home. Go home to this deaf and blind woman. Sutton won't cheat his fate."

"She's not deaf and blind."

"She has to be," Dreamer said with twinkling black eyes. "In the spring I will return to see for myself."

The two men faced each other in the winter cold, both wishing for more time to renew the friendship forged in the wilds of civilized Philadelphia, but the snows would begin any day now, and Dreamer's ride back to Pine Ridge in Dakota Territory would be a long one.

"Did you ever think twenty years ago about where we'd be today?" Chase asked, thinking back on the past.

"Frankly, I expected us to be dead already, killed by some outraged father or husband."

Chase had to smile at that. They'd been the educated, runaway Negro and the educated Sioux, paraded around the fundraising circuit as examples of why money should be raised for Indian and Negro relief. Two tall handsome exotics dressed in formal wear, drawn into bedrooms at every opportunity by dazzled society hostesses and their daughters. "We were lucky."

They smiled the smile of shared experiences, and then Chase held out his hand. Dreamer grasped it firmly.

"We'll talk next time," Dreamer promised.

Chase nodded. "Say hello to She Who Sings and to your sons."

"I will. You work on untangling the knots with the woman who is deaf and blind. You're getting to be an old man. You need sons."

Chase grinned, shaking his head. Dreamer and his outrageous wit were always good for the soul. "I'm going home."

"Take care, my friend. I'll stay awhile and wait for Mr. Sutton to wake up. I have a few words of wisdom to impart."

"Fine with me."

Chase started walking away, only to be stopped by Dreamer calling, "What is your blind woman's name?"

"Cara Lee," Chase called back. "Cara Lee."

Cara raised up sleepily when he entered the room carrying her breakfast tray. For a brief moment she wondered if he could tell she'd spent most of the night crying over their parting.

He could.

When he set the tray down she noticed the bandage on his hand. He'd obviously injured it sometime between last night and this morning. She looked up at him questioningly.

"Nothing for you to be concerned about. Eat. When you're done, get dressed to go out. Something I want you to see."

She knew from his manner not to ask for any more information, but where were they going?

He was now at the door. He stopped and turned back, saying, "And wear your drawers, Mrs. Jefferson. It's cold outside."

Cara didn't dwell on his cutting remark. Outside! She was going outside!

It was a cold gray November day, and one would think that most people would be far more concerned with getting out of the biting wind than standing around watching the newly married Jeffersons, but the schoolteacher and her soldier were news. Speculation about the two was fueling gossip around dinner tables and the cracker barrels of general stores all over the Valley.

Chase sat Cara carefully in the buggy beneath big blankets before rounding the back of the vehicle to get in on the driver's side. He spotted the curious, staring townspeople watching from the walks and store entrances, but he ignored them and climbed in. He picked up the reins and set the team in motion.

A small knot of people were standing in front of the charred and blackened remains of Miles Sutton's Liberian Lady. Cara stared in surprise as the buggy rolled by. "When did this happen?"

"Last night," Chase answered, keeping the horse on pace. "Sutton wasn't lucky enough to be inside, however."

"Does anyone know how it happened?" Cara asked.

"Sheriff's still investigating."

Chase said no more about it, though he had his own theory on what had happened to Miles's saloon.

A few miles outside of town Chase brought the buggy to a halt.

Confused, Cara stuck her head past the awning and looked around. "Why'd you stop?"

"Because we're here."

He set the brake and jumped down.

Puzzled, she placed her gloved hand in his, and he helped her step out.

They were in front of the Pennyman place. Parker Pennyman had built the house for his wife, Victoria, during the first spring of the settlement of Henry Adams. When he died of pneumonia two winters back, Victoria and the three children moved East. The house now belonged to Virginia's bank.

"I figured you'd want a place of your own."

Cara turned to him and stared.

"You go on in," he told her. "I want to put the buggy and the team in the barn."

Speechless, Cara walked up the plank steps and onto the wide, welcoming front porch.

Inside, she took a slow look around. It was a fairly large place for the plains, with a big parlor and an ample kitchen. The stone wall that ran the length of the front rooms held large fireplaces for the kitchen and the sitting room.

Cara was only slightly winded after climbing the staircase to the upper floor. She found three well-laid-out rooms, and what looked to be a partially finished bathroom—what a luxury.

Victoria Pennyman had left nearly all the furnishings, evidently not wanting to undertake the enormous logistics and expenses necessary to ship everything back East, so it all stayed except for a few treasured pieces. As a result there were beds and dressers, rough-hewn chairs and tables. With a little work Cara could make it a home again.

Cara could hear Chase yelling from downstairs.

"Up here," she yelled back. She walked down the short hall and stopped at the top of the stairs. An obviously angry Chase stood at the base.

"What in the hell are you doing? Are you supposed to be climbing stairs?"

Cara didn't know whether to be touched by his concern or angry because he was angry. She decided it would not do to have a fight their first day in their first home. "I'm fine. I just wanted to see what was up here."

"And do you approve?"

She sensed he was asking about more than the house. Gun shy, she left it alone. "You truly want to do this?"

Chase felt his mask slip in response to her sincerity. Her intensity made him answer in kind. "Yes."

"Then I approve," she confirmed softly.

"Well, then, come back down here before you hurt yourself. I want you to see the rest."

Smiling, she complied.

With Asa's help Chase readied the house in only two weeks. The windmill and some of the windows needed repair, and snakes and other varmints had to be cleared from the cellar and beneath the front and back porches, but the place proved to be in sound condition despite being vacant for so long.

A little over a week after they moved in, Cara was in the upstairs bedroom reading by a lantern on the stand next to the bed, when the front door slammed so hard the house seemed to shudder. He was back.

The echo of his entrance had barely died before the silence was once again split—this time by the sound of him yelling her name. Tight-lipped, she closed the book, set it aside, and swung her legs from beneath the warmth of the quilts. She'd seen him very rarely lately. His only priorities seemed to be fixing up the house and stocking needed supplies. In the mornings he would be up and gone at the crack of dawn, and before tonight he had never returned until after she'd gone to bed.

"You bellowed?" she asked, standing now at the foot of the stairs.

His look said he didn't much care for the sarcasm. 'Sophie sent some things for the house." He indicated a couple of large trunks by the door. "The supplies from town are outside on the board."

He went back out into the night.

In one of the trunks Cara found a treasure trove of linen: sheets, table covers, towels, pillow slips, and the like. But when she opened the second and looked inside, her first thought was that there had to be some mistake. Sophie had filled it with lingerie: flimsy gowns, delicate camisoles, flowing robes. The silky garments came in all colors and lengths, and as Cara carefully unfolded a few to view, she noted a variety of sensual styles. What could Sophie have been thinking? she wondered, marveling at the beautiful lacework and delicate stitches. Each piece had been fashioned to please a man's eye. These garments had no place here. Chase had not approached her in a loving way since they'd married, and she'd no idea if he ever would.

As she unfolded a few more gowns and held them up, she admitted, yes, his seeming lack of interest hurt; no woman wanted to go through life with a husband intent upon ignoring her existence. But she'd convinced herself the emptiness didn't matter. This marriage would be strictly a means to an end. Without his name she stood very little chance of teaching anywhere ever again. They were living in the 1880s; society dictated the standards, and, if one didn't conform, one found herself married to a pony soldier! No one cared that she truly enjoyed opening the world to eager young children—she'd made love to a man not her husband, and small minds would continue to harp on the indiscretion until she went to her grave.

At the bottom of the trunk, Cara found numerous pairs of erotic pantalets. Scandalized, she stuffed them back in quickly, then turned her mind again to the problems of her marriage. Supposedly this marriage would silence some of the gossip, but if not, that didn't matter to Cara, either. Only returning to her students mattered. She'd marry the devil himself if she could continue teaching.

Cara heard his footfall on the porch outside and hastily began to refold the gifts, hoping to repack them before he entered.

Too late.

He carried a sack of potatoes in his arms and set it by the door. "What's in the trunks?"

Cara answered truthfully, "Linen."

He came to stand over her, looming like a mountain. She didn't like having to look up at him. It spoke too much of what he perceived as their relative roles.

"What else?"

"Nothing. Female clothing. You wouldn't be interested."

"Open it."

The hard set of his unshaven jaw told Cara he was bent on making this an issue. Irritated, she flipped up the trunk's lid and picked up the gown folded on top.

Chase blanched at the beauty of the transparent cream-colored gown she held up for his inspection. The straps were as thin as moonbeams; fragile, delicate pieces of rolled silk designed to slide off a woman's bare shoulders like a caress. The straps led his mesmerized gaze down to the scalloped edges of a scandalously low-cut bodice held together by tiny white ribbons. Below the ribbons, the flowing, floor-length gown had no seam. The wearer would have to do nothing more than walk across a room to give her lover a teasing view of the bareness within.

The arousing mental images brought his manhood slowly to life, a reaction he could not control. And because he could not, anger tightened his jaw. "You're right," he said finally. "I'm not interested."

He turned and walked back out the door, slamming it for punctuation.

At his abrupt departure, Cara smiled sarcastically as she folded the gown and placed it back in the trunk. He didn't fool her at all. She'd seen his jaw tighten and his eyes go dark when she held up Sophie's creation. The jaw coupled with the prominent bulge below the waistline of the tight-fitting work pants told her quite plainly what he refused to say aloud; the gown aroused him. Cara was honest enough to admit he'd more than likely envisioned some other woman wearing the gown, but his reaction helped to salve the pain.

Outside, Chase stood in the cold, unforgiving wind of the December night and took a deep breath, willing his manhood to halt its breakneck galloping. In spite of everything, the desire to bed this treacherous little wife had him in knots. His vow to keep his hands off her had placed him in hell.

But he'd come out here to do a job, so, cursing himself, the woman inside, and the fates that had joined them together, he began unloading the sacks and crates stacked in the back of the board. They contained foodstuffs and supplies for the long winter ahead. The mercantile had received probably its last big shipment before the Valley closed down for the winter, and Chase, armed with six months' pay, took full advantage. In addition to the food he'd returned with feed for the animals, lantern oil, and some new cooking pots. A number of the women in the Valley made scented soaps, also sold in the mercantile. He'd purchased the last bar for Cara in what could only be termed a fit of weak-minded insanity. It rested now in his shirt pocket, wrapped in pretty silver paper.

Thinking about the soap gave rise to visions of Cara in the bath, sliding it slowly across her glistening wet skin, while he sat in a chair by the fire, watching from the darkness.

Chase angrily wrenched his mind away from the scene, cursing again. He couldn't ever remember wanting a woman this much, so much he ached all day long. But he wouldn't give in, he swore, violently snatching down another sack and adding it to the growing pile on the ground. He had only to remind himself of her selfish plans concerning his child, and all fiery thoughts of making love to her were doused by the storm of his fury.

It took him four trips to bring everything into the house. When he finally finished, he removed his coat and hung it on the peg beside the closed door. Being outside had given him the time to solidify his determination to resist the pull of passion.

Cara paid little attention to his mood. Instead, she concentrated on examining the things he'd brought back from town. They looked to be sound purchases: the potatoes weren't rotten, the lantern oil smelled fresh not rancid, and the cooking pots were of good weight and free of dents. The quantity and quality of the goods admittedly surprised her. He seemed to be very experienced at determining the items needed to stock a household, something she would not have guessed.

She also uncovered crocks of pale sweet butter, rashers of cured bacon, coffee, and flour. There were jars of put-up vegetables and spiced fruit and jams.

She was startled to discover he was standing in the kitchen watching her. The dark eyes, cold as the winter plains, held no emotion, yet seemed to burn across the distance. "There's stew on the stove," she offered, trying to shake the nervousness suddenly trembling in her veins.

For a moment, it seemed as if he hadn't heard, then came the words "Thank you." He moved over to the stove, and she let out an unconsciously held breath.

Chase helped himself to the thick hot mix of dark broth, vegetables, and meat simmering in the kettle while she began putting the food and supplies away. This would be his first opportunity to taste her cooking and he'd no idea what to expect. He hesitated a moment trying to decide how much he should put on his plate. He stoically opted for a healthy portion because, after chasing around in the cold since dawn, he'd eat anything as long as it was hot.

To his surprise the stew was good—damn good. And the fat golden biscuits had to have come from heaven. His soft yet audible groan of delight drew her sharp attention.

"Something wrong?" she asked in the process of storing the new cook pots in the bottom of the kitchen's big standing sideboard. She placed the last pot and stood, waiting for his answer.

"No, nothing's wrong."

She didn't believe him. Her eyes strayed to the large bowl of stew set before him on the table. "I distinctly heard you groan. Is my cooking that bad?"

"No, your cooking's fine. So fine, in fact—"

"You groaned."

He nodded.

"I'm glad." She went back to storing the supplies, thinking to herself, so he liked her cooking? That was hardly enough to base a marriage upon.

Chase could see the crossness lining her face. Dammit, he'd paid her a compliment, but evidently all he'd succeeded in doing was ruffling her feathers. Refusing to waste any more time worrying over her and her moods, he went back to his meal of thick savory stew and the light-as-angle-wings biscuits.

But all the while he ate, he watched her as she moved about; drawn in spite of himself by the lines of her body in the nightgown and robe, the way she moved, the faint scent of her passage. The sensations evoked memories that threatened to slide past the gates of his resolve, but he refused to let them rise. She'd made a fool of him once; he would never give her the chance to betray him again.

In the days that followed, Cara and Chase moved through the house like ghosts, passing each other without a word. When verbal communication had to be employed, the conversation was kept as brief as possible; neither of them used two words when one would suffice.

She took care of the cooking, washing, and day-to-day tasks of keeping their silent home clean. He worked on reports, cared for the animals, drew maps for the army surveyors, and chopped wood from sunup to sundown.

They came together as a couple only during the evening meal. He sat and ate; she sat and ate. On this night in particular, Chase pushed aside his plate after stuffing himself with her chicken and dumplings. He wanted to groan, he felt so full, but he didn't want her to know how much he'd enjoyed the meal, so he merely purred and hoped she wouldn't hear it. Damn, she could cook!

She cleared the table while he watched her over the lighted tip of his after-dinner cigar. They'd been here nearly two weeks now. In that time she had not begged him for attention, never come to him for anything personal, or demonstrated in any way that she felt hurt by his pointed display of disinterest. In fact, she seemed quite content with the way things were going, a reaction he would not have guessed but should have anticipated, considering the woman in question. She'd probably never begged for anything in her life, especially not a man's affections. He could not help but admire that backbone of hers. He'd challenged her to draw and so far she hadn't blinked.

But what stood between them was much more substantial than a metaphorical gunfight. He still had not forgiven her for planning to deceive him about the child.

Chase tamped out the cigar on the stones fronting the grate, then threw the butt in the fire. "Saw Sophie today."

"How is she?" Cara asked from the sink where she stood washing the dishes from dinner.

"She's fine. Sends her love."

Cara went back to her task, assuming that to be the whole of tonight's conversation. She was wrong.

"She wants to give us a reception."

"What kind of reception?"

"Marriage reception."

Cara studied his expression for some clue as to how he felt about participating in such an event, but she found it unreadable. "What did you tell her?"

"That we'd come."

Cara turned back to the sink, uncertain how she felt about the invitation. "Did she say who she invited?"

"No, but I don't think Sophie would invite anyone who would be cruel to you, Cara, if that's what you're worried about."

It was.

Then he added, "The folks who turn up their noses now are probably the same ones who turned up their noses before, if you think about it."

She decided he was right and agreed to go.

Chapter 12

Sophie held the reception for Chase and Cara on Christmas Day in her front room. It was well-attended and a great success. Cara and Chase received warm welcomes and a variety of gifts, ranging from preserves and canned vegetables to a beautiful snow-white bed covering, that the Three Spinsters must have been quilting for weeks. Cara cried.

More than a few folks came up to Cara and said she'd have their support if she wanted to start another school; evidently, neither the children nor their parents were pleased with Reverend Whitfield's fire-and-brimstone approach to education, and the board had been unable to hire a replacement.

And Chase? Throughout the evening, he stayed at Cara's side. He fetched punch for her, opened gifts with her, deflected some of the more snide comments, and even waltzed with her, to the delight of the true friends of theirs in attendance. He gave the gossips absolutely nothing to talk about, except perhaps how handsome he looked in his uniform. He played the role of an attentive, considerate husband to perfection.

On the cold buggy ride home through the snow, Cara thanked him. "For what?" he asked.

"For making people think we have a normal marriage."

"Like I said, purely selfish."

"Meaning?" she asked, not sure if she really wanted him to reply.

"Meaning that I'm getting pretty tired of people coming up and asking after you in such a way you'd think I'm keeping you chained in the cellar."

"You haven't exactly been polite since you've been back," she pointed out.

"And am I supposed to be? Sophie told me the cruel things people said about you the night you were dismissed. And Miles Sutton is lucky to be alive."

Cara could see his angry face in the moonlight reflecting off the snow. "Sheriff Polk told me you—how'd he put it?—'beat the hell out of Miles Sutton.'"

"I take care of my own."

Cara's reaction flickered, just as it did every time he directly or indirectly claimed her as his own. "He also said that was the night the Lady burned to the ground. Did you do that, too?"

"That I didn't do. Though I'd like to hang a medal on whoever did."

"So would I," Cara echoed.

Back at the house, Cara went inside, taking with her as much of the reception's bounty as she could carry. After putting the team and buckboard in the barn, Chase would bring in the rest. Shivering from the cold, Cara was stoking the fire in the grate when he entered, stamping snow from his boots. His arms were filled with a crate loaded with gifts. She came to relieve him of his burden. "I'll take that."

He gave it over without protest and removed his boots, though like Cara he kept his coat on, waiting for the house to get warm. She went about the task of putting away their presents. "Did Asa say when he would deliver that tub?"

"Sometime in the next few days."

"Wonderful. I've almost forgotten what it feels like to take a leisurely bath."

The big tub was a gift from Asa and Sophie. Because of its size, it wouldn't fit on the buggy with all the other items she and Chase brought home. Cara couldn't wait for its arrival.

"I have something for you," he told her.

Cara looked his way, surprised.

"Today is Christmas, so here, these are for you."

Cara took the two wrapped items from him and stared.

"Well, they won't open themselves," he prompted.

"I . . . have something for you also."

Now it was his turn to be surprised. She ran upstairs and returned with a wrapped parcel. He took it with wonder.

"Well, it won't open itself," she said softly.

They both spent the next few seconds unwrapping their gifts. Cara beamed at the bar of scented soap. "I will use this the moment that tub arrives. Thank you, Chase." When she opened the other, much smaller one, she had to fight her tears. "This is so lovely . . ."

"I hope it fits. You're my wife—you should have a ring."

Cara lifted the small gold band from the tissue paper and slid it on her finger. It did fit, remarkably well. She turned to him, her eyes filled with emotion.

Chase, overwhelmed by her reaction, looked away and concentrated on removing the paper on his gift. Inside he found a leather-bound journal. He was touched by the beauty of the volume.

"Do you like it?" she asked.

"Cara, this is—where'd you find something so fine?"

"I sent to Chicago for it. I thought you'd prefer something like that to all those loose pieces of paper you do your reports on. This way, everything is in one place."

"It's been a long time since I got something personal for Christmas. The army sometimes sends coffee, extra rations, but nothing personal."

"When was the last time you received something for Christmas that was especially for you?"

"Probably the last year I spent in New Orleans with Sophie and Asa."

Cara made a vow then and there that regardless of how this marriage went, she would always make the effort to give him something special for the holiday. She would also ask Sophie about his birthday.

"Do you like the ring?"

"Yes, I do." The band was simple, yet delicate and beautifully crafted. The gold sparkled in the light.

"Good," he replied.

There was awkward silence as they both tried to think of something else to say.

The house was noticeably warmer, so Cara removed her coat and hung it on the peg by the door. "Do you want a piece of this cake before I put it away?" She'd set the cake left over from the reception on the kitchen table.

"Sure, I'll have a small piece."

She took two plates and forks down from the sideboard and cut a small wedge of Dulcie's chocolate cake for each of them. They ate in silence at the table, too aware of each other.

"Cara?"

She looked up.

"I wish you'd written me about the child, that's all."

"Chase—"

"Hear me out, please?"

She nodded.

"Cara, I've been carrying around all this anger because of how I felt when I found out you'd planned on denying me my child. A free-born child means a lot to a former slave. Being free all your life, I doubt you know just how much."

The pain in his voice drew her eyes back to his, and he did not hide the hurt in his heart. Never, never had it crossed her mind that because he had been a slave, a free-born child would mean so much.

His voice softened as he continued. "It has to do with legitimacy, Cara. Remember the story I told you about my grandmother, that night you fell off the sawhorse and hurt your ankle?"

She did. His grandmother had called him a dirty black African bastard. Cara would always remember that tale.

"Well, I swore I would never father a child I could not give my name. When I found out you'd planned on leaving, I wanted to hurt someone —no, hurt you."

"And you have," she whispered without shame. Tears were stinging her eyes.

Chase felt his heart rising to his throat. "Cara, look—"

"Chase, I didn't think about what the baby might mean to you. We'd never discussed the possibility of children. I mean, you told Sophie to tell me where I could get in touch with you in case I needed you, but you never said a thing to me. When I found out I was carrying, I didn't know how you'd take to the idea of fatherhood. You said you were never going to marry, remember?"

He did.

"So I decided I had to look out for myself and the baby."

"I would have helped, Cara."

The passionate conviction in his declaration drew her gaze back to his. "You would have, wouldn't you?"

He nodded. "Yes. When we first met, I told you my intentions were honorable."

"Yes, you did, but it was such a game between us. Chase, I've relied on myself for so long . . ." Her voice trailed off.

"I know how hard it is to put your fate in someone else's hands, Cara. I'm the same way." He reached over and laid his hands atop hers. She laced her fingers with his. When he spoke again, his voice was soft. "Can you forgive me, these last few weeks?"

Cara looked down at their entwined fingers and whispered, "Can you forgive me?"

He stood slowly and held out his arms, "Come here."

Cara went to him and he held her tightly. "Chase, I'm so, so sorry."

"So am I, darlin'. So am I."

Cara wanted so much for them to start anew. She dearly loved this man. The last month had been a nightmare, but now maybe it was over.

Chase spoke into her hair, "I've spent the last few days asking myself what kind of marriage I wanted us to have. I don't really know, but I do know it can't be one with all this bitterness."

Cara agreed.

"Cara, I know we don't love each other, but in the beginning, before everything got so complicated, we did enjoy being together, didn't we?"

"Yes, we did." The echo of his words rang loud in her ears. *I know we don't love each other.*

He looked down into her face. "Why are you crying?"

She backed up and hastily wiped at the telling tears. "I'm not crying. I —you're right. Just because we're not in love doesn't mean we can't make this work. Other couples have done it."

"I asked myself something else."

"What?"

"I've never made a secret of how much I desire you, Cara Lee. And I asked myself if I wanted to spend the rest of my life looking at you, but never touching you . . ."

The hot whisper of his voice, the thought of touching him again made her go weak with desire.

"Will you share my bed? I'm not asking that we be intimate right away. We still need time to adjust to each other, but I don't want you sleeping down the hall away from me, schoolmarm. Not anymore."

Cara's heart soared. His mask had disappeared. She looked up into the eyes of Chase, her Chase, and said, "Then I suppose we should start moving my things."

It didn't take them long to get Cara moved into Chase's larger room down the hall. Her additional furniture made the room seem very small, but for Cara the slightly cramped quarters exuded the intimacy she imagined a husband and wife would share. Husband. He was all she could have hoped for: honorable, handsome, caring. She wanted this marriage to work. The truce they'd forget tonight made her feel as if that were indeed possible.

He smiled. "We'll move the rest of the things in tomorrow. Ready for bed?"

She was. It had been a long day.

While Chase added wood to the fire, Cara began her preparations for bed by taking the pins from her hair. The thick mass unwound slowly, and she slid her fingers in to massage her scalp. She glanced up at Chase and saw that his eyes were riveted on her. She smiled at his interest, got up, and retrieved her hairbrush from the top of her dresser. She sat with her back to him at the small vanity table and began to brush her hair. She could see him reflected over her shoulder in the mirror. He hadn't moved. She combed through her hair and braided it, then under his watching eyes, began to undo the buttons of her shirt.

Holding his attention, she opened the buttons at her waist. She shimmied out of her skirt and stood there in her slip and drawers as she took off the blouse, then she moved past him over to the wardrobe and pulled out a long flannel nightgown.

Chase's manhood swelled as he watched her. He supposed he, too, should get undressed, but he couldn't pull his gaze away from his beautiful wife. The removal of the blouse revealed the camisole underneath and the sweet brown curve of her bare shoulders. She hung up the blouse on one of the pegs nailed into the back of the door. She looked good enough to eat. When she sat on the bed and began to remove her stockings and shoes, Chase got a good enough look at the expanse of her legs to keep him awake for weeks imagining and remembering the feel of them entwined around his waist.

"Something wrong?" she asked innocently.

"No, just adjusting to you."

"I see. Would you rather I undress in the other room?"

"No. Here is fine." Then he added, "I'm going to go out and make sure the pump handle's high. Don't want it to be frozen in the morning. You go on and get into bed."

Then he left.

Cara viewed his exit with a knowing smile.

When he returned she was snug beneath the quilts. She'd left the lamp by the bed lit but had doused all the others. "How's the pump?"

He swung his eyes to her and smiled. He began on the buttons of his uniform. "Pump's fine. How's my bed?"

"Bed's fine," she replied, grinning.

He sat to remove his boots, then stood and shucked off his trousers. Dressed now in his union suit, he walked over to the door and hung his uniform next to her skirt and blouse. "It's better if you sleep on the other side, schoolmarm. The man should sleep closest to the door."

She moved over and felt the chill of the sheets. "You just want my spot because it's all warmed up."

"Smart woman." He chuckled as he slid into bed. He settled in and said, "Ah, nice and warm like I like it."

She punched him in the shoulder. He laughed.

Chase turned down the lamp, and they both lay there listening to the soft cracking of the fire.

"Know something, Sergeant?"

He smiled, realizing he'd missed her calling him by rank. "What?"

"This is going to be hard."

He turned and leaned on his elbow. "What's going to be hard?" Chase already had an answer: his manhood, but he doubted his answer had anything to do with the conversation.

"This adjusting you talked about. How long do you think it should last?"

"I don't know. We'll see, I suppose. Why?"

She turned and looked up at him. "Oh, I don't know, just curious is all."

He leaned down and kissed her lips. "You think you could hold out for three or four days?"

She savored his kisses and whispered, "Probably not. Two days is all I can promise."

He chuckled. "Two days it is. Now, let's get some sleep. In two days, you're going to need your strength."

"So will you," she countered.

Then they slept.

Chase awakened the next morning alone but with the smell of bacon and coffee in the air. All he could do was lie there and smile. Finally he got dressed and went downstairs.

Cara greeted him with a smile, then set on the table a stack of flapjacks that were still hot and running with syrup and butter.

"You make a man seriously consider deserting, Mrs. Jefferson, feeding me like this. When I go back, army food's going to taste worse than ever."

"When are you leaving?" she asked, taking a seat and passing him the coffeepot.

"The day after the new year."

"So soon."

"Yes."

Cara fought to keep the sadness from her voice. "Then I guess I'll have to be a good wife so you'll hurry back."

"I'll always hurry back."

His eyes were as potent as flame, and Cara told him so. "It's a little early in the day for you to be setting my clothes on fire, Chase Jefferson."

"Is it? Sorry about that. When would it be more convenient?"

"You're an outrageous man. Eat before your food gets cold."

He did, but did not turn down his eyes.

And as a result, when Cara got up from the table after finishing her meal, she seriously doubted her ability to hold out for even one of the two days they'd agreed upon. Her nipples were hard from his devilish stares and heat had began to pulse between her thighs.

After breakfast he went out to check on the animals. When he returned he said, "Let's have some fun today, Mrs. Jefferson. What would you like to do?"

Cara gave him a saucy smile.

"Not that, schoolmarm. We agreed. Two days, remember?" Then he added with a blazing gaze, "You were right. It's getting to be damn hard."

"Then we should spend the day adjusting. Let's go have some fun."

First order of business was a ride through the snow. Cara thought the idea grand when he suggested it. She hurried up to the room to pull on her warmest clothing and joined him outside. The cold fresh air was as invigorating as the kiss with which he greeted her. Just when she thought she was going to swoon, he withdrew, and they were off. The runners on the buggy made for a smooth ride across the snow. The weather was cold but not so extreme that it endangered the horses pulling them along.

Since they had no real destination in mind, Chase just headed the horses up the road.

It turned out to be a memorable morning. They saw snow hares and deer. They talked; they had a rousing snowball fight.

When they returned home laughing and cold, Cara ran into the house two steps ahead of his pelting snowballs. Laughing so hard it hurt to breathe, she positioned her body against the door to prevent him from entering. "Go away!"

"Open this door, woman!"

Cara jumped away from the door and took off at a run up the stairs. He was at her heels with a handful of the balled snow.

She yelled gleefully. "You quit throwing snow in the house!" He caught her in his arms and brought her back down the staircase. "You can't get away from me."

She threw back her head and laughed not only at the silliness of their play but at how good she felt inside.

They warmed up with cups of hot coffee and bowls of leftover stew.

Chase settled into the front room to work on a survey report for the colonel, and Cara took to the kitchen to make bread.

She was in the process of kneading when he came in behind her and slipped his arms around her waist. He nuzzled her neck, and she lost all contact with the dough under her hands. "We're supposed to be adjusting, Sergeant, not . . ." Her voice failed when she realized he was opening her blouse. When he pushed her camisole aside and filled his hands, she moaned. He ran his thumbs over the nipples until they tightened and pleaded.

He turned her then, lowering his mouth to her breasts. Sweet, hot pleasure filled her. He loved her for a few lightning-filled moments more, then closed up the blouse, and turned her back to the bread.

He left the kitchen without a word, leaving Cara dazed.

For the rest of the day he teased her like that, kissing her, caressing her in and out of her clothing, only to leave her dazzled and pulsing in response. By the time she set the plates out for dinner, he had her so flowing with warmth she could barely walk.

She had just set the last of the chocolate cake on a plate in front of him when his gaze let her know cake wasn't the only item on his menu. He pulled her down into his lap, eased a hand into her hair, and guided her mouth to his kiss. He slid a caressing hand up beneath her skirt, then very gently, yet boldly pushed her drawers down and ultimately off. "You won't need these," he whispered hotly.

Cara could not help but ease her thighs apart under the fiery impetus of his touches. His kisses on her parted lips, his questing fingers, and her own need merged into sensations so potent she began to moan low in her throat. He opened her blouse and reacquainted himself with the nipples barely recovered from his last ardent sucking. She trembled passionately as he looked into her eyes, then trembled again as his fingers slowly rubbed a bit of the cake's icing on first one dark bud and then the other. He bent and took an inordinate amount of time sucking and licking her clean. Cara swore she would die right then and there.

The only thing that saved her was the door pull's ringing chime alerting them to a visitor outside. Chase kissed her lips in parting. He eased her from his lap and headed to the door as she hastily readjusted her clothing. As he opened the door, Cara spotted her drawers lying scandalously atop the table. She snatched them up, stuffed them into the pocket of her skirt, and turned to greet the guest.

It was Asa delivering the tub. Chase helped with the unloading, then he and Asa carried the tub upstairs to Cara's old room. Asa left soon after, wanting to get back to town before the new falling snow made the road more difficult to negotiate.

After his departure, Cara grabbed her shawl. Pulling on her gloves, she stepped outside and began filling buckets with the snow in the yard. Chase came out to help, and soon they had more than enough to melt down on the stove for bathwater.

While Chase hauled the buckets of hot water up to the tub, Cara tended the fire in the room. When the combined warmth of the steamy water and the heat from the fire raised the surrounding temperature enough to make the room comfortable, Cara slipped down to Chase's room to gather the things she would need. She smiled as she added the scented soap Chase had given her for Christmas. When she returned he was adding a final bucket of steaming hot water to the tub.

"Who's first?" Cara asked.

"You are."

The tone of his voice rippled across her heightened senses. She began to undress slowly. They'd been playing a sensual game all day. Now it was her turn to see how he liked being on the griddle.

She planned on pushing him over the edge. She refused to wait another day to make love. Delbert had said she had to wait six weeks after the accident before resuming conjugal play, and more than six weeks were past. She wanted her husband, and she wanted him tonight.

Cara undid the buttons at her throat, then down her front. She asked, "Are you staying?"

"Yes," he told her. In fact, he pulled up one of the chairs in the nearly empty room and took a seat, then added, "This is the warmest room in the house."

Cara planned on it getting much warmer. To that end, she shook off her blouse, undid the ribbons on the front of her camisole, and stepped into the glow cast by the fire. She could see him seated just outside the circle of light, his face hidden by the shadows.

"Is the water still hot?" he asked.

She tested it and nodded. She slid the camisole off her shoulders, baring herself sensually for his eyes, then slipped her skirt slowly down her hips. The sharp intake of his breath made her smile. She'd bet he'd forgotten he'd taken her drawers earlier and that beneath her skirt she was still as bare as he'd left her. Without a word, she stepped into the tub.

Chase remembered fantasizing about sitting in the shadows and watching her bathe, but this . . . He could barely stay seated. The sight of her standing, then flashing him a bewitching little smile was hard enough to take, but when she began to slide the soap lazily up and down her body, he had to grip the arms of the chair. The scent of the soap and the wafting fragrance of the salts she'd added heightened his response. It was for Chase the most erotic interlude of his life.

"Would you do my back, please, Chase?"

"Sure."

When he walked into the light, Cara feared that the water would begin to simmer just from the heat of his dark eyes. He came to the tub and knelt, gave her a lingering kiss, and took the cloth and soap from her hand. He made her kneel with her back to him.

The initial feel of the cloth moving gently over her shoulder blades was glorious. She purred as it traced down her spine and circled the small of her back and the sides of her hips. His cloth-covered hand meandered up again, attending to those areas he'd neglected on the first pass. He dipped the cloth into the warm water to clear the soap from it, then used it to cascade a warm rinsing waterfall down her back. She arched responsively to the kisses he trailed up her damp spine. While his lips worked their way to the nape of her neck, his hands slipped around to gather up the weight of her breasts. She leaned back and let his strong chest support her. His hands played her like a delicate flute. And her body sang for him, rising and falling to the rhythm of the only man it had ever known.

Chase knew he had to take her tonight or die. Her damp skin under his lips and hands made him certain another day of denial would be impossible. He pulled back, leaving her only long enough to remove his clothes, then he returned to savor her soft nakedness pressed to his own.

Cara sensed herself being lifted from the tub. She turned her head to his lips as he carried her. She'd no idea where they were going and didn't much care as long as the kisses didn't stop. She came to rest atop the white cotton runner covering the surface of what she vaguely recognized as the top of her writing desk, but she was more interested in placing her kisses against his solid chest and flicking her tongue languidly over the flat brown buttons of his nipples. She was rewarded for her devotions by his fingers opening her like a flower to bestow devotions of their own. And she loved every brazen stroke, every circling pass that made a moan slide from her lips. She supported herself on braced arms, legs parted to offer him better access, and felt her hips begin to rise in answer to his call. He bent to circle the tip of his tongue lightly over the whirl of her navel. Soft kisses were placed against the damp skin of each thigh. He moved lower to pay tender, wanton tribute and she let loose a lusty strangled cry.

He filled her a heartbeat later and her eyes closed. He didn't move. She could feel herself pulsing around him and savored having him in the place she most wanted him to be. When he began to move he started slowly. The strokes were enticing, the first opening notes of a serenade she knew so well, and she responded by arching to receive more.

Chase obliged her. Watching her braced on her arms, the arch in her body offering her breasts so tantalizingly, added to the erotic memories he'd have of this night. The cotton runner beneath her slid in tandem with his thrusts. That sight also added to the blaze in his blood, making him increase the tempo to match the rise of his desire. The way her hips were answering him, enticing him, spurred him to lift her off the desk so he could guide her more commandingly.

The blazing contact sent Cara's passions higher. She tightened her arms and legs around him to increase the smoldering sensations. She pressed against him meaningfully and without shame. She loved the slide of their bodies as she feasted on his raw male power. It didn't take long for the climax to explode powerfully within her, making her cry out his name.

Watching her succumb with such fierce abandon, Chase smiled. Seconds later his hoarse cries were filling the silence as he gripped her hips in the glory of his release.

Cara, groggy with desire, had no idea how or when they'd come to be standing in the center of the room, but her legs were still wrapped around his waist, and he was holding her easily and without visible strain. They were also still joined, she realized. He began to move again. She sighed, and her head fell back as he stroked the lingering remnants of her desire.

"This part of our marriage will be very real, Mrs. Jefferson," he said raspily, guiding her hips with a tender vigor that made her twist for more. "Very real."

She gripped his corded arms, and then buckled as the world shattered into brilliance once again.

When Chase came down to breakfast, Cara greeted him with a shy smile. This was the first time she'd ever been with him on the day after making love; on the previous two occasions, she'd awakened alone. After being so wanton last night, she was a bit unsure how she was supposed to act.

He set her at ease by coming up behind her and pulling her back into the circle of his arms. He kissed her ear. She tilted her head up to look into his face and he craned his neck so he could set a kiss upon her lips. "Good morning, schoolmarm. I didn't cause you any pain last night, did I?"

Cara, touched by his concern, reached up and stroked his cheek. "No. Delbert said after six weeks I'd be good as new, and he was right."

"One for the good doctor then," Chase replied, sounding pleased. He kissed her once more and then patted her on the butt. "What's for breakfast, wife?"

Cara placed before him a plate of well-seasoned potatoes, scrambled eggs, slabs of ham, and three of her golden biscuits. "Cara Lee, you keep feeding me like this and Carolina's going to have to put in for a new rider."

"Good. Then you can stay home with me."

She turned back to the stove to fix herself a plate, and therefore missed the odd look that came across Chase's face. "Do you mean that?" he asked quietly.

The tone of his voice made her turn back. "Sure. Every woman wants her husband home, I think." The look on his face gave her pause. "Did I say something I shouldn't've?"

"No, I suppose not."

Cara sensed that something had happened and that she'd missed whatever it was. "Chase?"

"It's nothing, darlin'. Come sit and eat. I'm going to need a bath. Care to come and wash my back?" he asked with a grin and a couple of exaggerated winks.

Cara laughed, wondering if all married couples had so much fun.

Cara awakened the morning of January first, 1883, with Chase sleeping at her side and tried not to think about his leaving tomorrow. She'd been forcing her mind to skirt the subject all week, because of the pain it caused her heart. Instead she chose to dwell on his smile, his eyes, the way he'd made love to her the night, morning, or afternoon before. She replayed in her mind the rides through the snow they'd gotten into the habit of taking after breakfast, and the intimacy they'd discovered in reading to each other at night.

But she couldn't put it off any longer. Tomorrow he would be gone. Gone until the army let him come back to her. He'd admitted the other day he had no idea when that would be, but he'd vowed to make it as soon as it could be arranged.

She trusted him to keep that promise, but he would be so far away. He had no plans to transfer to a unit closer to Kansas, and she wouldn't be so selfish as to ask him to, though it would please her. She loved him now more than ever, and because she did, she would not ask him to choose. If she did, in the end he would resent her, just as she would had he decided to interfere in her work as a teacher.

Cara usually enjoyed the tradition of New Year's Day, but Chase's looming departure took some of the joy out of it this year. As always, all who were able came into town to visit with neighbors and to take advantage of the treats and drinks set out by the shopkeepers on Main Street. The residents also used this as a way to break up the cold and sometimes lonely winter.

Cara saw a few of her students, but only waved to them, and moved on. She didn't want to make her day any sadder.

She and Chase stopped and had lunch in Sophie's dining room, and Dulcie fed them until they couldn't move. Cara had tears in her eyes as Chase said his goodbyes to Asa, Dulcie, and then Sophie. He'd be riding out at sunup and would not be seeing them again for a long time.

When they left Sophie's and went back out into the gray January day, Chase turned to her and asked, "Do you mind if we go on home?"

She searched his face. "No, not at all."

"You'll have to apologize for me to the Three Spinsters for not stopping in to see them, but I want to get you home and spend every minute I have left holding you, looking at you, making love to you. Do you think they'll understand?" he asked, sliding a gloved finger over her brown cheek.

She nodded yes.

Chase tenderly kissed his wife right there in the middle of town, then took her home.

Back at the house, Chase spent the balance of the afternoon doing just as he'd said: holding her, looking at her, making love to her. By evening he began gathering and packing his gear. Cara had vowed not to cry and so far had done a good job keeping her tears inside. However, seeing him pack the journal she'd given him for Christmas into his saddlebag was almost her undoing.

"I don't want you to be sad, Cara Lee," he said, looking at the tears standing like jewels in her eyes. "I'll be back."

"I know, Chase."

They made love again that evening with a bittersweet tenderness. He took his time bringing her to the pinnacle of desire. She clung to him as they rode out passion's storm, and, when he finally let her sleep, she did so soundly.

When she awakened alone, she was a bit disoriented. It took her a second to shake off the cobwebs. She *was* alone, she realized, seeing the empty space beside her. Still hopeful, she sat up to listen for the echoes of Chase's presence somewhere within the house, but heard only silence.

Chapter 13

In the days and weeks following Chase's departure, Cara's sadness turned into a kind of acceptance. She kept herself busy during the day by helping Asa repair the floor in the biggest bedroom, and at night by writing long letters to her husband in care of Fort Davis.

One afternoon in late February, Cara responded to the chime on the door pull to find Virginia Sutton standing on the porch. Cara toyed seriously with the idea of slamming the door right in the Black Widow's face.

Virginia seemed to read Cara's mind. "If you don't want to invite me in, I'll understand."

Again, Cara's instincts were to send her packing, but the reason for the unprecedented visit made her curious. Since no one, not even fur-draped, mean-spirited Virginia Sutton, deserved to be left standing in the February snow, Cara stepped back to let her enter.

"Nice place," Virginia remarked, taking off her expensive gloves and looking around.

Cara closed the door.

"Your husband provided well for you," she added, tossing her big fur over the settee. "Paid me the asking price in gold. He tell you that?"

"Mrs. Sutton, I'm sure you didn't come all this way to talk about my husband's method of payment, so get to the point."

Virginia smiled. "No, I didn't. I'm here to offer you your job back, and I hope you will accept."

Cara was stunned, but eyed the woman suspiciously. "Why?"

"Why am I offering or why should you accept?"

"Both."

"Well, I'm offering because I'll need people like you if this town's to have any chance at a solid future. And you should accept because I'm willing to pay you sixty dollars a month."

Sixty dollars a month! Only men received salaries in that range. "Four months ago, I wasn't decent enough to teach anyone. Why the sudden reversal? And if it's because of your son, keep your pity. I don't need it."

"Only Miles can apologize for Miles. When he turned seven years of age, his father took over his raising. I've had no influence since." With a compelling look Virginia continued, "Do you know how much I envy your college education, your intelligence, your independence? I disliked you from the moment we were introduced because you're all the things I'll never be."

A dumbstruck Cara wondered if the woman before her could be an impostor. The Virginia Sutton she knew, or thought she knew, would never have said anything like this. In the past, the woman scarcely ever parted her lips, other than to make Cara's life miserable.

"Surprised?" Virginia asked.

"Frankly, yes. How in the world can you envy me? You have everything: money, prestige, power. You own half the town, for heaven's sake."

"I can't read."

Cara's shocked gasp sounded too loud in the silence of the room.

"Not a letter."

Due to the restrictions of the prewar South, there were thousands of the race who by law were not allowed access to the printed word. Cara had never imagined Virginia was one of them. "How do you run your businesses?"

"All my businesses revolve around counting and sums. I have a gift for that. Mae handled all my correspondence until she went off to school this past summer. Miles helps out a bit also. When I first started out here, banking consisted of making loans and handling deposits. Now times are changing. Those fools in Washington City are issuing conflicting edicts every time I turn around, and if I can't keep pace, I'll be plowed under. Jim Crow may take everything I have in the end anyway, but I'll be damned if I let them have it just because I can't read. I want you to teach me."

Cara stared. Virginia had never been anything but unpleasant in their dealings. She'd been uncooperative and opposed to every idea Cara had ever had, but Cara knew it must have taken a lot of courage for Virginia to come here today and confess what she had just now. "Why me? Why not the teacher over in Nicodemus, or the reverend?"

"Because even I know you're the best the area has to offer. I'll pay you, of course."

Of course, Cara thought to herself.

"So? Will you accept?"

"On one condition."

"Which is?"

"Build a new school. Do that and I'll tutor you for free."

Virginia looked mildly surprised. "Most people would want the money."

"I'm not most people."

Silence settled as the two women assessed each other.

"You have a deal," Virginia conceded, "but I'll only provide the building."

"That's fair."

"Well, then, have Sophie's man draw up some plans. We'll start the construction in the spring, agreed?"

"Agreed."

Virginia donned her coat, then pulled on her gloves. "Oh, and I would prefer to keep this arrangement about my lessons just between us. If my competitors find out, I won't last a week."

Cara concurred. "When would you like to begin?"

"As soon as possible."

After they agreed on times and days, Virginia started toward the door. "You're a decent woman, Cara Jefferson. Thank you for hearing me out. And although I can't speak on my son's behalf, please know how sorry I was to learn about the babe. Miles is still recovering from the beating your husband gave him, which Miles deserved. Your husband loves you very much. I envy you that also."

On a blast of February wind, she departed.

Cara came to learn a lot about Virginia during the mornings they spent together. Although Virginia had been born free, she'd been sold by her mother, Simone, a blue-eyed octoroon seamstress, to a man named Ezra Sutton, a former slave on a nearby Virginia plantation.

"Ezra was in love with my mother," Virginia told Cara one March morning over coffee at the kitchen table. "Because of his status he could only see her once or twice a month, so he didn't know he was just one of many men, black and white, who paid for Simone's company. The Union Army was close, and the planters were deserting the plantations in droves. Ezra, being a head houseman and carriage driver, helped his master bury all the valuables to keep them from the Yankees."

"Did many of the planters do that?"

"Quite a few," Virginia replied. "They couldn't carry gold plate or all their jewelry on the trains North, which is where most headed, for fear of being robbed or stopped at the rail stations patrolled by Union forces."

"The planters expected these things to be there after the war?"

"Yes. They planned on coming back, digging up their plate and gold coins, and going on with their lives."

Cara simply shook her head.

"Well, after Ezra helped bury the gold, he took the master and his family to the train station to go to relatives in New York. When he returned, he waited until dark, went out, and dug up the valuables. He brought the hoard to my mother and asked her to marry him."

"What did she say?"

"She laughed in his face. Told him she didn't care if he had rediscovered King Solomon's mines. He was a dark-skinned slave and she would have nothing to do with him. She, too, was headed North, but with one of her gentlemen friends. He was also a blue-eyed octoroon, and they were going North to live out their lives as white."

It was a common story. No one knew how many fair-skinned members of their race had "passed" before and after the war. It was a phenomenon very much prevalent even these days.

"My mother hated the restrictions that forced her to live in the small free-Black section outside Richmond, and she hated even more the drops of African blood in her veins that made the restrictions enforceable by law. However, there was one thing standing in her way—me, her fourteen-year-old daughter. Her lover didn't consider me, with my brownish eyes, 'bright' enough to make the passing ruse a success. He gave my mother an ultimatum. Either get rid of me in some way or stay in Richmond."

Virginia's voice lowered. "So she gave me to Ezra in her stead. I'll never forget the humiliation of standing naked in her front parlor while she and Ezra haggled over the price. He bought me for four gold candlesticks, a diamond necklace with matching earbobs, and a brooch. My mother put on her finery, told me I belonged to Ezra, and showed us both the door."

To punish Simone for her treachery, Ezra raped Virginia as soon as he got her back to the deserted plantation, Cara learned when Virginia picked up the narrative later that week. The abuse became a horror he repeated over and over again in the years that followed. Young and uneducated, Virginia stayed with him out of sheer fear at first, but eventually grew into a thick-skinned woman who took his nightly visitations and backhanded cuffs without a word. After Miles's birth, she was determined to survive. And she had survived, long enough to see him into his grave.

"How did he die?" Cara asked.

Virginia chuckled for the first time. "Funniest thing. He'd been around animals all his life and got kicked in the head by a mule named Opal. Only creature on this earth meaner than he was. I didn't mourn at all."

Cara awakened and smiled. Virginia's lessons had been rescheduled because she'd left town on business. So today, Cara's time was her own.

Shivering from the early morning chill in the room, she pulled on a heavy robe over her nightgown and was thankful for the warmth of the red flannel ankle-length drawers beneath the gown. Donning a pair of woolen socks, she left her bedroom.

She was halfway down the hall when she stopped. She smelled coffee. Hoping she wasn't being paid a visit by some drifter, she tiptoed back into the bedroom for the rifle.

From the top of the steps, Cara had a clear view to the floor below. A man dressed all in black sat at her kitchen table, drinking coffee. He had his back to her. Cara set the rifle against the wall.

"Chase!" she screamed with joy, running down the steps. She flew into his waiting arms, and he caught her up and swung her around to his kiss. They passionately greeted each other as if the months had been years. When they finally parted, he held her tight.

"Oh, it's so good to hold you," he whispered.

Cara was hanging on to him fiercely. All the worries she'd harbored over his safety melted away, along with her loneliness. "I'm glad you're home."

And that's exactly how Chase felt, as if he'd really come home for the first time in his life. He hugged her with every fiber of his being and never wanted to leave her again. Ever.

Cara looked up into his face and smiled, so glad that he was really home. "I see you made coffee. What do you want for breakfast?"

"You." As he placed soft hot kisses over her jaw, his firm hands slowly rubbed her nightgown up and down her hips. He purred like a cat and captured her parted lips. "I dreamed about doing this . . ."

Cara backed up against the wooden table and used her arms to brace herself as he covered her throat with his kisses. He opened her robe, then the gown underneath, and slid his hands into the opening, grazing her tightened nipples, rolling them slowly between his fingers. "Oh, Chase . . ."

"Yes, darlin'. I'm home now."

His mouth replaced his fingers and she bloomed with the sweet ripples flowing from his ardent appreciation. He raised her gown and slipped his hand inside her long drawers to caress the enticing flesh of her hips. Cara nipped his ear with love-gentled teeth while he circled his hand lower to tease the warmth already flowing between her thighs. He backed up a moment and undid his belt before shucking his pants. His dark eyes alone were enough to send Cara to completion as she stared up at him. And he was ready for her she saw, glancing down. The mahogany glory of him drew her hands to stroke the velvet-covered iron. She leaned forward and kissed the brown tip, lovingly using her tongue to pleasure him as he had done to her in the past.

He drew her head up after a few torrid moments, growling as he placed her atop the kitchen table. He drew her forward to his kiss, then coaxed her to lie prone, sending the sugar bowl crashing to the floor along with his coffee cup. Neither of them cared.

Just when Cara felt on the verge of pleading, he stripped the red flannels down and off her legs and took her right there on the tabletop. She rose to kiss his mouth, his jaw, his eyes, as he filled her. He felt wonderful, powerful, male. And when he began to move, he felt like bliss to her. He worshipped her with his hands, teasing her lips, stroking himself in and out, showing her in all his many talented ways why she would never love any man but him. He increased the tempo and her hips rose in response. The sensations exploded in her body like a flare, making her gasp his name as the passion grew sharper. She stiffened as release claimed her, the shudders bringing forth her surrendering cries.

For Chase, the sight of her riding her completion, so uninhibited and responsive, broke the tenuous hold he had on his own passion and moments later he, too, surrendered with cries of his own.

When they came back to themselves, Chase kissed her lips in parting and gently withdrew from her warmth. Cara just lay there spread out on her kitchen table like an offered dessert, wondering if she would ever move again. "I will never be able to look at this table the same way again," she confessed wearily.

He chuckled and leaned down over her prone figure, "Neither will I. So you'd better get up before I order another helping of breakfast . . ."

Cara smiled and rose. "What is it with you and furniture? You know I can't write at my desk anymore? Every time I sit there, all I can think about is me, you, and the runner sliding back and forth. We ruined that runner, by the way."

"You complaining?" he asked, drawn to taste her lips once more.

"No," she whispered, kissing him back in long, humid snatches. "I just never considered furniture to be a place to make love."

"Wait, I can show you uses for furniture you never thought possible."

"I can't wait," she purred as he swung her up into his arms and set her on her feet.

"How about some real breakfast?" she asked. "Won't take long."

"If you could somehow work a bath into the offer, you got a deal."

They had a deal.

While the water heated on the stove, Cara whipped up eggs, fried potatoes, and bacon. She'd made bread yesterday, so she added a fresh-cut hunk of that to his plate and served it to him with a smile.

"Lord, I missed your cooking," he said, picking up his fork and digging in. "My men don't believe me when I tell them how you feed me. They also think I'm lying about how pretty you are."

Cara responded to the compliment with a shy smile as she filled a plate and sat down. She wondered again how she and Chase measured up against other married couples. Did other husbands make love to their wives on the kitchen table after lengthy separations? Did other wives enjoy being made love to on the kitchen table? Cara certainly had. Just looking at Chase now made her want to repeat the interlude.

"Is there more?" he asked, holding out his plate.

She nodded, and he fetched himself another large helping.

When he was done, he pushed back his plate and sighed. "Now I can sleep for a week."

He did look tired, she saw. Earlier she'd been too ecstatic at just seeing him to notice the weary eyes and the tired slump of his broad shoulders.

"After you take your bath you can sleep for as long as you like."

"That would be wonderful."

Cara stood and came over to where he sat. He looked up at her with his tired eyes and she reached out and stroked his clean-shaven face. "Welcome home, Chase."

He took her hand and turned the palm to his lips. "It's good to be home, Cara Lee."

Upstairs, she was going to show him the bedroom, but he stopped her before she could enter. "Hold it," he said. "By law, I have to carry you over the threshold."

Cara snorted and rolled her eyes, "By whose law?"

"By the Jefferson rules of marriage. Law number five says: When entering shared quarters for the first time, the male is obligated to carry the female inside."

"Law number five," Cara repeated skeptically.

"Law number five." He scooped her up. She locked her hands around his neck and smiled up into his teasing gaze.

"Law number five makes it easier to do this." He bent down to kiss her passionately.

Cara immediately saw the advantages of law number five.

"How do you like the room?" she asked from her perch in his arms. He turned her this way and that as he took a look at all she'd accomplished. There were curtains at the windows, the newly sanded floor sparkled, and the walls had been painted a soft blue.

"You did all this by yourself?"

"No. Asa helped with some of it. I finished the floor alone, though."

"You did a great job."

"Why, thank you."

He set her on her feet.

Cara looked up at him and asked the most pressing question in her mind. "How long can you stay?"

"Fourteen days, then to Fort Leavenworth. The army has some new guns they're considering buying, and Colonel Grierson wants me to take a look at them."

For Cara, two weeks of having him near seemed like a lifetime after all the time he'd been gone. She would take the two weeks and be content.

Later that morning after the fire had been stoked to warm the room and the water was hot in the tub around him, Chase lay with his head back and drank in the pleasures of coming home to a good woman. He'd ridden four days, the last two without sleep, to get to her, and it had been worth every long, cold mile. He couldn't have asked for the companionship of a woman more passionate or more playful than his Cara. He'd bragged about her so much and so often to his men, they'd had to tell him to shut up about her. Chase made them envious, they said in explanation.

In Chase's mind he had to be the most envied man in the country.

"Chase, are you asleep?" Cara asked him softly.

He opened his eyes, saw her beautiful face, and smiled, "No, darlin', just relaxing."

"Well, please don't go to sleep. There's no way I can pull you out if you do."

"Then we need to fix that."

Before Cara could blink, he'd lifted her and placed her atop him in the warm water.

"Chase!"

"Now if I go to sleep, you can sleep right here with me," he said, nuzzling her neck. "How does that sound?"

"That sounds fine," she replied, paying no attention to her now-soaked nightclothes and robe or the soggy feel of the woolen socks on her feet.

"Chase?"

"Hmm?"

"Will you do something for me?"

"Anything."

"Will you wake me the next time you leave? I don't like waking up and finding you gone."

Chase saw the seriousness in her eyes. He replayed his departures from her in his mind. "I've done that, what, three times?"

She nodded.

"I'm sorry. When I left after the first time in May, you were asleep. I barely had time to get my men geared up to leave, thanks to you," he accused with a smile.

Cara smiled shyly; that had been a particularly vivid encounter.

He continued. "In August, I wasn't even supposed to be spending the night. I was supposed to be attending to army business, not you. And I had to leave you the way I did after the first of the year—had to."

"Why?"

"I'd've spent the winter here if I hadn't. Army calls that desertion, you know."

"You're not serious."

"Yes, I am. Your cooking by itself is enough to make me go over the wall. Throw in this lovely little body and it isn't so hard to imagine."

Cara didn't know what to think or what to say.

"But I had no idea I was hurting you, leaving that way. I'm sorry."

Cara knew then and there that he was a very special man. His allusions to how her presence affected him made her feel as if maybe she'd already won her quest for a place in his heart. He reached out and touched his finger to the crescent-shaped scar above her brow. She went very still. He traced its shape for a moment, his eyes serious.

"Are the memories bad when I touch this?"

Held by his power, she shook her head no. His touch, so potent, sent all thoughts of sadness and pain very very far away.

Chase's vow to keep her safe flared as he moved closer to brush his mouth across the pale sliver. He wanted to transform the spot; kiss it, heal it until it became a reminder of his passion for her. When she looked at the scar in the mirror, he didn't want her to think of Sutton, or horses, or how close she'd come to dying. He wanted her to be reminded of the feel of his lips upon it and how it had led to them making love the night or moment before. If he could have his wish, the sight of it would bring sensual memories, not sadness. "I should have killed him the first time he put his hands on you."

Cara could sense the shadows rising between them. "Chase, none of what happened was your fault. Can we not talk about him?"

He assessed her a moment, then acquiesced with a slight nod. "What do you want to talk about?"

She relaxed again. "Did you get my letters?"

"I got two. Did you get mine?"

"No."

He looked surprised. "Are you saying you didn't get the bank drafts I sent?"

"The drafts I received fine. I never received any letters."

"Cara, the letters were with the drafts."

Confused, she tried to sort out the mystery. In her mind, she replayed how'd she'd opened the envelopes and removed the contents. There'd been the draft and—narrowing her eyes she punched him in the shoulder, "That was your letter? 'Dear Cara, use the draft for whatever you need. Chase.' You call that a letter? I've seen telegrams with more words. Chase Jefferson, you should be ashamed of yourself."

But she was laughing and so was he. "I tried, Lord knows I did, but every time I tried to put words to what I wanted to say . . . Cara Lee, you have no idea how you make me feel. There are no words."

He stroked her bottom lip, then tilted her face up for his kiss. As it moved over her, lighting fires as it deepened, she thought the kiss was worth more than a thousand letters.

He ran a wandering palm over the point of one breast through her dampened gown, and when the bud hardened shamelessly and he could see the unbridled passion flaring like ripples across her face, asked, "Did you miss me?"

Cara's eyes slid closed as heat and fire took hold. "Terribly."

"I missed you, too, schoolmarm," he confessed, slowly reclaiming her lips. "Terribly."

They ignored the cooling water in the tub and came together, hands exploring, soft sounds echoing, taking their time to enjoy the feast of passion. They'd each dreamed of moments such as these over the last two months, and for the next fourteen days they had all the time two lovers would ever need.

Plying her mouth with his kisses, filling his hands with her breasts, Chase began to undo the soggy buttons centering her gown. The fabric, too drenched to enable him to conquer the buttons with ease, caused him to pull away from the honey of her lips.

"You're overdressed."

When he had the gown unfastened to her navel, the clinging cotton sticking to her lush lines, he toured a big hand inside over her damp skin, then pulled her closer until she knelt between his open knees.

With a slowness that only intensified Cara's anticipation, he removed the gown from one shoulder and then, after a soft kiss on her parted lips, the other. He worked it down until it hung at her waist, leaving her bare to his brilliant gaze. "Stand for me, darlin' . . . then hold up your gown."

Cara did and trembled as his hands pulled her long drawers down her legs. She lifted one leg, bracing herself on his strong arm so he could free her of them and the socks. He tossed them onto the floor.

"Now just stand here a minute . . ."

Chase ran his hand over the soft damp hair crowning her thighs, and his manhood pulsed sharply as he watched her respond. She was naked but for the held-aside gown and he pleasured her lustily, tenderly, erotically, making her moan beneath his fingers, and then he brought her forward to the heated delving of his mouth and tongue.

"Now . . . you can come back down here."

Cara did not trust her legs to obey his invitation. She was swollen with her desire for him, and his fingers hadn't stopped. They were slyly stroking the burning center of her world, coaxing her to the very edge of her control. "I can't sit if you won't stop . . ."

"Me? What am I doing?"

He brought her forward and flicked his tongue over her navel, then backed away. "Are you going to sit, Cara Lee Jefferson?"

He'd taken his hands from her, but that did not stop her spiralling senses or lift the haze from her mind. The throbbing between her legs seemed to pulse from every cell of her body.

While he smiled at her like a pleased potentate, she went back down on her knees between the vee of his legs. "You are too talented for your own good, Chase Jefferson."

"I know a schoolmarm who tells me that all the time . . ."

In the long silent moments that followed, they lost themselves in the pleasure of each other, kissing, stroking, seducing. Chase thought he would die when her hand lowered to settle warmly around his straining prize, and Cara thought the same as his hand below the waterline increased her throbbing need.

They paid scant attention to the sloshing water and even less to the now tepid temperature. Desire leaped another notch, caresses became wanton, intense.

Somewhere in the distance, Cara heard a voice and footsteps. Her mind dulled by the drug of passion took a few seconds to clear so she could speak. "Chase, someone's in the house."

"I know, darlin'," he answered thickly. "Just hold still."

The bold play of his hands beneath the water, the wicked flirting of his tongue and her own need to devour him in return, kept her out of focus. "What are you going to do?"

"Besides this?"

Cara bit her lip to keep her moans from spilling out into the hallway.

"I'll take care of them . . . whoever it is . . ."

With one hand he fed himself the dark-nippled confection of her breast, while the other hand reached behind him to extricate his Colt from beneath his clothes folded on the chair by the tub.

He worked a trail of magic back up to her lips, claimed them possessively, and pointed the big gun toward the door.

When the door opened slowly, Cara, shielded behind Chase's big body in the tub, tried to make herself smaller.

But her eyes widened as William Boyd, of all people, stepped inside. "William?"

He blinked. "Cara?"

She forgot herself and would have left the tub had Chase not pressed her back. "Where the hell are you going?" he asked.

Her state of undress immediately came to mind, and she slunk back down. "Sorry," she whispered. But William? Here?

"Now let's start over," Chase said harshly. "You are?"

"Uh, Cara's friend. William Boyd."

Cara could see that the sight of her angry husband and the dangerous-looking long-nosed gun in his hand were making William more than a bit nervous. She sought to smooth the waters. "Chase, this is my friend William from New York. William, this is my husband, Chase Jefferson."

William seemed to swallow nervously. "Pl-pleased to meet you."

Chase offered no such pleasantries in return. "You always walk into a bedroom unannounced?"

"Chase!"

"Uh, no," William said hastily. "You see, I just got into town and the man at the mercantile said Cara lived here, and, well—the door was unlocked. I called from downstairs. No one answered . . ."

William looked as if he couldn't decide which scared him most: the gaping bore of the firearm or the wintry scrutiny and large physique of the man pointing it his way.

"Back out of the door," Chase instructed.

When William made the mistake of looking to Cara for verification, the loud click of the Colt's hammer immediately sent his attention back to Chase, who warned quietly, "Keep your eyes off my wife and do as I asked."

Cara could feel the tenseness in her husband's back and prayed William wouldn't argue. Dragging her gown tighter, she urged, "Wait downstairs, William, please?"

Cara and William greeted each other with hugs. "It's so good to see you," Cara told him.

"It's good to see you, too, Cara Lee. Sorry about walking in on you and your husband like that."

"I know it wasn't intentional. Come on in here and sit."

They sat at her kitchen table, sharing grins.

"It is real good seeing you, girl," William spoke again. "Real good."

The sincerity in his voice touched her, bringing back a familiar warmth reserved only for him. He was her closest friend, and seeing him now after so many years filled her with a special kind of joy. "So what brings you out here? Are you still working for Mr. Fortune's *Globe?*"

"Yep. I'm here to do a feature on Floral Hall."

"Floral Hall's in Topeka, city boy. You missed it by about two hundred and forty miles." Cara couldn't resist teasing him.

He laughed at the old endearment. "I've been to Topeka. I'm interviewing 'dusters in the area."

"Really?" Cara told him about her experiences at Floral Hall, and gave him the names of people in town he should seek out. She made a special mention of the Three Spinsters, then added, "I met my husband at Floral Hall."

"The big man upstairs?"

"The big man upstairs. I hope he didn't scare you too badly."

"No, not *too* badly. A lot badly."

They laughed.

"When I saw that gun, well—we city boys don't encounter guns like that much back East. All I could think was that I was about to be shot for looking in on an old friend."

"I don't think he would really have shot you."

"You weren't facing him, Cara. He looked like an angry African sea deity protecting his queen."

Cara laughed at his description. "William, I don't think African sea deities carry forty-fives."

"Yours does. How come you never wrote me about him?"

"We got married a bit suddenly, last November."

They shared a look.

"And that's all you're going to tell me."

She nodded. "It started out real complicated, William, but I think we have things sorted out now."

"Tell me this, and I won't pry any further: Do you love him?"

She'd never lied to him. "Yes, I do, very much."

"Well, he seems to love you, too, very much."

"How can you tell?"

"By the way he ordered my eyes off his wife. He wasn't laughing at the time. He loves you pretty fiercely, in my opinion."

"Fiercely?"

"Fiercely."

Cara made some fresh coffee, and while they waited for it to brew, talked about a myriad of subjects. All the while, she tried not to stare at the changes time had wrought in this special friend. The tall, reed-thin young man-child she'd known years ago, now towered over her by at least a foot. He'd grown into a strikingly handsome man. His caramel-skinned good looks and jet-black wavy hair reminded her in a small way of Miles Sutton. However, William had none of the spoiled boyish lines so prominent in Miles's face, and one had only to look into her friend's eyes to see the kindness Miles lacked.

"Are you heading back soon?"

"Not for a while. I'm due in Denver day after tomorrow. I'm also supposed to look into some other things while I'm out this way. What do you know about Oklahoma?"

"The usual things: Indian Territory, Boomers, Payne. I know the government is talking of opening the land to settlers, but other than that? Chase is the one to talk with about Oklahoma. He and his men were stationed there last summer."

At first, William didn't understand. "Stationed there?" His brain finally made sense of what she'd said and he asked wondrously, "Your husband's a soldier?"

Cara nodded. "With the Tenth—"

"The Tenth? Why, they're the most decorated—Cara, go get him. Mr. Fortune will have my hide if he finds out I met a buffalo soldier and didn't get a story. There are rumors floating around about the government making the territory a Black state. Do you think he's heard anything concerning that?"

Cara had heard the rumors before; no one in the plains set much stock by them, however.

"People back East don't really believe that, do they?"

"Some do, some don't. The Missouri, Kansas, and Texas Railroad Company is supposedly behind the push. A contingent of A.M.E. ministers met with the Congress last spring to ask the government to do for them what they wouldn't do for Payne and the Boomers."

"They aren't going to give the Territory to any colored people. Can you imagine what kind of fit the rest of the country would throw?"

"It could happen, Cara. At this late date, the railroads don't care who the settlers are. Their chief concerns are laying track and charging freight. They can't expand without people, and evidently they don't envision much profit in having only Indians as passengers. Go and get your husband, please."

Cara had no idea whether Chase would consent to being interviewed, but she excused herself and went up to see.

Chase had intended to get dressed and go downstairs, but had made the mistake of sitting down on the bed. The soft mattress offered a seductive invitation to lie back. The bed seemed to sense he hadn't slept in two days and further beckoned him to savor stretching out on something other than a hard bunk or the damp, cold ground. He closed his eyes. Two beats later, sleep swept him away.

Cara found him asleep, sprawled naked across the bed, snoring as loud as a locomotive. The sight brought forth a soft smile. Careful not to cause a break in the resonating yet rhythmic snores, she covered him gently with the quilt. Then, unable to resist, she bent to place a whispered kiss on his brow, and slipped out.

Downstairs, William plainly showed his disappointment. "Look, I'm sorry if I'm making an ass of myself over this, but being able to meet a buffalo soldier is indescribable."

"You're as bad as the children. You should have seen them the first time they met him." And she thought to herself, Hell you should've seen *me.*

"Well, he is quite impressive," William allowed. Remembering the gun, he added, "Very impressive."

They spent a few more minutes talking and then William had to leave, but promised to return the next day.

While Chase snored on upstairs, the day slid into night. Telling herself the man was full-grown and therefore did not need to be checked on every fifteen minutes, Cara instead sat down to write letters soliciting donations for the new school.

When the clock struck midnight, Cara pushed her chair back from the kitchen table and stood, stretching once more. She doused the lamp in the center of the table, then walked over to the one she'd left lit in the adjoining front room. A tiptoe reach lowered it from the niche in the wall so she could carry it to light the way through the darkness and up the stairs.

Halfway up the staircases, she heard a polite "Excuse me" come from a voice below. It startled her so badly, she almost dropped the lamp.

A man stood in the shadows below. "Who are you!?" she asked in a panicked voice, almost tripping as her foot blindly searched for the next step.

"A friend. Is my brother here?"

His brother? Cara wondered if she could run to the rifle in her room before the man pounced.

"May I light the lamp again?" he asked.

Her mind darted to Chase. Trust him to be sleeping like the dead while she stood there terrified by Lord-only-knew-who.

But the man hadn't made any threatening gestures yet. Maybe lighting the lamp would show him he'd come to the wrong house; later she'd deal with how he'd gotten in here in the first place.

Knowing this could be the worst mistake she'd ever made in her life, Cara instructed shakily, "Go ahead."

He stepped out of her line of vision, and a moment later the first floor once again glowed with soft light.

"I trust this will be better," he said, coming back to the foot of the steps. Cara could see him clearly now. His dress, though shabby, differed none from that of the other men in the area. The thick coat, trousers, and large, weather-beaten hat that threw shadows across his face were damp with moisture from the rain outside.

He slowly removed the hat, and Cara stared in amazement at the black waterfall of hair cascading past his shoulders. "You're an Indian!" she gushed stupidly.

"No kidding."

And he spoke perfect English! He also had the nerve to be a handsome Indian, Cara thought needlessly, still struggling with fright and wonder.

"I think you've made a mistake. No Indians live here."

Smiling, he contradicted, "No mistake, little sister." Cara bet that smile of his left maidens weak wherever he went.

"You are Cara Jefferson, am I correct?"

Cara nodded horselike in reply, but did not understand, then a small memory came back. The day Chase came to her classroom he'd mentioned— "You're Dreamer of Eagles." Good Lord, she had a Sioux brave standing in her front room.

"You know of me," he stated in pleased tones.

"You gave Chase his *siyotanka.*"

"Ah, the army dog has played the flute for you."

Army dog? "Yes, I mean, no, he played it for my students."

"The gift of the *wagnuka* is not for children. If he played the love flute, it was for you."

"Chase is asleep. I'll see if I can wake him."

"No, don't bother. Tomorrow is soon enough. I'll bed down outside if that's suitable?"

Cara couldn't very well ask him to leave; Chase would skin her alive if she turned his brother out. "Do you need blankets, bedding? There is an extra bedroom up here, and you're welcome to it."

He went silent for a moment, and Cara felt that dark gaze of his scan her before he asked seriously, "You mean that, don't you?"

"Yes."

"Even though you're probably terrified I'll scalp you in the night, you agree to let an Indian you've never seen sleep upstairs in your spare bedroom?"

Cara didn't move. No one deserved to sleep outside.

"Well, don't worry, little sister. You, I'd never scalp. I may risk my brother's wrath and steal you, but scalp you? Never."

Shaken, Cara gave him directions to the room and bid a hasty good night.

The Indian's last remarks, serious or not, ruled out any thought Cara had entertained of sleeping alone. Shoving at Chase's broad brown back, she whispered, "Move over."

He was still sprawled over much of the bed's surface, and despite the wood she'd added to the fireplace, the room was freezing. "Chase, wake up. I want to sleep, too."

Finally, the dragon rippled and came to life. "Hello."

His sleepy smile made her heart puddle into her knees. "Hello yourself. Move over."

He mumbled something, then slid over to the side closer to the door.

Cara burrowed under the covers, shivering. Beneath her the sheets still held his heat, and she slid around, basking in it, thinking he could warm her bed anytime.

"Chase?"

"Mmm . . ."

"Dreamer of Eagles is here."

In the firelit darkness, Cara waited for some type of reaction. It came in the form of one long arm pulling her close until their bodies nested together like spoons.

"That's better," he affirmed with a sluggish whisper. His manhood against her hip didn't seem sluggish at all.

"He said he might steal me, Chase."

Silence.

"Chase?" She turned over until she could see his face in the light from the roaring fire. "He wants to steal me, did you hear?"

"Don't worry. After he finds out you talk all night, he'll give you right back."

Twisting around, she tried to put distance between them, but the heavy arm around her waist held.

"Settle down," he warned, "or I'll think you're trying to keep me awake for some other reason. As you can tell, I'm more than up to the challenge. In fact . . ."

"I'll be quiet," she promised quickly, feeling his hands begin to explore.

"No, you won't, you're never quiet."

She stiffened and he chuckled against her hair. "You're so easy to tease, I just can't resist sometimes. Go to sleep Cara Lee. We'll fight in the morning."

A second later, his snoring resumed.

Chapter 14

Cara had awakened to her husband's lovemaking, Dreamer's pounding on the bedroom door, and William's noisy arrival out front. The only saving grace of the morning was that Chase had taken over, ordered her to dress at her leisure, and rushed from the room. He'd even organized their guests to help him cook breakfast.

Now, washing up, Cara listened to the men discuss a wanted poster that William had brought.

"Cara," Chase said, "please come take a look at this."

Drying her hands on her apron, Cara walked over and stood beside her husband to get a look. The man pictured in the drawing was dressed as a member of the clergy.

"William brought this with him from back East. The man's wanted for gulling a bunch of folks. Posed as a representative of one of the big colonization societies."

"It's a pretty common dupe back East," William explained. "A man like this one will come to a small town pretending to be a member of a society. Once he convinces the people he can gain them a berth on the next boat to Liberia or wherever they want to go, he takes their money for passage and disappears. Few of these swindlers are ever caught, but this one bilked an unusually large number of people, and Mr. Fortune wants him found. *Globe* agents all over the country are showing his picture around."

"Look at the picture closely, Cara," Chase prompted. 'Recognize him?"

The thin-faced man had light skin, wore glasses, and sported a beard and mustache. "Nope. I've never seen him before." She turned to William. "What happened to the people?"

"Thinking the representative to be legitimate, they sold valuables our friend had not already taken for their passage, then they came to New York or Maryland to board the ships. Since no arrangements had been made, whole families wound up on the docks penniless. Only a small percentage had enough funds to return home. Others had given him the deeds to their land as collateral and had no home to return to. The benevolent societies were able to help a few, but when the numbers were overwhelming, people were forced to fend for themselves."

Cara looked at the poster again. With all the horror and stumbling blocks inflicted on the race, she could only feel contempt for someone getting fat by ruining his own people. Like Mr. Fortune, she wanted him caught. "I really wish I could help, but I don't recognize him."

Chase glanced up at her. "Take another look, but this time try to imagine him without the beard and eyeglasses."

Moments later her eyes widened in recognition. "Miles Sutton!"

"I think so." Chase said. "Especially since William said the swindled folks he interviewed described the man as having light gray eyes."

Cara picked up the broadside and viewed it again carefully.

"Granted, it's only a drawing," Chase pointed out, "but take a look at this . . ."

William shoved another likeness across the table. "We had one of our artists do just as Chase suggested to you a moment ago."

Cara studied the "new" face.

"Damn close, don't you think?" Chase asked.

She agreed, damn close. "I have to sit down," she confessed, overwhelmed by the implications. Without a thought, she sank onto Chase's broad lap. Had Miles really swindled all those people? The description fit, but there were gray-eyed, light-skinned Black men all over the country. Yet something inside told her he had. Call it woman's intuition, but Cara knew Miles was guilty.

From the other side of the table, William asked, "Do you really think this Sutton could be the man the authorities are looking for? Because if there's even the remotest chance, I need to wire New York."

"William, this definitely could be Miles Sutton," Cara said. She wondered if Virginia was aware of any of this. "And from what I've heard, he did come out here from back East, not South." She turned to her husband. "Have you spoken to Virginia?"

"Not yet because Dreamer and I think he's involved in something else."

"Wait," Cara said, putting up a halting hand. She turned her attention to the Lakota. "How do you fit into this?"

He told her and William the story he'd told Chase last winter about the vaccine on the ambushed gold coach. Cara then thought of something. "Chase, remember the night of the dinner last spring when those two gamblers came in looking for Miles?"

Chase nodded. "Yes. They said he owed him money"

"And they kept referring to Miles as Reverend. Do you think that's why—and when—these robberies started?"

"We can certainly go back to the banks and have them check the dates of the first few robberies and see if your theory fits."

"And he made a lot of improvements on the Lady last summer. I wonder if robbing those coaches is how he got the money to do all those repairs." Another shocking memory surfaced. "Oh, dear. He gave me money for the school expansion fund. Do you think it was part of the stolen loot?"

"Probably," Chase said.

"Well, I hope the banks won't want it back. I spent it all."

Chase chuckled. "I'll talk to Colonel Grierson."

"Did the Army know about these ambushed coaches, Chase?" William asked.

"Yes. The banks seemed to think someone had gotten hold of their schedule because the gang seemed to know which coaches to hit and the routes they were taking. So they asked us to look into the matter."

"But how would Sutton have gotten access to that information?" Dreamer asked.

Chase shrugged. "If we can answer that, we'll have the last piece of this puzzle."

"Did your people ever get their medicine?" Cara asked Dreamer.

"Eventually," he replied, "though not in time to save my sister's youngest son."

Chase looked up in shock. Dreamer had not mentioned this loss before now.

"Miles Sutton has much to account for," the brave finished quietly.

"What happened after you saw the ambush?" William asked.

The question seemed to lighten the Indian's mood because he smiled wryly. "I figured the information on the men might be valuable to someone and Chase came to mind. I knew the Tenth was in the Oklahoma territories last summer so I wrote. My letter came back with a note from one of his men. It seemed Mr. Army here had gotten himself sent back to Texas."

Chase glared across the table. "Is there anything you don't know?"

Dreamer simply smiled.

In answer to Cara's puzzled gaze, Chase explained. "The troops had a confrontation with some of Payne's Boomers who were squatting on Indian land. When the Boomers started gathering to voice their disapproval with the soldiers' orders, our new fresh-from-West-Point lieutenant got scared and ordered the men to open fire on the Boomers. Everybody in camp knew the college boy didn't know his ass from a prairie dog hole, so the troops looked to me and the other sergeants for confirmation of this order to fire. We shook our heads no, and they drew down their guns."

"How many Boomers were there?" William asked.

"Close to nine hundred."

"Nine hundred?" Cara echoed. "How many men did you have?"

"Not nearly enough. Had the men obeyed the order, more than likely we'd've been slaughtered."

"What did the lieutenant do?"

"Calmed down mostly. After that, probably to save face, he sent me back to Davis. Said he didn't need anyone from the Tenth undermining his command."

"I think you did the right thing," Cara defended. "He could have caused a bloodbath."

Chase met his wife's fired-up gaze and replied softly, "Why, thank you, Mrs. Jefferson."

"You're welcome." She saucily inclined her head.

The silent interplay was not lost on the table's other occupants. Dreamer broke in by grumbling, "Army dog, you do not deserve such a woman."

Chase smiled. "You're just mad because I found her first. She's not blind, either, I hope you notice."

Blind, Cara thought, bewildered.

"My offer still stands," the Indian replied cryptically.

"I don't want your ponies."

"I'll give you thirty of the finest this side of the Mississippi."

"No."

"Forty."

"You are serious, aren't you?" Chase answered with amusement.

"She'll have fine sons."

"That she will, but they'll be *my* sons."

"Would you two stop it? I'm not some deaf brood mare."

"She has great spirit."

"Great spirit," Chase acknowledged.

Cara had to look away lest she be burned by the heat in her husband's eyes.

William said, "I think you gentlemen should continue the story. How'd you find out Sutton's identity?"

"After the robbers divided the gold," Dreamer resumed, "they took their shares and separated. I followed one of them to a town on the Colorado border. I caught him coming out of a saloon one night and he happily volunteered the information I needed."

Writing furiously the whole time, William stopped and looked up, confused. "He just gave you Sutton's name?"

Chase interjected with dry amusement, "A person with a knife at your throat inspires you to be talkative."

William nodded and smiled.

Dreamer continued with a gleam in his eye. "I eventually traced Sutton here."

"Did you confront him with what you knew?"

Dreamer chuckled. "Nope, I couldn't. When I found him, he was about a raven's wing away from being beaten to death by one of the Tenth's finest." His tone became serious. "That's the night I learned about what Sutton had done to you, little sister."

A confused William looked to Cara. "What's he mean?"

In the ensuing silence, the sure comfort of Chase's hand rubbing softly at the tension in her back helped ease the painful memories of that time. In a quiet yet clear voice, Cara told William the story.

When she finished, William cursed softly, adding, "An even greater reason to find this bastard. God, I'm sorry, Cara."

"Thank you, William."

Chase's mildly quelling look from across the table said, Let the matter drop. William complied, but Cara knew William; after he'd heard about the tragedy, his desire for justice would be burning with a personal light.

Cara directed her next question to the handsome Lakota. "Did you burn down his saloon that night?"

Dreamer's smile did not reach his eyes. "At the time, it seemed a fit ending to the revenge my brother was exacting."

"But, Chase, you said you didn't know who torched the Lady that night," Cara reminded her husband.

"I truthfully did not know the night you asked. My Lakota brother didn't offer that bit of information until just now."

"I counted coup," Dreamer explained nonchalantly. "Besides, I knew I could always return and kill him later."

William looked from the Indian to the soldier in surprise. Neither man seemed the least apologetic.

The talk then moved back to the matter of apprehending Sutton. Chase hoped the banks, Colonel Grierson, and the mighty resources of Mr. Fortune's *Globe* would combine forces and there'd be a lot of people standing in line to get a piece of Sutton's hide.

"Has Sutton been seen?" Dreamer asked Chase.

"Sheriff Polk said he's been holed up somewhere outside Nicodemus since right after his place burned down, but nobody's seen him lately."

"Think he'd come back and try and hurt Cara again?" William's expression clearly showed the concern he was feeling.

"Not unless he wants to die," Chase promised.

"Very slowly," Dreamer added.

They all talked for a few moments longer, then decided a visit to Sheriff Polk would be the best next move. William began to gather up his notes, pens, and ink. Chase gave Cara a pat on the hip and she stood. "You coming?" he asked Dreamer.

"Nope. Now that I've done most of the real work, I feel safe leaving the rest to you."

Chase replied with a sarcastic "Thank you."

"Besides," the Lakota replied, "watching you makes me miss my wife."

"Good," Chase retorted. "I hope she's put pine needles in your bed mat by now."

"Such a kind brother." Dreamer turned to Cara. "If you ever tire of this army dog, remember me."

Cara chuckled. "But you just said you have a wife."

"I do, but it's not uncommon among my people to have more than one."

"No, thank you," Cara said, smiling. "I don't think I'd make a very good second wife. I don't like sharing."

The look she turned on her husband held just enough wantonness in it to make Chase dearly wish he could put off going into town.

Watching him, a grinning Dreamer of Eagles said, "You need to step outside."

"I think you're right," Chase confessed.

While Cara and William said goodbye, the two other men went out to saddle their horses.

"You'd better write me," Cara fussed as she and William strolled slowly out to the porch. Tomorrow he'd be catching the train to Denver.

"I will, and you do the same, and please, be careful. This Sutton sounds like he could be very dangerous."

"Who taught you to shoot a rifle, William?"

"You did, Cara, but you also have a tendency—"

"William, do you see that man sitting out there on horseback?"

He turned to view the waiting Chase. "I do."

"Then stop worrying. Sutton may be dangerous, but he's not stupid. I will be careful, though, I promise," she finished earnestly. She stood on tiptoe to place a kiss on his cheek. "That's to keep you safe."

Astride Carolina, a slightly impatient Chase viewed the chaste kiss and loudly cleared his throat, but Cara ignored him. She pulled her shawl tighter against the cold and kept talking to William.

"A little green around the eyes, are we?" Dreamer asked. When Chase refused to rise to the bait, the Lakota, also astride his horse and waiting, leaned around to look into his face. What he saw was a man not pleased. "That bad, huh?"

"That bad."

"Well, if it's any consolation, she does love you. She loves him, too, but in a different way."

"Doesn't help."

The Sioux smiled. "He's got what, five or six years of knowing her on you?"

"About that."

"What do you expect her to do, act like he's a stranger?"

"Maybe."

Dreamer shook his head. "You do have it bad."

"I already said that."

"Have you told her?"

Chase swung around in the saddle to glare at him. "What is this? You're as nosy as an old woman. Weren't you leaving?"

"I take that as a no."

Chase turned back around and refused to speak.

"Well, you should. Saying those three little words can work miracles, believe me."

"This," Chase remarked, still watching the scene on the porch, "from a man who used to count women like coup. Aren't you the same one who had a pot of stew dumped on his head because you went to see She Who Sings in a courting robe that had figures of your other conquests on it?"

Smiling, Dreamer could only nod in agreement. Like Cara, his wife, She Who Sings, also possessed great spirit.

"Well, advice notwithstanding, I do want to thank you for your help with this Sutton mess," Chase confessed honestly. "I couldn't have done it without you. If we get a chance, we'll come up for a visit in the summer."

"If your government hasn't massacred us all by then, you know you and Cara will be more than welcome."

Chase, not proud of the army's role in the government's ongoing destruction of the Indian way of life, thought the Sioux's bittersweet assessment justified.

The men rode off soon after: Chase and William to town, Dreamer of Eagles north to She Who Sings and their home near Pine Ridge.

When they were out of sight, Cara hurriedly reentered the house and closed the door on the wind and cold. The silence that greeted her, once a friend and comfort during the months she'd lived alone, now seemed alien, almost sad in the wake of the activities and voices of the last two days. She could look over at the kitchen table now and see Chase standing there. The memory of a Sioux brave at the foot of the staircase referring to Chase as an "army dog" would remain, as would the look on William's face when he walked unannounced into the bedroom upstairs.

As she hung up her shawl on the peg by the door, something else came to mind, self-possessed loner or not, she missed people: Sophie, Asa, the Three Spinsters, her students. She missed the children's squabbles, the comings and goings. Admittedly, Virginia's twice-a-week tutoring sessions did much to break up the solitude, as did the occasional stop-bys of Sophie and the Reverend Whitfield's wife, Sybil. But only now, with the presence of the men still hovering in the room like ghosts, did she come to grips with how terribly lonely she'd really been.

"Cara?"

"Up here, Chase."

After removing his hat and gloves and placing them on the shelf by the door, he hung his coat on the same peg that held her blue shawl, then climbed the stairs. He'd spent a lot longer time in town than planned; night had fallen hours ago. The information on Miles Sutton had been wired to Colonel Grierson at Fort Davis and to Mr. Fortune's offices at the *New York Globe*. In reply, both men expressed pleasure with the progress and pledged to start investigating on their ends. Colonel Grierson also indicated that he'd relayed the findings to the U.S. marshal's office in Wichita. The colonel requested Chase wait for their further instructions.

The marshal's office wired back three hours later: Miles Sutton was now wanted for questioning by the U.S. marshal's office. All the law enforcement officers in the area were asked to assist in his immediate apprehension.

Chase had come upstairs with the intention of telling Cara the good news, and to apologize for the long delay in returning, but when he reached the open door of the bedroom, it became plain his wife had intentions of her own.

The sight of her standing by the fireplace left him speechless.

"William ready to go tomorrow?" she asked.

Chase couldn't decide which made his blood roar louder: the sultry look in her eyes, or that absolutely wicked nightgown she had on. It was the color of cream and had two thin straps bisecting her shoulders. The bodice, cut low, barely covered the dark crown of her nipples. Between her breasts were two tiny ribbons just waiting for him to untie.

Chase thought he nodded yes in reply to her question about William, but he couldn't be sure. Behind her, the blaze in the fireplace crackled and spit, filling the room with a rosy glow and a skin-stroking warmth. A mesmerized Chase reached back and closed the door.

She stepped away from the grate and slowly began to close the distance between them. Her unbound hair flowed around her face and down her back. Watching her continue to come closer, he saw with amazed delight that the front of the gown was split from just below the ribbons beneath her breasts to the floor. As she walked, the lace-edged opening undulated and parted, arousing him with teasing glimpses of the bare brown legs beneath.

Any shyness Cara might have harbored over wearing this particular gown vanished before the desire dancing in her husband's eyes. Knowing she had the ability to elicit such a response filled her with a sensuous power, a power that gave her the confidence to approach him as she'd never done in the past.

When only inches separated her bare toes from the tips of his boots, Cara stopped, reached up, and began to undo the buttons of his shirt. If he noticed her shaking hands, he didn't comment.

Chase did notice but was too fascinated to care. "You're awfully forward this evening, Mrs. Jefferson."

The remark made heat rise in her face, but she didn't speak. Instead, with the last shirt button above his belt undone, she turned her attentions to the worn leather belt circling his waist. She'd never undressed a man in her life, and it showed as she tried to work the belt free from the denim trousers.

"Here," he told her, "let me, otherwise we might be at this all night."

Very late in the morning Chase awakened first. The sunlight mingled with the colors of the bedding, splashing it with patches of brightness. Careful not to jostle the small, quilt-covered form at his side, he left the bed and padded naked over to the dying fire. The chill made goose bumps rise on his skin, but he paid them little mind. He'd experienced colder mornings on the trail.

He placed some kindling on the faint embers. After a few stabs with the poker, it caught nicely. Chase used the same slow care reentering the bed, sliding beneath the sheets and quilts noiselessly, but instead of lying down again, he sat up, back against the headboard, to await Cara's awakening.

He thought back on another time when he'd watched her sleep; she'd been at death's door, and he'd been far too worried about her dying on him to derive any pleasure from the sight. But this morning, watching her filled him with a peace he'd never experienced. It seemed natural, right to wake up with her near. Her measured breathing barely ruffled the silence, quite unlike any army morning when one could count on the noisy chaos of men and beasts to start the day. This quiet she wrapped herself in might take some getting used to, but he thought he could learn to like it.

Cara stirred, as if sensing his thoughts. Her eyes opened and found his, and her sleepy smile garnered one in return. Not ready to face the day just yet, she burrowed back into her quilt cocoon and tried to drift back to sleep.

"Wake up, *mariposa*. Sun's up."

She murmured something unintelligible but didn't surface.

"Come on, Cara Lee, I've been waiting for you for a while."

Fighting off the lure of sleep, she struggled to a sitting position, pulling the quilts up against the chill, and rubbed her eyes. "Why've you been waiting for me?"

She appeared so tousled and vulnerable, he was half tempted to say something like, he wanted her to wake up because her snoring kept shaking the bed, but he didn't. He had the rest of their lives to tease her; he might have only one chance to tell her the thoughts in his heart at this moment.

His silence puzzled her, and she turned to get a clear view of his face. "Chase?"

"You know, I've very rarely seen you wake up."

"I'm a fright, aren't I?" She smiled, running a hand over her wild riot of hair. After Chase's loving last night, braiding it for sleep had been the last thing on her mind. "Surely you haven't been waiting just so you could see what I look like when I wake up?"

"Well, that, too, but mainly I waited so you'd wake up and know I didn't leave you last night."

For Chase, the idea that this woman professed to love him continued both to amaze and to humble him. In tribute to that trust, he'd vowed last night, holding her as she slept, that she would never find him lacking.

Cara reached up and put her hand against his unshaven cheek, once again moved by his sincerity. "You know something, Sergeant?"

He moved the palm across his cheek, then kissed the quilt-warmed center. "No, schoolmarm, what?"

"Beneath all that army crust and arrogance you have a very soft heart."

"I know. Don't tell anyone."

"I won't."

On that note, Mr. and Mrs. Jefferson began the day.

Chapter 15

Chase stayed three weeks instead of two. Admittedly, he spent the better part of each day scouting the area for signs of Miles Sutton, who seemed to have vanished into thin air, but nights and evenings he spent with Cara.

The time passed quickly, and on the night before he was scheduled to leave, they made love again in front of the fire. The poignant, furiously tender farewell left them both sated, but no less sad at the prospect of another separation. He had no idea how long he would be gone, but the next morning, after they shared a lingering, parting kiss at the door, Chase promised to return as soon as he possibly could.

Watching him ride out, Cara waited until he disappeared into the crimson dawn before she let the tears roll down her cheeks.

In mid-April, three weeks after Chase's departure, Sophie and Asa rode out to check on her. When Cara opened the door, surprised and very glad to see them, she nonetheless admonished them for venturing out on such a potentially stormy day. The dark gray sky, fat with ominous clouds, threatened to send down buckets at any moment.

Sophie thrust a package into Cara's hands. It was wrapped in brown paper, and Cara studied it while Sophie and Asa removed their coats.

"Open it," Sophie advised.

Cara could only stare in wonder at the sender's writing. "It's from Chase!"

Asa and Sophie smiled at each other.

Cara hurried into the kitchen for her sewing basket. Her scissors cut through the twine and layers of paper easily. With shaking hands, she peeled away the outside wrappings and lifted out the small note which read: "Because I knew you would enjoy these more than anything else. Chase."

"Are those newspapers?" Sophie asked.

Cara was choked up. "Yes, they are." Chase knew of her keen interest in the state of the country; during his most recent stay, they'd spent many evenings discussing the political situation. He also knew she incorporated news events into her lesson plans.

There were only three, and from the looks of them, all had been well read, but they were no more than four months old, and they had been sent by her husband. She couldn't have asked for a more precious gift.

"If I sent you newspapers, would you get all misty-eyed like this one here?" Asa asked Sophie.

"Not a chance," she replied.

Cara's predictions on the weather proved accurate. A little over an hour after she exchanged farewell hugs with Sophie and Asa, it poured and poured. She knew from experience that a rain this fierce would turn the outlying roads and the streets in town into impassable quagmires, so she hoped they'd made it back safely.

It didn't take long for the force of the deluge to cause leaks in the low-slung roof over the kitchen. She spent the next few minutes scurrying around placing pots and bowls in strategic positions. When she found the upstairs dry, she breathed a sigh of relief.

Later that evening, Cara lay snug in her bed. Outside, the storm continued to rage, wind and rain lashing at the panes as if wanting it, but she ignored it. With her fire blazing in the grate, her body nice and warm beneath the mound of quilts, and her husband's gift spread out on the bed, Cara didn't care if it rained until next week.

She pored over the papers most of the night. That Chase took the time to acquire them gave further proof of his soft heart. Sophie and Asa may not have found the unusual gift endearing, but Cara did.

He'd sent copies of the *People's Advocate,* published in Washington City; the *Cleveland Gazette;* and a February 17th issue of Mr. Fortune's *New York Globe.* None of the editions was lengthy, but what they lacked in quantity, they more than made up for in quality. Like a majority of the other two hundred African-American newspapers in the country, they were true to the tradition set in motion by John Russwurm and Reverend Samuel Cornish. These two men, Cornish a militant young preacher and Russwurm the second man of African descent to graduate from an American college, published the first Black abolitionist paper, *Freedom's Journal,* in 1827 in New York. Previously, the cause of Blacks, both slave and free, had been championed by publications owned and operated by white abolitionists. *Freedom's Journal* debated the issues in a Black voice.

Now, over fifty years later, their descendants continued to carry the banner. Justice was the rallying cry, justice and expressions of outrage over the government's hands-off attitude toward the escalating violence in the South.

The papers also carried news of events on the African continent. Cara glanced over a story on the exploits of the explorer David Livingstone. Under the auspices of Leopold II of Belgium, he'd begun establishing bases in the Congo Basin. Also reported on were the French, who after reestablishing themselves on the coast of African Dahomey, were now expanding into the interior. Cara solemnly shook her head and read on.

The most pressing concern of the Black press and Black people in general revolved around the upcoming Supreme Court decision in the case involving William R. Davis. On November 22, 1879, Davis, a Black resident of New York, had been denied entrance to a matinee at the New York Grand Opera House, even though he had a ticket. The ticket, purchased by his mulatto girlfriend, was deemed no good by the Opera House doorman, Samuel Singleton. Singleton offered a refund, but Davis refused it, demanding entrance instead. In the end, the police were called and Davis was evicted from the premises.

Davis felt he had a clear criminal complaint. The Civil Rights Law, passed by Congress after the war to strengthen the Fourteenth Amendment, guaranteed equal access to public accommodations, transportation, restaurants, and places such as New York's Grand Opera House. So the Black man, along with a United States Attorney, sued.

The doorman Singleton was indicted on December 9, 1879. When the case was heard on January 14, 1880, Singleton's lawyer, Louis Post, argued the unconstitutionality of the Civil Rights Law, saying it "interfered with the right of citizens and their private property."

The judge presiding over the case couldn't decide and sent the matter on to the Circuit Court. When they were unable to come to a decision, Davis's suit went to the Supreme Court.

The newspapers said the high court's ruling would be coming soon. Some people held hope; after all, it was the law of the land. Why else had the country waged war?

Others were not so optimistic. The Supreme Court had been no friend to Blacks during *Dred Scott v. Sanford* in '56 and '57. That judgment and the recent establishment of the hated Black Codes were only two items on a long list of court-sanctioned injustices that dated back to colonial times.

Both the pessimists and the optimists agreed on one thing: If the Supreme Court did indeed find the Civil Rights Law unconstitutional, segregation would become the law of the land for generations to come.

Cara thought about the future. She and Chase had not discussed the possibility of another child, but she assumed there would be one and perhaps more. What kind of world would they inherit? Sometimes her heart ached for thinking about it.

By April's end, spring finally wrestled winter to the ground.

Unlike the first winter when whole families died from exposure in sparsely heated underground dugouts and others might have found the same fate had it not been for the generosity of the Indians in the area, the Valley population came out of hibernation relatively unscathed. Preparations for planting began. Neighbors cut off by the fierce Kansas snows could visit one another again, checking to see if anyone needed help in shoring up winter-damaged homesteads—or in burying their dead now that the ground had begun to thaw.

With the break in the weather, the merchants of Henry Adams found the thirty-mile trip to Ellis and its railroad depot a less arduous journey. They restocked their depleted shelves with everything from bolts of cloth and farm implements to newspapers, washtubs, and seed. Wanted posters featuring Miles Sutton were plastered on fence posts and barn walls all over Graham County, but he had not been seen.

Cara received a page-long letter from Chase around that time, and its arrival thrilled her. She was disappointed to read he wouldn't be home until late May or early June, but he'd written, and that made her smile.

Another thing that made her smile was being able to resume teaching. The Reverend Whitfield had wisely closed the school back in February because of the toll winter had taken on the old place. The ground-breaking for Virginia's new school, which Cara, with reservations, had agreed to name the Virginia Sutton Free Public School of Henry Adams, would not be held for another few weeks, because planting came first. Cara held classes in the A.M.E. Church in the interim.

Cara's tutoring of Virginia also continued, though in the evenings, now that Cara's days were once again busy. Speculation ran rampant as to Miles Sutton's whereabouts, but Virginia never mentioned him, nor did Cara.

One evening in early May, they were in Virginia's sumptuous study going over the lesson for the week. Virginia had made tremendous progress over the winter, which Cara attributed to her strong will and determination. While Virginia was reading to Cara, the study door suddenly opened.

"Excuse me," said Frances, one of Virginia's servants. "I know you said not to disturb you," she added in an apologetic manner, "but—"

Miles Sutton appeared from behind Frances and explained drolly, "What she's trying to say is that I wouldn't go away. How are you, Mother?"

"Thank you, Frances. I'll take care of things from here," Virginia said, eyeing Miles.

Frances nodded and withdrew, closing the door quietly.

Cara viewed him with contempt and some measure of satisfaction. Being on the run had not served him well. He no longer looked like the rich dandy who owned a saloon. He was unshaven and his clothes were soiled. His face bore the scars of a fight, and it's handsomeness had been permanently marred by the breaking of his nose. Must have been some fight, Cara mused, pleased. She looked away from him and began to gather up her things. "Mrs. Sutton, we can finish this some other time."

"No, Cara, please don't leave. Miles won't be staying."

As if his mother hadn't spoken, he came over and took a casual look at the books and papers spread out on the table.

"What's this?" he asked, picking up one of the primers. 'Well, since *I* can read, and we all know Cara can, too, does this mean you're finally trying to educate yourself, Mother?" He tossed the book back onto the table. "It's about time. No telling how much you've been cheated over the years because of your ignorance." And he laughed.

Cara saw Virginia's jaw tighten and her eyes flash. However, when she spoke, her voice was calm. "Why are you here?"

"I'm a wanted man, Mother. Wanted men need money."

"And you expect me to hand some over?"

"You're my mother. Of course I do."

Virginia shook her head. "No more money, Miles. Not for gamblers, or pregnant girls, or anything else. I won't be bailing you out anymore. You cost this woman her child. Doesn't that mean anything to you?"

His eyes held Cara's. "Well, I think we're about even. Cara, did Mother tell you what your soldier did to me?"

"No," Cara responded. "But be grateful he let you live, Miles. He didn't want to."

"Grateful? For what? The broken nose and shattered jaw? Or maybe you mean the three busted ribs and the blood that I pissed for four days? Yeah, I'm very grateful."

Cara gave him a smug smile.

"Smile all you like, Cara, but if I meet him again I'll kill him."

"I'll be sure to tell him," Cara replied.

"Would you listen to yourself talking about killing someone?" Virginia snapped. "Why don't you turn yourself in to Sheriff Polk and put an end to all of this?"

"No, Mother, territorial prison is not for me."

"Then you did cheat those people?"

He didn't answer immediately. Cara wondered how Virginia would react when she found he had also been involved in the robbery of the mail coaches and the death of the drivers. So far, the warrants issued for Miles pertained only to his activities back East. The investigation surrounding the robberies was still ongoing, though close to closure, according to Sheriff Polk.

"Let's just say, not even your money can buy me out of this one," Miles was saying in answer to his mother's question. "But you have to understand that after they dismissed me from school I had no money."

"More gambling," Virginia snapped.

"Yes," Miles echoed in feigned weariness, "more gambling. I'm sure everybody in the state of Kansas knows I was dismissed for running games in Howard's dormitories at night."

"Crooked games," Virginia pointed out.

"Touché. But those sissies got what they deserved. Do you know what they nicknamed me the first day on campus? Seed." He sneered. "Short for Miles Cottonseed. They laughed at my Spanish-cut suits, my boots, the way I spoke. I hated them." His gray eyes flashed. Then he turned to Cara and smiled as he said, "But they didn't laugh at the way I played poker or my success with their pampered women. Unlike you, my precious Cara, Eastern women loved me."

"Why didn't you find a job, Miles?" Cara asked. "You took people's life savings."

Virginia offered an explanation. "Because before he started running the Lady, he'd never worked for a thing in his life. Your father saw to that, didn't he, Miles?"

"Yes, he did. Pity he's not still alive. He'd put you in your place soon enough."

Cara had never heard anyone speak to a parent so scathingly. She thought the remark especially cruel knowing the abuse to which Ezra Sutton had subjected Virginia for so many years.

He turned away from his mother's icy anger and spoke to Cara. "So, you see, I didn't look for a job. But I got lucky. I was walking through a park in Washington one afternoon, trying to figure out where my next meal would come from, and I happened upon an emigration rally. I listened for a while and at the end they passed the hat. I was impressed by how much they hauled in, so I became a missionary. It was easy. And in reality, I did those people a favor. What did they know about Liberia or South America? They were better off staying here where at least they know what they're facing."

"Oh, Miles," Virginia said in a tone that was part pity and part disgust. "I'm not giving you any money. The only thing I can do for you is not tell Sheriff Polk you were here until morning, and that's only because you are my son. But don't come back here. I don't ever want to see you again."

He observed Virginia a moment and drawled, "Such dramatics. Next you'll be threatening to disinherit me."

Virginia smiled bitterly. "You always were smarter than you let on."

"You wouldn't dare."

Virginia's expression did not change.

He became angry then. "That money is mine!"

Virginia was angry, too. "Not a cent of what I've earned is yours."

"That money's *supposed* to come to me."

"Why? Because you say it does? Miles, I'll give it to the Democrats before I leave you a dime. Now get out of my house before I have someone ride for Sheriff Polk right now."

Cara thought he would explode. "This isn't the last card, Mother dear. Not by a long shot."

He turned his blazing eyes on Cara and said in a softly sinister tone, "I'll see you again, too. I promise."

On June first, a star-filled night, Chase returned home. He let himself in quietly so as not to awaken his sleeping wife, put down his gear, and silently mounted the stairs.

At first, Cara thought it was just another of her vivid dreams. Her nocturnal imagination had conjured him up on many many occasions in nights past. She felt the caress of his hands, the fleeting pressure of his lips, the heady rasping of her name. His strokings were as potent as any reality and she arched her body for more.

"I should awaken you this way all the time," he murmured hotly against her ear. The feathery warmth of his breath pierced the dream. Slowly, she opened her eyes.

His mustache was the first thing she saw. Still groggy with sleep, she sat up partialy and asked, "Is that really you?"

His hands beneath the covers were doing wanton things to her.

"What do you think?"

Her answer was a soft drawn-out moan.

He spent the rest of the night convincing his wife that he was indeed real. By the time the sun rose, Cara had no doubts at all.

The raising of the new school was held the next day and turned into a community affair. People from all over the Valley came to help, bringing with them their families and a dish to pass at the potluck. Chase and Cara were among the first to arrive at the cleared field behind the church. Ignoring Cara's statement that she could swing a hammer as well as some of the men and would not be relegated to women's work, Chase helped her down from the buggy, then, with a firm yet polite guiding hand under her elbow, escorted her over to where Sophie and the other women were gathered. He left her in their care and went off to find Asa. Sophie silenced Cara's fuming by showing her Asa's final drawing of the school. It bore little resemblance to Cara's original idea of a modest one-story structure. Asa and Virginia had gotten together and added rooms, breezeways, and a steepled roof. The drawing left Cara speechless.

As the morning sun climbed to afternoon height, the day took on a beauty that was exclusive to the month of June. The sky was an endless blue above, and the sun bore down gently instead of with the blistering vengeance of the summer months to come. More and more people arrived with more and more food. Soon two long tables were filled with offerings.

The floor of the new school had been lain and completed, and now the walls were being raised. The children were running back and forth, and more than a few had to be cautioned about getting in the way of the workers. In the end, Cara rounded up all the children. With a ready, set, go, she raced them to a point out in the field some distance away from the main gathering. With Cara leading the way, they played kickball and baseball and tag. They had a grasshopper hunt and played leapfrog. By the time they were waved in for supper, Cara was too tired to join the foot race back. She let those with the energy run; she and a few of the younger ones chose to walk. She sent the children straight to the pump behind the church to wash up. When they were finished, she took her turn.

With so many people milling about and standing in line for the food tables, Cara gave up trying to locate Chase for the moment. Once people had their plates and began to find seats at the tables set up on the field, the crowd would thin enough for her to locate him. She waited in the line for her turn, filled her plate, and went off in search of her husband.

Cara saw him across the field seated at a table with the Three Spinsters and Mae Dexter. Having heard that Mae had come home from her first year at Oberlin, Cara was anxious to learn how the year had gone. There was a woman seated next to Mae. Cara almost dropped her plate in astonishment when she saw who it was. Laura Pope! The same Laura Pope who'd claimed to be Chase's fiancée back in Topeka three years ago. What in the world was she doing in Henry Adams? Chase was saying something to her but looked up with a smile when Cara neared.

"Hi, darlin'."

Mae also had a smile. "Oh, Oberlin was everything you said it would be. I can't wait for classes to resume."

Cara acknowledged the Three Spinsters with a kiss on each of their cheeks. Chase slid down the bench a bit to make room for her at his side, and she sat, looking into the cool, brown-eyed gaze of Laura Pope. Cara took in the little confection of a hat perched so pertly atop her glossy braided hair, and the expensive cut of her matching dark green jacket and skirt.

"Cara, you remember Laura Pope?" Chase said.

"Yes, I do. We met in Topeka, if I'm not mistaken. What brings you to Henry Adams, Miss Pope?"

"I'm here to look over some property for my father's bank."

"I met her on the train ride to Ellis last night," Mae said.

Laura took up the rest of the story. "I'm staying over at the hotel. When Mayor Dexter told me about the new school, I asked if I might join the gathering."

"Welcome," Cara said, trying not to dislike the woman. 'I hope you enjoy your stay."

Cara began to eat.

"I was surprised to find Chase here, of all places," Laura said.

Cara stopped eating, fork poised in midair, and looked into Laura's beautiful face. It wasn't the remark so much that rubbed Cara the wrong way, but the tone. Cara turned to her husband, who shrugged, then back to the woman. Rather than be the cause of yet another ruckus, and speak out of turn, Cara ignored the remark.

The Three Spinsters did not.

Lucretia was eyeing Miss Pope with a look that said she, too, had taken offense. She asked, "And just where would you expect our Sergeant Jefferson to be, Miss Pope? He and his wife do live here, after all."

Daisy added, "One wouldn't expect him to be in Paris."

The Spinsters laughed at their own cleverness. Cara smiled around a mouth filled with some of Dulcie's fine potato salad.

"And you know," Rachel said, leaning down so the young woman could be certain to see the censure in Rachel's black eyes, "if there's something wrong with our town maybe your father's bank should look elsewhere."

Laura had drawn up as stiff as a statue.

Mae spoke up for her guest. "I'm sure she didn't mean there was anything wrong with our town."

Laura finally found her voice. "Mae's right, of course. Your town is charming. I've spent most of the past two years in Boston. This is my first trip back. I'd forgotten how rustic everything is. Have you ever been East, Cara?"

"Ohio is as far East as I've gone."

"Ah, you're from the South then?"

"Georgia."

"Sometimes Southern people have a hard time adjusting to the East. A country girl like yourself probably wouldn't like it." Then she turned to Chase and asked him about a mutual friend in Topeka.

Cara knew that her personal dislike of the beautiful Miss Pope stemmed from the lie she'd told about being Chase's fiancée, but that notwithstanding, Cara had the distinct feeling that Laura was being difficult for a purpose. Laura's eyes were filled with contempt as she gazed at Cara. Cara hoped the woman wasn't planning on trying to reclaim Chase's affections, because she would not allow it. She and Chase had finally achieved the peace they'd both been seeking in their marriage. If Laura tried to mess that up, she swore there would be a ruckus this town would not soon forget.

Lucretia launched into a description of a trip she planned on taking to Denver later in the summer to see her sister. "My sister and her husband remind me of the two of you," she said, pointing at Cara and Chase.

"In what way?" Cara asked, feeling her husband taking bits of grass from her hair. Cara brushed her hand over her head and drew away a small sliver of cornstalk, a remnant of romping with the children all afternoon.

"You and Sergeant Jefferson share what used to be called a grand passion," Lucretia said wistfully. "My sister Anna and her husband have been married for over fifty years. They have a grand passion for each other also."

"How quaint," Laura said drolly.

"A grand passion," Chase said, as if trying the phrase on for size.

"Yes," Lucretia said. "I've been watching the two of you the last few months and I must say, it's wonderful to see."

"See what?" Mae asked curiously.

"The way he watches her walk across a room, the way he glows when he sees her. Do you know that you have two different smiles, Sergeant?"

Chase grinned. "No, ma'am. I didn't."

"Well, you do. You have one that you give faded roses like us, and then you have another that's reserved only for your beautiful wife. I've noticed it many times."

Cara turned to her husband. The tenderness in his dark eyes sent her heart soaring.

"Love is a glorious thing," Lucretia went on softly. "Treasure each other, because what you have is truly rare."

Laura stood up. "Thank you for the company, everyone."

Cara couldn't decide whether Laura could no longer mask her hostility or if she just didn't care to hide her true feelings anymore. Either way her anger was plain for everyone to see. "Chase, I wish you luck with your—your grand passion. It's been nice meeting you ladies. Mae."

With nothing more than a contemptuous look at Cara, Laura left the table and walked off across the field.

"Well," huffed Rachel. "She didn't even say goodbye to you, Cara."

Daisy giggled. "I wonder why."

"Oh, she should be glad we let her leave the table alive after the way she kept sneering at Cara," Rachel added. Then she looked down the table to her friend. "Lucretia, when you began talking about that grand passion, I thought she was going to choke."

The spinsters all laughed.

Cara smiled and waggled a teacherly finger as she said, "You girls have been very bad. Double homework for you tonight."

Mae looked around the table with wide eyes.

"What's the matter, Mae?" Chase asked, chuckling softly at the wonder on her face.

"Sergeant Jefferson, this is the first year I've been able to sit with adults at a gathering, and—is this what the adults do—act catty—while we young ones are sitting at the children's table? I had no idea there was intrigue like this in Henry Adams."

Laughter erupted from everyone.

"This has been much more exciting than watching the boys make lemonade come out of their noses!"

Cara thought about that remark as she lay in bed in her nightgown, waiting for Chase to return from washing up at the pump out back. Mae had certainly grown into a fine young woman in the past year. For a while Cara had despaired of Mae becoming anything more in life than a consumer of gowns from St. Louis. But Cara had talked with her about her studies and her goal of being a newspaperwoman when she finished Oberlin. She didn't think Mae would have any trouble handling whatever career she chose.

Chase returned then, his upper body wet, his lower body covered by the towel fashioned around his hips. Cara looked at the strong long legs below the towel and marveled once again at the beauty of the man she'd married.

The next morning after breakfast, Chase and Cara took their traditional ride to begin the day. They'd been out for nearly an hour and were sprawled atop a blanket spread out on the open plains, a checkerboard between them. "You know," Chase said, moving one of the few remaining pieces on the board, "that was something running into Laura yesterday."

Cara watched where he placed his piece. She frowned. He was trouncing her—again. She had never beat him. "Yes, it most certainly was something."

"I don't think she likes you."

"Could she really be that angry because you're married? It's been three years. Surely she's not still pining."

"I suppose she could be. I am quite a catch, you know."

"And so modest," Cara pointed out. "I know how talented you are, but she acts as if she has something else stuck in her craw. Call it a woman's intuition."

"I don't know, Cara. But I do know not even your woman's intuition can get you out of the mess you're in on this board here."

Cara shot him a look.

She directed her attention back to her dilemma. She made what she hoped would be the least damaging move to her dwindling forces, only to have him jump another of her men, and come to rest in royalty row. She sat up and folded her arms in disgust.

He grinned. "Well, don't pout. King me."

She did. "Don't gloat." She pushed her last man out to its death. She faced total defeat as he slid the new king down to sit judgment with his other four, pausing only to take her man as it did.

The game was over.

"Well, let's see," Chase said, and closed his eyes as if he were deep in thought. "Since we've been married, that's about five thousand games for me, and how many for you?"

She grinned and punched him in the arm. "None. And you know it."

"Just checking my figures," he told her. "Well, don't worry about it. Your cooking makes up for your not being able to play checkers any better than Carolina."

Cara yelled her outrage. "Carolina!" Laughing, she launched herself atop him, intending to battle to the death. They rolled around on the tarp, laughing and enjoying each other while the sun shone down above them.

That afternoon, Cara went into town with Chase so he could help with the work still needed to be done on the school. The outer walls were up, and today the men would hoist the roof into place. Cara ran her eyes lovingly over the structure. She couldn't wait for it to be filled with books and desks and, especially, her students. She had quite a year planned when the new school opened.

Chase kissed her on the cheek and hopped down from the buggy to the ground. Cara slid over to take the vacated seat behind the reins. He walked off to the field with a parting wave and she headed the horses up the street.

Cara did some visiting with the Three Spinsters, then stopped at the mercantile to check for mail and peruse the recently received newspapers. With those things accomplished she left the mercantile and crossed the street. She nodded to her neighbors as she passed, stopped to talk to a few she hadn't seen in a while, and started out toward Sophie's. As she walked by the bank, she was almost bowled over by a woman coming out of the door.

"I can't shake you, can I?" Laura said.

Cara watched the woman make minute adjustments to her beautiful navy jacket and black skirt and pat her black hat. "My apologies," Cara said coolly, determined to take the high road. "I obviously wasn't paying attention."

"Obviously," Laura replied.

"What is your problem with me, Miss Pope? Are you angry because I married Chase?"

Cara waited for her to deny there was a problem, but Laura surprised her.

"Yes, that is part of it. After you left us that morning at Floral Hall, he gave me holy hell for lying and saying he was my fiancé."

"I see."

"I knew my parents would never have let me marry a man like him, though," Laura said, pulling on her gloves.

"Why not?"

"Because he was a slave," she said. "Didn't you know?"

"Yes, I knew."

She seemed mildly surprised. "Then it must have not mattered where you were raised."

"No, it didn't matter where I was raised," Cara agreed.

"Well, it certainly did in my parents' circles. A slave. In your family. You'd never be asked to dinner again. It was wonderful to be seen on his arm at the parties around Topeka that year, though. Chase is a handsome man."

Cara hadn't encountered such blatant intra-race prejudice since her days at Oberlin, where there'd been a small number of students who'd chosen not to associate with those members of the race they deemed unsuitable.

"You said Chase's marrying me was only part of your problem. What else is bothering you about me?"

"I'd rather not discuss it out here, if you don't mind."

Cara was intrigued, to say the least. "Then let's go someplace where we can discuss it."

Cara took her over to Sophie's. Cara's old room had not been let, and with Sophie's permission, Cara escorted Laura up there to talk. Void of her many books and crates, the room appeared empty. She motioned Laura to a chair, and Cara took a seat on the bed.

"Now," Cara said, "let's hear what you have to say."

"You're quite the man-catcher, aren't you?" she began icily. Her eyes were blazing.

Cara had no idea what she was talking about. "Man-catcher?"

"First Chase. Now Miles Sutton."

Cara froze and stared. For a few moments Cara tried to convince herself she'd simply misunderstood, but she knew she hadn't. A million questions went off in her head all at once. "How do you know Miles Sutton?"

"We were to be married last fall."

"I see," Cara said, though she didn't see at all. "Do you know he's wanted by the law?"

"Yes, I do. I also know it's your fault."

"Is that what he told you?"

"Yes."

"Laura, I had nothing to do with his cheating people out of their life savings and their land."

"That isn't what I'm talking about. That is a simple case of mistaken identity. He'll straighten it out."

Cara was a bit taken aback but said, "Possibly you're right, but until Miles comes in and talks to Sheriff Polk, it won't be straightened out. Do you know where he is?"

"Of course." And she said no more.

Cara hadn't really expected an answer. Laura had the demeanor of a competent woman, even if she had swallowed the pot of fool's gold Miles had fed her. "What is it you think I did to Miles?"

"The baby."

Cara went still. Her voice was barely above a whisper as she asked, "Are you talking about my baby?"

"Yes, the one you claimed Miles fathered."

Cara felt herself turn as cold as stone. "I never told anyone that Miles was the father of my baby."

"Miles said you had his mother convinced, along with half the town. And then that tale about you falling from the horse. If you hadn't been hanging on to the saddle, begging him to marry you and give your bastard a name, you wouldn't've been hurt."

Cara stood slowly. She knew if she stayed in this room one more second, grief and rage would make her do something she would regret. She looked at Laura's smug expression and walked from the room.

Cara didn't stop walking. She came down the stairs, ignored Sophie calling with concern, and went outside and down the walk. She didn't see any of the people she passed. The utter falseness of the story hurt her immensely. That he would dare to twist the facts of her tragedy to fit his schemes made her want to grab a rifle and hunt him down like a rabid animal. Her anger climbed to fury. Tears were rolling down her cheeks. By the time she reached the end of the wooden walk, she was running.

Chase and Asa were up on the newly raised frame of the school's roof, checking the fit of the support beams. "Well, I'll be damned," Asa said sounding amazed. "Isn't that Miss Cara, Chase?"

It was his wife, all right. Alarmed, he looked at the area behind her, but saw no one in pursuit; still he knew something was wrong. "Be back."

The other men stopped work and turned to watch as Chase took off at a run, yelling Cara's name.

When he caught up with her, she was sitting in open prairie, plucking grass. "Hello, darlin'," he said gently. He hadn't seen her this sad since they lost the baby.

"Hello, Chase."

"Why're you crying?"

"I'm angry."

She plucked more grass and he waited.

"Chase, Laura Pope just told me that I lost the baby because I was holding on to Miles's saddle begging him to marry me." She looked up and saw her anger reflected in his stare.

"What?"

"Yes. And she also knows where he is. He told her I had told everyone the baby was his."

"To what purpose?"

"I don't know," she replied softly. "I left the room. I didn't want to hear any more." Cara tossed a few blades of the long grass into the air. "Why would he say that?"

"When I find him, I'll be sure to ask him," Chase promised angrily.

Chapter 16

It was pouring rain the next morning when Chase rode into town on Carolina. The army-issue slicker he had on protected him from the elements, but did not stave off the chill that seeped beneath it. He'd come to town to talk with Sheriff Polk about Cara's encounter with Laura.

Over a cup of coffee, Chase told him the story. The sheriff suggested they pay Laura a visit. They walked down to the Sutton Hotel where they were informed by the desk clerk that she'd checked out the previous night. Chase slammed his hand down on the desk.

They questioned the clerk further, but he had no idea where she might have gone. All he knew was that Miss Pope was no longer a guest.

At the livery station, Chase and the sheriff talked to the owner, Handy Reed. The big blacksmith said that Laura Pope had hired a coach early the evening before. He'd had a man take her to the station at Ellis. Handy had no idea where she was headed from there.

Chase and the sheriff thanked him. They walked the rain-muddied streets back to Polk's office. After a discussion of the options available, they decided to wire Laura's description to the Federal marshal in Wichita. Chase also wired his commanding officer requesting leave so he could protect his wife until Sutton was found.

The next two weeks were filled with a series of mishaps in and around Virginia Sutton's properties. It began with a fire in the mercantile one night. The volunteer bucket brigade was able to bring the blaze under control, but not before most of the contents were damaged. It inconvenienced everyone in town when the place had to be closed down for repairs, but there'd been no loss of life, so folks didn't grumble very loudly.

The next incident happened two days later. One of the wheels on Virginia's carriage came loose as she and her driver were returning home. In the resulting crash both she and her man were thrown from the vehicle and injured. Sheriff Polk said the wheel bolts had been sawn through.

Cara went to see her the next day to bring her some books to read during her recuperation.

"How're you feeling?" Cara asked as Virginia, hobbling with the aid of a cane, led the way to the study. Her face was covered with the bruises she'd gotten in the fall. She moved as if each step was painful. "I have been better, believe me. That damn Miles."

Cara opened the door to the study and they went in and sat down.

"You think Miles had something to do with your accident yesterday?"

Virginia set her cane against her chair. "Of course he did. He set the fire in the mercantile, slashed the throats of my mousers in the barn. Oh, yes, it's Miles. I'd bet every bit of railroad stock I own."

"Why are you so sure?

"I've seen this before. When he was younger, he hurt things—cats, the horses—especially when he was angry about something. The year he turned fourteen I refused to let him send to Mexico City for an expensive saddle he'd wanted very much. We'd had a poor crop of cotton the year before, and I needed every penny for seed. I told him he could have the saddle the following year, but he didn't want to wait and stormed out. The next morning two dogs that I truly loved were found poisoned. Their bodies were on the front porch."

Cara shook her head sadly.

"To this day," Virginia continued, "I believe he killed those dogs. Oh, I asked him about it, and he denied it, but something in his eyes . . . I never attached myself to another animal after that. So, yes, it's Miles. I know it is."

"What did Delbert say about your ankle?"

"Broken. He said to stay off it. I doubt I can. Too many things to do. Speaking of which, I've done something you may or may not approve of."

Cara observed her quizzically.

"I'm leaving my money to you. All the money my son thinks should be his."

Cara stared. "Why?"

"Because you'll do good with it. Miles will spend it on women and drink. I didn't work all these years to have my money spent on harlots."

"Virginia, I can't accept your money."

"I really don't care what you can or cannot accept, Cara. I made the decision months ago. In spite of all the hell I put you through, you were still decent enough to teach me how to read. Do you know what that has been worth to me? It's more valuable than anything I ever owned. And I own quite a lot."

Cara shook her head. "No. I can't accept."

"I told you it's too late to decline. And the reason I'm telling you now is in case something happens to me. Miles isn't going to be content to just walk away. I've hired additional security staff because he's broken into the house."

Cara was shocked. "Were you here?"

"No, I wish I had been. Everyone was at the school raising that day."

"How do you know it wasn't some drifter?"

"Every room in the house had been turned upside down except the room he used when he was here."

Cara wondered if Miles had become so desperate he hadn't realized how obvious it was to leave his room untouched. Or maybe he wanted his mother to know he'd ransacked her home. "Was he looking for money?"

"Probably, but he found only the pin money I keep in a sugar bowl for the cook. I'm sure it made him furious. The next day the cats were killed."

"Have you told the sheriff?"

"No."

"Why not? Virginia, he should know."

"I know, but Miles is my son. It's hard to turn your back on your child, even a child like Miles. At first, maybe I was hoping he'd come to his senses. Not anymore. I have only to look at these bruises on my face to know how serious this has become."

"So you will tell Sheriff Polk?"

Virginia nodded.

Cara returned home later that same afternoon, but Chase was no-where to be found. She did find a note he'd left for her on the kitchen table saying he'd gone to town to check the mail. Cara looked at the time he'd written on his note and compared it to the clock above the fireplace. He'd been gone a little over an hour. It was nearly dinner-time, so she started to cook.

When he came in she had just taken the last of the cornmeal cakes out of the skillet. She put a bit of butter on each of the small golden rounds of bread and covered them with a lid so they'd stay hot.

"Was there mail?"

"Yep. There's a letter here for you from William."

Cara wiped her hands on her apron and took the envelope. She smiled and stuck it into her apron pocket to read later.

"How's the Black Widow?" Chase asked, pausing to give her a kiss before going on through the kitchen and out the back door to the pump behind the house.

Cara followed. "She broke her ankle. You should see her face. It's covered with bruises. She thinks Miles is responsible for all the problems she's been having."

Chase wiped the water from his face and looked up. "Why?"

Cara told him of the incidents Virginia had related.

"I can see why she would think that," Chase said after hearing the story. "Are you certain she's going to tell the sheriff?"

"I think she will. The coach accident made her realize how serious the situation has become. I think it scared her."

"Well, when I go into town tomorrow, I'll be sure to let Polk know anyway. She probably isn't going to be doing much traveling if her ankle's broken. She might not get to town for a few days. What do you think?"

"I think that's probably a good idea."

After Chase related Virginia's information to the sheriff, they stepped up the search. For the following three days, Chase and the sheriff spent every waking hour in the saddle trying to track down Miles Sutton. They talked to people, chased rumors, and searched every deserted soddy and shack for miles around with no result.

Chase came home on the evening of the third day, tired and frustrated.

"We've turned over every damn rock in three counties and he hasn't crawled out yet," he told Cara angrily as they lay in bed. "We're not looking in the right place."

"Chase, you're doing as much as you can."

"Something's going to happen. I can feel it."

"What do you mean?"

"Sometimes on the trail you get a sense like this. Something in your gut signals danger ahead. I've had that feeling all day."

He turned over and looked at her. "I want you to pack some things in the morning and go into town and stay with Sophie or the Spinsters until this is done."

"Why?"

"Because when I'm gone, I worry about you. I can't look for Sutton and be here to watch over you."

"Chase—"

"Cara Lee, please. Don't fight me on this. I'll feel much better knowing you're safe. I don't want anything to happen to you, darlin'."

Cara wanted to argue with him. Lord knew she did, but he couldn't do his job if he was worried about her. She could understand that. "I'll pack first thing in the morning."

"Thank you. I promise you won't have to stay in town long."

"It better not be long," she whispered, leaning over to give him a kiss, "because when I'm away from home it's going to be real hard for you to get peach cobbler and real real hard to get this . . ."

Sometime later, a thoroughly loved and sated Chase closed his eyes with a smile. His last thoughts as he drifted into sleep were a vow to get his wife back home as soon as possible. He could do without her peach cobbler for a time, but not this . . .

So Cara moved back into Sophie's boardinghouse to Chase's old room. Everyone was glad to see her, though they wished the circumstances were different.

Cara dropped her carpetbag into a chair and walked over to the open window. The curtains flapped in the breeze. On Main Street people were going about their errands. The town looked and felt different to Cara. Nothing had changed, really, but this was no longer her home. Her home was with Chase outside of town.

She turned away and surveyed the room. It hadn't changed, either. The finely appointed room with its highly polished furnishings bore no evidence that a dark-eyed, mustached cavalry soldier had ever slept here, but Cara had little trouble conjuring up that wicked grin, or remembering how he'd looked walking toward her that night . . . tall, naked, and splendidly ready. He'd been in much the same condition last night. She'd left the house that morning aching with the erotic rememberings of the caress of his strong callused hands, his bone-melting kisses, and the shameless way she had begged to be filled again and again.

Smiling, she pushed the thoughts away, unpacked, and joined Sophie and Dulcie in the kitchen. Sophie wanted Cara to talk about the mess with Miles. Dulcie wanted Cara to peel carrots. Cara did both.

She passed the afternoon with them, discussing theories about where

Miles might be, and where the elusive Miss Pope fit into the puzzle. When dinner was ready, Cara took hers in the kitchen with Dulcie. Sophie went off to her suite of rooms to have her dinner with Asa as she did every night.

"How are you and Chase doing?" Dulcie asked.

Cara smiled.

"I see the grin," Dulcie said approvingly. "You two must be doing well."

"Yes," Cara admitted, pleased. "We are."

"I knew things would work out once you came to your senses."

Chase charged into the kitchen, looking around wildly. When he spotted Cara, he seemed to calm down. "Oh, Cara, thank God. I was so worried—"

"Chase, what's wrong?"

"Virginia's been shot."

Cara and Dulcie both jumped to their feet. "Is she alive?" Cara asked.

"Yes. Delbert's with her now out at the house. It's pretty serious."

"When did this happen?"

"A few hours ago. Cara, you need to come with me. Virginia's asking for you. The doc doesn't know how long she's got."

On the ride Chase told her what he knew of Virginia's shooting. A child in the area had delivered a note to Virginia the previous evening. It was from Miles, stating he wanted to turn himself in to the authorities. He asked Virginia to meet him alone at a spot outside Nicodemus so he could discuss it with her. Virginia went to the field and took only her driver. Miles never showed. On the way back, however, she came across a woman walking down the road. The woman said her father was badly hurt about a mile off, and she was on her way to Nicodemus to get help. Virginia was talking to the woman when Miles walked out of the sunflower field with a gun in his hand.

"The woman was Laura Pope, right?" Cara asked.

"From the description Virginia gave of her, we're pretty certain it was."

"Why did he shoot Virginia?"

"Well, Miles ordered her and the driver down from the carriage, took the driver's firearm, handed it to the woman, then gave the driver the choice of either walking or dying. The driver chose life and took off down the road."

"Leaving Virginia alone with Miles and Laura."

"Exactly."

"What happened next?"

"They argued. Miles demanded money. She told him no. He stuck his gun in her face, she hit him with her cane, and the woman, Laura Pope, probably, shot her."

"Laura Pope shot her? My Lord."

"She probably panicked. When the driver heard the shots, he ran back. Miles and Laura were gone, and Virginia was bleeding on the ground."

At Virginia's house, they were ushered in by a somber Frances, who showed them to the room where Virginia lay on the bed. Delbert and the sheriff were also in the room.

Delbert approached and said softly, "Thanks for coming, Cara. She doesn't have long, so be easy with her."

Cara approached the bed. The others hung back to give her some privacy.

Virginia's skin was as pale as vellum. She opened her eyes and whispered, "You came. I knew you would. Looks like you're going to be a very rich lady, Cara Jefferson."

"Virginia—"

"Shh," she whispered. "I don't have much time. My solicitors in St. Louis have already received the changes in my will. Have a good life, Cara. Thank you." She closed her eyes. Two hours later, she died.

Cara wore black to the funeral the next day. A uniformed Chase, Asa, Delbert, and Sheriff Polk served as pallbearers. They buried Virginia in the cemetery outside town, and the Reverend Whitfield spoke the words as they lowered her into the ground.

Cara and Chase returned to the room at Sophie's after the short service. Cara tossed her hat on a chair and said sadly, "She didn't deserve to be murdered like that, Chase."

"No, darlin', she didn't. Come here . . ."

Cara went into his arms and he held her tight.

He kissed her hair and whispered, "The day she was shot, I just knew he was coming for you next. I was so glad to see you sitting in the kitchen with Dulice."

Cara badly needed his strength and his love.

"Lucretia was right," he said. "You are my grand passion, schoolmarm. If anything were to happen to you . . ."

Cara looked up at him. "It won't. You won't let it. And neither will

I." She raised up on her toes and kissed him. "I want to change clothes."

Cara took off her funeral dress and substituted a somber gray shirt-waist that buttoned down the back. There was a memorial dinner being held at the hotel. Virginia had made many enemies over the years, but no one would have wished her such a tragic and senseless death.

It rained for the next two days, big bucketfuls that filled the streets with rivers of mud. On the third day following Virginia's burial it stopped. The sun came up bright and strong as if it wanted to remind everyone that it was still June.

Cara awakened that morning in the big bed next to her husband. It took her a moment to orient herself, then she remembered that she and Chase were at Sophie's and not in their bedroom back home. She saw the sun and was glad the rain had finally stopped, but she was homesick. She turned her head on the pillow and looked into her husband's open but sleepy eyes.

"Mornin', schoolmarm."

"Mornin', Sergeant."

"I see the sun's back from furlough," he said, yawning.

Cara turned over and propped herself on her elbow. "Chase, I want to go home."

He reached out and pulled her braid around in front of her shoulder. "Okay."

She was surprised by his instant agreement. "You're not going to lecture me about Miles and worry and keeping me safe?"

"Nope."

"Why not?"

"I miss my peach cobbler."

Cara shook her head, smiling, then said very softly, "Well, you take me home, and I promise I'll give you peach cobbler till you can't move."

"Start packing."

But they couldn't leave because of the mud-clogged roads. Cara was very disappointed when Chase came back to the room with the news.

"Don't pout," he said, smiling.

"I'm not pouting. I just want to sleep in our own bed."

"Cara Lee Jefferson, the last thing on your mind is sleeping."

Cara looked down to hide her embarrassment.

"It's nothing to be ashamed of, darlin', I want you just as much."

Cara grinned.

"I'd make love to you now, but I want it to be at home where I can take my time and show you how much I miss you."

Cara's nipples had hardened from his tone and the look in his eyes. Desire wove through her body like smoke.

They went downstairs and shared a late breakfast in Sophie's dining room. His eyes were so hot and his talk so lusty with promises for tomorrow, Cara's heart was beating fast and her senses were heightened by the time the meal had been consumed. He escorted her from the room with a polite hand at her back. The slight weight of his palm against her dress was as warm as a flatiron.

Cara expressed a desire to go to the partly reopened mercantile to check on an order of books. Chase agreed, but Cara changed her mind after looking at the mud-filled streets once they stepped outside.

"I think I'll wait until tomorrow. I'll sink to my knees in that slop."

The words had barely left her lips before she felt herself scooped up into her husband's broad arms. "Chase!" She giggled. "Put me down."

But they were already moving and being watched by smiling people on both sides of the street. He set her down on the walk and people began to clap. Cara watched her husband bow in response to the applause before she grabbed him by the arm and pulled him into the mercantile.

Later, they stopped by the sheriff's office and learned the banks were offering a two-hundred-dollar reward for Miles's capture and conviction.

"We need to find him quick," the sheriff said. "I don't want my county swarming with a bunch of bounty hunters and drifters sniffing around trying to earn some easy money. Someone is liable to get hurt."

Chase nodded vigorously in agreement.

"Chase, I contacted your commander. We both agreed you're needed here, so you've been assigned for another thirty days."

"Very good, Sheriff."

"Well, I know Miss Cara is happy with the news, but it was strictly a selfish request. I do need your help. Sutton and his lady friend are bound to surface sooner or later."

"We've been saying that for weeks," Chase pointed out.

A thought occurred to Cara as she listened to the sheriff say the word "surface." "Chase, have you searched any of the old dugouts? The countryside is filled with them."

"We did search a few of the ones that we knew weren't totally collapsed, but as you just said, there are probably a hundred or more in the area."

Chase could feel the rightness of his wife's theory in his gut. If Sutton had been hiding underground, that would explain how he was able to appear and disappear so easily. "Are there any old maps of the colony's first year? That might give us an idea of how many original plots there were."

"Rachel and the other Spinsters keep things like that," Cara said. "I'm sure if there was such a map the ladies would have it. If not, you might want to bring in the children."

Both men turned to her and stared. Cara explained. "Think about it. If there are dugouts around here that you can hide in, who would know better than the children?"

Chase exchanged a look with the sheriff. "At this point," the sheriff said, "I'll try anything."

Instead of spending the rest of the day thinking about how the weather had cheated her out of her peach cobbler, Cara spent the time going through the paper-filled trunks and crates stored in the basement of the house of the Three Spinsters.

Over dinner that evening at the Spinsters' house, Cara showed Chase and the sheriff what she and Lucretia had found in the basement. The crude map had gotten wet sometime during the five years of storage in a trunk and could hardly be deciphered. Chase spread it out on the table. The sight of the plots inked into the vellum brought back memories for the older people in the room. Sheriff Polk pointed out the plot he and his sister Rose had shared the first year in town. She'd died as a result of a widespread crop failure the second year. Lucretia and Daisy pointed out plots of people who'd given up and moved on in hopes of finding their dreams elsewhere. All in all, they were able to reconstruct a map of forty of the sixty-five sites of the original colonists. That still left twenty-five places unaccounted for. They spent the rest of the evening seeking out individuals in town who might be of help. It was midnight before Cara and Chase finally made it back to their room at Sophie's. Cara was so tired of talking to people, and listening to tales, and searching through boxes for old diaries and letters, she fell onto the bed in a heap. Chase came and plopped down beside her. He gave her a gentle swat on her behind. "Get up, *mariposa*. Fall out on your own side of the bed."

She groaned wearily, then pushed herself up. She got undressed and climbed into bed. "I can't wait to get home."

If Chase had a comment, she didn't hear him because she went right to sleep.

*   *   *

The roads and streets were still a mess the next day, but by early afternoon the children Cara thought would know the most about the dugouts had been brought into town by their parents. The children, sitting in the chairs in the sheriff's office, were a bit apprehensive. When Cara explained why they were there, they relaxed noticeably.

The three boys and two girls were very helpful. After Chase rolled out the map and oriented the children to some commonly known landmarks he'd added, they amazed even their parents with their knowledge of the prairie. Chase was immediately able to eliminate five spots as possible hiding places because the children all agreed they were impossible to enter. Then they pointed out the locations of four other feasible dugouts that weren't even on the map. Chase, impressed and amazed, penciled in the information. All in all it took less than an hour for Cara's students to prove that they did indeed know every hiding place in the county.

When the children and their parents departed for a reward of ice cream and cake Cara had asked Sophie to supply, Chase, Cara, and the sheriff studied the map some more. There were still over fifteen of the original colony sites unaccounted for, and no one knew how many other unrecorded dugouts there were, but the map had much more detail, thanks to the children.

The sheriff kept the map. He planned on resuming the search as soon as he could round up his volunteer posse. Chase would be joining them, but not until tomorrow. Today he and Cara were going home. They said their goodbyes to the sheriff, and less than an hour later to their friends at Sophie's.

The ride home was a slow one. The roads were still axle-deep with water and mud in some spots, and twice Cara and Chase had to get out and push. It was nearing twilight when they finally stepped onto their porch.

Chase, ever cautious, entered the house first, Colt drawn. When he came back a few moments later, he held the door open for her to enter.

"A bath!" Cara pleaded loudly. "Then dinner." Both she and Chase were covered with mud from the adventurous ride home.

"First time I rescued you, you were covered with mud just like that," Chase pointed out, bringing in buckets of water from the pump. He poured them into the big caldrons atop the stove.

Cara looked down at herself. "You're right, but if I remember correctly you stayed spotless the whole time."

"I'm in the cavalry. Uniform's supposed to be clean."

"I thought you were so handsome."

"You didn't act like it. Spent the whole time yapping at me like a jay bird." Chase chuckled.

"But you liked it."

"That I did. Didn't know whether to put you over my knee or kiss that sassy mouth."

Cara's secretive smile and flirting eyes made him smile in reply, and he said, "Now, be nice and stop looking at me that way."

"What way?" she asked.

"Like you can't wait."

Cara, made brazen by their always uninhibited play, and the fact that she hadn't made love to her husband in six days, began to undo the buttons on her dress.

Chase grinned with hot eyes and asked suspiciously, "What do you think you're doing?"

"I'm all wet."

His gaze leaped with fire at the double meaning. "Naughty, naughty woman."

They eventually made it to the tub upstairs; eventually, but not before Cara learned the erotic magic of making love astraddle her husband in one of the kitchen chairs; and only moments later, she learned also the wanton peaks a woman can attain when her husband comes up behind her, and teaches her how to make love on the way up the stairs.

That evening proved to be the most sensual time Cara had ever spent with Chase. They made love in the tub, and then out of the tub. They never did get dinner.

They combined breakfast with their usual morning carriage ride. On the way, the sun rose in all its glory, burning away the haze and warming the air. Cara shook off her shawl and let the sun's rays warm her.

"Will you take morning rides with me when we're old and gray?" Cara asked, linking her arm into his as he handled the reins.

"If you promise to give me peach cobbler when I'm old and gray, I'll ride you anytime you like."

She playfully slapped him across the shoulder. "You know, after we have children you won't be able to make love to me on the kitchen table anymore."

He turned to her, slowly searching her face, and asked seriously, "Are we going to have children?"

"I would like to."

He gave his attention back to the road and the reins. "So would I, but I didn't know how you felt."

"Delbert says he sees no reason why we can't have babies. I'm kind of looking forward to having a brood of little cavalry soldiers."

"Throw in a few little schoolmarms and you have a deal."

Cara leaned over and kissed him on the cheek. She felt certain she was the happiest woman on earth.

Back at the house, Cara went inside while he took the buggy around to the shed. She went upstairs to retrieve the letter she'd written to William. She'd forgotten to post it yesterday. Chase could take it to town for her.

Downstairs she stood inside the screened door and watched him making the final adjustments to Carolina's saddle. When he was done, he stepped onto the porch and came inside.

"Will you take this and drop it at the mercantile?" she asked, handing him the letter to William.

She waited while he looked at the address.

"I still don't like my wife writing another man."

"After last night, how can you think I could so much as look at another man? But the jealousy's kind of flattering."

"Don't gloat," he told her, grinning. "Kiss me so I can go."

"Yes, sir."

Cara went up on her toes, and as his arms closed around her waist, William's letter fluttered from Chase's hand. Cara saw the letter glide to the floor and reminded herself to pick it up before he left, but at the moment she was more concerned with enjoying her husband's kiss.

Finally, reluctantly, they parted, and Chase, still holding her around the waist, walked her outside with him. She waited as he mounted Carolina.

"Be back tonight. Keep yourself safe."

"I will. You look out for snakes named Sutton. Oh, and there'll be peach cobbler tonight."

His eyes lit up.

"Real cobbler, Chase, from peaches."

"I love that, too. In fact, I'll take a big helping of both when I get home."

Cara smiled. "You are such a greedy man."

"Always, darlin', but only for you."

He leaned down and gave her a quick kiss, then rode off.

Cara stepped up on the porch and watched him until he disappeared from sight.

When she walked back inside she spotted William's letter. She shrugged and placed it on the table by the settee. Tomorrow would be soon enough.

Cleaning up from breakfast, she heard footsteps on the porch. She tossed her dishrag aside and picked up the letter. Chase had come back.

Cara was wrong. The man who stepped through the doorway was Miles Sutton.

Her gaze leaped to her rifle, propped beside the door. He reached over and picked it up. "Good morning, Cara. I saw soldier boy ride away. Thought I'd see if you could spare a wanted man a cup of coffee."

Cara fought down her fear and faced him.

"No coffee, huh?" He opened the chamber of her Winchester, saw that it was loaded, and snapped it closed. "Well, I guess you and I are going to have to go someplace else and get some."

He pointed the rifle at her and said quietly, "Move."

Cara stood her ground.

"Now, Cara, don't make me have to leave you here dead. Think how soldier boy will feel when he comes home and finds you on the floor all covered with blood. Not a nice sight. So come on, move."

Only the thought of Chase finding her as Miles had described got Cara moving.

She walked down the front steps and outside. She didn't have to turn around to know he held the gun on her back the whole time. Out by the porch was a small carriage. Laura Pope was at the reins, and when she saw Cara being escorted at gunpoint, she exploded. "Miles, have you lost your mind? You said this was the house of someone who could help us!"

"She can, Laura."

"Miles, I refuse to let you bring her along!"

"Get in, Cara."

Laura stood in the carriage and appeared intent on keeping Cara out. Then she went still as she looked at something on the horizon. "Well, Miles, Chase is riding back fast."

Cara smiled hearing the news. She looked at Miles and said, "He let you live before. You're not going to be so lucky this time."

He snatched her by the arm and gripped it painfully. "Shut up. We'll see who lives and dies."

"Miles!" Laura snapped. "What are we going to do?"

"Just watch."

Chapter 17

The letter! Chase suddenly remembered he'd forgotten Cara's letter to William that he'd promised to take into town for the post. Corresponding with her old friend was so important to his schoolmarm that he didn't give a thought to his convenience, even though he must be at least three full miles from the house. He turned Carolina and headed back to get the letter.

What he saw as he rode up to the house turned his blood to ice. Miles Sutton was standing on the front porch. His left arm snaked around Cara's waist and held her hard against his body; his right hand held a gun to her neck. He yanked on the reins and drew Carolina to a halt.

"Morning, soldier boy. Toss your firearms on the ground. Now! Laura, you go pick up those guns."

An obviously angry Laura Pope stalked across the yard and picked up the Winchester and the long-nosed Colt.

"Dismount, Jefferson, slowly."

Chase did as he was told, then stepped away from Carolina. He gave Laura an angry glance, then looked at the even angrier face of his wife. "Has he hurt you, darlin'?"

"No."

"And she won't be hurt, Jefferson, if you do as you're told," Miles offered easily.

"Let her go."

"Nope. She's going to come with me."

"Leave her here, for heaven's sake," Laura screamed at him. "We don't need her."

"But I do!" he snapped back. He looked down at Cara and asked in a guttural tone, "Don't I, love?"

Cara shivered at what she saw in his cold gray eyes. She looked hastily at her grim-faced husband.

"So she comes," Miles stated. "Goodbye, Sergeant." He forced Cara over to the carriage.

"You're not taking her with you, Sutton. You'll have to kill me first."

Miles didn't hesitate. Cara's scream was lost in the roar of the two shots that exploded at her ear. She craned and saw Chase lying in the dust. She struggled against Miles's hold, desperate to get to Chase. Miles snatched her back, viciously jabbing the gun into her ribs. He forced her inside the carriage. She fought, squirming violently in his hurtful grasp.

"Let me go to him!" she screamed.

She couldn't tell whether Chase was dead or alive. As if in answer to her prayers, she heard him moan, then watched him struggle to turn his torn body over. Blood soaked the upper right side of his shirt. Cara bit her lip to keep herself from wailing. Chase was wounded in the right leg as well as in the chest, and she involuntarily cried out as he lost a battle to drag himself to a sitting position. Thanking God that he was still alive, she renewed her struggle with Miles.

Miles released the hold on her waist, grabbing her arm for better purchase. "Now, unless you agree to come with me willingly, I'll finish him off right here. Your call, Cara."

Cara turned to Miles and pleaded, "He'll bleed to death if we leave him like that. Let me get a doctor, then I'll go wherever you want."

Miles looked over at Chase, still attempting to rise despite his injuries, and said through a cold smile, "Yes, he probably will bleed to death. Your decision?"

Chase tried to voice his protest, but the searing, ever-advancing pain had him hovering on the brink of passing out. All he could do was issue garbled, delirious sounds.

Chase's helplessness tore at Cara's heart. She didn't want to leave him, but if there was any chance of his surviving, she'd gladly follow Miles into hell. Steeling herself, she said, "I'll go."

They rode for about an hour before Miles pulled off onto a rut that ran through a forest of sunflowers along the road. As the carriage bumped its way along they were enclosed on all sides by sunflowers that grew well above their heads. The leaves slashed at their faces and the horses had to go very slowly. Cara looked over at Laura Pope. She hadn't spoken a word since leaving the house. What did the girl feel?

Did she care at all about Chase's plight? Cara doubted that Laura was concerned about anything except herself . . . and Miles.

The steady pace of the horses drew Cara's attention away from Laura. They were entering a small clearing. A worn-out soddy sat in the center. She heard Laura sigh. "Finally." Cara supposed this was home for the two fugitives. Cara had never seen this place before and wondered if it was on the sheriff's map.

Miles and Laura climbed down and made Cara do the same.

"Tie her up out here," Laura snapped. "You and I have to talk." She strode into the doorless soddy.

Miles turned to Cara and said, "I don't think Laura's going to be staying with us much longer. Do come inside, love."

It was dark in the soddy, and Cara's eyes took a moment to adjust. It looked as if they'd been living here for some time. Clothes were draped over trunks. There were dirty plates atop the lifeless black potbellied stove. Pallets, raised off the earth by stacks of lumber, were covered with frayed blankets.

Laura bristled. "I thought I told you to tie her up outside."

"Laura, when did you start running things?"

She opened her mouth, then closed it.

"You've been screaming at me like a fishwife for days. If you don't want to continue on this adventure, there's the door."

Cara watched the angry young woman back down. "I'm sorry, Miles, it's just that we have enough problems as it is. Why add to it by bringing her along? I thought we'd already decided I would pose as her in St. Louis."

Miles chuckled. "Poor, naive Laura. Do you honestly believe that now that I've got Cara, I would want you?"

Laura's eyes widened.

"Laura, darling, you were just a means to an end. Cara and I are fated."

Laura looked at Miles in disbelief. "Miles Sutton, I stole those route schedules for you!"

"Yes, you did, and I greatly appreciate the risks you took, my dear. When we met back at Howard, I knew your daddy being a banker would be of immense help one day. And it was. Now I'm going to leave you two ladies together while I go and hide the horses and the buggy."

And he walked back outside.

There was silence after his departure. Cara thought Laura looked devastated. Cara almost felt sorry for her—almost. She went to the doorway and looked out. How far had Miles gone?

Laura said from behind her, "If you're thinking about running, I wouldn't advise it. Those sunflowers go on for acres all around. You'll be lost for days."

Cara knew she was probably right, but wanted to escape. The memory of Chase lying injured on the ground burned vividly in her mind's eye. She felt the desperate need to get help for him and be at his side. But that would never come to pass unless she could get free. Her eyes narrowed as she began to formulate a plan.

"So, Laura," Cara said, turning back to face the dark room, "you were the one who stole the schedules of the gold coaches."

Laura didn't say anything.

"Why, Laura?"

"Why should I tell you anything?"

"Yes," Miles said, walking in out of the sunshine. "Why should she tell you anything? Laura, you just keep your pretty little mouth closed about that gold."

"Does she know how many people died on those gold coaches?"

"We knew there would be risks," Miles said.

"Those were real people, not risks."

"I didn't care anything about those real people. I cared about those gamblers. You were there the night they came waltzing into the church."

"So you and your bandits killed all those people just because you couldn't pay your gambling debts? What happened to all the money you swindled from the people back East?"

"I spent that establishing the Liberian Lady. I had suits to purchase, houses to buy for some lady friends, my quarters to furnish above the saloon."

"So you spent it *all?*"

"It went like corn through a mill, but now with your help, my dear Cara, I won't have to worry about money ever again." He stared at her for a moment, then ordered Laura to give him two of her scarves.

"You're asking too many questions, love, and jabbering far too much," Miles explained as he gagged Cara with a silk scarf he took from Laura. With the other scarf he tightly tied her wrists behind her. He forced her to sit on the dirt floor in the far corner of the room.

Laura and Miles went outside to talk. At first they were conversing too softly for Cara to hear. Soon, however, they were arguing loudly. Cara heard nothing for a moment, then Laura was yelling at Miles to come back. Laura called again, louder this time. Her voice became fainter as she evidently ran after him.

* * *

Chase owed his life to Sheriff Wayman Polk. When he hadn't shown up at the appointed time, the sheriff had ridden out to find him. He managed to get Chase into the house and rode back to town for help. Now, a few hours later, Chase was determined, if hardly ready, to ride.

"Goddammit! You've patched me up, Doc, now get the hell out of my way."

Delbert looked up at the snarling Chase and said, "You've been patched up, Sergeant, but you're in no condition to ride."

"The hell I'm not. That bastard has my wife."

According to the doctor, had the bullet in Chase's chest been any lower, he would be dead; the splintered bone in his leg would take weeks to heal, but Chase was still struggling to get dressed and go.

"Dammit, Sophie, help me get this shirt on."

She didn't argue. She gave him the help he needed.

As Chase lifted his heavily bandaged shoulder and arm into the shirt, he ignored the pain and the sweat beading on his forehead. "Now the buttons," he ordered crisply.

While she complied, he looked over her head at the sheriff and Asa. "Asa, when you and Sophie get back to town, have Miss Rachel wire the marshal in Wichita and Colonel Grierson at Fort Davis. Tell them what's happened and that the sheriff and I are going after Miles and Laura."

Delbert spoke up. "Sergeant, you really have to wait until—"

"I've ridden with worse injuries. I can sit Carolina long enough to catch the man who stole my wife."

He stood on his splintered leg with the aid of a cane Sophie had provided. Asa came over and offered a shoulder for support. "Thanks," Chase said, hobbling out to the porch. He whistled for the stallion. Carolina came running and stopped at the base of the steps. Asa and the sheriff helped Chase negotiate the steps and get over to the waiting horse. Chase gave a command in the Sioux language, and, to the amazement of those watching, the big animal went down on his front knees, which made it easier for Chase to mount.

"Now that's something," Asa muttered.

Chase patted the horse's neck in approval. "I've had him since he was a colt. He'd ride me into the devil's own kitchen if I asked, wouldn't you, old boy?"

Chase looked at Sophie's concerned face. "If I'm not back in five days, have Miss Rachel wire Dreamer of Eagles at Pine Ridge Reservation in the Dakotas. Let him know the full details of what happened. He'll take it from there."

Sophie nodded.

"Stop worrying, Soph. I'll bring her back."

If Chase was dead, surely she would know, wouldn't she? Because of the untimely deaths of loved ones in the past, Cara had spent most of her life alone. Would fate be so cruel again?

"Thinking about soldier boy?"

Cara didn't reply. She and Miles had left the soddy on horseback at first light. They'd been riding for so long she'd lost track of time and direction. She'd even stopped speculating on the absence of Laura Pope.

"Well, stop thinking about him. You're never going to see him again."

They rode on.

Chase and the sheriff rode west. They were able to track Miles's vehicle fairly easily through the still-soft earth because one of the carriage wheels had a crack on the edge of its rim. It left a very distinctive mark when it rolled. Chase hadn't wanted to wait for the sheriff to round up his makeshift posse because of how long it might have taken. Every moment he'd have spent waiting let Sutton put more distance between them. However, Chase felt good about having Sheriff Polk riding hard at his side, because he knew the lawman could be counted on in a tight situation.

Chase and the sheriff followed the tracks until they led off the road and into a field of giant sunflowers. Chase guided Carolina on the rutted track, pushing aside as best he could the large petals and faces of the flowers. He kept his senses alert for anything that could indicate danger as he and the lawman made their way through. They found the small soddy in the clearing, but no one was inside. "Is this place on our map, Sheriff?"

"I doubt it. This area is way beyond the boundaries of the original settlement."

"Well, let's take a look around."

Walking was extremely painful for Chase, but with the help of the cane, he was able to move, albeit slowly. Inside they found evidence that someone had been residing there recently, but nothing to verify that it had indeed been Sutton. While Chase continued to survey the interior, Polk went outside to look around. When the lawman called, Chase hobbled out as quickly as possible.

Polk was making his way back to the soddy. "I found a woman's body about a hundred yards back up in the sunflowers. Looks like Laura Pope. She was strangled. The buggy's back there, and the tracks of two horses."

Chase dropped his head. He was sorry Laura had come to such an end, but glad the body had not been his Cara Lee's. Chase looked up at the sun to gauge the time. "It'll be dark soon. What do you want to do, Sheriff?"

"I think we need that posse!"

"I'm going on," Chase told him firmly. "Sutton already has almost a day on us. Get your posse, if you want, but I'm not going to get off this trail."

"You sure you can make it alone?"

"No, but I have to find Cara."

The sheriff nodded. "Well, I'll take the girl's body back to town and rustle up the posse, and we'll catch up to you somehow."

Chase had Carolina kneel so he could mount.

The sheriff walked back toward the sunflowers and Chase rode on.

Chase picked up the tracks of the two horses, following them west.

By the time Miles halted the horses it was near dark. Cara's arms and shoulders were burning from the strain of being tied. She'd tried to get away from him earlier, but he'd caught up with her nag of a horse and as punishment, he'd tied her hands in front of her body, attached her to a lead, and made her walk behind her horse. She'd walked until she dropped, and only then did he let her ride again. When she'd re-mounted, he'd tied her hands to the saddle horn. Cara could no longer remember how long ago that had been.

She waited on the horse while he dismounted. He came over and helped her down. Her legs buckled instantly; but for his hands she would have fallen. When he seemed certain she could stand on her own, he untied her hands. He left her to stand beside the horse while he strode off about fifteen paces into the fallow cornfield beside the road, where he looked around for a time, then found the trap door of a dugout. He returned to her and dragged her roughly through the field to the raised door. The pain in her arms and legs made her wince, but she bore it silently, consoling herself with the fact that at some point an opportunity to escape would present itself again.

The steps leading down into the dugout were rotten and split, the earth anchoring them soft and eroded. Cara had trouble sensing the supports as she hesitantly made her way down, and her hands were incapable of gripping the step above her head for purchase.

She made it down without mishap, though. Her hands, face, and clothing were covered with mud.

Miles had lit a lantern before descending. "You look lovely," he offered. "Make yourself at home. Be right with you."

Cara ignored the sarcastic compliment and surveyed her surroundings. A pile of supplies stacked in a corner proved he'd used this place before. He knelt before them now, evidently deciding what to take. The lantern beside him offered just enough illumination for Cara to see the dugout's deteriorated state. At one time the place might have easily sheltered a family of five or six, but now one wall had completely caved in, cutting off access to whatever rooms lay beyond. Beside her stood one of the old black potbellied stoves. The rusted-out hulk had lost its signature stovepipe long ago, but Cara dearly wished it could be fired up to counter the shivers brought on by the chilly night air and the underground dampness.

"Miles, where is Laura?"

He turned. "Laura decided to return home. She'll meet us later."

Cara didn't believe him for a minute. Laura hadn't returned after Cara heard her calling Miles's name during the argument back at the soddy. Cara had been left alone for quite some time after their voices faded away, and when Miles returned, he'd returned alone. Cara had asked then about Laura, and he'd given her this same explanation. She tried another tack.

"Why don't you just let me go?"

"Because, my dear Cara, I need you to get my dear dead mother's money."

"And then what?"

"Who knows? Maybe we'll sign on for Liberia." He laughed.

"One more question?"

"Certainly."

"How did you know about the gold shipments?"

"My poor ignorant mother, of course. I was helping her with her mail, since she couldn't read, and I found a letter from a bank in Topeka. It showed a tentative schedule of when the coaches would be making the circuit to pick up or drop off gold. I waited about a week for the Topeka bank to send the definitive schedule they'd promised in the original letter, but I never saw it. Mae Dexter was also handling Mother's mail during that time. My guess is Mae got to it first and took

it straight to Mother. I searched her office and never found it, so I
called Laura."

"And she did it just because you asked her?"

"She did it because I told her I wanted to marry her."

Cara stared. So Laura had been duped.

"She'd fallen for me back at Howard. Loved the fact that I was
different from the men in her parents' circle. I came from Texas; I ran
poker games and had my firearm on the table when I played. She liked
that. One of the reasons I was dismissed from Howard was because
when the boys didn't pay their poker debts, I'd go to their dormitory
with my forty-five and persuade them to reconsider. She begged to go
along with me one night. Ah, how that appealed to the little minx.
Turned her wanton—especially on one of my debt-collecting nights."

His eyes probed Cara and she looked away.

"So," he continued lightly, standing now, "any more questions?"

Cara shook her head.

"Good. You can take this blanket and sleep over there. And while
you're dreaming of your soldier boy, remember this: Once we get my
mother's money and leave St. Louis, we're going to California to be
married."

Cara's eyes flashed.

"Wait, now." he said patiently. "If you don't want to marry me, I'll
turn you over to a friend of mine who owns a brothel on the Mexican
side of the border. He'll pay me top dollar for an educated brown
beauty like you. Of course, once he gets his investment back, he'll probably sell you to someone else, who will sell you to someone else. But by
then, your looks will be gone—health, too, more than likely, and you
won't care."

She couldn't hide her shudder.

They were mounted and on the trail again just after sunrise. Cara was
exhausted after a fitful night spent on the blanket in a corner of the
damp dugout. Miles hadn't offered her anything to eat and she hadn't
asked. She refused to give him the satisfaction of seeing her cringing
and crying. Even with her hands tied to the pommel of the saddle, her
face streaked with dirt, and her head dizzy from the lack of sleep and
nourishment, she rode beside him defiantly.

As the sun rose higher in the sky, Cara tried to determine in what
direction they were traveling, but the ordeal had begun to take its toll.
She could no longer determine south from west or east from north. The
horse beneath was moving, and that's all she knew.

Blessedly, early in the evening, Miles stopped. Cara had ridden the last few miles like a corpse, slumped in the saddle. Only being tied to the pommel kept her from falling.

"Pretty hard ride," she heard Miles say as if from a distance. "But you need to be broken like a wild filly. If it takes a week out here in the sun to do it, so be it, Cara dear."

She felt the tension ease around her wrists, now tied with rope, then her arms were free. She moaned in pain as they were moved and her body was lifted from the horse.

"I'm going to set you down over here while I make camp. Don't run away now." He laughed.

And then later, "Cara, can you hear me?"

She opened her eyes slowly. Through cracked and swollen lids she stared up at the man's face. She searched her mind for some explanation. Then came recognition, and she attacked him, clawing and screaming at him in a dry, hate-filled voice with all the strength she had left. She felt his hand hit her sharply across the face, sending sparks through her brain. He cursed her as he retied her hands and pushed her back down.

Leaving Carolina hidden in the tall grass, Chase approached the camp cautiously. His slow progress had more to do with his injuries than with a desire for stealth. Each step was agony as he dragged the broken limb along the uneven terrain. Sweat poured down his face; breathing had become hell, but he'd be damned if Cara would spend another hour in Sutton's hands.

Tracking them had been a relatively easy task. Either from ignorance or overconfidence, Miles had not bothered to mask his trail. The prints of the horse had been clearly visible in the earth of the old Indian path. He'd expected to lose the tracks when it got dark, and he had for a while, but he'd stayed on the trail. He figured Sutton would do the same until he came across a place to hole up for the night. Luckily, Chase's intuition proved correct.

They were camped outside an old homestead not more than a few hundred yards away. Were he in better shape, Chase could simply walk down there, shoot Sutton, retrieve Cara, and be done. But he was in no condition for a fight. His only hope lay in going in after Sutton dozed off.

Chase gained the old shack without incident. His eyes swept the scene. Sutton lay snoring loudly on a bedroll by the dying embers of the campfire. It took all Chase's willpower not to jerk him awake and stick a rifle up his nose, but he reminded himself, his main concern was Cara's safety. He saw her, and his anger at Sutton warred with the blessed relief at finding her alive. She was seated with her back to an old fence post and her arms tied behind her. He could see the strain in her shoulders as she slept with her head tilted forward. Even in sleep she looked tired and defeated. Sutton would pay.

The hours Chase had spent on horseback had tightened his leg considerably, and the constant pain throbbed over every inch of his body. Cursing it, he moved as silently as he could around the sleeping Miles and over to his wife. Once there, he crouched as much as his injury permitted. Keeping a wary eye on Miles, he gently clamped a restraining hand across Cara's lips. She startled awake as he knew she would. She fought him with a strength numbed by sleep and fatigue.

"Evenin' ma'am," he whispered.

Chase felt her go stock-still. She turned her head to him, and in the moonlight he saw the look of wonder on her face.

Cara had never heard such beautiful words. Her only regret was that her hands were tied and she couldn't throw her arms around him or touch the lines of his face. He was alive!

Miles's attack came out of nowhere. One moment Chase had been holding Cara as if he'd never let her go, and the next moment they were bowled over by Miles's charging weight. The force slammed them to the ground. Cara came to rest a few feet away. She spent a few unfocused seconds trying to clear her head while Chase and Miles wrestled violently.

The injured Chase proved to be poor sport. Miles was glad. He owed Chase a lot, especially for the ass-whipping the night the Lady burned.

Cara could hear Miles's fist meeting the bones of Chase's face again and again. Certain she was not going to lie there and let Chase be beaten to death, Cara began to crawl toward Miles's bedroll.

Straddling Chase's chest, Miles snatched the barely conscious soldier up by the shirtfront and hit him again. He'd forgotten all about Cara—until he heard the angry click of the rifle at his back.

"Move off, Miles."

He turned slowly. The smile on his face was indulgent. Looking her straight in the eye, he pulled a knife from his boot.

"You don't have the guts to shoot a man in cold blood, Cara. Now watch. I'm going to cut your man into little pieces."

He brought the knife up high, intending to plunge it into Chase's bleeding chest, but he never got the chance. Cara pulled the trigger.

* * *

Chase was resting on Miles's bedroll. "You can take care of yourself, can't you, schoolmarm?" he whispered.

Cara nodded solemnly.

"Remind me to be more respectful in the future."

Cara, standing a little ways off, wanted to smile, but couldn't. "You've killed men, haven't you?"

Chase fought to keep from blacking out. She needed to talk. "In battle, yes."

"He would have killed you, Chase. I had to shoot."

The emotion in her voice made Chase feel a new and different kind of pain. "I know, darlin'. Come here."

She went to him, and with a gentle hand he tugged her down, then folded her into the crook of his arm.

"I killed a man," she repeated numbly.

"You did it because you had no choice."

"I took a man's life."

Chase thought a moment about how best to explain what Cara needed to hear. "Darlin', sometimes you do what you have to. It isn't easy, and it isn't something you forget." His eyes held hers in the flickering light of the campfire. "The sharpness of the memory will fade in time," he continued in a low voice, "but you will carry it with you for the rest of your life."

She looked back out at the horizon and saw the faint colors of dawn seeping into the heavens. She was filled with emotion—remorse over killing a man, relief that Chase was alive and the ordeal was over, and other feelings too jumbled to sort out at the moment. The overriding feeling, though, was one of quiet joy that she and Chase were alive. Alive!

"How do you feel?" she asked.

"Like hell." And he did. Miles had worked him over pretty good. There wasn't an inch on his body that didn't scream pain. He'd never be able to ride under his own power. "Sheriff Polk said he and the posse would be right behind me. We'll have to wait for them. There's no way I can ride."

"Then we'll wait. But if they aren't here by later today, we'll have to come up with something. You need a doctor."

"Oh, I don't know. The one I have here is pretty good."

After dragging Miles's dead body off Chase, Cara had rummaged through his pack for a clean shirt suitable for bandages. Using the knife with which Miles had planned to kill Chase, she'd cut the garment into strips. Cleaning Chase up had been impossible; he'd been covered with blood. It would have taken more water than they could afford to spare, so she concentrated on just his face, then wrapped the big gash on his head, repacked his shoulder bandage, and did what she could for the leg. In her opinion, it hadn't been nearly enough.

"It'll take more than a whipping from a two-bit gambler to put me in the ground, so don't worry. We'll make it."

Cara had to admit he did feel less feverish to the touch. The bark tea he'd asked her to make seemed to be doing its job. She, too, had partaken of the bitter-tasting brew and could feel the stiffness in her limbs fading away.

"Did he hurt you?"

"No," she replied softly. "Strangely enough, he was quite respectful, outside of tying me up and not feeding me. He did cuff me earlier this evening, but I'm fine."

She sensed his returning anger and moved to soothe it. "Relax, Chase, he can't hurt anyone else again."

Cara got under the covers with him. Careful to avoid his injuries, she nestled as close as she could.

"That's better." He sighed. Cara thought so, too.

After a few moments of silence, Cara asked, "Does it bother you, being saved by your wife?"

Some men, no, a lot of men, would rather have their lives taken than be saved by a woman. Did he count himself in that group? she wondered.

He raised his fingers to stroke her very dirty cheek with a tenderness that made her feel newly clean.

"What you did for me tonight . . . I will never ever be able to repay. A woman who possesses such courage is looked upon highly by Dreamer's cousins the Cheyenne, and by me. You have a heart of iron, Cara."

Cara had tears in her eyes. "You're very special, too, Chase Jefferson. Very special." She leaned down to kiss him, savoring it because he was both alive and near, then she slowly pulled away. Chase hadn't gotten enough, however. He eased her lips back to his, needing more of her vitality and warmth to melt away the anguish and fear that had ridden his soul since Miles dragged her into that buggy.

"Thank God I found you, schoolmarm," she heard him whisper. His emotion-filled words set off a fresh run of tears, and she clung to him.

They released each other only long enough for Cara to reposition herself beneath the blankets. When she was once again cradled against his side, he leaned over and kissed her on the brow. "Dreamer's invited us up to visit this summer. I'll see if he can arrange some type of naming ceremony for you."

Cara, in the midst of wiping away the remnants of her tears, asked, "What on earth for?"

"Because from here on in, schoolmarm, your Lakota name will be Heart of Iron."

Cara didn't know what to say. Tears seemed to be the only vocabulary at her disposal at the moment.

Her show of emotion moved him deeply. However, he couldn't resist the opportunity to tease her.

"If you don't ease up a bit on those tears, Dreamer and I are going to have to name you Heart of Rust."

Had he not already been injured, she'd have retaliated with a punch. Instead, she kissed him softly. "I love you, Chase . . ."

"I love you, too, Cara Lee . . ."

The sheriff and his hastily gathered five-member posse arrived late afternoon the next day. After making sure Chase and Cara were all right, the lawman surveyed the scene. He knelt beside Miles's blanket-covered corpse. He flipped back a corner and shook his head sadly.

Prefacing his request with an apology, Sheriff Polk asked Cara to tell him what had happened after Miles rode away from her house. She complied. But when she neared the end, she began to falter, and Chase related the rest.

If Cara's part in Miles's death surprised Polk, he didn't let on. Instead, he instructed the other men to begin preparing for the ride back. Before they could agree on a safe way to transport Chase, Asa, driving a buckboard, came out of the high grass. On the seat beside him sat Sophie and Delbert.

Cara smiled at her beloved friends, then at her beloved husband. They were finally going home.

Chapter 18

Three weeks later, while Cara was inside cleaning up, Chase sat out on the big porch swing watching the sunset. Here, where only the grass rustling in the breeze broke the silence, the evening had a different feel from the ones he experienced on the trail. He had spent more nights than he cared to remember huddled beside a fire, too exhausted to sleep, trying to make do with rations that were never enough. Most nights, especially after a forced march, were fraught with weariness, bad food, and short tempers. Now he'd had the experience of living with what folks termed "a good woman." He relished this peace and solitude. Sleeping on the ground didn't even come close to the comfort and bliss offered by the big feather mattress upstairs. The smell of Cara's biscuits in the morning, the cold lemonade she had a habit of bringing him just when he needed it most, the sounds of her humming, the taste of her lips, all added up to something he wanted to treasure for the rest of his days.

"You know, Sheriff Polk's talking about retiring to his daughter's place down in Mexico," he called to Cara in the kitchen.

"Oh, really? I didn't know he had a daughter."

"Yeah, she's married to some Spanish grandee down there."

Cara dried her hands as she joined Chase on the porch. She sat on the swing and enjoyed the peace of the beautiful evening.

"You've been awfully quiet the last couple of days," Chase observed. "Are you worried that we haven't heard from Virginia's lawyers?"

"No, times being the way they are, there's probably some Black Code somewhere prohibiting what Virginia wanted done with her property. Sophie doubts I'll see a cent, and I agree."

"So nothing's bothering you?" Chase asked.

"Nope, not a thing," she lied.

"You sure?"

"Positive."

He continued to watch her as if trying to gauge the truth for himself. Under his scrutiny, her hands did a nervous little dance. She clamped them back down into her lap a bit too quickly before she looked away.

"Do the elders have someone in mind for the sheriff's job?" She wanted this conversation to dwell on neutral ground only. Why in the world did she have to love this particular man? she wailed inwardly for what seemed like the thousandth time.

"Just a few," Chase answered, watching her. "Some are more qualified than others."

What was wrong with her? Chase wondered. All day she'd been as skittish as a horse tied up next to a hornet's nest. Every time he came near her, she slid smoothly away. She always gave him an apologetic smile, but it was clear she was avoiding him. He took in her appearance in the fading light. Tendrils of hair had come undone during her chores. A few clung damply to her neck. Her blouse was wet and damp below her breasts where water had evidently splashed above the apron, and the top two buttons were undone. She looked hot and sultry from the July heat. Seeing her gave him an idea. She'd managed to stay one step ahead of him all day, but now he thought he had a plan that would most definitely slow her down.

"Tell you what . . ." He slid down the seat next to her. His positioning forced her to stay where she was. "I'll fix you a nice hot bath." His hands were slowly undoing the apron at her waist. The minute brushes of his fingers against the thin blouse covering her skin as he worked on the knot sent ripples of flame up and down her length. She knew he would be leaving her soon. She'd convinced herself that if he didn't make love to her, maybe she could survive seeing him only now and then. But the heat of him made her want to feel him everywhere and she couldn't protest. Yet she knew Chase; in his own subtle way he was trying to find out what she was feeling.

Chase didn't think she stood a chance. It had been three weeks since the last time they'd made love. Their combined injuries had kept them apart. But now he felt the shudder rippling her skin when his finger brushed against her back.

The knot finally surrendered and he took an inordinate amount of time easing the apron from her body. She shuddered again and he smiled. She was a passionate woman; he sensed they shared an equal hunger.

Through the thin fabric of her blouse he could feel the lightweight camisole and the heat of her skin. His fingers began to trace the line of her waist. "You're wet . . ."

"I . . . think I would like that bath," she said, trying to steer him back to safer ground. Her breathing had begun an all-too-familiar cadence under the seemingly innocent stroking. How did he do it? He ran a bold knuckle over the smooth undercurve of one breast, and Cara's insides seemed to buckle and weave.

He repeated the lazy gesture on the other breast.

"Chase, please . . ."

"I'll get your bath in a moment, schoolmarm."

He gently turned her so that her back pressed flat against the swing. "Sit there and watch the sunset. You've worked hard. Let me help you relax."

When the sun finally died in a ball of red and orange fire, relaxing had to be the farthest thing from Cara's mind. Her blouse was undone, her nipples were hard and tender, and her skirt was in scandalous disarray. She had no idea when or how her drawers had disappeared. She was conscious only of being deliciously naked under his intimate touch.

Her breasts came in for more delight as he eased down the camisole. One tug left her naked to the soft wind. His kisses soon followed. When he slowly withdrew, the air mixed with the moisture on her nipples to make them harden with need.

Hands followed by lips coursed over her skin both in and out of her clothing. Her nipples ached, her thighs burned with age-old fire, yet still he would not let her rise.

"Not yet . . ." he said in a low growl against her ear. His touches were working slow magic between her thighs. "I'll let you up in a minute."

His kisses then slid down between her legs. He moved her skirts aside. She inwardly crumbled when lightning tore through the tender bud of a shrine he worshipped at so beautifully. No matter how many times he loved her this way, the delicious wickedness always set her on the road to madness. Her hips always rose to the rhythm. Blazing heat always seemed to originate from his spark-tipped tongue. And the ending; oh, the glorious, glorious ending was always so powerfully explosive that she screamed his name. This time proved to be no different as he sucked, licked, and loved her over the edge.

Much later, in the silence of the darkened house, the big upright clock in the upstairs hallway chimed four. Dawn would come soon, but for now night still ruled. In their bedroom, the two lovers lay side by side. Happy. At peace.

"So, are you leaving?" she asked softly in the dark. She hoped her tone reflected the neutrality she was determined to maintain. He was not a man to be held by tears or pleading. And she had her pride.

Chase smiled in the darkness. His eyes were focused on the ceiling, but his being was focused on the woman who lay at his side.

"Do you want me to leave?"

"It isn't a matter of what I want—and don't answer my question with a question."

"Well, suppose, Mrs. Jefferson, I told you I want nothing more than to be at your side."

That got her attention. She turned to face him, and not even the dim light could mask the astonishment on her face. She was so overcome by his statement, she paid little attention to the sheet as it slid down. Her beautiful breasts and the flat trim lines of her waist and belly were bared to his eyes. His manhood rose to the call. Talking suddenly became a very low priority. He'd made love to her more than a few times tonight, and she, bless her wicked little soul, had reciprocated in kind. But it hadn't been enough, not nearly enough. He wanted more.

Cara was still waiting for him to clarify his words, but instead of an answer, he treated her to the coaxing pads of his thumbs and fingers, over, under, and around the nipple of one breast. A giddy joy spread sharply at the teasing manipulation. For the moment, her mind closed to everything but the pleasure. "Stop," she said raggedly, but didn't pull away.

"Such adamant protest," came his hot whisper, while his hand, moving now to the other nipple, slowly seduced. "Try again . . ." Raising up, Chase put his mouth to the sweet buds his hands had once again awakened and let his tongue feast on the spice there. She groaned in protest and delight. She arched to him, further aiding and abetting her own downfall. In a few more seconds, she knew she would be unable to muster defenses, nor would she even care to. Already she was succumbing to the wild magic his wanton sucking brought to the fore. He would sweep her away and she would love it if she didn't stop herself now.

"Noooo . . ." she moaned softly, backing away. Her breath, coming in soft gasps, filled the silence. "Now stop it," she warned.

"Why?"

"Because I can't think when you do that."

He accepted the compliment with sparkling eyes. "That's the general idea, isn't it?"

Cara had as much trouble smothering her smile as she did controlling her pounding pulses.

"Now, you were saying?" she prompted. She was still prey to his eyes, his humor, and her own desire to make love to him again.

"Very well," he replied in mock defeat, "we'll talk." He wanted to get this talking business completed as soon as possible. "Then we 'talk' my way, understood?"

"Understood."

"Gladly?" he dared to ask.

"Hotly," she threw back boldly.

He grinned.

When he finished speaking, Cara was so outdone she hit him in the chest with a pillow. He'd not anticipated the fairly forceful blow, and the thud against his chest elicited a muffled groan. Before she could strike him again, he pulled the weapon away, but the emotion in her face could not be denied.

"You knew all along you were staying?" she asked and accused in the same phrase. "You let me mope around all week, knowing you had the answer to my mood. You're rotten, Chase Jefferson, rotten as buffalo meat left in the sun. I'll never forgive you. Never!"

"Never is a long time, schoolmarm."

"Don't tease with me. How dare you let everybody in town know about you being the new sheriff and not tell me! Didn't you think I wanted to know?"

"It was going to be a surprise."

"Some surprise," she summed up. All this time she'd been agonizing because she thought he would be leaving soon. Her heart had ached miserably with the prospect of seeing him only three or four times a year. Yet he'd known he wasn't going anywhere.

"Well, then you probably don't want to hear the question I was going to ask next."

Her stiff profile answered, but he was undaunted. He slid over to where she lay. Once behind her, he pulled the sheet back over them, then gently parted the unbraided length of her dark, heavy hair and helped himself to a warm triangle of naked neck.

Determined to stay mad, Cara snatched her hair from his hands. She spun to face him, intending to let go with both barrels, only to find her face positioned only a breath away from his own. "I love you, Cara."

His nearness washed over her and the anger slid away. "What—what were you going to ask?"

He kissed her, pulling away with a tender, slow reluctance. "You didn't have any say last time. This go-round, you will. Would you be my wife, Cara Lee?"

Astonished joy widened her eyes. She couldn't speak.

"It's your choice."

Cara finally found her voice and said yes. Laughing, she launched herself into his waiting arms.

After they slowly broke a kiss, Cara whispered, "Now I have a question for you. Is this wedding going to be soon? Because we have a baby on the way."

Chase's jaw dropped. "A baby?"

"Yes, Sergeant, you're going to be a father."

"A baby?" he asked again, searching her face.

Cara nodded.

"A baby!" he yelled at roof-raising volume. "Hot damn!"

He grabbed her around the waist and they were soon rolling around on the bed. Cara was screaming with laughter and Chase was crowing like a fool.

When they finally settled down, he turned to her and asked, "When's the baby going to be born?"

"The first of the year."

"A baby. . ." he said, amazed.

"A baby that'll cross into the next century, Chase. Can you imagine that?"

He could.

"Do you think things will be better for our child?" Cara asked seriously. She didn't want her children to grow up in a Jim Crow world.

"We can only hope, darlin'," Chase said, looking into her eyes. "We can only hope." He kissed her softly.

"You know," Cara said later, when they sat down to breakfast at the kitchen table, "Delbert said the baby was probably conceived back in March."

Chase thought back to last winter and smiled devilishly. "Hmm. Probably that March morning when I had homecoming breakfast right here on this very table."

Cara shook her head, smiling. "Probably."

"That was a very good breakfast as I recall."

"You are outrageous. Do you know that?"

"Yep," he replied, the mustache framing his dazzling smile. "I know a schoolmarm who tells me that all the time. Pass me the preserves, please."

Cara smiled and passed him the peach preserves. "I love you, Chase."

He looked up and said softly, "I love you, too, Cara Lee."

Author's Note

Night Song is grounded in the little-known history of the Black migration to the West after the Civil War. "Kansas Fever" or the "Great Exodus" began in earnest in 1879 as over forty thousand Blacks fled the violence of Reconstruction, then the terror-filled era of the Redemption. In Kansas they founded all-Black towns, knowing hardship at first, enjoying success in succeeding times. The most famous of these towns is Nicodemus. Nicodemus and its nearby towns in the Great Solomon Valley lost population in the early 1900s, due mainly to the decision by officials of the Missouri Pacific Railroad to lay their tracks far from the area. By 1945 the town that had fueled the dreams of the Great Exodus of 1879 lay virtually deserted.

Today Nicodemus has had a rebirth. Once again, the mostly Black population is on the rise.

The 'dusters—all the descendants of the fictional characters of Cara and Chase in Night Song, their friends, foes, and acquaintances—would be proud.

Historically, the name buffalo soldier refers to four regiments of Black soldiers: the Ninth and Tenth Cavalry and the Twenty-fourth and Twenty-fifth Infantry. Between 1869 and 1890 they earned eighteen Medals of Honor for distinguished service to our country.

In 1981 when he served as Fort Leavenworth's deputy commander, General Colin Powell, later Chairman of the Joint Chiefs of Staff, began to dream of erecting a monument to the Buffalo Soldier. He thought the two gravel alleyways in Leavenworth named Ninth and Tenth Streets a poor tribute to men who'd played such a significant role in the nation's history.

In July 1992, the Buffalo Soldier Monument Committee made his dream a reality. The statue of a mounted buffalo soldier named *Scouts Out* was unveiled at the 126th anniversary reunion of the Ninth and Tenth Cavalry Association at Fort Leavenworth, Kansas.

If readers would like more information on the statue or any of the other ongoing projects of the Buffalo Soldier Monument Committee, write to the committee at P.O. Box 3372, Fort Leavenworth, KS 66027. The National Headquarters of the Ninth and Tenth (Horse) Cavalry Association can be be reached by writing P.O. Box 475, Junction City, KS 66441.

When I first began showing *Night Song* in manuscript to my friends a few years ago, they enjoyed the story of Cara and Chase and loved the history, which was new to them. I promised that if *Night Song* was ever published, I would list some of the sources I used when writing it.

So for those readers who want to know more about this fascinating part of American history or who want to build their own African-American history library, here's a list to start you on the journey to greater knowledge.

Cornish, Dudley Taylor. *The Sable Arm: Negro Troops in the Union Army 1861–1865.* New York: W. W. Norton & Company, 1965.

Dann, Martin E., ed. *The Black Press 1827–1890.* New York: Putnam's Sons, 1971.

Erdoes, Richard, and Ortiz, Alfonso, eds. *American Indian Myths and Legends.* New York: Pantheon Books, 1984.

Foner, Eric. *Reconstruction: America's Unfinished Revolution 1863–1877.* New York: Harper and Row, 1988.

Lingeman, Richard. *Small Town America.* New York: Putnam's Sons, 1986.

Painter, Nell Irvin. *Exodusters: Black Migration to Kansas After Reconstruction.* Lawrence, Kansas: University Press of Kansas, 1986.

Quarles, Benjamin. *Black Abolitionists.* New York: Oxford University Press, 1969.

Quarles, Benjamin. *The Negro in the Civil War.* Boston: Little, Brown, 1953.

Sterling, Dorothy A. *The Trouble They Seen: Black People Tell the Story of Reconstruction.* New York: Doubleday, 1976.

Sterling, Dorothy A. *We Are Your Sisters: Black Women in the Nineteenth Century.* New York: W. W. Norton & Company, 1984.

Thompson, Erwin J. "The Negro Soldiers on the Frontier: A Fort Davis Case Study," *Journal of the West* (1965) 7 (2): 217–235.